A MESSAGE
TO THE CHARNWOOD READER
FROM THE PUBLISHER

Since the introduction of Ulverscroft Large Print Books, countless readers around the world have confirmed that the larger and clearer print has brought back the pleasure of reading to an ever-widening audience, thus enabling readers to once again enjoy the companionship of books which had previously been denied to them due to their inability to read normal small print.

It is obvious that to cater for this ever-widening audience of readers a new series was necessary. The Charnwood Series embraces the widest possible variety of literature from the traditional classics to the most recently published bestsellers, and includes many authors considered too contemporary both in subject and style to be suitable for the many elderly readers for whom the original Ulverscroft Large Print Books were designed.

The newly developed typeface of the Charnwood Series has been subjected to extensive and exhaustive tests amongst the international family of large print readers, and unanimously acclaimed and preferred as a smoother and easier read. Another benefit of this new typeface is that it allows the publication in one volume of longer novels which previously could only be published in two large print volumes: a constant source of frustration for readers when one volume is not available for one reason or another.

The Charnwood Series is designed to increase the titles available to those readers in this ever-widening audience who are unable to read and enjoy the range of popular titles at present only available in normal small print.

THE STALIN ACCOUNT

London, 1925. The first-ever Russian trade-mission is set up in Moorgate. The head of the mission is Pavl Nakentov. Part of his espionage activities is to compromise secretaries —usually unattractive—and this he succeeds in doing. Jane Barnard, secretary to the managing director of a large engineering firm that handles government contracts, is among them. The only difference is that they fall in love. Nakentov finds himself compromised bewildered and with a special problem—for he is brother-in-law to Joseph Stalin.

KENNETH ROYCE

THE STALIN ACCOUNT

Complete and Unabridged

CHARNWOOD
Leicester

JUL 1 6 1986

First published in Great Britain in 1983 by
Hodder and Stoughton Ltd.,
London

First Charnwood Edition
published April 1986
by arrangement with
Hodder and Stoughton Ltd.,
London
and
Stein and Day, Inc.,
New York

British Library CIP Data

Royce, Kenneth
    The Stalin account.—Large print ed.—
Charnwood library series
I. Title
823'.914[F]   PR6068.O98

ISBN 0-7089-8328-6

Published by
F. A. Thorpe (Publishing) Ltd.
Anstey, Leicestershire
Set by Rowland Phototypesetting Ltd.
Bury St. Edmunds, Suffolk
Printed and bound in Great Britain by
T. J. Press (Padstow) Ltd., Padstow, Cornwall

1

EDDIE TYLER glanced over to where the old lady lay dying. She was quite still, her sunken eyes gazing up at the ceiling.

He crossed over to the bed and placed a hand on her forehead. She offered no reaction to his touch. "I'm sorry," he said aloud. "This shouldn't have happened to you. But I'll be here. Me or someone if I'm called away. You won't be alone, Auntie. Don't worry."

Useless words. She was really his *great*-aunt, the unmarried sister of his maternal grandmother. In spite of the age gap they had always got on well together. He had a great deal of sympathy for her; she was lonely and, as in manhood he had got to know her better, he had always felt that somewhere along the line she had suffered some terrible tragedy. Yet she never spoke of it, and he had not probed; he believed that she appreciated his restraint.

As he looked down at her, she seemed already dead. He wondered if she could hear or see him. He would ask the doctor when he called again, or the part-time nurse, at present having lunch in the kitchen.

Eddie Tyler took one of the frail hands. Again, there was no reaction. He lowered the hand and

1

wandered into the study. To fill in time he poked around the desk and the small bookcase. In the centre drawer of the desk, pushed to the back, he found a leather-bound book with a small brass lock. He tried to open it but it was firm. He went into the kitchen.

Nurse Hayes was sitting at the table with sandwiches and coffee. She appraised him carefully: he was still under thirty, with dark hair looking as if it needed a brush, grey eyes, sombre, but with humour lines around them that could deepen. Tall and untidy, she reflected, but not unattractive. At present, he had joined the millions of unemployed; university degrees gained no privileges during a recession and with decreasing circulations and closures reporters were in short demand. She knew that much about him. She fancied him too, but decided that it was dangerous to mix business with pleasure.

"What's that you've got?"

At first he did not know what she meant, then he realised that he was still holding the locked book. "A diary?"

"Ah! Secrets. It looks kind of old. Does it open?"

"Not without a key."

"So you've tried already?"

He grinned. "I'll take it back. Take your time over lunch. I'll be here for a bit."

He wandered back to where his aunt lay. He had moved into an upstairs room and the sitting room had been rearranged as her bedroom: it was easier for everybody.

He suddenly wished she would die—that would be easiest for *her*. He raised the book again and turned it over. It *did* look old. The covers were padded but soft now.

About to return it to the study he heard a terrible sound from the bed. He turned to find his aunt watching him. He noticed that her gaze was on the diary and that her mouth was working as the dreadful sound escaped. She was struggling to sit up.

Tyler hurried over, his face creased with worry. For days since her stroke she had been unable to move. Now, suddenly, she was moving her head and was even trying to speak. He put down the diary and tried to comfort her but she was attempting to turn her head to the bedside table where he had placed the book. The incredible effort she made frightened him. Sweat was standing out on her skin, and her hands twitched as she endeavoured to raise them. He thought quickly, then picked up the diary.

"Look," he said, holding it up. "It's unopened. The lock is firm. I'll put it back." He did so, closing the desk drawer loudly so that she would hear him—if she could hear at all. When he returned to her bed she appeared less distressed, her breathing easier. Her eyes met his and he believed that she tried to smile. The fact that she could move her eyes at all was incredible. What

3

was there about an old diary that could motivate her sufficiently to break through paralysis?

He took her hand again and this time there was a faint response. She was suddenly struggling to live—in order to tell him something?

"I'm sorry," he said. "I had no idea it would upset you so."

Later that night he looked in on her again and she was apparently asleep. He switched off the light and left.

Mary Hayes had gone home. Eddie went into the study and quietly closed the door. With equal care he took the diary from the desk drawer and searched for a key. There were bundles of old keys, none of which fitted the tiny lock. He searched again but could not find the right one.

Resigned, he held the diary in his hands. He could always force the lock, but he didn't want to go that far. In exasperation he unconsciously squeezed the covers; the pressure released the flap which immediately sprang up on its hinge.

He laid the diary on the desk aware that he was about to pry. Before he opened the book he paused, anxious to be sure of his motives. If there was some dreadful secret between the padded covers, something that might besmirch Jane Barnard's name, then when she died he would destroy it so that any shame would die with her. He would not allow anyone else to know.

Slightly reassured, he opened the diary and began to read, astonished that the entries started in early 1926 and ended in 1931. The handwriting was difficult to follow at times, and in parts had faded badly.

When he had finished he wondered what had disturbed her so much. Nothing he had read could have done that, surely? He went over the pages again then put the diary back where he found it. It was clear that, in her youth, Aunt Jane had had her moments, but there was nothing to suggest that any of it could harm her. There was also mention of an old bank account, but in no meaningful way. Perhaps her mind had gone.

As soon as Nurse Hayes arrived next morning he went out shopping. When he got back she had coffee ready for him. They sat at the kitchen table together and he told her what had happened when Aunt Jane had seen him with the diary.

She could not believe him. "I'd better tell the doctor; he'll be in later."

"It was incredible."

"He won't believe it either." And then archly, "Did you read it?"

"Read what?"

She laughed, teasing him. "The diary. You brought it into the kitchen yesterday."

There was no point in denial. "I read it in her own interests—I intended to burn it if it was something shocking. She was in love one time. Back in the mid-twenties."

"Maybe that's why she stayed a spinster. A

5

love must be deep to keep a record of it for so long. Does she say who, or what happened?"

"A man called Lubov. Sounds eastern European. In fact, there was an entry that she went to Moscow on a tourist visit. The entries finished shortly after that. But there was very little detail —as though she wanted only a bare outline; the rest would be in her head. She used initials a lot. Not at first, but increasingly." He looked across the table at the pretty Irish face. "Nothing bad in it or I wouldn't have told you."

"Good for her. God bless her, poor soul."

"She mustn't know," he stressed.

"Of course not. She has problems enough."

Eddie Tyler found Jane Barnard dead two mornings later. The bedclothes had been pushed down to her waist, her fingers still clutching them. So she had moved her arms. Had she been trying to get out of bed? The effort must have been superhuman.

As he stood in his pyjamas, looking down at her, he wondered if he should call the doctor straight away or wait for Mary Hayes who was due in about an hour. He decided to wait for the nurse and returned upstairs, saddened at the death yet relieved too.

When Nurse Hayes arrived Eddie told her what had happened and they went into the sitting room together. "Did *she* push the clothes down?"

"Must have."

"That's incredible." And then, briskly, "Leave everything to me. I'll let the doctor know."

He wandered into the study and immediately knew that something was wrong. He always checked and tidied up before going to bed at night. Now he could see at a glance that things had been disturbed; items on the desk top were not as he had left them, and some of the drawers were partly open. He opened the central drawer: the diary was missing.

Eddie sat down at the desk and began to tidy up, then realised that the police would not want anything touched. *Police*? Over a diary? Nothing else seemed to be missing. He called out to Mary Hayes and she came in.

"We've been burgled," he said. "The diary's gone."

She gazed round the room, startled and mystified. "Is that all?"

He got up slowly. "I think so. Did you tell anyone about the diary?"

She did not like the question. "I told the doctor what you told me."

"Anyone since?"

She glared at him. "Don't try to make me a scapegoat. Who else did *you* tell?"

He held up a placating hand. "Sorry. Someone found out about it who wanted it. It's been around for a helluva long time without arousing curiosity; one of us must have mentioned it."

"Are you sure the room's been burgled?"

"Look at it. Someone's been in during the night." He scratched an ear. "I didn't hear a thing."

She was about to speak again when she suddenly recalled that she had spoken to her boyfriend about it. It had been in passing and she had thought nothing of it. But the implications were ridiculous.

Eddie had wandered over to the old sash windows. The catch of the middle window was off. "I'm going to have to tell the police," he said. "It sounds crazy, but what else can I do?" Halfway across the room, he stopped and turned to face her. "Supposing my aunt heard something? Suppose she made a frantic effort to get out of bed? Couldn't that have killed her?"

Six days later General Pavl Nakentov was in his Moscow apartment watching a live television transmission of the Moscow Dynamos being beaten at soccer by an East German eleven when the doorbell rang. With his eighty-sixth birthday less than three months away he had outlived most of his friends and relatives and now received few visitors. His wife had died eight years ago but his daughter and, more often, his grand-daughter, dropped in on him from time to time.

The ring broke his concentration; it was an exciting match. He rose tetchily, his white hair falling forward as he pushed his stocky frame up from the chair. Once up he moved quite well. He

8

pulled down his crumpled jacket and went to the front door.

As soon as he opened it he knew that he was in trouble. So often had it happened in reverse, when he, with a colleague, had been the caller. He did not need to be told that the two stony-faced men blocking the doorway were members of the State Security. He had trained many such men and had himself been a member of the KGB for forty-seven years. He had joined during the GRU days before the newer and larger organisation had taken over.

"Gentlemen, come in." But he knew that they would not.

"We have been instructed to take you with us, Comrade General."

It was odd how the more senior man always stood on the right. There was no precise drill: it just seemed to happen. He had done it himself in the old days.

Nakentov smiled, but he had chilled inside. His old brain was churning but it was still sharp. Only one thing could have made these men call. After so long?

Years ago he had dreaded that this might happen. The passing of time had deadened expectancy until it had disappeared altogether, and in retirement he rarely worried about it. He was too old for a trumped-up charge, and anyway there could be no possible reason for one. Even now his advice was sought on European affairs.

Conscience stabbed his mind like a knife. He did not need to be told why they were here but too easy a submission would suggest guilt. "Why?" he asked. "Can't it wait until after the match?"

"Now, Comrade General." The man on the right was uneasy but that would not stop him from doing what he must. "Shall we get your coat? It's cold outside."

"I'll get it myself." Nakentov turned back into the room while the junior man followed him. He switched off the television before gazing round the small apartment as if to say farewell to it, knowing that he would not see it again. He struggled into a topcoat, brushing aside the attempt to help him, and donned a fur hat. "Where to?" he queried.

"Dzerzkinsky Square."

Nakentov buttoned up his coat, his trembling fingers not entirely due to age. Dzerzkinsky Square. They all said that, but what they really meant was Lubyanka prison. So he was not even to be granted the comfort of the Centre.

His escorts were courteous, helping him into the Volga, showing respect for his rank and reputation. But his rank would not help him now, and his reputation would soon be in ruins. He wished he could just sit back in the car and die. He sat next to the senior man and closed his eyes. He was old enough—it was time to go anyway. But it was not so simple. He felt fit for his age and reluctant to deny the will to live.

10

They did not speak to him in the car and he was glad of it. At no stage did he display dismay. Rigorous training dies hard and a lifetime of deception stood him in good stead.

The car moved past the long banana shape of the Headquarters of the First Directorate. The screen of trees that hid all but the top three floors were shedding rapidly now. The distant view of the building brought back memories—ironically, most of them pleasant.

They reached Dzerzkinsky Square and Nakentov showed no surprise when the car was driven to the older part of the building, on the corner and once occupied by the dreaded Cheka. Were they any more dreaded than their successors? Reputations stuck. Nakentov was filling his mind with inconsequential thoughts; it was best to keep his brain busy. When he was escorted from the car and taken down to the basement of Lubyanka, he accepted that the very worst had happened. This was where he would die.

He was taken to a solitary cell that was cold and damp. They took away his watch and emptied out his pockets, removing any object with which he might try to commit suicide. There was no sound through the thick walls and the silence was unnatural, as though he was meant to feel alone in this vast prison. Sitting on the edge of the bed he noticed that extra blankets had been provided.

He saw the irony of it: they wanted to make certain that he did not die from cold.

At his age too much privation could be fatal. He had caused them a dilemma and he reflected on how he would have handled it. He tried to prepare himself for what was to come, but more than anything he dwelled on what could possibly have gone wrong after so very long. The matter should be dead, buried with Stalin's son Jacob in 1942. His thoughts faltered; nobody knew for sure what had really happened to Stalin's son. It was generally assumed that he had died in Nazi hands. Surely, he could not still be alive?

Nakentov gazed at the heavy cell door, at the observation grill set into it. Were they watching, and was he showing too much already? He was tired and felt his age.

There were no windows in this underground wing. He knew better than anyone the disorientating effect that lack of natural light could have on people; not knowing whether it was night or day. The lights went out without warning. A total blackness surrounded him, as damp as fog. He sat on the edge of the bed, hunched in his coat, and gazed morosely into space.

The light remained off and nobody came. Finally he rolled over on to the bed, cold and exhausted. He drew his topcoat closely round his body and slept without interruption.

He awoke naturally, still in his clothes, and shivered, sorry now that he had not climbed into bed. The light was back on but there was no way he could judge the time. He swilled his face in the sink in the corner, feeling the stubble on his chin.

Nakentov felt dreadful and depleted and lay down on the bed again. He glanced at his wrist and was instantly annoyed with himself. Already he had forgotten his watch had been taken. He had thought he would be able to resist them better than this.

A meal was brought to him and he ate it on the fixed table against the wall. Sustenance was important. That the content of the meal could be described as breakfast did not deceive him: he had sent prisoners breakfast at midnight. He had no idea how long he had slept.

No sooner had he finished eating than the door opened again and a man he knew entered. In his mid-fifties, the man was well-built and quite handsome, his dark hair touched with grey at the sides. The features were heavy and friendly. He was dressed in civilian clothes but Nakentov knew that he was entitled to a uniform. They were meeting rank with rank.

General Georgi Stevinski pulled out the wooden chair Nakentov had used at breakfast and sat on it to face his captive who was now sitting on the bed. He leaned forward and grasped one of Nakentov's hands warmly in both of his.

"How are you, Pavl? It's been so long."

"I'm old and I'm upset." Nakentov spread his

13

hands to encompass the cell. "What could I possibly have done to deserve this? Me? With my service and record? Who's blundered, Georgi?"

Stevinski smiled. "You shouldn't have been brought down here." He pointed to the ceiling. "There's a flummox going on upstairs and someone took the easy way out. The youngsters these days always take the easy way out." He gestured quickly. "Don't worry about it. You'll be out before you know it."

"Well, that's a relief." Nakentov did not believe it. They were trying to confuse him. In a way it was a compliment, but one he could do without. And it showed how well he had trained Stevinski. "Why *am* I here, Georgi? At my age it's murderous."

Stevinski still bantered. "You're too tough to die. Anyway, we can soon clear it up. Does the name Jane Barnard mean anything to you?"

Nakentov was glad he was sitting hunched on the bed for his stomach suddenly convulsed. He tightened his arms across his abdomen but he could feel the pain as if he had been kicked. He said, "You've brought me here to ask me that? Jane who? American?"

"Barnard. English."

"English?" Nakentov stared in disbelief. "*English*? Do you know when I was last in England?"

"Summer 1927. The year I was born."

Nakentov faced Stevinski squarely. "And you

expect me to remember a name after so long? Over fifty years ago? Do you realise how things were in Britain at that time?"

"Oh, yes. Our first major spying mission in Britain collapsed. You were all sent packing."

"So you pick one name out of a hat and expect me to remember? I could have been asked that at my apartment."

"We thought the atmosphere here might help you remember. Like old times."

"This is like old times?" Nakentov laughed sharply. "From where you're sitting, maybe."

"You still haven't answered, Pavl."

"The question is too absurd. Of course I don't remember." Cunningly, he added, "If she was one of the old contacts surely she'd still be on file?"

"She isn't. Clear or coded, she doesn't officially exist."

"It doesn't surprise me. Things were chaotic before we left and a good many papers were burned. But you must know this."

"You were there. You saw it happen. Tell me about it."

"Why? Of what possible importance can it be after so long?"

"Possibly none. Bear with me, Pavl. I'm trying to do the job that you taught me to do. You'll understand that."

Nakentov pressed his arms into his body. "It's

15

damned cold," he complained. His stomach nerves were still kicking.

"We went to London to start the first Russian Trade Mission there. We called it Arcos and we leased two large blocks in . . ." he groped convincingly ". . . Moorgate. That was in 1924. A much bigger operation was opened in Berlin called Handelsvertretung in the Lindenstrasse. And Amtorg was set up in the USA. Although London was the smallest venture, it was important. I think we had a staff of over three hundred. Are you sure you want to hear all this? I might get some of it wrong."

"It's better than reading files. It brings it to life, Pavl."

"At first things went well. We recruited a fair number of British over a wide spectrum. And . . ."

"That was *your* job," interposed Stevinski. "You were always a charmer."

"There were others besides me. But we were very successful." Nakentov broke off. It would not do to make the memory too easy. After a while he continued, "It started to go wrong during the General Strike of 1926. Some fool in Moscow sent the British miners £25,000 for their strike fund. It was a stupid thing to do. It not only incensed the British Government but it angered the miners too and the British Trades Union Congress sent the money back.

"Churchill, who was then Chancellor of the

16

Exchequer, wanted to cut off all trade relations with us. All this enormous blunder of ours achieved was to bring Arcos under the surveillance of MI5. It was tragic when we were going so well."

Nakentov suddenly swayed and clutched the edge of the bed. "It's a wonder I remember so much; it's a great strain."

Stevinski was unmoved, eyeing Nakentov shrewdly. "You want a stimulant? Something to drink?"

"I want a rest."

"And you shall have one. Get this out of the way first."

Nakentov feigned annoyance. "You keep forgetting that I'm nearly eighty-six. My memory is clear until I get these tiny blackouts—everything goes and I have trouble remembering how far I got." It was a clever plant, a suggestion that his memory might lapse, and it was not unreasonable. Stevinski would decide what was reasonable.

"Take your time, Pavl; we have plenty of that." Stevinski smiled encouragingly.

"As long as you realise how difficult it is for me to remember so far back." In fact, it was as though it had just happened. Nakentov's visual memory could see the events in minute detail. It was a chapter of his life that he desperately wanted to forget, yet was the one he would always carry.

17

He was weary and his speech wavered, but he missed little out. "The British belatedly realised that we had a very large staff for such a small amount of trade. Do you remember Jilinsky?"

"I know *of* him. He died some time ago."

"He was with Arcos and the British found out that he was in the GRU. They also discovered that Khopliakin at our London Embassy was a member. When Khopliakin was sent back the British refused to grant diplomatic immunity to his successor; Khinchuk, I think it was."

Nakentov paused. His eyes were tired, his hands trembling a little, but his stomach seemed to have settled down.

"Then MI5 caught an RAF technician stealing drawings. He broke down and told them that he had planned to send them to Arcos as usual."

"What was his name?"

The trap was too crude for Nakentov to fall into.

"I can't remember. He wasn't one of my contacts, anyway."

Stevinski smiled. "You were more for the girls, weren't you? You must have had some fun."

Nakentov shook his head. "It's true I seduced a few. But none of them was very pretty, mostly on the shelf, but in important positions." He smiled feebly. "The things I did for the Soviet Union. It wasn't easy, you know. I had to force myself."

"I'll take your word for it. Was that the beginning of the end?"

"Well, we didn't know about the arrest of the RAF man until it was too late. MI5 obtained permission from Prime Minister Baldwin to raid us at Arcos. The police surrounded the building on the 12th May 1927. They forced open the basement where Robert Kopling and Eva Malenkov were burning papers like mad. Anton Miller, the chief cipher clerk at the embassy, was with them and that was another dreadful blunder we made. The embassy should have kept out of it.

"Anyway, they managed to burn some papers but the British finished up with whole lists of agents and recovered a good few of their own documents, some of which they did not know were missing. We were all sent packing. Three years of highly successful work was ruined by Moscow's stupidity. Diplomatic relations were broken off and the whole delegation was sent home. Do you know, it was two years before another Russian was allowed into Britain?"

"Was Jane Barnard one of the names that went up in smoke?"

"How can I say? Kopling and Miller were never sure what they burned; they just shovelled what they could into the furnace. The only ones to know what was not destroyed were the British." Nakentov gazed mockingly at Stevinski.

19

"I don't think they did the courtesy of informing us."

"So the name means nothing to you?"

"No." Nakentov was pensive. "*No,*" he repeated. He shook his head slowly. "It doesn't ring a bell."

"Yet you precisely remember the date of the raid. May 12th, 1927. And some of the other names."

"Wouldn't you?"

"Perhaps. I don't think I would forget my agents. Not ever. I might need prompting but I'd remember. But then I had a brilliant tutor."

"Georgi, you keep assuming that I knew the name in the first place. She was no agent of mine. Why the concern for her?"

Stevinski rose and pushed the chair back under the table. He looked down at the old man; he could still learn from him and he was doing so at this moment. "She's dying in London." He watched for reaction but Nakentov showed none. "She has a diary and your name is in it."

"My name? *My* name?" Nakentov smothered a smile. "Well, well. I never used my name the whole time I was in Britain. Or anywhere else for that matter."

"Your code name."

"Lubov? Are you serious?"

"You remembered that well enough."

"I've used it a hundred times. I shall never

20

forget it. What does this Jane Barnard say about this Lubov?"

Stevinski hesitated and Nakentov quickly realised that there were gaps in his information.

"Meetings. That sort of thing. She came here as a tourist in 1931. She met you here."

"You mean there's an entry which states that she met Lubov?"

"You were the only one with that code name."

"And were there others with Lubov as an actual name? Like Layevsky, for instance?" Layevsky was dead and Lubov had been his second name. Nakentov doubted that there was anyone still alive who would know that Layevsky never used the name.

"That's something I can check. There's also an entry about a bank account."

Nakentov slipped to the floor, gasping for breath and holding his chest. He did not make it easy for Stevinski to lift him back on to the bed. He knew that Stevinski would be worried that he might have induced a heart attack.

"You all right?" Stevinski stepped back.

"Go ahead." Nakentov gestured weakly.

"The question worried you?"

"What question? I heard your voice but it was slipping away."

Stevinski pulled the chair out again and put a foot on the seat. He leaned on his raised leg. He felt no rancour and not a little admiration. It would make no difference ultimately but old Pavl was playing with him.

"There was a reference to a bank account but it really does not matter. You've been helpful, Pavl. I appreciate it, for I know it must be tiring for you." For a while he just gazed down at the old man. The twinkle was back in his eyes and he was smiling slightly as Nakentov spoke.

"I've told you all I can remember. If I think of anything else I'll tell you, although I can't see the importance. When do I get out of here?"

"The sooner the better." Again Stevinski put back the chair as he straightened. "Let me see what I can arrange. Meanwhile, lie down and sleep." He walked to the door, opened it, turned and said, "By the way, it's half-past eleven. In the morning. And the Dynamos lost last night. The boys did you a favour by interrupting your viewing. These East Germans are getting too good."

Stevinski closed the door and signalled a guard to lock it. He went thoughtfully upstairs. On the half landing a tall, bespectacled, white-coated man was waiting for him. They continued up the stairs together and entered one of the interrogation rooms.

"What do you think?" asked Stevinski, sitting on the edge of the desk.

"A remarkable man. Quite extraordinary. He still has all his marbles."

"Was he lying, Doctor?"

The doctor laughed. "You're far better qualified to answer that, Comrade General."

"He's cagey. Wily old devil. But we must get the truth and get it very quickly. There is no time for psychological programmes. My feeling is that time is important, and that he's holding back."

"You sense a can of worms?"

"Yes, I do. The feeling is strong. I've even considered using old-fashioned torture. How can we get it out of him? Quickly?"

"Torture would almost certainly kill him. He would not stand up to the shock."

"Drugs, then?"

"Anything you try on a man of that age could be fatal. Anything."

"We haven't the time for days and nights of interrogation. We can wear him down, but I want the answers now."

"They may not be as important as you think. It would be safer to take your time."

Stevinski nodded in acquiescence. "It's a matter of judgement. Right or wrong, I must back my own."

"There's nothing I can suggest that does not carry a high degree of risk. If he dies it's no use being sorry afterwards."

The telephone rang on the desk and Stevinski reached to get it. He listened, his features unchanging. He put the receiver down slowly. "The only other person who might have helped has died. Had she made any sort of recovery we might have tricked it out of her. But I suppose it was really wishful thinking." Suddenly he made up his mind. "We'll have to risk it. Give him a shot of sodium Pentothal—but be careful with the dose."

The doctor did not need telling, he was not at all happy for he could see where the blame would land if Nakentov died.

When Stevinski returned to the cell with the doctor Nakentov immediately knew what was about to happen. "It will kill me," he stated flatly.

"That's the last thing I want to happen," the doctor assured him. "Believe me, my intention is to keep you alive and well."

Nakentov turned to Stevinski, "So, you don't believe me?"

"Of course I do. Every word. We just want to make sure there's no mental blockage, something you would willingly tell if it would surface."

Nakentov was clearly agitated as he rose to his feet. "Take that needle away. I'd prefer to die in my own bed. Anyway, if you give me time I might come up with something else."

"Pavl, my dear friend, you've taxed yourself enough. The doctor knows what he's doing. Don't humiliate yourself. Don't make me call the orderlies to hold you down. Come on, take off your coat and roll up your sleeve."

Nakentov had banked on them not risking drugs. Stevinski must be desperate; if he ever

24

broke Nakentov's resistance he would realise the value of his instincts. Stevinski had changed from an apt pupil; now he was master of his craft. Nakentov felt old and tired. He wondered if it really mattered at all. Yet life was still sweet. He backed against the wall as they advanced on him.

2

RAYA DUBROVA ran up the stairs with the shopping bag over her arm. She opened the door of her grandfather's apartment with a key that she and her mother shared, and let herself in. She called out as she entered the cramped hall.

She went into the living room to find the curtains drawn across, although it was now lunch time. She smiled, thinking Nakentov was still in bed, put down her bag on the table and pulled back the curtains. She went into the bedroom a little apprehensively to find the room empty and the bed made up. Raya quickly discovered that Nakentov was not at home.

At first this did not surprise her for he often went for a walk. She unpacked the items of food that she had brought for him and stored them in the tiny kitchen. She rummaged until she found pen and paper and scribbled a note for him. It was something she always did to make sure that he would know the food was there.

Raya would have left it at that had she not suddenly wondered why the living-room curtains had not been pulled back. She stood in the middle of the room and gazed about her. The only unusual thing she noticed was a used tumbler left on the table. She sniffed it. Vodka, his usual tipple. It was a minor point but normally Nakentov would have washed it up before turning in: he was a tidy-minded man.

She went back into the bedroom. A striking girl, she had closely cropped black hair, her grandfather's straight nose and his deep brown eyes. She had even features and high, slavic cheek bones. Tall and slender, she had at one time been a contender for the Olympic swimming team, and still had the firm body of a swimmer. But she had just missed making it to the top and now, in her mid-twenties, was considered too old to compete.

Raya Dubrova had one thing in common with her grandfather. As he had grown older, and as she had matured and had dropped the heavy discipline of training, they had found that they shared a sense of fun.

It had not always been easy; she had known of his old career but had not thought too much about it. However, as his job had become more routine as he had neared retirement, the young girl had found him humorous and relaxed.

Raya had been only fifteen when Nakentov had retired at the age of seventy-four, so she had not known him during his years of heavy duty and he had never spoken about them. They had always got on well together; much better than he had got on with his own daughter, Raya's mother. Raya had never understood why. He had been as attracted to sports as his granddaughter and in his day was a wonderful pistol shot. The trophies he had won were tucked away somewhere in his apartment. At one time he had taught her to shoot.

Raya gazed at the bed and reflected that it was possible that he might have dozed in the chair all night. As she considered that, it was still difficult to believe that he would get up and go out without drawing back the curtains. The bedroom curtains *were* drawn back, but that could simply mean that he had not been to bed.

She was not unduly concerned. Her grandfather was a very self-contained man; there was nothing more that she could do. She washed up the glass and left the note for him in the usual place, under a corner of the bread bin on the kitchen counter. She left the apartment, puzzled but not over worried. She would call back later.

Nakentov lay on the bed and they put his coat over him. He could barely see the hazy outlines of Stevinski and the doctor standing beside him.

It was pleasant drifting like this, and the cold disappeared. He was floating, unconscious of body weight and unaware of menace. If this was dying then he had no objection to it. Everyone should sign off like this.

"Jane Barnard."

The voice was like his own conscience, prodding and demanding him to face what he had for so long avoided. He tried to open his eyes

28

but someone had told him to close them and no matter how he tried he could not raise the lids.

"Jane Barnard."

A whisper that barely penetrated. Nakentov was at peace with himself. He could dream without them knowing; savour the best of the past without intrusion. Perhaps it was like drowning, his life floating past him. But not all of it. There was only one small part he really wanted to remember, a highlight he had always cherished and yet had tried so hard to erase from his mind.

He could feel her body, warm, soft and eager, moving against him, feel her hands clutching his back and shoulders. And he could hear the passionate endearments whispered in his ear. Moments of extreme bliss hung suspended and he wanted to live through them again and again.

She was different from the others. Almost from the first meeting he had known that he was in deep water. The motive with which he had contrived to meet and to court her had been in danger of being ignored from their first dinner date. What had started out as a political expediency had finished up as an emotional awakening. She was not exactly pretty but her personality, once apparent, was alive and joyful; her nature was beautiful, like her young body.

He had fought it at first. Years of indoctrination could not be overcome easily. Each time he left her he confronted himself with what was happening, with the trap he was creating for himself. Yet as soon as he was away from her he wanted to be with her again.

It was unwise to see her too often, it would be noticed and he would be sent back to Moscow. The separation made it worse for him and for her, too, for Jane had accepted him at face value and it was difficult for her to understand that his spare time could not always be his own. She realised, of course, that Russians were political animals all kept under tight control, but even so it was often hard to accept.

When Nakentov reached the stage when his destiny was so entwined with Jane's that the consequences didn't seem to matter he knew that a decision had to be taken to avoid calamity. He could not ask to be sent back, for he did not want to leave her. And he did not want to seek political asylum, for that would almost certainly mean betraying his comrades and he could not go so far.

The solution he considered terrified him so much that at first he discarded the idea. His background, training and beliefs should preclude such thoughts. He was related to Joseph Stalin, the brother of his dead first wife Ekaterina. He was uncle of Stalin's son, Jacob, or "Yasha" as he was more affectionately known. When he considered these facts he thought his mind would burst, that he had gone mad. And yet his yearning for Jane Barnard was almost impossible to bear. Absence from her tortured him. When they were together he was in paradise.

The rationing of their meetings became more drastic and he was having difficulty in masking his feelings from his comrades. It was fortunate that everyone was so busy and there was a good deal of travelling round Britain to do: contacts to develop, payments to make, information to gather.

What had started out as another conquest of a woman to be exploited had finished as something for which he was totally unprepared. He could not tell her why he had first planned their meeting and he believed it no longer mattered, for he did not intend to exploit her innocence.

Jane Barnard was secretary to the deputy managing director of a large manufacturing company which dealt almost exclusively with Defence Ministry contracts. She had sense enough to realise that her relationship with the man she simply knew as "Lubov", and who had told her that his surname was totally unpro-nounceable, might be frowned upon in some quarters. She realised, too, that her own job was sensitive to national security. To be in love with a handsome young Russian, who worked for the Soviet Trade Mission, carried dangers. So she had reluctantly accepted the gaps between their meetings.

She had done nothing wrong, revealed no secrets nor had she been asked for any, and did not doubt that it would remain so. But if her affaire was discovered some people would think the worst.

Jane understood Nakentov's dilemma without knowing that he was a member of the GRU. She encouraged him to stay in Britain without understanding the enormous complications confronting him.

Nakentov had considered every avenue open to him in order to live a peaceful life with Jane Barnard, but he could see no way out of the dilemma. The Russians would not let him loose and the British would want something in return. His family connection with Stalin was not a help but an enormous hindrance. He had no doubt that, if he stayed in Britain, he would eventually be eliminated by the GRU.

Nakentov had never liked Stalin, an opinion he kept to himself. He despised the way Stalin had treated his wife, Nakentov's own sister, and their son, Jacob. But Jacob was another matter; there was real affection between them. As a teenager, Jacob had tried to commit suicide but Nakentov had succeeded in preventing him. He did not like the idea of deserting Jacob, who needed all the help he could get.

Emotionally, Pavl Nakentov was being torn apart. His political roots were deep, but were they stronger than his love for Jane? And could he cope with all the other problems that would arise if he joined her? When he thought it out, torturing himself with doubt, he was finally left with a single, unarguable fact: he would not leave Jane Barnard.

It was at this point that the possibility he had previously found quite terrifying opened up again as the only escape. The young GRU officer laid his plans. If he had money he could desert rather than defect. None knew better than he that there were many ways to obtain false documents, provided one had cash. He and Jane could elope, go where they pleased and begin a new life. With money they could start a business together somewhere on the continent.

Whenever he had doubts about his plan, they would be quashed as soon as he saw her again, and his resolve strengthened from the moment they embraced.

In the spring of 1926 he put his proposals to her. They must both save as much as they could. He sounded her out about living abroad, explained why he must change his name, but none of this mattered to her as long as she could be with him.

They would need time to save; a year or so, even longer if it could be managed and if they could avoid having a child meanwhile. It meant a great deal of patience; there was frustration when they could not meet and the constant danger of discovery but, in the end, it would all be worth it for everything they could offer each other and the tremendous love they shared.

Nakentov had no idea how long he would remain in Britain. He assumed that, provided he continued to be successful at his job and that Arcos remained good cover, his stay could run into several years. Neither he nor Jane wanted to wait that long. His pay was not high: serving the cause was considered sufficient reward in itself. But expenses were good, and were necessary if he and his colleagues were to be successful.

Payments to contacts had to be commensurate with the risks; inducements to betray had to be tempting. Of course, receipts were signed to keep check of the money and to ensure that the recipient could henceforth be blackmailed. But it was easy—and risky—for Nakentov to cream off the top. He tried not to think about the penalty for discovery.

He was careful, not retaining too much and covering the amount on receipts with thumb or fingers as the traitors signed. In any event, after a while signing receipts became a routine and it was doubtful if the figure was ever checked. It was also possible to get agents to sign in circumstances that would make them hurry. Nakentov used any ploy open to him.

Periodically he would hand the money he had embezzled to Jane to bank. It never occurred to him that she might cheat him, nor did it ever occur to her. He always brought cash and she once remarked on the size of the amount but he explained it away by saying that he had been put on a commission basis and that trade was improving.

They entered 1927 with a little nest-egg but not sufficient to break loose. Instinct warned Nakentov that his time was limited. Already committed to a fraud that could cost him his life, he decided to speed up the process and that, inevitably, meant increasing the risks. He was courting disaster.

He had four really profitable contacts who produced highly classified information. There were others who were overpaid for minor snippets on the grounds that their value might increase if their jobs improved. From the main four he began to extract some important information and set it up as if it had come from a different source. He invented two new agents, paid himself high sums, and signed the receipts in fictitious names.

Knowing that Jane might become suspicious of these larger sums, Nakentov opened a bank account himself, using a French name and Jane's address. He wanted no statements sent, a strict instruction. He chose a small branch of the Midland Bank in the East End of London and left the money on deposit.

Starting agents off often meant paying out disproportionately high sums but he was depleting his best informants and this, eventually, would be noticed. He decided to give it to the end of May.

He told Jane his deadline so that she could give

her employers a month's notice at the end of March. That would leave a month for them to prepare to disappear.

Nakentov's employers were expert at supplying false passports but on this occasion it was necessary to turn elsewhere. Soho was the place to make enquiries and he was no novice at finding contacts. It turned out to be the easiest part of his plan, but also the costliest, for he wanted a first-class job.

At the beginning of May he sensed danger, but couldn't identify its source. He didn't believe that he personally was under suspicion but nevertheless decided to take precautions.

On 8th May Nakentov made a final visit to the East End Docks and closed his bank account, drawing out the money in large denomination notes. He then went to the nearest Post Office, wrapped up the notes in brown paper he had taken with him, sealed the ends, tied the parcel, addressed it to Jane and posted it. He rang her that evening to explain but there was no reply.

This did not worry him over much. They were not due to meet for another ten days, and he knew that Jane had served her notice and now had time on her hands. She'd probably gone to visit her family in Norwich.

It worried him that a parcel of money would arrive with nobody there to receive it. He should have made sure she was at home before posting. His impulsive action was untypical, but highlighted his increasing strain. There was nothing he could do and few safe opportunities to telephone. He fought off the impulse to go round to her apartment.

The holocaust struck four days later, on 12th May. Nakentov, along with others who had thought the British police to be amiable but naive, suddenly found themselves surrounded. Policemen were everywhere, breaking down doors and catching red-handed the three who had dashed down to burn incriminating evidence in the hastily lit basement boiler. But masses of papers and files were saved from being burnt. Arcos, hot bed of spies, had come to an end.

The rest was a nightmare. Recriminations and abuse bounced around the Arcos offices as each member tried to justify his own position and to place blame elsewhere. What made it far worse was the Soviet Embassy getting themselves involved. Had they stood aside they might just have scraped by.

With all personnel confined and under close surveillance, Nakentov found it impossible to make contact with Jane. There were always colleagues around and the mood was grim and suspicious. Expulsion was one thing; accountability once back in Moscow quite another. It was not just a matter of the exposure of a big spy ring but of a diplomatic collapse which was to rebound throughout the Western World. Russia had been caught out publicly for the first time, and on a huge scale. She was to suffer for her sins.

Jane Barnard could not fail to notice the front-page newspaper reports. She hurried back to London on the first train. There was a slip through her letterbox stating that a parcel was waiting for her at the Post Office. When she collected it, she was astounded at the amount of money it contained.

Jane felt frustrated and deeply afraid for her lover. She had no way of contacting him. She knew where he worked, of course, and the switchboard number would be in the telephone directory, but she could get him into even deeper trouble if she telephoned. Her love for him protected her against believing that he was a spy. She did not accept the newspapers' claim that this was true of all Arcos employees.

She was afraid to go out in case he telephoned her. The Russians were all under notice to quit. Some had already started on the long journey home, and she did not know who still remained in London.

Nakentov telephoned the next evening and she cried with relief. From his formal tones and occasional hesitancy she realised that he was afraid of being overheard. There was no way he could avoid going back to Russia. He was ensnared with the rest. The British would laugh at any request for political asylum; they were in no mood to trust any Russian and he could not blame them.

But once he was back in Moscow and the dust had settled, he would be sent abroad again—and would then contact her. Could she stay in her flat for a year? Perhaps longer? So that he would know precisely where to write or telephone?

Their conversation was short and unnatural. He managed to declare his love, at which she broke down, but he stressed the importance of what he said next. He then gave her exact instructions on what to do with the money. He told her first to take what she needed, for she had no employment. She listened tearfully, until suddenly he hung up and she knew that he would not ring again.

Jane Barnard's world had collapsed. She was not concerned with losing her job; she was too good a secretary to stay unemployed for long. But she simply did not know when she would see Nakentov again. A year or so, he had suggested. It seemed a lifetime. But he had told her what she must do and she would follow it to the letter.

Distraught and nearly suicidal she pulled herself together because he had held out hope. He had entrusted the money to her. No one must ever find out where it came from for, if the information reached Moscow, she would have killed Nakentov as surely as if she had fired a gun at his head.

She produced her bank book and began to tot

up what they already had on deposit. She then counted the money from the parcel. When she had finished she could barely believe it. In all there was just over £21,000. Although she herself had been highly paid, her own contribution was tiny compared with his. How had he raised so much? There had been an enormous accumulation over the last eight months.

She dare not dwell on it. Re-wrapping the notes she pushed the parcel under her bed and left it there, intending to do nothing about it until all the Russians had gone home. Only then could she accept that the links with her young lover had been broken. She never doubted that, in due course, he would make contact again.

The newspapers carried pictures of the Russians leaving at the docks. A Soviet ship had called in to take them back. In none of the pictures could she see Nakentov and in a way she was relieved. She would rather carry her own image of him as he had appeared when last they met.

Jane Barnard did her best to sort out her life. After closing her deposit account and withdrawing the money in cash she had £21,000 in fifty-pound notes in her flat. She treated the money casually, placing it in a paper bag under her bed. The money itself did not inspire her; she was not the type to spend a lot on herself, nor were her needs expensive. The money was for them both; when Nakentov finally became free.

She booked a first-class ticket on the Golden Arrow to Paris with a Wagon-Lit sleeper connection on to Zürich via Basle. She allowed herself this luxury so that she would feel safer while travelling alone.

She left London from Victoria Station on the 18th June 1927 and arrived in Zürich the next morning, the money packed in a small attaché case she had bought for the purpose. She had no problems with customs; it was impossible to imagine that this pleasant-looking, plainly dressed English woman carried with her a small fortune.

She booked a room at the Dolder Grand—her second concession to luxury but mainly for assured privacy—and again placed the money under her bed. It did not enter her head to use the hotel safe. Jane still had a great deal to learn in the ways of the world, but now her innocence remained her best protection.

After a light lunch she retrieved the case of money and went to look for a bank. In a narrow street not too far from the hotel, she came across the Zeitlinger. As she did not know one Swiss bank from another, it seemed unimportant which one she used. When she entered the place seemed small, smaller than an English suburban bank. She went to the first empty teller's bay and, speaking in German, said she wanted to open an account; could she see the manager.

The manager, a plump man in his mid fifties, received her politely enough, humouring her, although not seeing much profit in the meeting.

"How much would you like to deposit, madam?"

Jane placed the case on his desk, snapped back the locks and opened the lid. "Twenty-one thousand pounds," she replied quietly. "In fifty pound notes."

The manager stared; that was a very large sum indeed. He reached for a signature card and payment slip and then stopped as Jane added, "I want the account to be completely anonymous."

The request was by no means unique, but he was still surprised. "I will need a signature, madam. We must be able to protect your money."

"Total anonymity," stressed Jane firmly.

He sat back and mused over her demand. "An account number will not be sufficient protection. I need to have additional identification."

"Protection against what?" asked Jane naively. "Will the money be in some danger in your bank?"

The manager smiled. "It will be perfectly safe here. But we must have some sort of authorisation for withdrawals. Simply quoting the account number will not be enough. Someone might find a payment slip or cheque stub and use the account."

"No one will know but me. And I don't intend

to withdraw anything for a year or so. I won't need a cheque book."

He was patient with her. "I am sure that is your intention, madam. But intentions sometimes go. astray. I think we should have a code as well as the account number."

"Instead of a signature, you mean?"

"It would replace a signature. We are fully aware that some of the signatures we have do not relate to the true names of clients. But we must have something additional for your own sake. Can you give me a name?"

"Any name?"

He could not resist another smile. Clients wanting the protection of anonymity usually had everything cut and dried; this girl was totally unprepared. He nodded.

Jane thought quickly. "Dranrab," she said. Spelling her own name backwards seemed easy to remember.

He showed no surprise. "Then let us say Dranrab 627. The six for the month, twenty-seven for the year. That will be your signature. Now we need an address."

"No address. No statements. I will contact you."

Now that was unusual. He began to wonder if the money had been stolen, though that would not have stopped him taking it. When he studied Jane across the desk he found such an idea incredible. No thief could be so ill-prepared.

"Can you make an arrangement for an address? It doesn't have to be your own, just somewhere to contact you if needs be. Send one on to me quoting the account number and, of course, the code. Is that agreeable?"

Jane nodded.

The manager continued, "I will draw up a document instructing that whoever presents the account number, *together* with the agreed code, shall be presumed to be the owner of the account. You must then sign it to give us our authority." As Jane hesitated, he went on, "You sign as you mean to go on. Dranrab 627."

For the first time Jane had doubts. This was more complicated than she had envisaged.

"May I suggest," her banker said gently, "that you return tomorrow at this time. It will give you a day to think things over: whether this is the best way for you or whether you might have other instructions for me. Take your time. I will give you a receipt for the money now and have the document prepared for when you call in."

Jane left the bank feeling thoroughly confused. Surely a signature was meaningless—she could have given him any name. At no stage had he asked to see her passport. And signatures could be forged.

She considered simply using her own name but Nakentov's warning came back to her. It was almost all Nakentov's money, and he *must* be protected. How would she stand in relation to the

Inland Revenue? She did not believe she was doing anything wrong. The amount she herself had contributed had already been taxed so her conscience was clear. She was cheating nobody. Yet she was now uncertain. Somehow a code seemed sinister.

The next day she decided to leave matters in the manager's hands. After all, a code was just another form of signature. An identification. He had prepared the document in such a way that the bank was absolved from responsibility if anything went wrong. She duly signed herself "Dranrab 627" in the presence of the chief clerk who witnessed the document. She now had £21,000 in an anonymous, numbered account with an additional protection code.

Jane Barnard shook hands with the manager and his clerk and left, never to see either of them again. In her handbag was the paying-in slip which quoted only the account number. On a separate slip was the code, meaningless on its own. She had now only to occupy herself with work and dream of hearing from her lover for whom her heart ached.

3

THE second half of 1927 was perhaps easier to bear for Jane. She desperately missed Nakentov but she did not expect to hear from him so soon. They had arranged no method of communication and there was a complete clampdown on Russians entering Britain. Repercussions, in the form of trials and arrests, abounded as the documents taken from the Arcos basement were studied. Each time there was another exposé, she was filled with bitter sweet memories.

By the spring of 1928, Jane began to have her first real doubts. She did not know why. Her own love was as strong as ever but the long silence was unsettling on her. There was no one in whom she could confide.

Jane was not only deeply in love but she was loyal, and saw nothing extraordinary in her total dedication to one man. But, increasingly, she doubted that she would hear from him again; she couldn't even be sure that he was still alive.

She took a holiday and changed her job. She had no financial problems and she could always go home to Norwich but she chose to bear her increasing uncertainty alone.

1928 passed in a dull ache of all too slowly

passing time. Yet she never gave up hope completely. Surely there must be some way Nakentov could communicate? But even if he had a friend he could trust, no Russians were being allowed to enter Britain.

Jane lost over a stone from a frame already slight. She could not quite accept that it was all over, yet, in her heart she did not now believe that she would ever hear from Nakentov again. The torture for her was in not knowing why.

Before the end of 1929, the Russian Diplomatic Delegation was allowed to open again in London. Slowly, political contact was restored. And still she did not hear from Nakentov. Gradually her longing for him became less painful to bear but it was always there. She remained a spinster. Other men did not interest her, just as they had failed to before Nakentov had aroused her passion.

In the early thirties, there was some attempt to attract tourists to Russia in small, tightly controlled groups. Jane decided to go there to try to establish whether or not Nakentov, still only known to her as Lubov, was still alive. She went in the same innocent spirit as she had gone to Zürich to find a bank. She had no preconceived plan, no idea how she might shake off the attentions of the Russian lady courier who, most certainly, was a member of the State Security. She believed that somehow she would find him if he was there.

It was the summer of 1931. Nakentov was now a Major in the OGPU, Obiedinennoye Gosudarstvennoye Politicheskoye Upravlenye. After the Arcos debacle in London, his work had varied since returning to Moscow. His reputation was still sound and he had been sent to Germany to set up a cell, but had been recalled shortly afterwards for safety's sake. It was a period during which the Russians had suffered too many exposés for comfort.

During periodic spells in Moscow Nakentov trained other agents. Visa applications from any foreign country in which he had served came his way. There was always a possibility that he might recognise a name, and he was always looking for someone he might subvert. It was a system that had on occasion provided a backdoor method to recruitment and to blackmail. All visa applications were referred back to Moscow and took some time to be approved or refused.

Jane Barnard's name was presented to him long before she arrived in Moscow and it rocked him to the core. Memory of her had tormented him. But, once back in Russia, the insidious clamp of indoctrination and immense security had slowly closed in on him until he could clearly see the insanity of thinking he could ever have successfully eloped with Jane. Her name in front of him, on the complicated visa application form, the small photograph staring up at him, brought back the happiest memories of his life. He realised that he still wanted Jane more than anything. What had he done to her?

For a long time Nakentov just sat there with the forms shaking in his hands. He was ridiculously close to tears and was grateful for the small office he occupied alone. His first reaction was to reject the application. But his clear duty was to see Jane. He could have got in touch with her from Germany. But he had thought it best for them both that he did not. When he looked down at the passport-sized snapshot, he reflected that he had perhaps been wrong.

It was not going to be easy to see her again and virtually impossible to avoid causing her pain. His feelings for her were just as deep as hers were for him. But he had the unrelenting strength of a totalitarian state behind him to support his difficult decision. There was also the fear of doing the wrong thing and the absolute certainty of reprisal if he did. If he was afraid for himself, he was also afraid for her. If he were caught out, it would be expedient to eliminate her and he knew only too well how easy that would be for his colleagues in London.

To show interest in a visiting tourist or business man was nothing new to Nakentov or his colleagues; all would be under surveillance anyway. Special hotel rooms were allocated to particular languages, and most waiters, concierges, guides were all members of OGPU. So that Jane was not selected alone, Nakentov

49

expressed personal interest in two others on the tour. But it would be difficult for them to meet without apparent recognition on either side.

He had the tour guide report to him and nominated those tourists with whom he wanted to make contact. He questioned the guide about them, and spoke about Jane as if she was a total stranger. The assessment he received from the girl worried him: the guide saw Jane as withdrawn, not a good mixer, and sometimes agitated. He made an arrangement with the guide for the next evening and made further plans for the other two tourists.

The Hotel Moskva was used almost exclusively for overseas visitors. It was medium sized, solid and plain with a slow service and indifferent food. The pillared lounge was spacious and annexed to it was a bar.

When Nakentov entered the hotel, he quickly located the tour guide and Jane seated at a corner table where there was maximum privacy. The guide had invited Jane to a pre-dinner drink before others in the party came down from their rooms.

Nakentov crossed the lounge, catching the eye of the guide who was facing him. The girl made an excuse to Jane and left the table, ostensibly to return. Jane had her back to Nakentov as he approached. As he went past her to take the chair the guide had vacated, he said quickly in English,

"Whatever you do, don't show that you know me."

As he sat down opposite her, Nakentov thought that Jane was going to faint. She clutched the edge of the table. Nakentov looked around quickly. The lounge was sparsely filled and Jane had her back to the room.

"Oh, my God," she said. "I've come all this way to find you and here you are, just like that." She was recovering quickly, colour returning to her cheeks and a new light in her eyes.

"Be careful, my darling," Nakentov said softly. "We must act as strangers and my smile is to persuade a girl I do not know to accept my presence."

She had been about to stretch out her hand to him but now she withdrew it slowly. She was trembling, unable to believe that he was with her.

"I'm sorry to shock you. I saw your visa application and arranged to meet you. The guide invited you here on my behalf. She won't be back."

"Won't she wonder . . . ? You are no longer in trade?"

He smiled and shook his head. "No. No more."

She picked up her drink nervously, gripping the glass with both hands. She drank deeply. "I've waited all this time to hear from you." She spoke with relief rather than anger.

51

"I know Jane, and there's nothing I want to do more now than hold you in my arms. But I dare not."

She stared back at him, bemused.

"We'll sit here for a few minutes, have another drink, give the impression that I am making your acquaintance for the first time. After a while you will agree to come out with me, to the park and then to dinner." He signalled a waiter.

He took her to Sokolniki Park. Their fingers touched as they walked and the temptation to hold hands was almost irresistible. They found an empty bench and sat down. Muscovites were enjoying the evening sun, lying on the grass or sitting on benches; the birds flitted in and out of blossoming trees.

Jane had eyes only for him. It was of no interest to her that children played and parents called out to them; that the weather was fine and the park looked beautiful. She could have been anywhere. It happened to be Moscow where Nakentov was sitting so close to her.

"What went wrong?" she asked him at last.

He told her what he believed to be the truth, that his return to Moscow had made him realise how crazy they had been even to consider elopement. When he looked at her, saw the way she had aged, the weight she had lost, the indifference she had to her appearance, he could only think in abject despair what he could not say aloud: My

God, what have I done to you, how could I have hurt you so?

Jane saw what he told her as half-truth. With perception she said, "Your country means more to you than us?"

"It's not quite like that. It will be difficult for you to understand. This country could destroy both of us."

"Because we're in love?"

He explained as best he could, gave her opinions that were less than prudent. He felt desperate and trapped and wanted her to understand. "Could you not have contacted me?" Jane felt that life was being squeezed from her.

"I had no chance. It is impossible from here." He felt dreadful about lying to her.

"You mean you are not allowed to send a simple letter?"

"Jane, my love, I beg of you, please try to understand."

"I can only understand that you should have relieved my misery and that you did not. Not knowing is worse than receiving bad news. I would have got over it. Now, after three years of hanging on, I learn the truth. You are afraid for yourself."

"No. For both of us. Nothing must happen to you."

"It has already happened. *Look at me, Lubov.*"

He could not. He wanted to hide his face in

53

shame but he could not do that either. "Forgive me," he begged. "Try to forgive me."

She almost stretched out her hand to him, but remembered in time that she must not. Were there watching eyes all over this cursed country? "Is it really too late for us?"

"I could only give you the same promises. And then, when you had gone home, I would find myself under the same impossible pressures."

She considered what he had told her about those pressures. "Were you a spy? In London?" Previously she could never entertain the possibility. Now she was confronting him with it.

"We weren't all spies at Arcos."

"Is that why you met me? Because of where I worked?"

She was being so calm about it, as though these were thoughts that had been kept on ice. "I loved you, Jane. I still love you. And I always will."

She nodded slowly, her eyes red but her tears held in check. "I believe you. What I shall never know is whether you did before or after you took me to bed."

"You're destroying yourself. Please don't. Did I ever ask anything of you? Did I use you at all?"

"No, my dear. Thank you for that." She paused, gazing blindly across the grass. "It's over," she said softly to herself. And suddenly she was crying. The tears flooded down her face but she did not move nor did she sob; it was a

54

quiet release of pain and anguish which had been bottled in her like an emotional bomb.

Nakentov felt his own tears welling as he watched her. He almost threw caution to the winds and moved to embrace her. Then, he stopped. It would make it worse for her. Let her cry. She needed it and perhaps he deserved the torture of seeing her suffering.

Jane wiped her eyes undemonstratively. Straight backed and dignified she presented the perfect image of an English lady. Nakentov admired her for it.

When she had finished, he said, "I know what I've done to you. I shall always have to live with it. Jane, if I thought there was the remotest chance of us getting away with it, I would ask you to take that chance with me."

"You did in London."

"But this is Moscow, my dear." He paused while he struggled to phrase what he wanted to say. "I hold a position here that would make it imperative for them to track me down if I disappeared. And that would mean tracking you down too."

"I would rather die with you, Lubov. Living without will be a more painful way of dying."

Nakentov hung his head; there was no satisfactory answer he could give.

Jane suddenly felt resigned; he loved her, but his love fell short of hers for him. It was resolved, painfully, but finally. She opened her handbag and took from it a sealed envelope which she handed to him. He took it from her quickly concealing it under his hands.

"In there," she said, "is the number of the Swiss bank account which I opened for you. The ownership of the account is anonymous but there is a code to cover the authority of transactions. It is my name spelled backwards plus the month and year of opening. Dranrab 627. It is written down together with the name and address of the bank."

"The money is yours, Jane. Do you think I would take it from you?"

"I don't want it." She told him the story of how she opened the account and of the years since.

"I can understand. But your savings are here too. You may need them later. Take the envelope back."

"I want nothing to remind me of you. The account represents the wonderful days when you had the strength of character to fight for our love. I want no part of it now."

"Give yourself time to think it over. Don't reject it out of pride."

She turned to him, studied the face she loved so much. "Pride is all I have left. If you have any love for me at all you'll make no attempt to change my mind. The money is yours. Your name is irrevocably linked to it."

He wanted the account no more than she. Yet

to accept it was the last thing he could do for her. He slipped the envelope into his pocket, aware of his madness.

Sadly, he asked, "You're not coming to dinner with me, are you?"

"No."

"Not a last meal together?"

"What for? Must we prolong the agony?"

She was showing such immense strength of character he almost broke down. "Thank you for everything, Jane. One day I hope you will *really* understand."

"Will you take me back to join the others? I'm lost here."

They walked slowly back to the hotel, each preoccupied with their own thoughts. They parted like strangers.

Jane saw the tour through with considerable effort. Nakentov kept a distant eye on her until she left the country. He made no record of the meeting, though it should have been normal practice to make out a report.

Meanwhile, in the privacy of his room, he examined the contents of the envelope: the receipt for £21,000, the name and address of the bank, and the account and code numbers. If ever he was found with this information on him, it would be his death warrant.

He could burn the contents of the envelope and that would be that. But eventually the Swiss would try to trace the account holder. Had Jane left a poste restante address with the bank? He should have asked her. Her words came back to him: "Your name is irrevocably linked with it." He felt a twinge of panic. Did she mean that it was traceable to him? Surely not? But he needed to be certain; somehow he had to find out.

There was no safe hiding place that he could think of for the account slips. Then he thought of a solution. It was not uncommon for men to wear gold rings, so he bought a second-hand, broad-banded eighteen-carat ring to fit his little finger. Elsewhere, he bought an engraving tool.

Before applying himself to the ring, he practised with the tool on odd pieces of metal. After a good deal of effort, he worked on the inside of the ring. The result was crude but he managed to scratch the legend: *ZEITLINGER. ZH. 72–598–8764 DRANRAB 627*—ZH represented the first and last letters of Zurich. It took him considerable time and he used two lines for the engraving, but at least it was legible. Finally, he burned the papers and dropped the engraving tool in the Moscow river.

To a layman, the inscription was meaningless. He rubbed round the edges of the figures with abrasive to give an impression of prior wear.

As a bank account was not something that could be given away without raising considerable speculation, Nakentov accepted that he would have to live with it until there was a way to dispose of it. Only then would he have complete peace of mind.

As a major in the OGPU, Nakentov was successful and his superiors considered that he had a very bright future. Pavl Nakentov would go right to the top.

This premise was not unaided by the fact that he was the younger brother of Joseph Stalin's first wife, Ekaterina Svanidze. For Nakentov it was an uneasy relationship, for he was never sure of Stalin's real opinion of him. Nakentov had only been eleven, and his nephew Yasha barely two, when Ekaterina was buried but they had both heard from family friends about Stalin's neglect of his wife. The stories had a profound effect on Yasha who despised his father—and Stalin in turn had no regard for his son. Nakentov never understood why Stalin had brought Yasha to the Kremlin, and then neglected him. It came as no surprise to those who knew him, that Yasha had tried to commit suicide whilst in his teens.

It was from this point that Yasha, who refused to use the name of Stalin and retained the family name of Djugashvili, drew closer to his uncle Pavl Nakentov.

Nakentov made great efforts to break down the barriers that Yasha erected. And he, more than anyone, succeeded. When Nakentov was sent to England with Arcos, Yasha had missed him considerably. Nakentov had become the only person that Yasha was willing to turn to in total confidence. That Nakentov was in OGPU made no difference; their loyalty to the State was not in question. The problem was domestic and emotional and Nakentov gave him the reassurances he needed. They were good friends.

But Nakentov could not turn to Yasha for counsel about Jane Barnard and a secret Swiss bank account, as Yasha could turn to him about the hatred he had for his father.

It was fortuitous that, at the time Jane went back to England, Yasha was going through a bad patch and Nakentov was partially occupied by comforting his nephew. Yasha had heard that Stalin was going to send him to the Caucasus to manage an out-station for farm machinery. He saw this as his father's revenge, because Yasha had not succeeded too well in his training as an electrical engineer.

Nakentov was well aware that Stalin knew of the deep friendship between nephew and uncle and probably recognised its cause. Nakentov shrewdly judged that Stalin also saw his influence, more than anyone else's, having a good effect on Yasha, and keeping him out of trouble.

For a time, family affairs and involvement in his work kept Nakentov fully occupied. He didn't take up the matter of the account at Zeitlinger until, late in 1931, he was posted to Berne as second secretary, and the new "resident" of OGPU.

He worked for some weeks in Berne before making the short journey to Zürich. And even then he was careful not to go immediately to the Zeitlinger Bank. It was over-caution but he could not remove the feeling that this particular posting might have a sinister background. He was being influenced by his own guilt.

The manager he saw at the Zeitlinger was not the one Jane had seen. His name was Brun. To Nakentov, his neat, polite image represented the suave capitalist class which he despised so much. It did not register with him that these beliefs had been badly shaken during his spell in London but, since his return to Moscow, had intensified to a degree well beyond the bounds of indoctrination and had become an armour against what he had done to Jane.

After Nakentov's credentials, in the form of the code, had been examined, Brun sent for details of the account to find that for almost four years the money had been stagnating and that no contact had been made by the client. Well then, how could he help?

Nakentov had considered the matter carefully. "I want you to invest the entire sum in any way that you think fit, on my behalf but in your name."

Brun was astounded. "I can't do that. We're bankers, not brokers."

"Is it not the same thing?"

"Totally different."

"Well, that's what I want you to do."

"Why not invest it yourself?"

"I shall make mistakes. I'll leave it to you."

"We, too, can make mistakes. Believe me. Get some advice on it."

Nakentov had not expected obstruction. All capitalists were decadent and crooks and bank managers were the biggest crooks of them all. He was relying on that assumption.

Nakentov had to be careful. He spoke fluent German but he knew he had an accent and he did not want it identified; the Swiss were so used to dealing with foreigners. At last he said, "I am perfectly willing to take your advice."

Brun considered this. "All right. I can give you advice which I believe to be sound, but it will be no guarantee of good investment. There are many safe possibilities but the growth rate will be much slower. However, you must do the actual investing yourself."

Nakentov shook his head. "Your job is handling money. If you can't handle mine, I'll take it to someone who can."

The possible loss of the account left Brun unmoved. It was no threat to the bank but, even so, no manager likes losing an account and this one presented a new challenge. He carefully considered Nakentov's request; the man was obviously quite serious. "I'm willing to put it forward to my directors. Can you come back in a week's time? I can have an answer for you by then."

Nakentov was annoyed but he could not see what else he could do. Coming back would be a risk.

"It is inconvenient, so I trust you'll have the right answer on my return. So that there is no misunderstanding let me make it clear what I want." He tapped the desk to emphasise his points. "I want no safe investment. I want a gamble. I'm not interested in slow development. Speculate. The money will be of no particular loss to me if you are unlucky. I will not complain. Just use your own judgement." He spoke as if the account was a tiny part of his financial resources.

Brun looked at him across the desk. Nakentov wondered if he had gone too far. But Brun smiled politely. "An interesting prospect. I'll see what can be done."

Nakentov left the bank wondering, as Jane had, why was it all so difficult. But, when he returned a week later, Brun greeted him affably.

"We're willing to do it, sir. There was much heart searching for it presents us with an enormous responsibility. Our job is to protect your money not to gamble with it."

Nakentov nodded impatiently. He had given the bank an open opportunity to embezzle him out of the total amount. The money would dissipate, the bank would gain, and the account would die. He failed to see why they must go through this charade of meetings.

Brun produced two typed sheets.

"This has been drawn up by our lawyers. You must sign and it will be witnessed. You had better read it."

"I trust you. Give me the essence."

"We will invest for you on the authorisation of this document. We are absolved from all responsibility if we invest badly. The investments will be in our name, even the anonymity of your account code will be protected. On all profits made for you, we will want a commission. The amount is stated."

"It is understood that I want no investment in slow growth?"

"That adds considerably to the risks but it is understood."

Unknown to both men, Brun was launching the pilot scheme to what, in later years, was to be known as a fiduciary account. To bank in secrecy has always been a prerogative of Swiss banks. Dranrab 627 was the first account to be *invested* in secrecy with the real investor remaining anonymous.

Nakentov glanced through the forms; he was not really interested in them. "There is one point I must stress, Mr. Brun. I want a clause stating that the account is to be automatically closed and the code destroyed should the money be lost."

Brun sent the document out for the clause to

be included. He thought Nakentov's attitude cavalier, almost as though he wanted the money to be lost. When the document came back, Nakentov signed in the code and two bank employees signed as witnesses. It was done.

Before he left, he tidied up the ends. He discovered that Jane had supplied a poste restante address in London and this he had annulled. He did not provide another. The only contact between client and bank would be from Nakentov alone. He could see no way that the account could be traced to him but he would be much happier when it was dead.

Nakentov left the bank satisfied. He was quite sure that he had given the Zeitlinger a carte-blanche to steal his money, for he had placed himself in the position of being unable to protest. He was convinced that eventually the account would terminate.

As General Georgi Stevinski sat on the wooden chair listening to the low mumbling of his old comrade Pavl Nakentov, his face was grim. The tape was running quietly, the microphone close to Nakentov's moving lips. The coherence of Nakentov's speech fell far short of the vividness of his drug-induced dreams. Nakentov was reliving a part of his life and the suffering of the English woman he loved so deeply; she must have been constantly on his mind.

Stevinski had the essence. He could not be sure

of what the tape had picked up until he played it back and he was not ready to do that. There were gaps but, armed with what he had already learned, he expected no difficulty in extracting the rest once Nakentov came round and was confronted with what he had already revealed.

But if Stevinski had obtained enough bare bones to make a framework which disturbed him considerably, he was yet to hear the worst. As Nakentov rambled on Stevinski leaned closer, pleased that he had had the foresight to dismiss the doctor.

A shudder ran through Nakentov and Stevinski pulled the topcoat higher round the body, tucking it in to give his old chief more warmth. The action was not one entirely of compassion; Nakentov was living in the past and Stevinski did not want the intermittent flow interrupted.

There was a hiatus in Nakentov's mind; a void where nothing happened for a long time. It was a natural mental break because his recollections so far were geared to that part of his life which had been influenced by love and guilt. From the moment he left the Zeitlinger Bank, a weight was lifted from his shoulders. He found he was better able to put Jane, and the fortune he dare not keep, from his mind.

After serving three successful years in Switzerland, Nakentov was brought back to Moscow for a spell and was promoted to colonel. He later served two more years in Austria but was recalled because, for the first time in what had developed into a distinguished career, he was felt to be at risk. One of his agents was a possible double.

Back in Moscow he took up his old friendship with Yasha whom Stalin had brought back from the Caucasus. There was a strong smell of war in the air and Russia, along with others beyond the Nazi orbit, was not prepared. Yasha was a Red Army reservist.

As Yasha and Nakentov re-kindled their deep-rooted friendship, Nakentov could see that Yasha's exile had done nothing for his nerves nor endeared him any more to his father. This created a problem, for Yasha loved his country but hated his father more than ever before.

Just after Britain and France declared war on Germany, Nakentov felt that Yasha would really crack up. Having tried to commit suicide once he seemed poised to attempt it again. Nakentov, deeply worried about his nephew, kept in constant touch.

And then one day Yasha's young wife contacted Nakentov to tell him that Yasha had threatened to end it all. Nakentov hurried round to see what he could do. When the two men were alone Yasha confirmed that he felt he could not go on living; he believed that his father was ruining the country and had become a mass murderer, killing off many of his own and Yasha's friends.

They drank and talked through the night but the drink merely made Yasha more depressed.

Nakentov could see that he was losing his influence, that their friendship was not enough to stop Yasha committing suicide. He tried a desperate measure because, at the time, he believed it to be safe and he knew that Yasha would not betray him.

They were in Yasha's apartment in the Kremlin, perhaps the safest place for what Nakentov was about to do. He looked around the dull room that so much reflected the resentment and the dark moods of Yasha himself. Yasha was sitting in an armchair opposite his uncle, empty glass in hand, long face gaunt, cheeks sunken, and lank hair, usually combed right back, falling forward over his face.

"Listen to me, Yasha," Nakentov made his last effort. "If things are so desperate, you don't have to stay here."

Yasha gave a sickly grin. "Where then can I go? Where can I escape the long arms of the pillaging bear?"

Nakentov knew that Yasha was referring to his father. "Out of Russia. It doesn't matter where."

"Russia is my home. This is where I belong."

"This is where you belong—but to live—not to die as you intend to. If an alternative is open to you it leaves a loophole, somewhere to run if the need is strong enough. If you know a door is open for you, it might help you to bear it here—knowing that you can escape if necessary."

Yasha sighed and reached for the bottle. He

had enormous respect for Uncle Pavl. It was a friendship without which he would probably not be here now.

"This time you can't save me," he said morosely. "Don't try. I've had enough. Anyway to leave here is not easy and I would need money."

"I can fix it for you to get out. Just shout and leave the rest to me. As for money, well . . ." Nakentov slipped off the ring and held it up with a smile. "I'm not simply offering the ring—it's not worth much anyway—but the information it contains. Now listen carefully, Yasha, I must have your full attention."

Yasha stared across the room; the ring was like a magnet, holding his gaze hypnotically. Just for a moment, his depression lightened as the metal glowed under the light.

"This belonged to one of my German agents I used as a paymaster. He had this account in Zurich into which he fed funds I supplied. He was killed quite accidentally by a tramcar. I had some difficulty in finding the details of his account and had to burgle his apartment after his death. I had the detail scratched into this ring to pass on to someone else the next time I go back there. Good paymasters are not easy to find."

Nakentov made sure that Yasha was listening, and then he went on, "The account was in code. On the inside of the ring is the name of the bank in Zürich, the account number and the code which is substitute for a signature." He passed the ring over. "Can you read it?"

Yasha held the ring under the light and peered at it, turning it round until he could make sense of the inscription. Nakentov was already pleased because Yasha was concentrating on something other than his own problems.

"It's very worn," said Yasha. "But I can just about make it out." Hesitantly, he read the scratched details aloud.

Nakentov smiled. It was important now to keep Yasha occupied. "I don't know what's in the account. Possibly little. But if you ever feel the strain is too great to bear here, there will be some funds there that you can use. It's a way out, eh? Something to fall back upon in an emergency. Put the ring on."

Nakentov was hoping that the ring would fit one of Yasha's fingers and it did, the little finger of his right hand. Yasha took it off again. "I can't take this."

"Of course you can. The account isn't mine."

"But the money belongs to the State."

"Not entirely. The German Communists provided quite a bit in the way of funds. This was a method of disguising the fact and that was why it was banked in Switzerland. Nobody knows about it but me, and now you, and the man who opened the account is dead. Keep it as a lifeline, no more. When you feel depressed like tonight, you look at that ring and say to yourself here is the key to the escape door if ever I need to open it."

And that was the psychological basis of Nakentov's gesture. He did not believe that there was any money left in the account. He was not even sure that the account still existed for, if the money had gone, it would have been closed. Nor did he believe for one moment that Yasha would attempt to leave Russia. What he had done was to provide hope for his friend and an anchor to hold on to in times of stress. He noticed that Yasha put the ring back on his finger.

"I don't have to tell you, old friend," Nakentov added, "that if anyone finds out about that we will both be shot."

Yasha, still fingering the ring, gave a faint smile. He pushed his hair away from his eyes. "You are right, Pavl, but you don't have to tell me. I'd never get you into trouble. You are the only person I trust."

The war continued and Russia was sucked into the vortex in spite of her peace treaty with Nazi Germany. Yasha Djugashvili was called up and posted as an Artillery Lieutenant on the Byelorussian front. He was captured by the Nazis at Ljosno on the 16th July 1941 as the Germans drove for Smolensk and Moscow. He was still wearing the ring.

4

NAKENTOV stopped talking. His eyes fluttered. For him the long secret episode of his life had ended; he had just lived through it a second time. There was no more to dream about, nothing to relate.

Stevinski sat on the chair, elbows on knees, hands clenched. The only sound was the whirr of the tape. He leaned forward to switch it off, the click like a small explosion in the damp cell. He sat still for several minutes sometimes looking at Nakentov, sometimes with head lowered. His face was taut, his breathing slow and heavy and his deep eyes worried. Who could believe it? Old Pavl. For over fifty years he had carried this secret. What had happened to the account?

Stevinski rose like an old man. He stood over Nakentov who was now stirring. There were still points that had to be clarified. The name of the bank had come over clear enough but the figures that had followed had sounded jumbled. Would Nakentov have remembered them after so long? The tape may have picked up the account number and the code more clearly than Stevinski's ears but it was a risk he was not prepared to take. Whenever Nakentov had spoken of his lover he had referred to her as Jane. The code name had sounded like Arabic and, as yet, Stevinski hadn't recognised it as an anagram of her surname. It was best to be sure.

Stevinski went to the door and called the doctor who was waiting. The doctor entered the cell, stared down at Nakentov. "He's tough, my God. Eighty-five and struggling out of it. Look at him."

"Give him another shot. I'm not finished."

The doctor shook his head. "It will finish him."

"That's what you said before. Do it."

"That's an order, Comrade General?"

"I'll give it to you in writing afterwards, if that's what you want. A mild dose should do. There are just one or two more questions I want to put to him."

The doctor opened his bag. "I would like it on record that I do this against my better judgement."

"Get on with it, man. If he dies, he dies."

"With what you need to know, General?"

The doctor examined Nakentov first, peeling back the topcoat. The pulse was surprisingly strong. Nakentov was tough, all right, but there was a limit to what he could withstand. As Stevinski was watching closely, the doctor dared not give *too* mild a dose though. He believed it might finish off the old life system by arresting the heart. He injected, packed his syringe, and left the cell.

Stevinski made sure the door was properly

closed before returning to Nakentov. "Right, old friend. You've shaken me to my boots and that's not easy." He switched on the tape, adjusted the microphone and quietly demanded, "Tell me the account number and code again. Speak slowly and clearly."

Nakentov's lips moved. Then his eyes opened wide and stared straight at Stevinski. He could feel death creeping over him. He quietly accused his one-time pupil: "Murderer." He made a supreme effort. "How well did I teach you, Georgi? How many marks have you scored? Where have I lied? Where is the truth? It is not the account that should worry you but what has it been used for? And is still being . . ." Nakentov's lips did not move again.

Stevinski felt the icy chill of uncertainty. The last few sentences were not the rambling of a drug-filled old man. Nakentov had placed in doubt the validity of everything he had recounted. Stevinski shook him by the shoulders. Nakentov's mouth remained open, the lids half closed.

Before calling the doctor Stevinski unstrapped his watch and held it over Nakentov's mouth; there was no breath mist. The doctor came in and made a perfunctory examination before proclaiming Nakentov dead. As he gave Stevinski his diagnosis, the doctor kept his expression blank. It was clear that Stevinski had just received a severe shock.

"You want me to make out a death certificate of heart failure?"

"No." Stevinski was gazing thoughtfully at the corpse. "I'll have him taken back to his apartment. In due course he'll be found; then I shall want a death certificate."

"His own doctor will be called in."

"Then find him and warn him."

The doctor left, these were matters he understood but he could not help wondering why Stevinski wanted such a cover up.

Stevinski made arrangements for Nakentov's body to be taken back to the apartment that night. He wanted nobody to witness its return and he stressed the point to his men.

Stevinski returned to his office at the Centre and instructed his staff that he was not to be disturbed. He sat with arms folded on the desk and gazed into space. Nakentov's last words filled his head. He realised that this was something he could not keep to himself. It was a matter that must be discussed at the highest level. Stevinski would speak to the Secretary General himself who would decide whether or not it should be raised with the Politburo. He was quite certain that it would not be an issue for the Council of Ministers, nor even the Central Committee. But first he had to find out precisely what he had on record.

He played the tape back and, as so often on these occasions, the reproduction was anything but perfect. The strength of Nakentov's voice varied considerably and often faded.

The bank details did not come over sufficiently clearly for him to decipher the codes. He cut out the section of the tape concerned, and rang for one of his specialists. "Get that down to the audio section and unravel it. I want it now." There was equipment in the laboratory that could amplify and separate the sounds.

While he was waiting, he considered the implications of what he had learned. Perhaps the most revered figure the KGB had ever known had turned out to be a possible defector and a criminal who had siphoned off government funds.

For over fifty years Nakentov had succeeded in concealing his crimes. And the stunning prospect was that the account had, after all, been used over the years. For what? Had corruption continued? Was it still continuing? If Nakentov's last words were to be taken seriously, then the rottenness may have spread well beyond him. The thought made Stevinski shiver. Whom could he trust now?

For a moment Stevinski was consoled by the possibility that Nakentov's last words had been deliberately misleading. But he dared not take the chance of believing that, not with someone as wily as Nakentov had been.

Nakentov's successes in his long service were quoted to all recruits. Nakentov had probably covered more ground than anyone; he had become a living legend. It was an image that must be protected at all costs. To expose one of the most successful and most trusted officers of the KGB, a man who had been Chairman of the State Security as Stevinski was now, would have a disastrous effect on morale, be of enormous propaganda value to the West and do nothing to reassure Russia's friends.

Stevinski was well aware that the Soviet Union was suffering more than it had done for very many years. Economically she was in a bad way. There were still problems with Afghanistan and Poland, and signs of unrest elsewhere which enemies of the State were closely watching. The effects of exposing Nakentov, once possibly the most powerful man in Russia, could be far reaching. There had been too many internal scandals.

But his treachery went beyond his love affair, his embezzling of State funds and his fraudulent handling of agents. It appeared that he had corrupted Stalin's own son, Jacob. If ever that was discovered, Russia would become a laughing stock. It was true that Stalin himself had been discredited some years after his death. But not in this way. Nakentov and Jacob Djugashvili—his brother-in-law and son—had not only been traitors in their actions and in their collusion; they had become *capitalists*. It was unthinkable.

The more he went over it, the more Stevinski realised that this was a matter to be nailed down and buried. But he must find out if the account still existed and, if so, who was using it and whether it was traceable to Nakentov. If it had been closed, he would be both relieved and satisfied. If it was still open . . . The thought of what he might uncover unsettled even Stevinski's strong nerves.

He sent for the file relating to Stalin's eldest son and, to confuse the issue, asked for some others concerning POWs during World War II.

Yasha had been interned at Sachsenhausen concentration camp. Stalin himself had been informed and an exchange of prisoners suggested. It was then that the intense dislike that Stalin had for his son became openly evident. He refused any form of exchange and claimed that his son was guilty of treason for defying orders to defend Smolensk to the last man, and ordered the arrest of Jacob's wife for helping him to desert.

It was not pleasant reading. Stalin had died in 1953 without knowing for certain what had happened to Yasha and apparently indifferent to his fate.

It seemed that Yasha had, at last, committed suicide, but there was no real evidence of it. There was also a strong rumour that he had escaped. Stevinski put the file down. It was just possible that Yasha was still alive—and using the account. Somehow he had to find out what had happened.

The short section of tape took longer to

decipher than Stevinski had hoped and it was late afternoon before the tape and the slip of paper with its message were laid before him. He picked up the paper, and read: 72–598–8764 CODE DRANRAB 627.

Stevinski glanced up at the research assistant. "Are you sure?"

"Absolutely, Comrade General. It was tricky raising it but that is what's on the tape."

Stevinski nodded a dismissal. It should be easy. If the account was still alive, he would simply take it over and change the code, effectively blocking off anyone who might be using it. He felt a little better. But the lid still had to be nailed down tight.

He rang for Colonel Utenko who often executed personal tasks for him. When the tall, lanky colonel came in Stevinski asked, "You received the information about Jane Barnard's diary direct from our London resident?"

"Yes."

"No one else knows?"

"Just the two of us, this end, General."

"How did he get hold of it?"

"Apparently one of our more fervent pseudo-intellectual English supporters has a girlfriend who is a nurse looking after Miss Barnard and he heard from her about it. It didn't amount to much but the name Lubov intrigued him and he insisted that someone at the embassy should hear about it."

"So who at the embassy was so smart?"

"Anton." Utenko used the code name of a KGB man. "Lubov was a name to be respected by those who knew. Anton checked back on the period. Arcos. Miss Barnard was dying but her diary would go on living—and could be important. It was worth a routine check. Anton used an English burglar who does odd jobs for him."

"Lucky, then?" commented Stevinski.

"That depends on what you found out," said Utenko guardedly. "But Anton must take credit for using his initiative."

"Who else knows?"

"The nurse, obviously. And there's the great-nephew of Miss Barnard. I don't know if there's anyone else."

"Find out. I want anyone who knows about that diary located and eliminated."

Utenko was shaken. He had not expected such a dramatic turn from Stevinski. "Including our informer?"

"Especially him. Tell them to use as many staff as necessary. And I want the diary brought here to me."

Colonel Utenko left wondering what the general was keeping so close to his chest that warranted the removal of innocent British citizens.

When the door was closed Stevinski reached for pen and paper. He made a list of those people who knew of the diary. The nurse and her boyfriend had been disposed of; the great-nephew was still floating. In his own department, Colonel Utenko knew of it but had reported to him. In London, Anton had done the same. Neither man, if implicated in any of Nakentov's schemes, would have been so foolish as to declare their knowledge of the diary. Tentatively, therefore, they could be trusted.

Who else could he trust? Nakentov had raised a huge question mark over the bank account. Was it being used as a pay office for doubles? Traitors? Stevinski stared at the paper with its pathetically few names and cursed Nakentov for so clear mindedly uttering his last words.

Raya Dubrova called at her grandfather's apartment late that evening. On opening the door she was relieved to find the lights on. She could hear the television.

She called out, closed the front door and entered the lounge. Nakentov was sitting in an armchair with his back to her watching an agricultural programme. That surprised her.

"Where have you been, Poppa? I called this morning." When he did not reply she smiled, thinking he must have dozed off. She patted the top of his head as she rounded the chair but he gave no response. His eyes were closed.

Raya crossed over to switch off the set. "Wake up," she said. "I'll make you some tea."

But Nakentov did not stir and it was then that she realised he was not sitting naturally. It seemed as if he was propped up. His mouth was slightly open. She gently shook his shoulder and he fell sideways.

Raya jumped back, alarmed. Tentatively she felt his face; it was cold. She made herself raise an eyelid and a sightless eye stared back at her. She swallowed and tried his pulse. Then she straightened. It was hard to accept that so vital a man had died. Her eyes pricked with tears; she had admired and loved her grandfather.

Raya struggled to lift him in the chair again so that he did not loll so dreadfully. And as she did so she wondered how long he might have been sitting there.

She checked the phone pad and called Nakentov's doctor. As her mother was not on the telephone, Raya couldn't tell her until she reached home. While she waited she made tea. As she leaned against the counter in the kitchen, she noticed the message she had left that morning. It was still under the corner of the bread bin.

Raya found that odd, for it had been routine for him to check for messages. It implied that Nakentov had not come into the kitchen to eat or even to make himself a drink. Had he come straight in, switched on the television and sat down? It was possible. But unlikely.

She checked the bedroom. That was the same

as she had last seen it, curtains drawn back as they were in the kitchen. She checked the food cupboard; the items she had put there were as she had arranged them.

In the hall, his topcoat was hanging on a hook instead of the customary hanger. She told herself she was being stupid, making something out of nothing, yet the fact remained that there were several small inconsistencies in the flat that she couldn't make sense of. They reminded her of the shadowy life her grandfather must have led as Chairman of the KGB. It was best not to dwell on it.

The doctor arrived surprisingly quickly, bearded and reassuring. He told her he would attend to everything. It made her realise just how important Nakentov had once been.

The doctor examined Nakentov while Raya went back into the kitchen. She did not want to watch her grandfather being handled like a carcase.

The doctor called her in, he was buttoning Nakentov's shirt. He smiled at Raya. "Almost certainly a heart attack. He was a good age."

"Yes. I suppose we've been expecting it but he was so full of life."

"He was lucky to go like that." The doctor closed his bag. "You need do nothing. I will arrange everything for you."

"Shouldn't my mother make the funeral arrangements?"

The doctor pulled on his coat. "Normally, my dear. But this is Comrade General Nakentov who holds almost every major distinction the State can offer. He will be buried with full honours."

Raya had not thought so far ahead. The personal little chats and the many laughs she had enjoyed with her grandfather had not prepared her for the national display of mourning that would follow his death. "You mean military bands? That sort of thing?"

"Of course." The doctor stared at her across Nakentov's body. His tone was friendly as he said, "You are surprised? Then let me tell you that it will not stop at military bands. The President and the Secretary General with other dignitaries will be at the funeral. Your grandfather will not lie in state, but it will be the next best thing."

"I see." Suddenly, Nakentov had ceased to be a grandfather. Now he was dead he was being handed back to the State. He would have wanted a quiet funeral.

"How long has he been dead?"

The doctor looked at Raya sharply. "It's difficult to tell. But sometime this evening. A few hours."

"Is it possible to tell whether he'd eaten anything recently?"

The doctor put his bag down on top of the television. "That is a very strange question."

Raya realised that she had been imprudent but

equally she was determined to go through with it. "He liked his food. He always told me that age was supposed to subdue the taste buds but it had never done so to him. He hasn't been into the kitchen to eat."

"My dear girl, that is something you cannot possibly know for certain unless you were here." The doctor was pulling thoughtfully at his beard.

Raya saw the dangers of what she had raised. What did it matter? Nakentov was dead. "It was just a thought," she said lamely.

The doctor smiled again. "Well, it would be impossible to tell whether or not he had eaten without an autopsy and there is no justification for one." He cocked his head and stared down quizzically at Nakentov. He reached for his bag again. "I must go. There is much to do." And then as he reached the door. "Can I give you a lift?"

"No thank you. I'll stay a little longer to pay my last respects."

After he had gone she wondered why he had not used the telephone to call an ambulance to remove Nakentov's body and why he had not asked for a key to the apartment? Perhaps he didn't need one.

Raya asked the neighbours if they remembered when Nakentov had returned. Her feeling of disquiet grew when they all denied seeing him, but at this stage she considered it best to keep her suspicions to herself.

Eddie Tyler had made the funeral arrangements for his great-aunt. He somehow felt that she would prefer to be buried than cremated. Old values had been important to her. He had checked with her solicitor and searched most of her papers to find relatives who should be told; there were surprisingly few on record.

It was three days after her death and he was still living in his aunt's house as a matter of convenience until she was buried. The door bell rang. When he opened the door his first reaction was to think: another bloody copper. A warrant card was flashed at him. "DS Savage, sir. Can I have a word?"

Eddie let him in. The two men were of similar height but the policeman was thicker, heavier, and a little older.

"DS?" queried Eddie.

"Detective sergeant."

They went into the study where Eddie had been trying to find insurance policies. "Things are improving," commented Eddie dryly. "I've only had a detective constable, so far."

The sergeant smiled. "Then you can expect an inspector next."

"Tea?"

"Why not? It's about the burglary."

"I keep telling them; only a diary was taken."
They went into the kitchen.

"You considered it important enough to report."

"Sure. The house was broken into and the shock probably killed my aunt. What else could I do?" Eddie flicked the kettle switch.

"And you only told the nurse about it?"

"That's right. Strong or weak?"

"As it comes. Tell me what you remember about the diary." As he saw Eddie's look of exasperation, Savage added, "I know you've said it all before but we're flummoxed as to why someone should only nick an old diary."

Eddie found himself warming to Savage. There was no officiousness about the sergeant. "I'm sorry I ever mentioned it to Mary Hayes but I couldn't foresee any of this happening. It's crazy." He told Savage the little he remembered. Only the name of Lubov stood out from the rest.

"Sounds Russian," commented Savage as if it was the first time he had heard the name.

"I don't know." Eddie passed over a cup of tea. "She was terribly upset when she saw me holding the diary. She probably loved him. There was always a sadness about her that I couldn't fathom."

They stood to drink their tea. Savage peered above the rim of the cup, steam distorting the shape of his eyes. "You thought a lot of her?" he observed shrewdly.

Eddie nodded. "I liked the old girl. She'd suffered somehow."

"But she knew how to hold her tongue, though."

Eddie raised his head. "Hadn't thought of it like that. But you're right. Whatever bugged her she kept to herself."

"Makes you wonder why, doesn't it?" Savage put down his cup.

Eddie fingered the roll neck sweater at his throat. The sergeant was raising his curiosity again when he had almost put the diary from his mind.

Later, Savage swilled his cup at the sink. Over his shoulder he said, "While you're going through your aunt's stuff look out for anything unusual."

"What sort of unusual?"

"If I knew that it wouldn't be unusual. Anything that doesn't gel, that fits no pattern. I know it sounds trite, but anything at all you can't explain or understand."

"Can't we let her rest in peace?"

"*You* called us in."

"Yeah. Well, it seemed the right thing to do at the time."

"Don't you want your aunt's diary back? It obviously meant a good deal to her."

Eddie took his own cup over to the sink. "We'll not get it back, let's forget it."

Savage put down his cup. "Y'know, for a

journalist you're not showing a frantic amount of interest."

"An out-of-work reporter; a cast off from a local rag. Big stuff. Anyway, I have the feeling that Aunt Jane would prefer it to be buried with her."

"Okay." Savage straightened. "But I do need your cooperation. Is there a room upstairs with net curtains?"

Eddie stared at the sergeant in mock surprise. "You mean you didn't notice? All the upstairs front rooms have net curtains."

"Take me up to one. Any one."

Mystified, Eddie led the way upstairs to the room he was using. Savage went round the bed to the bay window and peered down obliquely into the street. "Come over here," he instructed. As Eddie joined him, he continued, "Don't touch the curtains. See the cream coloured Ford? There, behind the Rover. There's a bloke in it watching this house."

"You're barmy."

"I know him. I spotted him on the way in."

"Why, for God's sake?"

"I don't know why. But I bloody well want to find out."

"You're crazy," Eddie commented scathingly, following him down the stairs to the hall.

"So humour me." Savage pulled out a note-book and tore out a page on which he scribbled briefly. "Have a good look through her stuff. If anything strikes you, give me a ring at the Yard —Special Branch. Don't worry about wasting my time. Anything. That's the number and my extension."

Eddie stared incredulously at the slip of paper.

"And don't let chummy know that you know he's watching you." Savage opened the front door. "I'll be in touch."

Eddie carefully locked the door. It was a peculiar feeling to be in a house that was being watched; life had suddenly stopped being humdrum. Clearly, Aunt Jane had had a secret, but he wasn't sure that he wanted to know what it was.

He went into the room where his aunt had lain. Her body had been removed by the undertakers, the bed stripped. Nurse Hayes had left as soon as the doctor had confirmed the old lady's death and the house felt empty and lonely.

Special Branch? Eddie went into the study again and continued to go through the drawers, trying to sort out the various papers.

He found nothing unusual in his methodical search. Old letters were mundane and unrevealing. Recipes were piled neatly in folders. He went from room to room, poking about in drawers and cupboards, and then made a search of the upstairs.

In what had been Aunt Jane's bedroom before her stroke, was a Victorian wardrobe with a high-topped pediment. He had already rummaged through her hanging clothes and the drawer beneath. He stood on the dressing-table stool to look over the pediment.

There were three ancient, dust-covered suit-cases and, as he lifted them down one at a time, they all seemed to be empty. They were also locked, and he had to sort through a mass of keys before he could open them.

Two were empty, the silk linings faded and filled with the musty smell of age, and the smallest case had nothing in it but yellowed newspaper clippings. Eddie put the cases back on top of the wardrobe and took the clippings downstairs to the study.

By now it was dusk. He pulled the curtains before putting the light on, unable to get used to the feeling of being spied upon. He sat down at the desk, and went through the clippings.

They all related to the raid on Arcos in 1927 and the subsequent repercussions. There were pictures of the Russians leaving. Names from recent history came to life during the reading: Baldwin, Churchill. Some of the Russians were named, too, but nobody called Lubov. In the space above one of the articles he noticed some pencilled remarks which were too faded to read.

Eddie Tyler prepared himself a hasty meal and, when he had finished eating, went back to the study to read the clippings again in an effort to obtain a running story. He had never heard of

Arcos, or realised that major Russian spying went so far back in Britain.

Long before he had finished it was clear that this was the sort of information Detective Sergeant Savage wanted. But Eddie needed time to think. *Could Aunt Jane have been mixed up with spies?* He tried to imagine her as she might have been way back in the twenties. There were no early photographs of her except one in an old passport and she had appeared rather ordinary.

Whilst he did not like the idea of her being a spy, the possibility offered a new dimension to her character. He had always believed that she did not lack courage and it seemed that he was right. As he turned over the clippings he found himself smiling. She must have fooled everybody. And yet he had always found her so stoically British.

In Eddie's mind, she would never be the same again. Yet he felt a strong need to protect her. He was not sure why except that he had always been close to her. He felt emotional, as if he had not done enough for her while she was alive, and now he must make amends.

They sat in the Mini which was parked in the quiet lane and, as they cuddled, Mary Hayes tried to discourage her boyfriend's rising passion. His mysterious intensity and dark good looks had always attracted her but now she was annoyed with him over the diary and angry with herself for telling him.

Although she lay in his arms and half-heartedly responded to his caresses, Mary was sorry that she had agreed to meet him. She had meant to ask him whom he had told about the diary but it now seemed pointless.

"Take me home," she said suddenly. They were to be her last words. The ten tonner grew from the darkness and bore down on them without lights. They did not see it until it actually crashed into them—and then only fleetingly and far too late. It was like a tank running over them. Mary screamed both in fright and in agony as they were crushed to death in the concertinaed Mini. The lorry backed off, then made sure of the job, until there was just a mass of crumpled metal and broken bone, lubricated by a flow of petrol, oil and escaping blood.

By the time the screech of ruptured metal drew people from nearby houses, the ten tonner had disappeared.

A few people gathered at the house, relatives and friends. A funeral brought together people who would not meet again until the next one.

At the graveside it was cold and blustery and Eddie glanced around to see if there was anyone on the fringe of the small gathering who might have him under observation. His gaze spread out to the nearby trees.

She was gone forever, six feet down; her past buried with her, for Eddie had made up his mind to tell Special Branch nothing. He muttered a silent prayer, groping for unfamiliar words and forgotten beliefs, knowing that Aunt Jane would have wanted them. He said his goodbyes and trudged back to the house.

On the way back a car veered, just missing him as he crossed a road. His own quick reflexes saved him and he shouted abuse at the disappearing car. Mad bastard, he thought, but the anger passed as he walked on.

The house was full of her presence. He groped around in the kitchen until he found some cooking sherry. As he drank the coarse wine he was reminded of his own plight. He guessed he would get something from Aunt Jane but he did not expect much. His attitude to money was so casual that he had no idea whether the house was hers, or rented, or mortgaged, or loaned. He had found no papers relating to it. Perhaps they were with the solicitor, and everyone knew that lawyers took their time.

He made a final tour of the rooms and tidied up. After his father had died, his mother had remarried and gone to Canada, and Eddie had moved in with friends. It was time to return to them yet he felt a strange reluctance to leave. It was almost dark when, on sudden impulse, he took the old newspaper clippings from the desk

94

drawer and put them in a pocket. He did not want strangers or lawyers reading them.

The telephone rang, cutting through the silence and making him jump. He picked up the phone, rather breathless.

"Is that you, Tyler?"

"Who the hell do you think it is?" Eddie was angry at being so startled. "Who are you?"

"Sergeant Savage. Are you alone?"

"Of course I'm . . . Yes, I'm alone."

"Lock all your doors and windows. Don't let anyone in. *No one.* I'll ring two shorts and three long. *Stay there and do as I say.* We're on our way."

Eddie found himself holding the receiver long after Savage had rung off. He felt shaken, the sergeant's tone had not been one to argue with. He put down the phone and looked around quickly. He was pretty sure that everything was locked up but double-checked, trying doors and examining window catches. He peered through the upstairs net but could not see the cream Ford. What the bloody hell was going on?

The door bell rang. Eddie stood rooted. He gazed around as though someone might already be in the house. One long peal followed by a dreadful silence. He went into the hall and stared at the solid pine door. There was no sound from outside.

The bell rang again, more persistently, and the shrill sound filled the house with an electronic scream. When it eventually stopped Eddie was tempted to call out to ask who was there and then he noticed that he had not slid the heavy bolts across the front door.

He crept along the hall and reached up to push the top bolt. As he eased it across, he saw the big brass knob turn and felt pressure against the door. No longer caring what noise he made he rammed home both bolts as fast as he could.

He stepped back, pulse racing, and worried about the windows. He wished that Savage would hurry up but it was a fair distance from Scotland Yard to Bayswater, and it was peak traffic time. Hurrying back to the kitchen, Eddie took another swig of cooking sherry.

He felt helpless and looked around for some kind of weapon, settling for an old-fashioned brass-handled poker which was propped up on the Sussex firedogs in the lounge fireplace. He felt better. He went round the ground floor checking everything again. The back door was locked, the fanlight above it closed. It was something to do, for now that the ringing had stopped the continuing silence, broken only by the occasional creaking of the old house, was unnerving.

Eventually he sat down on the edge of a chair, poker in hand, applying sinister meanings to every small sound. How could the fear he felt stem from the past antics of his aunt? Had *she* suffered this sort of feeling?

The bell rang again and he jumped from the

chair; two shorts, three long like a segment of morse code. Eddie went into the hall and approached the door. Taking no chances he called out, "Who is it?"

"Police."

"*Who*?"

"Savage." This time the shout came through the letter-box. Eddie pulled back the bolts and unlatched the door and Savage and another, tall, fair-haired man pushed their way in.

Savage asked brusquely, "Anyone try to get in?" He noticed the poker Eddie still carried.

"Someone rang the bell twice and tried the door. What the bloody hell's going on?"

"You'd better leave here or they might try to kill you. We'll put you up for a while."

"Kill me? Who, for Christ's sake?"

Savage did not answer directly. They were still standing in the hall as if there was no point in going any further. "They got the nurse and her boyfriend, ran a heavy truck straight over their Mini. The remains weren't pleasant."

"The nurse? *Mary Hayes*?" Eddie paused to take it in. He and Mary Hayes had mildly flirted, no more. But she was now dead and it came as a shock. "Are you saying she was murdered?"

"Difficult to prove but that's what we believe. At best hit and run." Savage noticed Eddie's eyes glaze over. "Something occur to you?"

"Almost. A car nearly hit me on the way back from the funeral. No, it can't be."

"It can. And it probably was. If you are ready you had better come with us."

Eddie collected his case from the lounge. "Where to?"

"A safe house. We've got to shake off chummy first but Ted will see to that." Savage indicated his colleague who was standing almost indifferently with hands in pockets and close to the front door. He gave a brief smile.

Safe house! The words were almost comical. But there was nothing funny about the death of Mary Hayes. Ted opened the door once the hall lights were switched off, and he stepped into the porch before signalling to the others. Eddie locked the door behind him and the three men went down the steps to a car parked further along the street.

Savage told Eddie to climb in the front with him but Ted made no attempt to join them. Noticing Eddie's suspicion, Savage explained, "Ted has another car. He'll cut off the tail."

"I can't believe this is happening."

"You'd better."

"All because of Aunt Jane?"

"Looks like it." Savage pulled the car out, watching his central mirror.

"You mentioned a boyfriend. Nurse Hayes," prompted Eddie.

"A layabout. Fancied himself as a do-gooder. Extreme left. Friendly with the Russians."

"Doesn't sound like the type Mary Hayes would encourage."

"He had charm. And he might have been good in bed. Who knows? Anyway he died with her."

Eddie looked back over his shoulder but they were now in the main Bayswater Road and traffic was heavy. All he could see was a chain of dimmed headlights trailing behind them. Savage made periodic checks in his mirror and Eddie could not understand how the sergeant could make sense out of what he could see. Suddenly Savage turned left, double parked and switched off the lights.

Savage sat behind the wheel watching the mirror, uncaring of the congestion he might be causing in a narrow street. After a while, he said, "Good. Ted's fixed 'em." And he switched the lights on and drove off.

Eddie felt inadequate. How could Savage be so sure?

Savage started to talk as if they were out for a spin. He seemed quite relaxed, but constantly watched his mirrors, and never once glanced at Eddie. "I'll tell you what's struck me about you," he said casually. "I've been rattling on about Russians and cutting off tails and safe houses, yet you've shown no real surprise."

"You're kidding," replied Eddie vehemently. "My hair's standing on end."

Savage was expertly cutting through side streets. "Oh, you were shocked about the nurse, and didn't like being left in the house alone, but you've not taken me up on the Russian involvement. As if you knew they were in it."

"Balls," snapped Eddie. "You never said that they are in it."

"I think you found something to indicate they are tied up in this."

"Then you're a lousy detective."

Savage grinned, passing lights alternately illuminating and shadowing his face. "That's been said before. By experts. What did you find?"

"Sweet Fanny Adams."

Savage pulled up in a street near Highbury Fields; tall, Edwardian houses flanked the road like molars, some decayed. Two lines of parked cars lay like dormant beetles, the street lights glossing their shells.

The rows of terraced houses were not unlike the one they had left in Bayswater but were larger. Some had become boarding houses, others were divided into apartments.

The two men climbed steps to a canopied porch. Savage unlocked the massive door with two keys and pushed the door open. Eddie was not certain, but he thought the sergeant pressed the bell before entering, although there was no peal from inside.

They went into a hall illuminated dimly by a night-light in the ceiling. Savage led the way up two flights of stairs and showed Eddie into a bedroom. There was a single bed, a collapsible table and two chairs, a small bookcase and a wash-basin. The big windows were, at the moment, shuttered.

"Prison," observed Eddie dryly.

"You'll be lucky to get one like it. Loo and bath the next door along. The other side is a stocked kitchen. Only three of the cooker hobs work. We're waiting for a replacement of the fourth."

Eddie put his case on the bed. "How long do I stay here?"

"Until we've sorted something out for you."

"Do I get a say in it?"

"Sure. You can walk straight out and get your head bashed in, if you want." Savage grinned. "But we'd rather extract what you have in it first. Anyway, you'll be safe here for the moment. The grub's not bad. I'll bring you in a television set and some books and newspapers."

Eddie said carefully, "You seem convinced that I need protection. You wouldn't be conning me?"

"Ah, you're beginning to think again. Good. We've no reason to con you. If they find you, they'll kill you. By the way, don't shave in the morning."

"Why?"

"The point's dodgy." Savage winked. "Don't want you electrocuted and, yes, we do know that you use a dry shaver. Think over what I've said. We're not out to destroy your aunt's image or desecrate her memory. Bear it in mind."

5

THE monotonous slow beat of the muffled drums, the depressing deep notes of the funeral march, the painfully slow pace over the short distance to Red Square, the crowds who had turned out to line the route in solemn silence of bowed heads as the gun carriage, the flag-covered coffin mounted on its bier, went past: all these things filled Raya Dubrova with a deep sense of occasion.

Russia was honouring one of her dead heroes. The fact that most people had long forgotten General Nakentov did not matter. The State had brought memory of him back, for it did not forget its high-ranking loyal servants, and it must be shown that it did not.

Raya was filled with awe at the magnitude of it all. Nakentov had managed to keep his fame from her but that was perhaps because he was past his peak before she was old enough to understand.

Now his services were being publicly acknowledged and she was proud for him, even if not convinced that this massive public display was what he would have wanted. She could not equate her own image of him with the pomp and circumstance around her.

As she walked behind the carriage, dressed wholly in black from boots to her hat, she found it impossible to keep in step with the ponderous tread of the massed troops behind her, and the military band behind them. With her mother on her left holding on to her arm, and her two elder brothers on her right, she felt that they were being spotlighted.

The agony of the long walk caused Raya's mind to drift. She reflected on her mother's lack of feeling on hearing that her father was dead. Perhaps she had never really recovered from the death of her own husband whom Raya had barely known.

Raya glanced right and left, at her mother's grim, tearless face behind the veil and at her brothers' unemotional severity. She did not think that either of them had ever had a real feeling for Nakentov as she had done. Leading the group behind her was General Georgi Stevinski who now held the position that Nakentov once held and who had insisted on joining the funeral procession because of his deep love and respect for Nakentov. It was a touching tribute from a man who owed so much to her grandfather, and constantly reminded her family that he had once been his pupil.

The beat thumped through her head. The constant repetitiveness was like an amplification of her own pulse. The width of Kaunin Prospect was daunting as they approached Red Square and the triangular mass of the Kremlin where Nakentov would be laid.

They passed the canopied dais where the country's rulers saluted, in solemn respect for the man once more powerful than most of them. Raya heard the shouted commands as the troops saluted, flattened hands held horizontally across automatic rifles, heads turned as one in an impressive eyes right. She saw the sloppy acknowledgement from the elderly group on the dais. Ahead lay the Kremlin gates through which they would have to turn left.

The reception afterwards was a well attended, quiet, dignified affair at which the entire Politburo was present. The Secretary himself came up to the family group, to have a few meaningless words with her mother and to give Raya and her brothers a nod and a brief greeting. Nakentov was going out in style.

When the Secretary retired to a corner of the ornate, chandeliered room, nobody tried to join him except the one man whom he expected. General Georgi Stevinski unhurriedly approached the man to whom he was directly responsible, though the balance of power between the two was not so clearly defined at times. In this relationship they were perhaps unique; others in their circle had to be very careful indeed of the two of them.

The Secretary stood with glass in hand, the liquor rarely touching his lips. His hair was still black in spite of his seventy-odd years but his huge bushy eyebrows were grey. His shrewd eyes watered and his heavy face sagged.

As Stevinski joined him, the Secretary remarked: "Well, Georgi, we've done what we should. I hope it doesn't rebound on us."

Stevinski stood beside the Secretary so that both their backs were to the wall and they could take in the gathering of mourners without effort. "What else could we do? News of his death could not be kept secret. And, if Pavl did not receive his due, the Western press would be quick to notice and to speculate."

The Secretary's gaze was slowly roaming the room. "I agree there are more waverers in the Third World than is comfortable."

"Nearer than that, Comrade."

The thick brows lifted fractionally in acquiescence. "Have you decided what you are going to do?"

"Not entirely. We've partially tidied up in London but there is still a problem remaining."

The Secretary knew that Stevinski had understated the case and this worried him. "Are they on to it?"

"There's a great-nephew of Nakentov's lover. He's the one who first found the diary. It's doubtful if he made any sense of it. Indeed, apart from Lubov, there's no sense to be made of it by a layman. It was really a matter of taking from the scene anyone who knew the diary existed at all in order to prevent the SIS eventually learning of it, or at least hearing of the Lubov section."

The Secretary stirred uncomfortably. "Are you saying that British Intelligence now know?"

"They have certainly contacted the nephew and, therefore, I must assume that they know. It's a pity. The matter should be dead and buried."

The Secretary studied his drink. "I don't like the sound of it, Georgi."

"Nor I. But remember, we have the diary, and the British will have to rely entirely on what the great-nephew of Jane Barnard can tell them about it. It won't mean so much to them. The woman was a nobody. Nakentov was a different proposition entirely. Also, there is no mention of the bank codes in the diary."

"Perhaps, then, your tidying up in London should have been left alone?"

"No. The nurse's man was a dangerous gossip with an inflated opinion of his own importance. The fact that we kept the diary and paid him would have influenced his beliefs. He had to go once I realised the importance of the information he had supplied. It was too late to play it down. And it was convenient to take the nurse with him. It's the nephew that worries me. We tried too late."

"Do you intend to persevere?"

"If he can remember what he read I must assume the worst, that he's passed on what he knows. The name of Lubov might be sufficient to get the SIS digging. If their spade gets stuck, well and good. The position is fluid but we are watching it closely. What we must do is to get hold of the account if it still exists and cover what tracks there may be back to Nakentov and possibly to others. Perhaps there are none."

"A dangerous assumption, Georgi."

"Yes, I can't afford to assume it."

The Secretary sipped from his glass at last. "You know your own business. I leave it to you to ensure that this whole sorry affair will be as effectively buried as Nakentov today."

Stevinski nodded gravely. The balance of power had, for the moment, shifted away from him. A warning was a warning, however phrased. "I'll see to it that we will remain the only two men in the Soviet Union who will ever know of Pavl Nakentov's treachery."

"Not only in the Union, my dear Georgi." The Secretary smiled and moved off briefly to circulate before leaving the gathering. Funerals depressed him, his own could not be too far off.

Raya smiled at General Stevinski; he had sung Nakentov's praises so unstintingly. Stevinski was not much taller than Raya herself, but his build was solid. His eyes were pleasant and kindly as he spoke so affectionately of her grandfather.

"When this is over, Raya, come to my office. I'd like to talk to you privately. You know where I am?"

"Where grandfather used to be."

"Fine. This must be very trying for you." Stevinski gave her a wink. "I'm going to slip out quietly. I'll see you sometime after lunch, but before four. After that I shall be impossible to reach."

Raya watched him go, feeling that at least one man really cared. A lot was said about the KGB but they could be very nice at times, like her grandfather used to be.

She was glad when she was finally able to break away. Her mother had seldom shown her real affection and her brothers had long since married and had gone their own ways. The only person who had ever given her a sense of being part of the family was now lying in his coffin.

She went home to change, aware that this would be interpreted by some as disrespect for the dead, but she hated black, her spirit was too buoyant, her disposition too cheerful.

Raya had been so influenced by Nakentov that she had long taken for granted what his job had meant. He had softened its outline for her, removed the sinister and the fearful. Security was necessary and only affected enemies of the State. Loyal citizens need never have cause to worry. She had grown up with it.

Even so she was a little in awe of visiting Stevinski. She had been too young ever to call on Nakentov at his office. The phenomenal security was the first thing that struck her on arriving at the gates. It was surely worse than a prison. Stopped and searched at the barrier when she told the guards that she had an appointment with General Stevinski, she thought they were going to arrest her on the spot. Guns were unhooked and the attitude was so severe as to be frightening.

After a phone call from the guardroom, during which a gun remained pointing at her, the atmosphere changed completely. The guards saluted and escorted her across the wide forecourt to the building which grew increasingly forbidding as she approached.

She was screened again inside but now with some respect. More checks, more delays and at last Raya was in an elevator which took her to the top floor. She was escorted by two armed guards all the way.

She had to wait some time in an anteroom with low tables and chairs and cultural magazines, before being shown into General Stevinski's office. The size of the room and its furnishing was immediately indicative of the importance of the man. She had never imagined Nakentov against this background, yet belatedly realised that she should have done.

Stevinski was standing with his back to the window, smiling broadly. "Come in, Raya. I hope they did not scare you."

"I didn't expect all the checks. I suppose I should have done."

"Sit down. There. The best armchair in the

room. Here, of all places, security has to be infallible. Or as near infallible as we can make it. And that means considerable inconvenience to everyone, including me. I'll send you a copy of one of the photographs they took of you on the way in. Sometimes they're quite good."

He was making light of it but the humour did not reach Raya; she was alarmed that she had been photographed without her knowledge. Now, just below her eye level, was the desk with its battery of coloured telephones and intercommunication equipment. The inevitable portrait of Lenin hung on one wall and, on another, was what seemed to be a framed gold medal.

Stevinski saw Raya's glance stray towards it. "Your grandfather's," he explained. "He won it at pistol shooting, but he was good with any weapon." He unhooked it from the wall. "For some reason he left it here, although he could have taken it at any time. I let it hang as a reminder of the aim to which the occupier of this office should strive: to be the best. Here, take it, Raya. A memento."

Raya stared at the framed medal, recoiling back in the chair. She did not touch it.

Stevinski was surprised. "He would want you to have it. After all, he taught you, too."

"It belongs here, where he worked."

"Does it remind you that he achieved at shooting what you did not at swimming? A gold?"

She shook her head, unable to say precisely

why she had refused it. Perhaps it reminded her of Nakentov's profession, rather than of the man himself; of the security and cameras and passes and guards she had just encountered.

Stevinski hung it back on the wall. "It was only target shooting, you know. There it is if ever you change your mind." He went to the high-backed leather chair and sat facing her.

"I particularly wanted you to come here to impress upon you the importance of the work your grandfather did for his country for so long. I wanted you to taste the unpleasantness of security and of the power behind it. I wanted you to be reminded that the Soviet Union has many powerful enemies whose one aim is to undermine and ultimately to destroy this country. The result of that foreign and malignant pressure is all around you. This is what we have to do to protect ourselves. Your grandfather understood that better than anyone."

"He often explained it to me."

"Are you still swimming?"

The sudden switch confused Raya. She was beginning to wonder why she was here at all. Stevinski had effectively cast an aura around himself. Behind his benign and friendly attitude he quietly exuded power and she was meant to feel it. "Only for pleasure. I'm too old for competition."

"Too old?" Stevinski chided her. "Why aren't you married?"

"There is plenty of time for that."

Stevinski leaned back on the tilting chair. The springs creaked. He toyed with a steel paper-knife he had lifted from the desk. "Raya, you might be able to help me. I don't intend to put pressure on you but you have your grandfather's linguistic ability, which is why you are employed as a translator. I've checked. You are very good."

Raya was wary and flattered at the same time, knowing that she was not important but that Stevinski was. The only link between them was Nakentov. "What do you want of me?" She was pleased with the way she said that; cool and reserved, although she did not feel it.

Stevinski laid down the paper-knife and arched his hands below his chin, elbows on the arms of the chair. Raya noticed his expression change. His scrutiny was intense as if he was making up his mind about her. "What we say now will be off the record. There is no need to be alarmed, but nobody else must know of this conversation."

"I understand," She had almost called him Comrade General. The informality had gone between them.

"No one, Raya. That includes your mother and family. If you feel that you cannot guarantee total silence then we finish now." His eyes softened. "But in friendship, of course."

"Whatever you say will be kept quite secret. But you are beginning to scare me a little."

"There's nothing to be scared about. I would

not ask anything dangerous of you; there are professionals for that sort of thing. So. This is between the two of us." Stevinski relaxed a little as he came to the point. "Will you go to Switzerland for me?"

Raya was caught off guard. She had been expecting something sinister.

"The scenery is still unspoiled in spite of the utter capitalistic commitment of the people. They eat, sleep and think money there."

"Which part? My German is far better than my French."

Stevinski knew it already. "Zürich."

"I've been there before. To research foreign training methods before the European Games."

Stevinski knew this too; it was one reason he had considered using Raya. "Ah, of course. That could be useful."

"What do I have to do?"

"Oh, that doesn't amount to much at all. I simply want you to go to a certain bank and ask for a statement of account. Once you have it, you will give them sealed instructions on what to do next."

Raya was puzzled. "It sounds easy."

"It is." Stevinski added, "You would be doing me a personal favour. There are reasons why I prefer not to use a professional. There are also reasons why the information I want should not come through the post or by diplomatic mail. You will be on your own. I cannot tell you more."

"When do I go?"

"Tomorrow."

"I have to get an exit visa." She had imagined it would be some time ahead.

Stevinski laughed. "A passport and visa are being prepared this very moment. And your seat is already reserved on Aeroflot." He held up his hands. "You are shaken? Well, I had to be prepared for your agreement, Raya. Annulling everything is much easier than belated preparation. You can still say no."

It was all so soon. "I'd better go home to pack."

"You've plenty of time. You will have funds to take with you. I'll see that a hotel reservation is made and will let you know where, by this evening."

"What do I tell mother?"

"I'll have a word with her. I'll explain that you'll be doing a small job for me. This is between you and me. Now I'll give you the details."

Eddie Tyler lay on the bed watching the flickering television screen. He uncrossed his feet so that he could see the picture between them. Black and white, he reflected. Not even colour. And a portable at that. He had asked Savage whether a magnifying glass went with the set when the sergeant had carried it in.

Savage had taken the barb good-naturedly. "Getting our bottle back, are we?"

114

"If by bottle you mean courage, let me tell you that I never had any to lose. I'm trying to make the best of what I've got."

"It's all on the house," grinned Savage.

But when Eddie was left alone again his thoughts were more serious. He could not see where his present plight would end and at times he simply could not believe that any of it had happened. But for the persistent ringing of the door bell at Aunt Jane's he only had Savage's word to go on. The cream Ford could have belonged to anyone.

And then he remembered the newspaper clippings in his pocket and the near knockdown in the street after the funeral. Here he was in some strange house with a mass of rooms which Savage assured him he had to himself.

Eddie switched off the televison and went into the kitchen to inspect a well-stocked food cupboard and fridge-freezer. He boiled a pre-cooked Duck à l'Orange and added a can of new potatoes but his thoughts were constantly on his present situation. It had all happened so quickly, all stemmed from Savage's icy telephone call.

As he prepared for bed, he still did not know what he was going to do. At half-past ten there was a knock on the door and Savage poked his head into the room.

"Saw your light on. I'm off."

"I thought you'd already gone. It's worse than being at Aunt Jane's, alone in a house this size."

"It's wired up all round. If anyone tries to break in you'll have help before you know. Main danger is risk of heart failure when the alarms blow."

"Look," said Eddie, "were you serious about Aunt Jane resting in peace?"

"Why would we want to disturb her? If she's left anything behind of interest to us we'd naturally like to know."

"But you could keep her name out of it?"

Savage came in and closed the door behind him. "Let's get it straight. The last thing we want is a public exposé. We've had too many already and they do nothing for our image. But there has to be a reason why you've attracted so much interest and we'd like to know. Wouldn't you?"

"If I have your word that you'll leave her out of it, I'll help."

Savage compressed his lips. "There are people further up the ladder than me. I can't see why their thinking will be any different from mine. *My* word, you have."

Eddie went to the wardrobe and took down his jacket. "You did say you're Special Branch?"

"I did." Savage did not move a muscle. "You want to see my ID again?"

"No. I just thought you might be MI5 or 6."

"Our interests are the same."

Eddie knew that he would get no further. He took the clippings from the inner pocket and passed them over. "I hope I'm doing the right thing."

Savage took them, glanced at the first headline, checked the date, and whistled aloud. "Christ," he exclaimed. "How interesting. OK if I take them with me?"

When he was alone, the emptiness of the big house unnerved Eddie. He shivered.

The country was level beneath her, the undulations flattened by the height at which they were flying. The Dnepr River was an untidy blue line beyond Smolensk to be followed soon by the sprawl of Minsk. Raya wriggled herself into an acceptable position in the cramped seat and turned the pages of a magazine.

After a while the magazine lay opened on her lap, her hands covering it. The big man next to her was asleep, head back, snoring softly. He looked like a Pole. On her left a thin-faced Russian diplomat fidgeted nervously. He had told her he was returning to the Soviet Embassy in Warsaw.

But her thoughts were really on Stevinski and her grandfather. She could not dismiss the idea that the reason for her presence on this plane was in some way linked with *both* men.

Raya felt important at being asked to perform a personal mission for Stevinski but she was mystified as to why one of his own men could not do it for him, particularly as it was so simple.

And she did not much like the idea of bearing a Rumanian passport. *That* had come as a surprise. It made her realise the mission really was secret, and that took away its simplicity.

On arrival at Zürich, Raya was immediately aware of the change of pace and atmosphere. She had to admit that the style of dress was more expensive and elegant than at home. For a while she felt lost. She had not been alone on foreign trips before. She had always been in a party, with a controller who dealt with passport and immigration details.

She followed the crowd and the notices and arrows and finally found herself outside the airport building and climbing into a coach, which took her to the Bahnhof where she hailed a cab.

The hotel was called the Diana and was in a narrow rising street in the older part of the town. To ensure that she was not surrounded by too much luxury, Stevinski had wisely chosen a hotel at the lower end of the second-class scale.

After breakfast next morning she went to the bank but it was not yet open so she roamed about the quaint old streets to fill in time. She was conscious of being near to West Germany and Austria and France. None of these countries were far and the thought put her on her guard. She was a Soviet and should not be influenced by them, or by Switzerland.

Raya returned to the bank and crossed the same floor her grandfather had five decades before. She went to the counter marked enquiries, pushed across the slip of paper with the account and code number and asked for a statement of account.

She gazed around at the marble pillars, the ornate ceilings, the polished stone floor. She had never seen a bank like this before.

It was some time before the clerk came back and politely asked if she would step into the manager's office. She stood inside the doorway as the clerk closed the door behind her. The room was vast, bigger than Stevinski's office and much more luxurious.

"Fräulein, please, take a seat." The manager was suave and smiling as he stood politely behind the desk, indicating a chair to her. Raya sat, touching the expensive leather and feeling suddenly dowdy amongst the opulence.

"Would you like coffee, fräulein?"

"*Nein, danke.*"

Heinz Meisser sat down and picked up the slip of paper. He had been expecting it and now it had happened. "You want a statement? Of this account?"

"Please." Suspecting something was wrong, Raya pulled from her handbag the sealed instructions she had for the manager once she had the statement. She held the envelope and guessed that she was acting like a guilty person. That was how she felt: guilty. But of what? She could not take her eyes from Meisser's and she could see that he was uneasy.

"We have no such account here." Meisser spread his hands. "Are you sure you have the right bank, fräulein?"

Raya felt a fool. Stevinski had prepared her for the possibility of the account being closed, in which case she was to keep the envelope.

"Oh, yes." Her voice trembled a little. She was totally unprepared for her own reaction, certain now that the manager was suspicious of her. She must make a show, try a little indignation. "Are you sure?"

"Of course. There is no such account here."

She could see his gaze dissecting her, going over her clothes, and her cheeks were burning. She had never been so embarrassed.

Meisser held out his hand for the envelope. "If that is for me perhaps the contents will explain."

Raya hastily put the envelope back in her bag. "No. I'm sorry. Is the account closed then?" She realised the question should have been asked immediately after he had denied its existence. *But surely she was supposed to know?*

Meisser smiled politely, aware that Raya was ill at ease. He found her attractive, with high cheek bones and a disarming, if disconcerting innocence. "I can only repeat," he said, "that we have no such account here."

Raya rose, clinging to her handbag and making sure that it was closed tight. "I'm sorry to waste your time."

Meisser said, "It's been a pleasure, fräulein."

He had postponed another appointment in order to meet Raya, for seeing the slip with the code on it had alarmed him. As he rose, he added, "Perhaps you will tell me where you are staying so that I can contact you if something should come to light."

Raya stopped near the door as Meisser approached to open it for her. "If the account is not here, that is that." She had regained some confidence but had the impression that she was in some sort of trap.

"I can check with our other branches."

Raya did not believe him; he wanted to know where she was staying. She smiled sweetly at him now. "I think it is I who had better do the checking."

She crossed the wide floor feeling his eyes on her all the way and believing that others were watching her. Was this how it felt to be a criminal? She was glad to get out into the street and walked about aimlessly, her thoughts disturbed, until, after some time, she stopped and asked herself why she was feeling so uneasy. She had done nothing wrong.

Vice-president Eric Baumann was in his sixties, grey haired and as tall as Meisser, whom he eyed with some amusement. Meisser was an excellent manager, but sometimes he worried too much.

Meisser had coffee brought in and when the two men were alone he related what had happened. The vice-president listened without showing any sign of being perturbed. He sat on the edge of Meisser's desk, coffee in hand, "So, what's the problem?"

"The girl was trying to get information about a secret account. Doesn't that worry you?"

"But she didn't succeed; her information is outdated."

"But how did she get it?"

"Is that our concern? The account has been protected."

"The police should know. She attempted fraud."

Eric Baumann looked up sharply. "We leave the police out of it. You're panicking, Heinz. No harm has been done."

Meisser slowly roamed his office without looking at Baumann. "Don't you think we should at least inform our clients?"

"How?" asked Baumann quietly. "Through the usual poste restante? Or wait until one of them calls in?"

"That is the problem," agreed Meisser, "the account is *too* secret."

Baumann laughed. He put down his cup. "Isn't that what our banking is all about? I shouldn't have to explain it to you, of all people."

Meisser shook his head. "You know that's not what I mean. This is an old arrangement. It's not the only account that is safeguarded by total anonymity and it certainly won't be the last, in spite of the present laws. But I have never liked the way it was set up in the first place. I wouldn't have chosen this particular method."

"Presumably it was how the client wanted it. You're worried about the code being stolen? To a client who takes normal precautions, that possibility is more remote than someone trying a common forgery. At the time the account was opened the risks would have been pointed out. And any unlawful usage would have come out in due course. Let's face it, Heinz, if the client wants his own identity to be secret as well as the account then he has more to hide than either of these things. In such cases there is always a minimal risk."

"I've never been happy about this one," Meisser rejoined.

"I know you haven't, yet the account has been in operation for well over fifty years without problem. When the code was changed, what— six years ago?—you voiced the same doubts. And yet, in all that time there has been no problem, no argument about propriety, everything has run smoothly. Indeed, it's an account that has caused us very few problems, wouldn't you say?"

"Until now," pointed out Meisser.

"One ripple in fifty-odd years is no storm, Heinz."

Meisser shrugged. "Well, I've reported it. I thought I should."

"Do you know where this girl is staying?"

Meisser went round his desk to glance at the note he had made. "Her name is Gavor. Rumanian, according to the clerk. She showed no inclination to tell me where she is staying. And the name could be meaningless."

"As so many of them are." Baumann stood up. "It's strange how this account disturbs you so. It is probably the most successful account we have ever handled. We've made a good deal of money from it over the years."

Meisser smiled ruefully. "Nevertheless the girl *did* call, she *did* use the original code and I *must* advise our clients when they call. They've asked for an updated breakdown of investments so they might call soon."

"I won't argue with that," agreed Baumann. "But don't lose sleep on it. She missed by a mile; you won't hear from her again."

Meisser was not so sure.

6

EDDIE TYLER awoke naturally and was immediately disorientated by the strangeness of the room. He sat up quickly remembering the events of the last few days. Nothing had changed; he was still a prisoner.

By half-past ten nobody had called, so he went round the house trying doors, all of which were locked except those rooms he was allowed to use. There was a telephone on a stand in the lofty hall but when he tried it the line was dead. He tried the front door. It, too, was locked. There was no way that he could reach the back of the house because he could not open the door at the rear of the hall. He noticed that the night-light was out and wondered if it was on a time switch.

The isolation had begun to play on his nerves. Frustration was building up in him when the door opened and a well-dressed man entered, with Sergeant Savage just behind him.

"Ever tried knocking?" Eddie was annoyed because he had not heard them approach.

"I'm so sorry. Of course, I should have done. May we come in?"

They were already in. Eddie put aside the book he had been trying to read.

"My name is George Seymour, Mr. Tyler. I'd like to talk about a few things."

"Do I get to see an identity card?" Eddie asked, as Savage left the room and closed the door.

"Would it do any good?" Seymour slipped out of his topcoat and placed a document case on the table. He was of medium height and build, clean-shaven, with flabby cheeks that were reddened by the wind, and unblinking eyes that would have done credit to a bird of prey. The eyes were his only memorable feature; the rest, from the thinning hair to the well-cut but badly pressed dark suit, and the medium-clean shoes, were unremarkable. He sat at the table, his back to Eddie, and opened the case pulling out the press clippings about Arcos. "I imagine you would like these back. Terribly interesting."

Eddie went round the table so that he could face Seymour. He sat down opposite him. "Did you learn anything from them?"

The eyes coldly held Eddie's gaze, while the soft lips tightened. "Your great-aunt was obviously interested in the affairs of Arcos. Or at least in their personnel."

"You spent all night working that out?"

"Now, now. But we have spent all night going through old files and records. Lubov was the code name for an agent, Pavl Nakentov, who worked at the Trade Mission."

"So?"

"The same man later became a General, and head of the KGB. He was buried only two days ago. The timing of his death was extraordinarily coincidental to that of your great-aunt. Quite interesting."

"You mean there could be some sort of connection?" Eddie was trying to equate the head of the KGB with the frail image of Aunt Jane.

Seymour handed over the press clippings. "I don't know. Your aunt died naturally, though her death might well have been hastened by shock. We don't know how Nakentov died. The public release was that he died of heart failure. Well, he was eighty-five. But that diagnosis covers almost anything."

Eddie scratched his tangle of hair. "All this is over my head. What the hell has it got to do with me?"

The flaccid cheeks wobbled as Seymour shook his head, but the eyes remained penetrating. "It has nothing to do with you except in one respect. You read the diary and told someone else who told someone else. I could take you down to the morgue to see the gruesome result of possessing the knowledge you imparted."

"No thanks. It could have been an accident."

"And the late night knock on your door and the trying of the handle could have been the milkman."

"So I've been sucked into some sort of mess?" He tried to cover his anxiety.

"We'd like to know just what kind of mess it is. There were some pencil marks on one of the articles. Very faded, made with a soft lead. We've managed to raise the impression." Seymour handed over an envelope on which was boldly printed: ZEITLINGER BANK, ZURICH 72–598–8764 DRANRAB 627. 21,000.

"This supposed to mean something to me?"

Seymour blinked slowly. "I was hoping it might. Evidently I'm wrong."

"Doesn't mean a thing."

"Then let me enlighten you as much as I can. The bank part is obvious. The numbers could be an account at the bank. The DRANRAB 627 could be a code, perhaps issued to hide an identity. Swiss banks are very good at that sort of thing. And in those days perhaps even better than now."

Eddie, listening with interest, had expected Seymour to go on.

"That all?"

"You've missed the obvious. We didn't need a cryptographer to work out that Dranrab is an anagram of Barnard. Spelt backwards, in fact."

Eddie stared at Seymour in amazement. He began to laugh lightheadedly. "Aunt Jane with a Swiss bank account? You've got to be kidding. *Aunt Jane?*"

Seymour smiled politely. "You seem to find that more incredible than a possible connection between your great-aunt and a chairman of the KGB."

Eddie was grinning widely and shaking his head in disbelief.

"Good old Aunt Jane. You know, there was always something about her that I liked—always something there that I couldn't fathom."

"Doesn't the possibility that she was spying for the Russians disturb you?"

"Aunt Jane wouldn't spy for the Russians. She was English to the core. Straight as a die." When Eddie noticed Seymour's expression of scepticism, he added, "Think what you like. The old girl must have lived to the full at one time and I'm glad of that."

"There is the last figure; the 21,000. It's possible that that was the amount banked."

Eddie came forward on the chair with a thump. "Twenty-one thousand? Swiss francs?"

"Who knows?"

"Oh, come on. That note was scribbled between the wars. It can't mean anything now."

"There's only one way to find out."

"Write to them?"

"Yes, if you want them to know where you are. But it might be more satisfactory for you to call in person."

"Me? You do it. It's your idea."

"And you stand to gain as one of the beneficiaries if she has an account there."

Eddie had not really considered that he might

129

benefit; he had been thinking of Aunt Jane and what she must have been like in her younger days. Now he had to take the matter more seriously. "There's nothing, apart from that pencilled note, to indicate a Swiss bank account. I've been through all her papers. The solicitor might know but he's said nothing to me."

"I repeat, there is only one way to be absolutely certain."

"I can't go to Zürich. I've no money."

"We'll finance you."

Eddie was curious. "What can it matter to you after all this time?"

"The money doesn't interest us. But if there is an account, we would like to know why."

"To tell the tax people?"

"That's not our job. The whole background to this needs to be examined."

"Sergeant Savage promised to keep her name out of it."

"*Publicly* out of it; his word will be honoured."

Eddie stood up. "Okay. I'll go." He grinned. "Provided I can stay at a first-class hotel."

"You'll put up at a pension. With government cutbacks you're lucky that we don't fly you out and back in a day."

"Mean bastard," replied Eddie. But his flippancy covered an increasing concern.

Raya Dubrova packed her case. She was disappointed with her failure to achieve a positive

130

result for General Stevinski. She realised that it was not her fault but to come all this way for nothing seemed such a waste of time and money.

On arrival at Sheremetyevo Airport she made the long journey into town and went straight to KGB headquarters. Her suitcase was examined and taken to the guardroom while she went through the security checks.

She had to wait a long time before she was ushered into Stevinski's office. He greeted her like a benevolent uncle, conducting her to a chair before returning to his own. He asked about the flights and whether she had enjoyed herself, but she could not contain her disappointment. "The bank manager said there is no such account there."

Stevinski looked at her thoughtfully. Before he could ask the question, Raya added, "I asked if there had ever been such an account and the manager only repeated that there was no such account there."

"Did you get the impression that there had been?"

Raya examined her feelings. "I was a little flustered. I believe he was being guarded but I don't know why. I think he was suspicious of me. He wanted to know where I was staying but I didn't tell him."

Stevinski tried to put Raya at ease. "You did the right thing, but you must be tired, coming here straight from the airport?"

"You said it was important."

"It was. But if the account is closed then that's an end of the matter. Would you like coffee?"

Raya saw that he wanted time to think. "That would be nice."

They talked for a while about Zürich, which he seemed to know well, until coffee was brought in on a silver tray. When the attendant had left the room, Stevinski filled two cups and handed one to Raya. Slowly stirring his own, he said,

"I know that you got on particularly well with your grandfather. Did he ever tell you about his friendship with Jacob Djugashvili?"

Raya hesitated. She was a party member, her loyalties clear. But she had a loyalty to Nakentov too.

Stevinski was quick to see her dilemma. "Raya, my dear girl, I am not trying to get information about your grandfather, but about Joseph Stalin's son."

"From time to time he talked of Yasha. Always with affection."

"Of course. You know, no one knows how Yasha really died, it remains an open file. There are even rumours that he's still alive. You probably know that father and son didn't get on. Stalin didn't even want to know Yasha's fate. I wonder if Pavl took steps to find out? He was in a good position to do so at the time. Perhaps you can help me finally to put a lid on this particular issue."

When he saw that Raya was trying to think back, he smiled at her. "Drink your coffee before it gets cold. I don't want you to tax yourself now. Go home. Rest. And then just jot down anything you can remember; see if he made any notes, your mother or brothers may have heard something. And let me know what you've found out."

"What about my job?"

"The State Publishing House has been informed that you are on indefinite leave. Your job will be in no danger. Have you a key to your grandfather's apartment, by the way?"

"Mother and I shared a key. We still have it."

As he showed Raya out, Stevinski was thinking that it was much better this way than having his own men trampling all over Nakentov's apartment under the eyes of neighbours.

"You may even have to go out to his dacha at Socchi," he said as an afterthought. "Let's do the job properly." As he opened the door for her, he added, "There will be a car downstairs to take you home."

When Raya had left the office Stevinski sat down heavily into a chair. He felt uneasy. He wiped his face and stared at the door. Why had the bank manager been so evasive? Was the account still there? Had Nakentov told the truth? Stevinski realised that he might be surrounded by treachery.

As Raya sat in the rear of the Volga she gazed at

the uniformed back of the driver. Occasionally, when she could afford one, she used a taxi; but this was the first time in her twenty-six years that she had ever been chauffeur-driven in an official car. It made her important—that was obvious from the driver's manner and from the attitude of the guards at the gates. She sat straight-backed and held her head up.

And yet, as the novelty wore off, she began to think: she was confused by the two loyalties; one founded on tutoring and belief, the other on love for an old man who had counselled and cherished her. She simply could not understand why Stevinski was using her when he had a huge staff at his disposal. And why so benevolent, as if he were trying to take over Nakentov's close relationship with her.

It was due to Nakentov that she was thinking like this. In his efforts to befriend his granddaughter, he had toned down the massive role he had played over so many years, the power he had exercised over life and death. In seeking her love, he had softened the reality of his profession.

But Raya was flattered by Stevinski's confidence; she would do as he asked. Then, for no apparent reason, she recalled the little inconsistencies surrounding Nakentov's death.

When they arrived at the block of flats, the chauffeur took Raya's battered case from the boot of the car and saluted her before driving off.

When the car had disappeared, Raya mounted the stairs, case in hand.

Larissa Dubrova looked up in relief as Raya entered the room, she looked tired, there were rings of strain round her eyes. Raya dropped the case and came forward to peck her mother on the cheek and was surprised when she was embraced briefly but warmly.

"It's good to see you back, Raya. I was worried."

Raya carried her case into the small bedroom, lifting it on to the bed and unlocking it. "Worried, Mama? Why?"

"Because you were doing something for General Stevinski."

Raya came to the door, her mother was polishing the living-room table. "Did he tell you that?"

"He told me that he needed you for a few days."

"But he did not tell you what I was doing?"

Larissa leaned on the table, duster in hand, dark eyes on her daughter. "You are very naive, Raya. Men like the general don't explain things to people like me."

This was how it always ended between them, Raya reflected. Friction. "Mama, I don't understand your attitude. Your own father was doing what General Stevinski is now doing. You imply that it's something terrible."

Larissa Dubrova straightened wearily. They

had been over it so many times in so many different ways. She tried once more. "It's as well to remember who my father was. You worshipped him. But you never really knew him. Nor some of the things he did in the name of the great Soviet Socialist Republic. He's dead now. Keep what memory of him you want but don't be blind to everything that happened."

Raya was astounded and upset. "You hated him."

"No. He could be kind. But I despised him for what he stood for and for many of the things he did. You think you knew him. Nobody knew him. Nobody."

They had argued before but Raya had never known her mother to be so bitterly vehement. "Why do you think the general is using you?" Larissa asked bitingly.

"I don't know. The job was trivial. I think he respected grandfather and he's trying to be helpful to us."

Larissa threw down the duster in disgust. "I can't believe that my own daughter is such a fool. Stevinski has no more time for sentiment than my father had for my mother. And she died of a broken heart."

Raya was close to tears. Her mother was destroying everything she believed in. Her own doubts about Stevinski made it worse.

"Don't believe that Stevinski liked your grandfather." She went on. "He might have respected his ability but they were never friends. Stevinski wanted your grandfather's job. And after father retired, he had to wait years while Braga filled the post. It meant nothing to him when papa died. He was probably glad to be rid of the kind of legend that he himself will never become."

Raya, tired and disillusioned, leaned unhappily against the bedroom door jamb. "Please, don't do this to me."

Larissa was filled with compassion but she knew that if she moved to comfort Raya she would be rebuffed. The damage was done. Quietly now, she said:

"It's for your sake that I say this. I don't want you to get involved with Georgi Stevinski. You loved your grandfather, then respect his opinion of Stevinski whom he did not trust at all."

Raya pulled out a handkerchief. "I've done nothing to be ashamed of."

"Good. Have you finished with him now?"

Raya shook her head. "No. He's asked another favour."

"A favour? Or an instruction?"

"There's no secret. You can be part of it, the whole family."

While Raya dried her eyes Larissa gazed at her with deep suspicion. "I'll have no part of anything Stevinski wants. The hypocrite walked with us at the funeral, just to impress. What has he got you into now?"

"He's trying to find out how Yasha Djugashvili died."

"Stalin's eldest boy? Why now?"

"To close the file on him. He knows that grandfather and Yasha were close friends, and wonders if anything was ever said to you, or whether grandfather made his own enquiries after the war, whether he kept notes."

Larissa said slowly, "I'm sorry I upset you. In spite of what you think, I love you. I don't want you to come to any harm, Raya. Working for this man can be dangerous."

Raya was both moved and surprised by her mother's apology, but wanted to get things clear. "Isn't it natural that General Stevinski should ask for our help? I understand that Yasha and grandfather were really close friends."

"They were. What I can't understand is why it should be raised after all this time?"

"Does it matter?"

"Perhaps not. But nothing is ever as it seems with Stevinski. If he gave you a reason then it's not the right one."

"Oh, Mama. But do you know anything about it? Did grandfather look into it at all?"

Larissa wondered what harm her knowledge might do but decided it might be more dangerous to withhold information. "Yes he did. He was terribly upset when he heard Yasha had been taken prisoner. He used to talk to mother about it. The Germans wanted to arrange an exchange with Stalin but that monster didn't want poor Yasha back. Your grandfather tried to arrange the deal, and I know he despised Stalin for his indifference. When it was reported that Yasha had died, your grandfather was distraught. He did not often show emotion but he did then. I was only a child but I remember it so well."

Raya was appalled at the way Larissa spoke of Stalin but it was just one more surprise since her homecoming just a few hours ago. She wondered what else her mother knew. "Did he find out anything?"

Larissa's eyes had half closed in recollection: "He found some things out. He made notes for the official file but I don't know whether he handed them over. I think there were some aspects he preferred to follow through himself."

"Where are the notes now?"

Larissa broke from her trance. "If he kept them at all he would have kept them close by. Perhaps they're in his apartment."

Heinz Meisser sat rigid and grim faced. On receiving the message that someone else was enquiring about Dranrab 627 he had taken precautions. He had called Eric Baumann immediately and insisted that the vice-president should listen to the forthcoming conversation over an intercom system in another room. He had not sent for Eddie Tyler until Baumann was in position.

And now Meisser was going through exactly the same motions as he had with Raya two days ago. He did not have to look at the slip on his desk, he knew the account number and the code by heart. He studied the young man in front of him; in spite of a two days' growth of beard, the clothes were clean if informal. No tie but a good shirt. Strong face, but there was an irreverence about the eyes and a twitching at the corner of the lips as if he found the situation amusing. Well, it was far from that.

"I understand," ventured Meisser "that you wish to make a withdrawal from an account named Dranrab 627?"

"Only if there is some money there," replied Eddie good-naturedly.

"Have you a cheque book, Mr. Tyler?"

"No. But you can supply a blank cheque, surely?"

"Of course. But only if there is an account."

"Ah! That's what I thought. Finished is it? Never mind. It was worth a try." Eddie was about to rise when Meisser asked, "Try for what, Mr. Tyler?"

"Let me explain. I think that my great-aunt might have had an account here some years ago. Way back in the twenties. She's dead now, I'm afraid, so I couldn't ask her. The next best thing was to come to you. As I say, it was worth a try."

With dread in his heart Meisser asked, "What was her name?"

"Jane Barnard."

Meisser gripped the chair arm. It had been accepted for as long as he had been manager that the original Dranrab was an anagram of a real name and he suspected that this premise had been passed on to each manager in turn.

"*Did* she have an account here?" pressed Eddie. He could see that Meisser was struggling behind his urbanity.

"I cannot disclose that information. All I can say is that there is no such account in this bank."

Meisser was comparing Eddie's approach to Raya's. The girl had been uncomfortable; this man gave the impression that he was not concerned one way or the other. But there was one common denominator between the two. Both appeared to be honest to a point of innocence. And that simply did not make sense, unless someone else had recruited them to make the enquiries.

"Fair enough," said Eddie, cutting through Meisser's reflections. "I didn't expect any pleasant surprises." He stood up to go and Meisser tried the ploy he had used unsuccessfully on Raya. "I can get someone to check through old files, if you like. Where are you staying?"

Eddie smiled wickedly: "You've already suggested that old files are privileged information. But no sweat. I'm at the Pension Bella. Can't think of the alley, it's one of those being squeezed to death by the buildings either side, even the cobbles are being pushed up between them. Cheers." He left while Meisser was only halfway out of his chair.

The door to the secretary's office opened as soon as Meisser's door was closed. Baumann said, "A good deal of confidence, has that young man."

"You didn't see him," commented Meisser. "It's not confidence but indifference. I wonder how he would take it if he was left a fortune?"

"He clearly thought he had been. But it didn't seem to worry him that he had not." Baumann made sure that he had closed the secretary's door. "You'd better turn that thing off." He pointed to the intercom and, as Meisser flicked up the switch, added, "Talking of confidence, yours seems to have grown over this business during the last few minutes, Heinz."

Meisser sank back in his chair as Baumann sat down in the one Eddie had vacated. "A few things have slotted in. Tyler would seem to have more claim than the Rumanian girl if a claim were possible. Which it is not."

"Provided that Jane Barnard was indeed the lady who opened the account, and was his great-aunt. Whether or not she was, her initial instructions were explicit. But that can't be what has eased your mind."

Meisser explained, "The president came to see me after you had told him about the girl. I'm still not happy about the arrangement but at least it

142

confirms something I've suspected all along and feel I should have been told about."

Baumann stretched his legs. "He told me he would tell you, but you had just taken over as manager and we didn't want to involve you at the time. It boils down to this: Since the government pressure and the new laws that insist on all Swiss banks knowing the source of their clients' funds, we were faced with a dilemma over this particular account. Have you looked into its value lately?"

"Conservatively and in round figures, subject to current prices, it's worth over two hundred and fifty one million Swiss francs." Meisser sat back. "Almost a hundred and twenty million dollars. Or, converting it to its original currency, about seventy-five million pounds."

"So it's quite clear why we hung on to it in spite of the problems arising from government. It's all right, Heinz, for us bankers to state, hand on heart, that we know the declared identity of each and every client. If they really believe that they believe in fairies."

Meisser was pleased he had done his home-work. "Did Dranrab threaten to pull out?"

"Obviously. At that time bankers here were running round to show the world just how honest they really were. And the Austrians were waiting in the wings to pick up anything we lost and they acquired a good deal. You can open an account in Austria as Mickey Mouse and they'll ask not a single question. We had to do something."

"So you suggested a change from the code?"

"We had to wait to hear from Dranrab in the usual way. The woman came alone and we gave her the facts: it would be officially impossible to continue under the same code name unless all three with authority to draw out sums of money declared their identity. We discussed various ways round it and she said she would speak to the others. Behind her glasses and her wigs she seemed to be a very striking woman."

"She still is," endorsed Meisser.

"Anyway," Baumann continued, "she came back a few days later, still alone and straightaway pointed out that it would be much easier for all of them to transfer the account to Vienna where no questions would be asked.

"I pointed out that our investment record with the account was outstanding by any standard. From the original £21,000 had grown a multi-million investment. I think it was 1931 when we received carte-blanche to invest in any way we liked. Even over a period of fifty years there could be no cause for complaint. It showed we knew, and still know, our job."

"A powerful argument. What did she say?" asked Meisser.

Baumann smiled ruefully. "Well, obviously, they stayed with us. But I think she was really exerting pressure on us to accept a new formula. They would form a holding company with three directors each having equal powers for handling

144

Dranrab. The account was transferred to the company's name, Tinsal Holdings, and we have the three signatories whose names are meaningless, but enough to satisfy statutory demands."

Baumann added earnestly, "We should have told you, Heinz, but really it has made no difference. The situation is exactly as it was. Until now there has never been any other problem."

Meisser inclined his head in agreement. "We'll see what happens when they call." Then he looked across the desk at Baumann and asked sharply, "Why Tinsal?"

"Don't start more hares, Heinz, for God's sake. Any name would have done."

Meisser glanced at his pad. "Have you tried an anagram of it. One is *Stalin*."

7

RAYA let herself into Nakentov's apartment. His position had warranted a larger place than this but, once his wife had died, he had moved here and it was all he had wanted.

Raya had always believed that the absence of photographs of her grandmother was because Nakentov had found them too painful to live with. Now, after what her mother had told her, she was no longer sure. She resented having to re-examine everything she had always taken for granted.

Her peace of mind had gone. It would have been so much easier to cling to earlier beliefs and recollections but, though memory of him was still pleasant, another side of him was being forced on to her and she did not want to know it.

As Raya roamed the apartment, she stopped in front of the chair where she had found Nakentov and exclaimed in anguish, "Oh, why is everything so complicated since you died, Grandpapa?"

She felt he was watching her as she went through his things and, from time to time, found herself glancing over to the chair.

As she searched, she was aware that she wanted to find the notes to satisfy her own curiosity. It had become important to her to find out exactly what kind of man Nakentov had been, even if she was hurt by what she discovered. She could not go through life with doubts about an old man she had revered and a mother she had mistakenly believed did not love her.

When she had unsuccessfully been through every drawer and cupboard, every nook and cranny, she sat down on the edge of Nakentov's bed with a feeling of failure. Then she reflected that if Nakentov had hidden anything at all he would not have done it in an obvious place. Try to think as he might.

Nakentov had been clever. He might have used somewhere obvious. Where was a really unlikely place? The bread bin. There was nothing in it but part of a stale loaf but she knew that she was on the right track, for she was now utterly convinced that there was something she had missed.

When she eventually found what she wanted it was by a combination of luck and observation and the fact that Nakentov had been very fond of beetroot chutney.

She had twice been through the food cupboard before the almost full jar of chutney had registered with her. A jar of chutney never lasted for more than a week or two with Nakentov, it was one of his weaknesses and he had used it with almost any dish.

Raya took the jar down and unscrewed the

lid. She prodded the contents with a fork, felt something in the dark mess and, using two forks as tongs, pulled out a furled package.

She pulled a face at the gluey mess as she took the package to the sink and ran water over it. When it was clean she saw that it was a waterproof plastic envelope, well sealed, with some papers inside. She dried the plastic before opening it. Both excited and apprehensive, she took the contents into the living room and sat down to examine what she had found. There were several sheets of notes, all in Nakentov's difficult handwriting, but she waded through them.

Nakentov had indeed probed into Yasha's presumed death and had gone to considerable lengths. The notes were not dated. Clearly his enquiries had been made after the war, but when exactly? Immediately after the war Nakentov had been high enough up the tree to conduct enquiries of this kind without reference. Raya realised that what she held in her hands could well have been an official enquiry. So why had it finished up in a jar of chutney?

When she turned over the last page her heart pounded. There, on its own as if unconnected with the rest, was printed DRANRAB 627. Although there was no reference to it in the notes, she instinctively knew that there was a link. *And Stevinski must know it too.* He had lied to her.

She collected the plastic envelope, dried it off again and put the notes back inside. She had been tempted to throw it in the bin but something stopped her. She was acting as Nakentov himself might have acted, with caution and suspicion.

When Raya was sitting on the crowded bus on the way home, she sensed that what she had rolled in her handbag was something very important. She had not experienced real fear before. Apprehension, nerves, particularly before an important swimming event; these were sensations she knew and could cope with. Fear was something quite different. She was afraid, but for whom? Herself, her mother? She controlled a rising panic and was reasonably calm by the time she jumped off the bus.

Larissa was about to ask Raya why she had been so long when one look at her daughter's face stopped her. "What's the matter? Have you seen a ghost?" She slipped off her apron.

"Perhaps. On paper anyway. I found these." Raya took out the notes while her mother watched with concern. Raya handed them to her. "Read them."

Larissa read slowly, aware that Raya was watching her. When she had finished, she looked up. "What's the problem? I told you I believed he had looked into Yasha's death."

"What was it doing in a jar of chutney?"

"Chutney? Seriously? Perhaps Papa was so in the habit of being clandestine that he could not stop." But she felt some of the qualms Raya had experienced. The jar had been the current hiding

149

place, but where had the notes been before? From year to year?

Raya asked, "Why didn't he hand them over officially? Why hide them at all?"

Larissa was still holding the loose pages. "We don't know that he didn't pass them on officially. These might simply be his own copies. Information on which he intended to act but never got round to it for one reason or another. Once at the top of the ladder, Raya, he would have had to delegate and he might have had reasons not to do that." Larissa could see that Raya was still disturbed. "Why has it affected you so?"

"I don't know. I can't explain."

Larissa waved the pages. "All these give are two reports from witnesses of Yasha's death. Horrifying, I agree, and some names and addresses of guards at the camp where Yasha was last imprisoned. It doesn't amount to much."

"There is also a report from a man who said Yasha escaped, Mama. If they don't amount to much, why would grandfather go to so much trouble to conceal them? All this time? Why not destroy them?"

Larissa shrugged. "Knowing him he probably hoped to get round to it again. Yasha meant a great deal to him." Catching Raya's doubt she said, "I've never seen you like this." And then she held the papers up, "What can they be worth? After so long? The witnesses are probably all dead and the addresses would be hopelessly out of date, anyway."

"Maybe there was another reason why he wanted to find out what happened to Yasha."

"What do you mean?"

Raya shook her head in anguish. Her mother had not noticed the bank code on the back of the last sheet. She was glad, knowing that she could not explain. "I wish I knew."

"Are you going to give these to Stevinski?" Larissa went and put an arm round Raya.

"I'll have to. I'm no good at lying."

Larissa held her daughter's head on her shoulder. Uncertainty had brought them closer together.

Raya telephoned Stevinski from a call box the next morning. He would send a car round straightaway. And this was the extraordinary thing she began to notice. A man like Stevinski ran a massive empire and would be under constant pressure, yet he always found time to see her, even at a moment's notice; even her telephone call had been accepted straightaway.

She was tempted to try to erase the bank reference at the back of the notes so that Stevinski would not know that she had made a connection between Yasha and Dranrab. But Stevinski had sharp eyes, he would notice something had been removed. If she didn't mention the code, perhaps he would think she had missed it, as Larissa had done.

Raya was kept in the comfortable anteroom while an orderly took the notes into Stevinski who read them alone. He compared them with the official file on the fate of Jacob Stalin.

Stevinski did not miss the Dranrab code on the last sheet. Had Raya? He still needed her. To find out what had happened to the account, he had first to discover what had happened to the ring Nakentov had claimed to have given to Yasha.

To start an official enquiry into Yasha's death after so many years would cause questions to be asked. Stevinski needed someone who would have legitimate reason for the enquiry. That person was waiting for him in the anteroom. And, if Raya had seen the connection between the notes and Dranrab, it simply made her more expendable.

Stevinski took his time in making his decision. There was a certain justice in using a granddaughter who had doted on Nakentov to help uncover his unsavoury past and to discover if it affected the present. He went through it all once more before pressing his buzzer.

"Very interesting," Stevinski said, as Raya was shown in. He tapped the papers on the desk and smiled benignly. "You did well, Raya. Where did you find them?"

"In a drawer. They were not hidden anywhere." Already she was lying and that was something new to her.

Stevinski glanced at the waterproof envelope. It was too clean, and there was a faint moisture smear in one inside corner. She had not lied well, and she was trying to protect Nakentov.

"I suppose he had long since forgotten they were there. Does anyone else know about them? Did you tell your mother or brothers?"

"I haven't seen my brothers. Mother doesn't know." She saw his eyebrows raise slightly. "It was mother who told me there might be some notes. You remember you told me to ask her and my brothers? But when I found them, I did not tell her."

"Didn't she ask?"

"She and grandpapa did not get on too well. I don't think she's interested and I didn't volunteer to tell her."

"You felt it was better that she did not know?"

Raya was aware that she had not handled the lie too well. Every word she had uttered to him so far had been a lie but she felt a need to protect her mother. "No. Had she asked, I'd have told her. But she didn't." That was better.

"Good." Stevinski made a mental note that Larissa Dubrova had been told about the notes. Which meant she would have read them. Stevinski now exploited Raya's determination to protect her family. He tapped the papers. "There's a suggestion here that Yasha might not even have died."

"Yes."

"With his half-sister Svetlana in America, it's not a pleasing possibility, is it? The chance of *two* Stalins defecting to the West? It's not something we would like to be published around the world."

"I understand. But he's probably dead."

"You may be right. But I'd be happier if we knew for sure. Will you go to Austria for me? See if you can find out?"

Raya could feel the claws of fear again. Her stomach nerves were fluttering, worse than before a race.

"You hesitate?" Stevinski was reassuring, his voice quite gentle.

"I—I didn't expect it. I mean you have . . ." she tailed off, flustered and uncertain.

"I have staff who can handle it? Of course. But I don't want a result like this." Stevinski touched the official file. "Even Nakentov's notes are inconclusive. I want someone who has a real interest to dig away and to find out just exactly what happened."

"It will be difficult after so long."

"It will probably come to nothing, Raya. But I'd like to try. And it's not something I can spare men on over a long period." Stevinski gestured across the desk. "Isn't it better to keep it in the family?" He added slyly, "I'm absolutely convinced that Pavl would have wished you to continue what he could not. Yasha was very important to him."

Raya had no alternative but to agree, he had

the power to force her. "I must admit it intrigues me."

"I'll see that you're well funded and you'll be personally briefed by me." Stevinski smiled wryly. "It will be almost a holiday for you. And you'll be pleased to hear that this time you'll travel under your own name. No one has better reason to make these enquiries, no one will be surprised once they know who you are, and of your relationship to Yasha."

"And mother?"

"I'd rather she did not know where you are going."

"But she will worry about me, I must tell her something."

"I'll talk to her. It's best it comes from me or she will think I'm sending you into the jaws of hell. Mothers are all the same, Raya."

Stevinski was about to escort her to the door, when he added, as though it was an afterthought, "It's just occurred to me that Yasha carried a memento from your grandfather. In fact there were two." He stood in the middle of the room musing as if trying to recall the detail.

As Raya watched him, Stevinski snapped his fingers. "I remember Pavl telling me once of a watch he gave to Yasha. A pocket watch, of sentimental value." Stevinski inclined his head towards Raya. "Well, I shouldn't think there's much chance of getting that back, it would surely have been pilfered. And then there was a ring which Pavl had given him."

Stevinski stood still as though he was trying to take his mind down the years. "There was something special about the ring, something that meant a great deal to both Pavl and Yasha. And yet, I cannot for the life of me remember what it was. I know that Pavl intended to take it back if anything happened to Yasha. He would probably have left it to you."

Stevinski broke his pose of deep concentration and took Raya's arm. "See what you can find out about the ring. A simple gold band, I think. Meanwhile, I'll try to remember what was so special about it. I'm sure it was something connected with your family."

They reached the door. Stevinski gave Raya an apologetic smile. "I'm getting old, my memory is going."

It was the only observation he had made that Raya found impossible to believe.

A feeling of unreality seized Meisser. With their wide hats and dark glasses the two men looked like gangsters seated in front of his desk. But it was only their appearance that was sinister. Their attitude and speech were polite, not that they said very much. The woman, who was called Ulla Krantz, was as elegant as ever in a dark, classic suit clearly from a top Paris couturier. A white silk blouse softened her throat. Her long-fingered hands were ringless but her carefully manicured nails were tinted a light pastel rose.

She appeared to be around thirty-five but she could have been older. Her teeth and jawline were good and Meisser sometimes had a strong urge to take off her glasses to see the colour of her eyes. She would smile faintly as if she could read his mind.

The man called Gustav Wegel was in his forties and was lean featured, cheeks sunken under the bones. He was really too tall for his slight frame; a thin man but well dressed in a conservative way, in an expensive handmade suit. He spoke German with an American accent but Meisser had never heard him speak English.

The other man gave the impression of being physically strong, although he was not over large. About six feet tall and well built, the impression of strength came through small actions, such as the way he would suddenly lean forward to make a gesture, or clench his hands. These motions, with the tightening of his jaw, and the manner in which he spoke suggested an image of a barely contained dynamic energy. The face was full, like an aggressive power unit, the lips usually tight. When he did smile it was full bodied, his teeth showing a dentist's craft. Rolf Hartmann wore a well cut, dark suit and appeared to be in his early sixties.

As Meisser confronted the three signatories of Tinsal Holdings he was well aware, as he had always been, that the names he had before him were meaningless until they were written on a cheque. If the account belonged to Tinsal Holdings, these three, the woman flanked by the two men, were its only known directors.

Meisser had a stapled sheaf of typed papers on his desk, copies of which had been passed to his clients. The three seemed to have an unusual understanding. There was a complete lack of friction between them as Meisser systematically went through the lists of investments, item by item, pointing out profitability and recommending selling or buying. He was quite satisfied that they fully understood what he was saying even when some of the transactions were complex.

On occasion, certain investments had been recommended by them. It was the woman, for instance, who wanted to buy a majority holding in an obscure and small bank near Blackfoot in Idaho. He had wondered how she could ever have heard of it.

Meisser had argued about it at the time. The bank was virtually unknown, not corporate, and it didn't control large investments. The very ordinary cheque-cashing facilities of the bank held no appeal for him. But the woman was adamant, so he juggled investments and bought the bank in the name of Zeitlinger.

But these interventions into the investment policies of the Zeitlinger Bank were rare. There had been a few demands to be represented on boards of companies in which Tinsal had strong, and sometimes majority, shareholding. Ulla Krantz and Gustav Wegel had insisted on being represented on certain boards of overseas companies and had put up their own nominees, but there had never been adverse reaction to these moves and profits had been unaffected. Strangely, in Meisser's experience, Rolf Hartmann had not made any kind of demand. Each of the three had carte-blanche and acted separately. One signature was enough for any withdrawal. Yet it worked.

As Meisser watched them study the lists of investments, he reflected that there was no motive that he could see that might provoke any of them into embezzling the others. All three were immensely wealthy. What point could there possibly be in rocking the boat?

"The market, as you know, is very depressed at the moment." Meisser tapped the sheets. "This is a very pessimistic valuation." As this raised no comment, he added, "Our recommendations are listed on the final two pages. At the moment it is best to leave things as they are but there are one or two areas where sale and re-investment might be more profitable." One of those areas was the American bank but it was not listed and he had no intention of including it. He could not argue that the Idaho bank did not make profit, only that, in his opinion, more could be made elsewhere.

It was some time before they finished going

through the papers. Profits had fallen but not significantly and merely reflected world-wide recession. Finally, the three looked from one to the other in silence as Meisser waited anxiously. The woman spoke for them all. "Fine. Leave things as they are."

"And the recommendations?"

"We leave it to you, Herr Meisser. You suggest very modest changes. The risk is obviously minimal."

Meisser glanced at the woman, her voice was rich and deep but eminently feminine.

The investment lists were put away and there was nothing more to discuss on the issue. The clients were preparing to leave when Meisser said with difficulty, "It's my duty to tell you that there have been recent enquiries about your account under the old code of Dranrab 627."

A declaration of sudden bankruptcy could not have had more effect.

Meisser had not known what their reaction would be but he was unprepared for the strong feeling of menace that suddenly filled the office. "I thought you should know," he added weakly.

"You'd better tell us about it," said Ulla Krantz softly.

Meisser held up placating hands. "Please understand that there was absolutely no risk. The girl was Rumanian. The man was English. Both young."

"Tell us," repeated Ulla.

The intensity of their attention unnerved Meisser. He related the two incidents quite calmly but, on the three faces across the desk, half hidden by the absurd glasses, was a grimness he had not previously seen. They were suffering the first chill breeze of threat to the vast fortune they controlled.

When he had finished Meisser reiterated, "There is no risk. It is finished."

"Maybe. But we'd like to know how it started." The thin lips of Wegel barely moved and his voice grated. Meisser could feel his gaze through the glasses.

"I've no way of telling. Both were informed by me that there is no such account here. That's an end to it."

"Dranrab was changed six years ago," Hartmann's words were slow but each one was weighted.

"I know. It's a mystery. We would rather not call in the police and I'm sure you must all feel the same."

"No police," agreed Wegel. "Don't even think about them."

Ulla Krantz sat facing Meisser, hands clasped lightly on her handbag. She asked, "They presumably left an address where you could contact them? I'm sure you would have tried that much, Herr Meisser?"

"Of course. I got nowhere with the girl. She

161

was nervous of the whole situation. Here is the man's address if it will help you."

Ulla took the note and studied it. "A Mr. Tyler. Not very wealthy it would seem by this address. And you say the two incidents were unconnected?"

"That was my impression. I did not think it prudent to ask Tyler if he knew the girl. I don't think I would have received a sensible answer and he might have gained by the question."

Ulla Krantz rose, her movements gracious. "Thank you, Herr Meisser. As you say, the matter is probably dead."

Meisser noticed that Tyler's name and address was slipped into her handbag. He was relieved when they had left his office and patted his brow with a handkerchief.

The three stood on the outside steps of the bank. They had planned to separate and meet again in six months' time but now they had a problem to discuss. Hartmann called a taxi and told the driver to take them to the Baur au Lac.

The two men removed their glasses in the taxi, their semi-disguise no longer required.

Wegel's brown eyes now carried a frown above them. Hartmann's eyes were blue and restless like his body, and they searched his colleagues for some sort of answer which none was willing to offer in the confines of the cab.

They waited until they were seated at a corner table in the hotel's coffee room.

"How?" demanded Hartmann. "How could it have happened?"

"It's impossible, yet it *has* happened." Wegel stirred coffee he did not want. "After all these years. What do you think?" He turned to Ulla.

"I think that if someone can find out that much, they might find out the rest. We don't know where the girl is but if the Englishman is still here we must learn how he knows and then make sure that's where it ends. Book rooms for the night." Ulla rose as Hartmann said, "Do you want backup?"

"I can handle it," she replied, and strode across the room. She was fervently hoping that Eddie Tyler was still in Zürich but, if he was not, his home address should be in the pension's register. Either way, the matter must be resolved quickly.

8

THE clerk looked up and blinked. Women like this did not call at the Pension Bella. The diamond and sapphire bracelet she was wearing was worth more than three years of his income. The clerk adjusted his glasses and adopted an obsequiousness he had not used for a long time. "Madam?"

"I wish to see Mr. Tyler who is staying here."

The clerk knew Tyler, they had joked together. "I'll ring his room."

Ulla put out a restraining hand to touch his before it reached the phone. "If he's in I'd like to surprise him."

The clerk left his hand where it was, enjoying the soft contact of hers. "I don't know whether he's in, madam."

"Won't the keyboard tell you?" asked Ulla sweetly.

"Yes, of course." Well, he had enjoyed the moment. He turned round to glance at the board. "He's out. He goes out a lot. He's usually in for dinner."

Ulla glanced at her watch. "Give me your number. I'll ring you at six-thirty and you can tell me whether or not he's in. After that, I'll ring half hourly if it's necessary."

He gave her a card as Ulla took some notes from her bag. She passed them across as she asked, "And your name?"

"Bider, madam. I shall be on duty until ten."

"I don't want him to know about this, Herr Bider. That is important."

"I understand, madam."

Eddie Tyler had been eking out the meagre allowance George Seymour had given him in order to see as much as he could while he was in Switzerland. He had been down to Lucerne, crossed the lake to Burgenstock, taken the nerve-shattering elevator up the sheer rockface, enjoying the expanse of mountain scenery. The autumn weather had so far been kind and he had used his time well. But funds were running out.

He had only managed to stay on by half starving himself. He could eat when he got back to London and Seymour would pay for it. By the time he reached the Pension Bella he was very hungry.

Eddie wished Hans Bider a friendly good-evening, took his key and went upstairs. Once in his room he took his wallet out to check his money. He might have enough for eggs and chips or he might be reduced to a sandwich. Either way he would be forced to return to London tomorrow. He washed and put on his last clean shirt.

The tap on the door was so soft that at first he

thought he had imagined it. When it was repeated he called out, "Come in," in English although he spoke good German. He was standing in front of the dressing-table mirror trying to get a comb through his hair when Ulla opened the door. He did not turn immediately, thinking the maid had come early to turn down the bed.

"May I come in?"

English spoken in a foreign accent always fascinated him. Eddie turned to see a well-dressed woman standing in the doorway, gently silhouetted by the dim light from the passage behind her. He could see a pleasant smile beneath the tinted lenses.

"Certainly, if you think you have the right room. Don't let me talk you out of it, though."

Ulla closed the door behind her. "You *are* Mr. Tyler?"

Eddie gave up the battle with his hair. Suddenly he was wary, it was time to remember why he was here. "Eddie Tyler, yes. Who told you?"

"May I sit down?" Ulla indicated the only chair in the room; it was near the window.

"If you can find your way in the dark." He wanted to see the rest of her face, but his barb did not induce her to remove her glasses.

When she was seated, she crossed her legs in no way that could be described as provocative yet he was not insensitive to their shape·or to the expensive shoes that so neatly covered her feet.

"I always believed Englishmen to be polite," she gently chided him.

Left with nowhere to sit except the bed, Eddie leaned against the wall, hands in pockets. "Times change and I'm not your average Englishman, if there is such a thing. You did not answer my question nor did you introduce yourself."

"My name is Ulla Krantz. I am German and the concierge told me you were here."

Eddie liked her image, and she handled herself well. "Married?"

"No. And if at my age you find that odd, it is by choice. Why do you ask?"

"Well, I wasn't getting anywhere with anything else. You've still evaded my question, Miss Krantz."

"Ulla. I didn't think it mattered. I thought you might like to take me to dinner."

Eddie burst out laughing. "Before you came in I was working out whether I could stretch to a ham sandwich or buttered toast. Anyway, why should I want to?"

"That was ungallant. Then let me take you, if it won't embarrass you. And these days it should not."

The very suggestion of dinner was aggravating Eddie's hunger pains. "Where?"

Ulla shrugged. "The Baur au Lac? Anywhere."

"I'm wearing my only suit. I don't think it would stand up to that sort of opulence."

"That's of no importance. You have presence, Mr. Tyler."

"Eddie," he replied. He was flattered but suspicious. "You know, I'm enjoying talking to you but we're not really getting anywhere, are we? *Why* do you want to take me to dinner? Do we go to bed afterwards?"

"You are very direct. I want to talk to you about a bank account."

The nerve ends prickled at the nape of his neck.

"I haven't got one," he said flippantly. "Money doesn't interest me. By the way, I like your hat, the way it comes down over one eye."

"Thank you. The account is Dranrab 627."

Now his nerve ends screamed. Ulla was so relaxed, so sure of herself while Eddie had the sudden impulse to run from the room. He no longer felt hungry. "That sounds more like a drug or a new make of television."

"But you know that it's not. And I would like to know how you came to hear of it."

"And I'd like to know why you think I have heard of it. Ulla, you're a lovely lady—not my type, perhaps, but lovely just the same. I didn't mean the bed bit. I was trying to shock you. I'm afraid you're off your rocker, though. Someone, somewhere, has misled you."

"We both know that is nonsense. Come, Eddie, you surely can't be afraid of me? We can at least have a meal together."

"Sure. The last supper." Eddie suddenly leaned forward and removed her glasses. The quick action took her by surprise. For a moment she was cold with fury, and it showed through tightened lips and bright, brown eyes that were agate-hard. Apart from a hand involuntarily lifting to her face, she remained rigid.

"I like to see who's inviting me," said Eddie, somewhat shaken by his own bravado. As he scrutinised her he was absorbed by the deep expressiveness of her eyes which were beginning to soften as her lips relaxed. It occurred to him that the corn-coloured hair did not really go with the eyes. She should be brunette. Quite affably, he said, "Why hide them? They are beautiful." But he had glimpsed the brief stoniness before the warmth filtered back.

"That was a childish thing to do," Ulla remarked evenly.

Eddie handed the glasses back. "I don't like smokescreens. I'm an open sort of fellow. Now what's your game, Ulla?"

"Aren't you prepared to discuss it over dinner?" She held the glasses now. She remained quite still, aware that to try to vamp him would fall flat. She had already learned that shortage of money had not made him less independent, and doubted that Eddie Tyler could be bought. It was something to bear in mind.

"OK," he said. "The Baur au Lac. Why not?

I'm hungry. Give me an hour. I'm leaving tomorrow and must pack first."

Ulla rose, careful not to stand too close to him. "Can't you pack later?"

"I won't feel like it later. Anyway, it's too early for dinner so I'll meet you there. Half seven?"

Ulla stepped round the bed and put her glasses back on as she reached the door. "I was hoping we could have a drink first."

Eddie grinned. "On my empty stomach it would go straight to my head." He opened the door for her. "Just to show you that I have not forgotten *all* my better habits."

She smiled and inclined her head and said, "Seven-thirty, then. In the lounge."

"Fine. You'd better dress down to my level." Eddie saw her to the elevator then went back to his room. He sensed trouble. Pulling out his grip he packed quickly.

He went to the window and looked down. The narrow street was tight with rush-hour traffic and impatient drivers were blasting their horns. Leaving the room, he went down the stairs and stopped on the landing above the small foyer. He could hear Hans Bider's voice on the telephone. He waited until Bider had finished, satisfied himself that the foyer was empty, then continued on down.

Bider looked up as Eddie crossed the foyer. "Hi! Some dame, eh?"

"She is a high-class whore who was told I was

deep in perversion. She wanted me to put on a show. What did you tell her, Hans?"

Bider was alarmed. "I told her nothing. *Nothing*. She said she wanted to drop in and surprise you. I thought you must know her."

"I've never met her and someone has told her lies about me. No one else knows I'm here. What are you up to, Hans? Does she pay you commission if it comes off?" Eddie's false anger was convincing.

"You mustn't say things like that. For God's sake, it's not true."

"Well, I'm going to tell the proprietor. I'm not having this. You had absolutely no right to send her up to my room. How much did she give you?"

The question caught Bider off balance. His expression gave him away and Eddie's face darkened. Bider dived into his pocket and pulled out the notes Ulla had given him. "Here, take it. It's all a mistake. I never said those things. I thought it was OK."

Eddie picked up the money. "This proves it, doesn't it?"

Bider could only see that whatever he did or said now would place him in deeper trouble. "Please don't tell the proprietor."

Eddie glowered. "I'm checking out of this dump. I've paid for the room. What do I owe?"

"Nothing. Nothing. You settled your meals as you had them."

Eddie counted the notes he was holding. He glanced across the counter at Bider. "She pays well, doesn't she? This will help me to get to Geneva. Is there a late train?"

Bider scrambled for a timetable but Eddie said, "Forget it. There must be something. Is there a back way out? She didn't take kindly to what I told her. I don't want her thugs beating me up."

"Thugs?"

"She threatened me when I said I'd expose her racket."

Bider pointed to the rear of the foyer. "That door and then through the kitchen. I'm sorry. It's a terrible mistake."

Eddie took a few notes and handed the rest of the money back. "Don't do it again. You could have got me in real trouble." He went back upstairs, put on his topcoat, and carried his grip down the stairs. He waited until Bider was occupied at the counter before slipping towards the rear door.

He went through the busy kitchen oblivious of stares and wanting only to get away. Once outside, he found himself in a small yard with a gate at the end, unbolted it and went out into a narrow alley. There was a street at each end and he could see the slowly moving traffic. He paused to pick up his bearings, then walked briskly.

He hailed a taxi and asked for the Bahnhof. As he sat back, watching the early night movement of Zürich, he was certain that he had been right

172

to avoid a further meeting with Ulla Krantz. The one glimpse of her eyes had been sufficient, they had momentarily scared him.

The Bahnhof was bustling with activity and was a mass of lights. He located the Swissair counter and discovered there were no flights to London until the next day. A further check produced a flight to Paris with a possible transfer to London, too risky to be shown as an official connection. He booked it with the Paris—London sector unconfirmed.

He caught the airport bus and stood near the folding doors all the way to Kloten Airport, his grip between his feet. He was uneasy. He did not think that Ulla would be an easy woman to fool. He bought himself a sandwich and chose the most crowded part of the departure lounge, once he had checked through.

Eddie was not comfortable until the lights of Zürich were dropping away behind him, and even then he suspected that Ulla might have a long arm on the end of a telephone. He found the qualms she had raised in him quite extraordinary, but he couldn't reason them away. He sat uneasily throughout the flight.

Raya Dubrova found that she was not very good at waiting. Her return to Western Europe was being held up by delays over visas. Stevinski had left her in no doubt that strings were being pulled to speed the process, but even he had to be patient. A new passport in her own name, complete with a photograph taken at the Centre, had been issued in a matter of hours.

Her mother had asked no questions and had obviously been briefed by Stevinski, but her concern for her daughter was evident. Raya did not understand why her mother should not be told that she was going to make enquiries about Yasha's fate. It seemed straightforward enough. And yet she really knew that it was not.

She was learning that Stevinski was devious. Was this how Nakentov had been? The side of her grandfather that she had not known?

All she knew for certain was that her life had changed completely. The relationship with her mother had changed. They had drawn closer through concern for each other, yet there was a barrier through which they could not communicate.

Raya spent time studying Swiss and Austrian street maps, but always at the Centre so that her mother would not know. If Stevinski was aware of the increasing strain between mother and daughter, he gave no sign.

If Eddie Tyler could have seen Ulla Krantz's look of cold rage as she left the Pension Bella for the second time, he would have been certain that his fears were well founded.

When Ulla left him she had not been entirely satisfied that he would go to the Baur au Lac.

Once outside the pension, Ulla decided to wait. For three-quarters of an hour she waited patiently, half concealed in a canopied doorway, across the street, like a prostitute who could afford to choose her clients. She received many inviting glances. By six-thirty, the traffic had thinned and she was able to call a taxi.

She sat in the cab, having convinced the driver that she would not only pay any fines for illegal parking but would give him a bonus.

The hour went past and she believed her instincts had been right. Just before seven-thirty, the time she was due to meet Eddie, she told the driver to wait and she dashed into the pension foyer.

By the time she had finished with Hans Bider, he was pale and shaken, and wondering where it had all gone wrong. But she did compensate him again, and he held her money in an unsteady hand as she stormed out.

Ulla at once saw through Eddie's ploy of going to Geneva.

"Zürich Airport," she snapped to the driver. "Fast."

She made no attempt to find Eddie but checked on flights to London. Satisfied that he could not have caught the last direct flight she checked on the indirect ones.

Ulla possessed the kind of aura that commanded attention, but she still had to pay for the information that Eddie had booked on the Paris flight.

So he had fled. Ulla did not relax her pace. She took a taxi to the Baur au Lac, checked which room her colleagues had reserved for her, then tracked them down at a table in the bar. She refused an offer of a drink and came straight to the point, keeping her voice low against the general hum.

"He ran out on me." She told them what had happened.

"He wouldn't duck out like that unless he knew something," said Wegel.

Ulla glanced at the clock behind the bar. "I must make a call to London before he gets there."

The two men looked at her quizzically. "Are you asking for our endorsement?" Wegel appeared to be in pain, his thin face slightly contorted. "We have an understanding."

"About *our* actions. Now I have to subcontract to a London detective agency. We must stick together; each must know what's happening. It has worked for us well. We must not now desert the system that has been tried and tested, particularly under the first sign of pressure." Ulla glanced at the clock again.

"Go make your call," said Rolf Hartmann, "before it's too late. But it will still leave the girl. We'll talk when you come back."

Ulla hurried from the room. Hartmann and Wegel called for more drinks and ordered a dry

176

sherry for Ulla. The sherry rested on the table before the empty chair and became a point of focus for the two men, as though the reflection from the pale wine embodied Ulla.

"There's nothing anyone can do to us," asserted Wegel. "We've sewn it up too tight."

"Someone must have thought that of Dranrab. Yet look what's happening."

Wegel shook his head, bony fingers slowly turning his drink round. "That was a sloppy arrangement. The Swiss government did us a favour when they started to get tough."

Hartmann inclined his head in agreement. "I can't see how anything *can* go wrong. Unless it can be discovered how we got it."

"That's impossible," replied Wegel.

Hartmann stroked back his long grey hair and then picked up his drink. For once he was less restive, his gaze turned inward, but Wegel was still aware of the power of the man sitting across from him. Though now in his sixties, Hartmann was not someone to tackle physically. Wegel had seen him operate.

"We had better hope so," Hartmann responded at last.

The two men took stock of each other, almost as if they had only just met. The suggestion of a crisis made them realise that everything had run smoothly for over twenty years. Whatever happened, they were wealthy. The agreed amounts each took out from the Zeitlinger, without interfering with the capital structure, had accumulated over the years to fortunes in their own right.

It was at this point that the affairs of the three directors of Tinsal separated. What each did with the interest drawn was their own business. Their personal bank accounts were unknown to each other. Lack of money had not been their fear for very many years.

Their individual profits were so vast that greed was eliminated. But their very safety depended on stability and mutual trust. The trust itself was founded on necessity; it was no moral issue, no guide to character. It was a simple life-line for self-protection.

Arguments between them were rare. If the action of one raised a query, no questions would be asked, provided that the stability of the account that governed their lives was not affected. That did not mean such action did not provoke occasional thought, but once the trust crumbled, so might the rest.

Such a thought occurred to Hartmann now. "How are your tame directors getting on?"

At first Wegel was surprised by the question, unable to place its meaning. A nerve pulled at the left side of his face which brought back the slight contortion. It was a reaction the others had grown used to but it was a giveaway to stress. "What made you ask that?"

"Just wondered. Never really understood why you wanted jobs for your friends."

"Why not? There was nothing to stop you doing the same." Wegel knew that Hartmann was referring to his insistence with Zeitlinger to put a director on the board of two separate companies in which Tinsal had a large holding. The nominees had been put forward by Wegel but had been adopted as representatives of Zeitlinger who held the investments in their name. One company was in France the other in Sweden.

"I have no friends," said Hartmann simply.

Wegel knew it to be true and he knew why. He watched the pressure of Hartmann's hands as they wrestled against each other. "Anyway, Ulla insisted on having someone at that tame Idaho bank. It does no harm. The time to complain is when it does."

"I'm not complaining," said Hartmann irritably. "I was curious."

"More so now than at the time?"

Hartmann quickly saw where this was leading. He smiled awkwardly, "Of course, it's done no harm. As you say, why not?" He raised his drink. "I was out of order, Gustav. It was a foolish question."

And the system worked once again, but Wegel was quite certain of what had caused the near friction between them. After all these years people were digging around the foundations of their security.

Ulla came back a few minutes later and was quick to pick up their mood. But Wegel was pleased to see her, Hartmann's sudden questions had worried him. It was an area where such probing could do him most harm.

Ulla sat down eyeing them quickly. "I hate being rushed into a job. And I don't like using untried contacts."

Wegel and Hartmann silently agreed. They had relied on their own abilities for so long that delegation was difficult for them. Loose ends had been cut off years ago and yet, suddenly, here were some more.

"I take it you made contact?" asked Wegel, pushing her sherry forward.

"Yes. But there's no certainty Tyler will arrive on time. He's on an indirect flight."

"One of our problems has always been that we have never been able to find out who was the original Dranrab," Hartmann spoke with his head turning aggressively from one to the other.

"It's done us no harm," Wegel mused. "They could be dead."

But Ulla was only half listening. "Don't you think it a strange combination? A young Englishman and a young Rumanian girl both enquiring at roughly the same time but presumably unknown to each other? It's as though the same bomb has exploded in two different places."

They looked at each other uneasily.

Eddie Tyler threw his grip on the bed. He was tired and irritable and he resented the fact that he was now being criticised by Savage.

"Why the hell didn't you phone?" snarled Savage. "You had the number. We'd have sent someone out to meet you."

"If I'd known that, I would have done. Leave me alone for chrissake."

Savage relented but he had to make the point. "You might have blown a safe house. You come back here and sit on the steps on open view waiting for someone to pitch up."

Eddie undid the zip of his grip. "Yes, well, I'm not at my best. I missed the damned plane from Paris and spent the night at Orly half dozing on a seat. It was bloody cold and uncomfortable. I caught the first flight out this morning."

"You going to tell me what happened?"

Eddie flung himself on the bed, "No. I'll wait till George Seymour pitches up. It will save telling the same story twice."

Seymour arrived an hour later. "Trouble I hear," he breezed as he entered the room.

Eddie was still on the bed, his hands clasped behind his head. He swivelled his eyes towards Seymour. "Good morning," he replied pointedly.

Seymour appeared not to notice the rebuke.

He hooked a chair out with his foot, opened his coat and flopped down. "Tell me about it," he said.

Eddie noticed that Savage was standing near the door with a notebook and ballpoint like a policeman at a break in. He collected his thoughts and related, in detail, what had happened. Before he had finished Seymour gave Savage an almost imperceptible nod and Savage left the room, closing the door behind him.

Seymour rubbed his eyes with finger and thumb. "I'll say this for you," he acknowledged, "when you want to be you're quite lucid. I won't ask if you've left anything out. Why didn't you go with the woman?"

"I think she wanted me out in the open."

"To kill you?"

Eddie stared. He had not pushed his thoughts so far yet but he couldn't avoid the possibility. "It must have crossed my mind. I wasn't prepared to take a chance."

"Why would she want to kill you?"

"How the hell do I know? Someone tried it here didn't they? She knew that I knew about Dranrab."

"Did anyone follow you from the airport?"

"I hope not. I wasn't looking. And I don't suppose I would have known had I been."

"That was careless of you. I'll have this place checked out. We might have to close it."

"Look, I missed the connection. No one could

182

know which flight I'd catch from Paris the following morning. I didn't know myself."

"There is a certain breed of person who would willingly wait for hours. Your half-grown beard, your mop of hair, your height and your age, would be easy to relay and easy to pick up by an experienced man."

Eddie sat up on the bed. "So I cocked it up? Well, you hardly wasted any money, did you? I had to blackmail the concierge to raise enough cash to get a taxi to the air terminal. And the beard is your damned fault."

"Don't spoil things by repeating yourself. You did well in Zürich. You might have made your getaway *after* your second meeting with Ulla Krantz."

"No thanks. You know her?"

"Not at all." Seymour glanced at his watch. "Almost lunch time." He rose and went to the window to look down into the street. "Your aunt's house is still being watched, by the way. I suppose they're hoping you'll go back."

"Why don't you arrest them?"

"For loitering? We prefer to leave them alone, ties up some of their labour."

"Are they anything to do with Ulla Krantz?"

Seymour turned to face the room. He was fumbling in his pockets but whatever he was searching for never came to light.

"I don't know. I don't think so. Dranrab seems to have turned over a few stones."

"Including yours."

Seymour smiled. "You're determined to get at me." He glanced towards the door as he heard footsteps on the stairs. Savage came in, notebook in hand, and addressed Seymour. "No Ulla Krantz on any international list. We've done a computer run down and Interpol did a crash action job for us. We're waiting on the FBI but my feeling is that this is European."

"It might not be her real name, of course. You're talking of wanted lists?"

"Natch. A full run-down will take a lot longer."

"And we know of only one person who's actually met her?"

Seymour and Savage turned slowly to face Eddie.

"Oh no you don't," he said. "Whatever you're thinking, forget it. I'm a coward."

Savage was grinning wickedly and Seymour offered the suggestion of a smile. "Little wonder," remarked Seymour, "that you're an out-of-work reporter on an obscure local paper. That's exactly what you are. Unemployable."

"Social service keeps me alive. Just. Anything you two cook up, won't."

Seymour was holding his stomach, his expression mild; the flaccid cheeks shook as he sighed. Apparently Savage recognised the signs, "You want me to get you something? The kitchen's well stocked."

"I'm sure we all need a meal. There's some liquor in that cupboard that won't open. You know where the key is. I think Mr. Tyler needs a drink."

Watching this brief pantomime, Eddie swung his legs off the bed and stood up. "I'm no good to you," he insisted, "Zürich was a waste of time."

"Zürich was a master stroke." Seymour slipped off his topcoat and hung it behind the door. He put his hand on the radiator to make sure the heat was on, and then he sat on the chair again. "It produced a denial of Dranrab from the manager of a highly reputable Swiss bank. It brought the apparently lovely Ulla Krantz running to you. Now how do you suppose she found you?" And, when Eddie did not reply, "Surely, only the bank manager could have told her? Now managers of reputable Swiss banks do not pass on information of that kind. Swiss banks are still very secret. So our Miss Krantz is not only a client of the Zeitlinger, and I would suggest a very valued one, but in some way she must be tied up in Dranrab. Past or present."

"He said there was no Dranrab."

"And I'm sure he would not lie. Evasive to be sure, but not a liar." Seymour gazed at Eddie steadily. "Dranrab is still in there somewhere, in some form."

"Shouldn't you be discussing this with Bill Savage? It's nothing to do with me."

"It's everything to do with you. Your enigmatic Aunt Jane opened up a secret bank account . . ."

"We don't know that," Eddie interrupted.

"Let us assume so. And I believe you think so too. Twenty-one thousand could represent pounds. A large sum of money in 1927."

"The year is another assumption."

"A fair one, though. Now . . ."

"I'm not risking my life for twenty-one thousand quid. I'm not that interested in money."

"I believe you. It's one of the few things I find I like about you." Seymour remained unsmiling. "But would we be talking of that figure now? Eddie, we could be talking of a very large sum indeed. After fifty years or so? It could be your rightful inheritance. Believe me, it has everything to do with you."

"And you're just interested in my personal well-being?"

"I'd be a hypocrite if I suggested that. We're interested in where Lubov will lead us and that, quite clearly, is still a live issue. The two things are interlocked."

"Then use your own secret army."

"The account is the key to all this. And you are the one who can turn it. I'm convinced of it."

"A fortune is no good to me dead."

"A fortune could save you. And wouldn't it only be fair to Aunt Jane? If we don't handle this the right way she could finish up all over the front pages, however we tried to stop it. This should be kept in the family, don't you think?"

Eddie raised an eyebrow, "How much, do you think?"

"Who knows? Perhaps a million or two. People like Ulla Krantz won't try to dispose of you for petty cash."

Eddie showed no obvious reaction to the amount but he said thoughtfully, "A lot can be done with that sort of money."

Seymour eyed Eddie shrewdly. "I'll do you the compliment of suggesting that you weren't thinking of yourself when you said that."

"That's right. I wasn't."

9

THE nearest airport was Zürich. Switzerland's commercial capital had become the magnet of the affair although Raya's final destination was beyond it. On the flight from Moscow she had gone over everything Stevinski had told her. She had read up the background to the places she must visit and she had made notes of the train times.

The journey from Zürich was so awkward that it was necessary to stay the night there and she had been booked into a second-class hotel as before. This time her luggage was more presentable as she had spent the last two days in Moscow on a hectic spending spree. Stevinski had provided funds, apparently as a generous gesture to reward her for helping him. But in truth he did not want Raya displayed as an obvious, limited-budget, dowdy-looking Russian. His reasons were not solely propagandist, though; there was a more deadly reason should he have to fall back on it.

The early November weather was wet and wild when she started the tedious rail journey from Zürich to Bregenz in Austria, the next day, and on arrival at Bregenz, she took a taxi to the hotel.

As she peered through the cab window, she could see the rough spread of the Pfander Mountain.

She was glad to be staying outside the town, in a hotel of the old chalet style. From her bedroom window she could just see a tip of Lake Constance; it was all so peaceful, and seemed far removed from her Moscow apartment. Yet almost before her cases were unpacked she was worrying about her mother.

She had to face the fact that her distrust of Stevinski was growing and some of her fears on finding Nakentov's notes returned. There was nothing she could do while Larissa was in Moscow.

After dinner she put on a coat and went out into the wet blustery night. It was dark and it was some time before she reached the street lighting, but she had a small flashlight with her and passing cars helped illuminate the way.

It was a long way down to the lake but she wanted to think and breathe in fresh air and feel the slight rain on her face. She reached the open area by the lake and stood by the quay where the ferries berthed. A swell on the water broke up the lights that reflected across it. Out there, in summer, the festival was held on the largest floating stage in the world.

She turned up her collar and faced the broken darkness of the lake. She had to take up a trail that must surely long be dead. It seemed so hopeless, and now, so pointless. The distance from

Moscow destroyed Stevinski's credibility. Why now? Even Yasha's best friend, Nakentov, had given up.

Raya started out mid-morning. At breakfast she was aware of being a focus of attention. The word had got round. A young Russian girl travelling alone was unusual. She was self-conscious as she crossed the restaurant floor.

The rain had stopped but the streets were still wet and glistened as she walked. She had memorised the small town's layout, and she preferred not to use a taxi for there was plenty of time and it was better to find her way on foot.

Baumwolle Strasse may once have been part of the cotton industry, but there was no sign, that Raya could see, of a connection now. It was a short, cobbled street of terraced houses, charming in themselves, but which had seen better days.

She walked down the slight incline, trying to pick up the run of numbers on the painted, plain wooden doors. The odd car passed her and others were parked in the street, but otherwise there was little sign of life. As she hesitated between two unmarked doors she heard the tinkle of a cow bell, and a heavily coated woman with a protective headscarf came round the corner with a cow on a lead.

"*Kommen*, Sadie. *Kommen*," called the woman to the reluctant cow and Raya reflected that these people had long since forgotten the war and yet she was here to dig into it.

Raya knocked on the door of what she believed was number fifteen. As she stood there she felt foolish. A dark-haired woman in her thirties opened the door. She smiled pleasantly as she wiped her hands on a towel and Raya detected traces of flour. "*Ja?*"

"*Ich möchte bitte mit Herrn Retzer sprechen.*"

"Mit Herrn Retzer?"

"Herrn Kurt Retzer."

"*Hier? In diesem Haus?*"

"This is the address I have. Number fifteen?"

"This is number fifteen, fräulein, but there is no such person here. You have been misinformed."

It was worse than she had thought it would be. "Did he live here once?"

The woman gave it thought. "Perhaps, but not immediately before us. We have been here six years now."

"I'm sorry." That was an end of that.

Observing her disconsolation, the woman asked, "You have come a long way?"

"Moscow." It sounded better than the Soviet Union.

"*Moscow?*" The woman smiled, not sure whether to believe her. And then she laughed. "Perhaps you have the wrong country, too?"

Raya smiled with her, it seemed the only thing

to do. Then she said again, "I'm sorry to have troubled you."

About to close the door, the woman opened it again.

"*Einen moment, bitte.*" As Raya turned back the woman added, "Frau Linten has lived here for many years. She may be able to help you." She pointed, "Three along. The yellow door."

"*Danke.* You've been very kind." Raya retraced her steps, aware of one or two curtains being tugged. She knocked on the yellow door.

It was clear from the moment the door was opened that Frau Linten was eager to gossip. She insisted that Raya come in out of the wind as soon as Retzer's name was mentioned.

Raya followed her into a neat living room and sat in the armchair by the window. The Austrian was in her seventies and had lived in the Voralberg all her life. She was spritely and lean and still retained fine features. It was obvious that she was lonely. Raya stiffened as she learned that Frau Linten had lost her husband on the Eastern Front and had never re-married. Being a Russian was suddenly a big drawback.

With great patience and increasing understanding, Raya listened to the Frau's life story and the difficulties of widowhood. But at last her enquiry was being answered.

"Herr Retzer is German. From Bavaria. Settled here after the war. A fine strapping man." A belated suspicion crept over the lined features, bright eyes fastened more closely on Raya. "You are a relative?"

"No." Raya carefully considered what to say next. And then, because she wanted to terminate the whole business, she said, "I'm a Russian. I'm trying to find out what happened to a distant relative during the war."

Frau Linten became silent. She sat with her tightly bunned hair resting against a lace anti-macassar while her veined hands fiddled on her lap. Her lips had tightened and she was clearly sorry she had already spoken so freely.

Raya could feel the hostility; the old mind was creeping back down the years to the man she had lost. She was forced to say, "I am twenty-six. I know only what I am told about the war. I was not born until long after it." She leaned forward. "Frau Linten, my relative was killed too." She was not sure that it was true.

Frau Linten exhaled slowly. "Do you imagine I would blame you for what happened forty years ago? That is not the reason I hesitate. If you are Russian, what do you want with Kurt Retzer? To lock him up again? I will not help you to do that."

"I've no wish to harm him in any way. An uncle of mine has just died and he left some notes about people who might be able to help to find out what happened to his nephew. That's all there is to it."

Frau Linten was still suspicious. "And the

Russians let you out on your own just to find that out? You must be very important."

"I'm not. My name is Raya Dubrova and I'm a nobody. My distant relative was more important; he was Stalin's first-born son."

"*Stalin*? He claimed you lost twenty million people in the war. He must have killed more than half of them himself."

Raya was shaken by the hatred. She had not encountered the questioning of an official pronouncement before. The very challenge of such a claim staggered her. She stood up. "I did not mean to upset you. I must go."

"Sit down." Frau Linten waved Raya down with a bony finger. "It is I who should apologise." She waved a hand in exasperation. Memories returned. "I am bitter, but not at you. Are you sure you don't want to cause trouble for Herr Retzer?"

"None at all. Frau Linten, I'm on my own because they would not spare anyone of importance to look into this matter. Stalin and his son never got on. It would be unfair to confuse the two." Raya could now understand some of the reason Stevinski was using her instead of an experienced agent.

"I'm beginning to like you, young lady. But you must still be a paid up and highly trusted party member for them to let you go so easily."

"My mother and my brothers are still in Moscow."

"Ah! That is an old trick." Frau Linten sat back musing, her head against the antimacassar, eyes reflectively cast at the ceiling. "Is it so important to find out what happened to this man?"

"My mother would like to know. So would I. It will be better than going through life not knowing what happened to him."

Frau Linten's gaze moved slowly to a small sideboard against the rear wall. A framed and fading picture of a young corporal held her attention. Raya guessed that it was her long dead husband, it was time to be silent.

"Herr Retzer's in Lindau," said Frau Linten. "Don't bring harm to him for he's suffered for his sins. He has served his prison term. And his wife and baby were both killed in a car crash, he never really got over it." She paused, her gaze slowly leaving the photograph. "He was driving," she added simply. "Which is why he moved from here. It must be fifteen years now since he left us."

"I only want to know if he knew my relation and what happened to him."

"Let me find the address."

When Raya had gone, Frau Linten picked up the photograph from the sideboard and stared at it for some time. The young Russian girl had revived old memories. They were all she had left and she was surprised to find that, with the photograph in her hand, she could still feel both pain and joy. But some things were perhaps best forgotten. She put on her coat and a woollen headscarf and went out to the nearest telephone kiosk.

Raya took the train on the short journey to Lindau which spread over two islands on the north-eastern shore of Lake Constance. She had to endure customs and immigration, which, with her passport, always invited close scrutiny, before she could enter the Bavarian lakeside town. Frau Linten had told her that Kurt Retzer's small villa was on the Friedrichshafen road which ran north-west along the side of the lake.

Raya took a taxi. When the driver left the main lake road and started to climb to higher ground Raya realised that the area might be remote. The small villa was on an unmade road. Suddenly the taxi began to sway ominously and the driver pulled up. "I'll break my springs," he complained. "There's the villa. Not too far to walk, fräulein."

Raya paid him off and heard him reverse back as she picked her way through the water-logged gravel craters. Half-way along, white painted stones lined the rough drive to help motorists crazy enough to approach in the dark. As Raya came closer the villa appeared neat and was painted like the stones. Single-storeyed, it stood out like a white beacon amidst a high rock cluster. She turned to look down towards the lake: the view was magnificent. The lake craft left plumes of foam like aircraft vapour trails and sails stood out like coloured balloons on some of the yachts.

Beyond the wide stretch of water she could see as far as the snowcaps in the Swiss Oberland to the south west and to the Tyrolean ranges in the south east. It was breathtaking and, near to the villa, she stopped to take in the elevated view of the distant mountains with their mass of rain clouds suspended over the peaks and mirrored in the lake.

As she gazed out, Raya was aware of being watched but when she turned to face the villa the curtainless windows showed blank reflections. She trudged the remaining few yards up the incline and stood in the paved porch. Below, to her right, was another larger villa and she was somewhat comforted by it. Lindau itself was lost from sight by undulations. Raya raised the horseshoe knocker on the plain door and hammered it down. After a while she knocked again and, when there was still no response, she ventured round the back to find a terraced garden stretching up in well-cared-for stages. She had almost given up hope, and was wondering how she would get back to the hotel, when she tapped on the opaque glass section of the back door. The nearby villa was out of sight from where she stood and the fact just registered as the back door was opened.

Before Raya could move she was grabbed and pulled through the door with a force that sent her reeling. She lost her balance, crashed down, but before she could rise she saw a gun pointing at her head and a voice above it was saying, "Don't move, fräulein, or I'll shoot you dead."

Ulla Krantz was wearing the expression that Eddie Tyler had so briefly glimpsed when he had removed her dark glasses. Gustav Wegel and Rolf Hartmann had not seen it for a very long time. She called them to a conference in her hotel suite the evening following Eddie's flight. There was a tray of drinks on a table but no one approached it. The two men were not even seated before Ulla said, "London bungled it. Tyler got away."

She was pacing the room slowly, high heels indenting the pile. She was furious yet philosophical at the same time and for a moment they did not know which way to respond. The arrangements had been hers and, in part, she seemed to accept the blame as she said, "Perhaps I used the wrong agency. Anyway, he's still loose and cannot be found. At the moment."

Hartmann decided it was time to visit the drinks tray; it was difficult for him to remain still for long. "So what went wrong?" he asked, as he poured a schnapps.

"Tyler must have stayed overnight in Paris. That wouldn't have mattered if the London contacts had been at Heathrow Airport the next morning. They say they were. I don't believe them, or, if they were, they got there too late."

Ulla moved behind the huge settee on which Wegel sat. "We must find him."

Wegel said nothing. He could see them being forced to live in each other's pockets until this matter was resolved. They operated more efficiently when separated, and the system of meeting only occasionally added to security. He could see friction coming if they were not careful. There had already been signs of it.

"You're quiet." Ulla said to Wegel as if to confirm his own appraisal. There was criticism in her tone.

"Because, knowing you, you'll already have taken steps to track Tyler down."

"I have the biggest agency in London on it."

"That's what I mean. So what else can we do?"

"Have either of you any connections with Western intelligence services?"

Wegel had difficulty in controlling the nerve that suddenly tugged at the side of his face. He scratched his temple to cover the contortion and let Hartmann answer.

"Intelligence services? Us? Ulla, you have gone mad."

"I don't mean working connections, but someone with influence you know well enough to ask a favour."

Hartmann shrugged, "Money doesn't cut ice in that game."

"Money cuts ice in any game."

Feeling safer, Wegel ventured, "Why do you ask?"

"Because there is something odd about Tyler. London has already run down his address. He left it and moved to an aunt's house while she was terminally ill. Now she's dead, he has left there but not to go back to his own place. Apparently he has no money; it's too soon for him to benefit from anything his aunt may have left. We need more information. Tyler has gone to earth. And that means he has a good reason."

Hartmann said viciously, "We had better find and get rid of him damned quick."

The circle was complete. There was no argument to that.

Wegel wanted to be alone. Here they were staying in the same hotel trying to plan a quick murder. I've lost touch, he thought. But it was not only that Ulla would not leave things as they were. If Hartmann possessed the outward restiveness, Ulla certainly contained the inner. She would be plotting and scheming and the Englishman Tyler really stood no chance at all. Ulla would succeed but Wegel would be expected to add his contribution and that could mean anything from pulling the trigger to disposing of the body.

"You want me to go to London?" Wegel asked.

"Give it a couple of days. I'll keep in touch with Meisser just in case Tyler comes back."

"He'd be mad to do that."

"He might think the risk worth while."

Wegel entered an expensive restaurant without knowing its name: it drew him like a magnet. His claim was that he could find quality blindfolded, but it was really extravagance that attracted him. His wealth provided him with a secluded table at a peak period and he took his time over eating.

Wegel liked Zürich; not its charm but its prosperity. Success was evident everywhere. Banks, Stock Exchange, Conventions, Gold Trading. It was all here. And he could feel its commercial atmosphere more easily than the touch of the silk shirt he was wearing. He would like to live here but that might be misunderstood by the others so he lived in Frankfurt instead where he could thrive on the industrial emanations of wealth and power.

But power was not always entirely his. Sometimes it had to be shared, however reluctantly. And it was on this undoubted fact of life that Wegel centred his thoughts while he ate. When he finished his meal, he tipped liberally—there was nothing mean about him. As long as people recognised his very considerable financial status, then Wegel was satisfied.

He left the restaurant and entered the nearest hotel to find a call box. He dialled from memory a number it would be impossible for him to forget. "Wegel," he announced in English.

"You're late," answered an American voice.

"Unavoidable. I'll explain."

"Usual place," instructed the voice.

Wegel swore and put down the phone. He went outside and looked for a taxi but it was a difficult time of day. The nerve pulled in his face as his impatience built up. But at last he obtained a taxi and, almost angrily, asked for a remoter part of the older town. He was acting against his character and he did not enjoy it.

Wegel dismissed the cab a short distance from his destination and started to walk. He was now well away from the lake and the more fashionable parts of Zürich.

After a few minutes, he turned into a tavern and squeezed his way to the crowded bar. There was no refined hum here; voices were raucous with belly laughs and coarse humour.

He located Gates waiting in his usual spot at the corner of the curved bar, sitting on a stool with his back to the wall. Gates waved and Wegel wondered how the American managed to get the same position every time.

Wegel hated the place. It was filled with ordinary people enjoying themselves on beer, cheap wine and bar snacks. The place was the antithesis of all he had strived to achieve and he believed that Gates knew this and selected the tavern deliberately. Yet he had to admit that it was the most unlikely place to find Ulla or Rolf Hartmann, and therefore safe.

Gates was in his forties and looked like a boxer who had given up because he was too short for his weight. His nose was slightly askew, giving the false impression that it had once been broken. His hands could have belonged to a labourer, but the grey eyes in the rough-cast face were shrewd and bright. His speech was better than his appearance.

As Wegel reached the bar and made a space for himself, Gates passed him a glass of wine as he always did. And, as always, Wegel would only sip it for appearance's sake; it was too cheap for him to drink.

"What's the problem?" asked Gates without preamble.

Wegel told Gates as much as concerned him. The two men had perfected a method of speaking so that it did not penetrate the general noise but each could hear the other without raising their voices. They kept their heads quite close together and Gates's eyes would occasionally sweep round the room.

"I think we should put things on ice for a while," Wegel suggested when he had finished his explanation.

"Because an Englishman and a Rumanian girl are sniffing around your bank account?"

"It's dangerous."

"Only if they get hold of it. Is that possible?"

"No."

"Then forget it."

That was the same suggestion that Wegel himself had first mooted to Ulla. "We don't know how much they know or where they got their information. It's a dangerous situation."

Gates gulped at his lager. He wiped his mouth and loosened his tie; it was stuffy in the bar. "You're not by chance trying to unhook yourself?"

Wegel eased away as someone backed into him; he would be glad to get out. "I've thought of many ways of getting unhooked. Killing you is one. But I always came back to the same problem: the whole of the CIA is behind you. It wouldn't do any good; someone else would take over. You keep the threat hanging over me, but one day I'll think of a way out."

Gates nodded understandingly. "You're scaring me to death. You've got to face up to it, Gustav. You did knock off one of our guys. We've been pretty lenient."

"He shouldn't have been poking around in my affairs. You gained by it. I got the right person on to the board of the French company and as they are trading with the Russians you're benefiting from both ends. Anyway, you'd be hard pushed to prove I killed him."

Gates patted Wegel's arm. "You're scraping the barrel. You know how many times you've said that in different ways?" His eyes screwed up with humour. "Of course, if you knocked off an eye witness . . . But that wouldn't do either."

because we have a sworn and attested statement. Why do you make me go over this every time? You hoping I'll slip up? Show a loophole?"

Wegel did not smile back. "This problem is something quite new."

"It's your problem, not mine. Everything else is still fine."

"Phil, I'm warning you. If the others find out that you've forced me to infiltrate a French company engaged in secret government work we're in trouble."

Now Gates knew it was serious. Wegel never used his first name unless he sensed real danger. "If you're that worried, get rid of them."

"Would you help me?"

"Find them or kill them?"

"Both. It's in your own interests."

Gates lowered his drink. He did not trust Wegel, who might be trying to implicate him in something that could rebound. Wegel was of considerable use as things stood. And that was the crux.

"What do you know about the guy?"

"I have two addresses. Ulla got some outfit in London to dig them out."

Gates studied Wegel closely. "I hope you're not trying to pull anything. As you say, there's a lot of us. And enough money to make even yours look like a piggy bank."

"Make up your mind, Phil."

"I'll send the request to base. See what they say."

"It would be useful to know how this all started before they're eliminated. It might even be *vital* to know if we're to prevent it happening again."

Gates did not answer at once. He had the feeling that something more than Tyler and a Rumanian girl was involved and that somehow Wegel was playing his own game. Yet the issue could not be ignored. "OK. But keep things going until I say otherwise. We'll help deal with Tyler and the girl."

10

RAYA was afraid to move. From her position on the floor the man appeared huge. He had closed the door and stood with his back to it so it was difficult for her to see his features properly. But what riveted her attention was the aperture in the gun barrel; it was close to her head and seemed as wide as a tunnel, and it was so steady. After the shock of being brutally flung inside the house, Raya was trembling and terrified.

"Rise slowly."

There was no compromise in the voice. At first Raya could not move at all from her awkward crouch but, by pushing herself up against the wall, she was at last on her feet.

"In there." The gun barrel moved to indicate direction.

"Hands on head."

Too nervous to speak, Raya clasped her hands on her head and entered a room which overlooked the lake far below. "Stop. Keep your arms up." She went rigid as a rough hand traversed her body. She managed to say, "I cannot harm you."

"There are more ways of doing that than with a weapon. All right. Sit in that chair there and put your hands on your lap."

Raya eased herself on to a low armchair and, as she sank into it, she realised that the springs had gone. It would be difficult to jump up from it quickly. Very slowly she lowered her hands and intertwined her fingers on her lap. She was uncomfortable but felt slightly less threatened. She stared up. The gun was still pointing at her. But she could now see the man clearly.

He was tall and had perhaps once been handsome in a rough sort of way. His eyes were hard and his lips were thin and pressed tight as he eyed Raya. What was left of his hair grew out in grey tufts around his large ears. His trousers were unpressed and he wore a grubby white shirt with sleeves rolled up and an open waistcoat over the top. On the arm that held the gun Raya could see a tattoo mark of some kind. He could be aged anywhere between late fifties to mid-sixties. He looked tough and intimidating, yet Raya was sure that he, too, was afraid, and that made him more dangerous.

Stepping away from her he groped to find a ladder-back chair and lowered himself on to it without taking his gaze from her. He leaned forward, forearms on knees, gun now held with both hands. "I know how to use this," he said, moving the gun, "so don't tempt me."

Raya thought it best not to reply; it was obvious to her that he was familiar with the weapon.

"You're Russian," he stated as an accusation. How could he know? Frau Linten? The telephone was on a small veneered table behind the man. "I'm a Soviet citizen," Raya replied.

"Don't stand on your dignity with me. How do you know my name?"

"My grandfather left some old notes about his nephew who was a prisoner in Germany during the war. Your name was in them."

"Who is your grandfather?"

"He's dead now. Pavl Nakentov." Raya was relieved to see that the name seemed to make no impact on Retzer.

"And he was trying to find out what happened to Stalin's son?"

Now Raya was certain that Frau Linten had telephoned.

"He preferred to use the family name, Djugashvili. He did not get on with his father." Raya believed it to be important to break away from the image of Stalin.

"I know he didn't," replied Retzer and was then angry with himself for letting it slip out.

"You knew him then?" Raya moved in excitement and Retzer bawled, "Put your hands back on your lap."

Raya did so quickly. Retzer was unstable. He appeared hunted, and he was licking his lips anxiously.

"It will be easier to kill you," Retzer said desperately after an obvious period of mental agony.

"No, it won't." Raya was surprised at her

calmness. After the first shock she was being rational. "If you kill me you will have to kill Frau Linten and the woman who passed me on to her. The death of a lone Russian girl will raise a lot of enquiry and a great deal of anger in Moscow. You would never be safe."

"I'm not safe now. It couldn't be worse."

"It could. Much worse. You have lived here for twelve years? You would not live for another twelve weeks."

When he did not respond, Raya risked asking, "Why aren't you safe now?"

Retzer stared, suspecting a trap in almost everything she said. But all he saw was a young woman with attractive high slavic cheek bones, and deep concerned eyes. Why was it all starting again? "He thought he'd killed me," Retzer burst out. Suddenly he pulled back his waistcoat and pulled out his shirt to reveal a once muscular body now turned to flab.

"See that? The scar has faded but it's still there. How it missed my heart I shall never know. I think a rib must have deflected the bullet which went straight through me. It broke the rib and I bled like a pig."

Raya leaned forward as far as she dared. She could see the puckered skin like a small crater on the mound of fat.

"But who did it?"

Retzer roughly pushed his shirt back. "Who?" He laughed nervously. "That's the question I've asked myself ever since. He was masked." The gun levelled again. "He wanted to know about Stalin's son, too."

"For what reason?" asked Raya unsteadily. Retzer was wavering again, balancing on a hair-line of indecision.

"People like that don't give reasons. They squeeze the last drop of information out of you, then they kill you so that nobody else will get it."

"What information, Herr Retzer? I swear I can do you no harm." Raya's voice was shaking.

Retzer noticed the tremor, and for a moment the pendulum swung in her favour.

"I don't want to frighten you, fräulein. But I have to be sure of you." He gazed round the room. "Now I must move on again. I ran a bakery in Lindau and retired a year ago. I was hoping this would be my last home."

"Why didn't you change your name?"

Retzer shrugged. "Changed names can draw more attention than the originals. People who know you begin to talk and to wonder. There are other Retzers. I thought it safe enough, particularly as he thought I was dead. You may be right, but I'm too old to change now." He steadied the gun. "You found me, others can."

"You shouldn't have told Frau Linten where you were."

"I didn't. She has long ears and nothing else to do. She means no harm. Are the Russians

211

looking for me too? Someone you report back to?"

It was too near the mark. Stevinski would expect her to give a full account.

"All I want to know is what happened to Yasha Djugashvili. I can protect my sources."

"You are either a liar or very naive, fräulein. There is no way you can protect me if someone wants to know." Retzer paused, eyeing Raya curiously. "You said Yasha. We knew him as Jacob."

"Jacob is his proper name. The family knew him as Yasha." It was clear now that Retzer had known Yasha. She had to find out what he knew.

In the end it was her own quiet charm that persuaded him to talk. Retzer had seen her fear, her courage and her guilelessness. If she was hard she had shown no sign of it. She puzzled him, but he made up his mind that she did not want to harm him directly. The villa would go up for sale the next day and he could live elsewhere until it was sold. And he thought it might be worse for him if he left her uninformed; that could bring a pack round his heels.

He stood up wearily and pushed the gun into his waistband.

"Are you any good at making coffee?" he asked her. He showed her a kitchen that sadly needed a woman's touch. Raya prepared two cups while he looked on from the doorway.

When they were seated at the scrubbed pine table, Retzer told her what he knew.

"I was a guard at Sachsenhausen, near Berlin. I was in the Waffen-SS and had just come back from the Eastern Front with a leg wound. Nothing as bad as this one," he added, touching his rib cage. "Mortar shrapnel. Always got you in the legs. Jacob Stalin was already there when I arrived. Him and a nephew of Molotov's called . . ."

"Wasili Kokorin?"

"That sounds like it. They were in Hut A, inside a privilege compound. Our duties rotated. Sometimes I was assigned there—sometimes not."

"What's a privilege compound?"

Retzer eyed her in surprise. "Relatives of famous men and other special prisoners were not herded in with the rest. They were kept apart as a possible bargaining factor. Word got round that Stalin had been informed where his son was captive and we all knew that Stalin would not have him back. We felt sorry for Jacob, in a way, although he had special privileges." Retzer heaped white sugar into his coffee.

"What sort of privileges?"

Retzer arched an eyebrow. "Their food was better. They were pandered to in other ways. Chess sets were provided and sometimes books. And women. They had plenty of room and privacy when they needed it."

"Women?"

"Of course. We had to keep them happy." Now that he was talking Retzer's mind was filling with recollection. "Jacob was taken to see Field Marshal Goering. He was entertained and fêted. And Goebbels worked on him too, trying to turn him against his own country so they could use him for propaganda. But it didn't work. In spite of his father's rejection of him, Jacob stayed loyal, I'll give him that."

"What happened to him?"

"I wasn't on duty at the time, but a colleague told me what he saw. Afterwards there was a lot of confusion and a cover up by the authorities."

For a few seconds Retzer sat staring broodily at his coffee as if he did not want to go on, but his sadness was for Jacob. "They were pulling him apart. With all the soft soaping at camp, Goering and Goebbels trying to win him—it was rumoured that he even had a letter from the Führer—and his father accusing him of desertion, I don't think he knew where he was after a time.

"Jacob had a woman with him that day. When she had gone there was a row in the hut; no one knew how it started but some blamed Kokorin who was a shit. Jacob came dashing out brandishing a piece of wood. He dived straight at the electrified fence, there was a blue flash, and a turret guard shot him as he hit the wire. He hung on while the current kept going through him.

They had to switch it off before they could pull him away. We never found out whether he was killed by the bullet or the current. It didn't make any difference. He was dead."

Raya was appalled. "Did you see his body?"

"No. It was taken away damned quick."

"Who was your friend who saw it happen?"

"Gerhard Julich." Retzer sat back. He looked ill, as if the memory was too painful. "Gerhard was killed by the man who shot me. And so was Jost Schnell."

"Schnell was another guard?"

Retzer nodded. "I don't know why they wanted to kill us. We had all served prison sentences after the war, just for being in the SS and for being short-term camp guards."

"How can you be certain that Yasha was killed?"

"That's a silly question, fräulein. Nobody could hang from high-voltage wire and have a bullet in his head without being dead."

"But was it *Jacob?*" insisted Raya.

Retzer stood up, gulped back the remains of his coffee and left the kitchen. Raya heard him rummaging in a room beyond the lounge but she stayed where she was, fearful of provoking him again. Retzer returned with an old metal cash box and a bunch of keys. He unlocked the box and emptied its contents on the table.

War souvenirs, military buttons, cap badges, medal ribbons, and two lightning flashes from the lapels of an SS jacket, scattered over the table. Retzer groped at the bottom of the box and pulled out some papers and envelopes, from one of which he produced a photograph. He tossed it across to her.

Raya straightened it but thereafter did not touch it. She counted eight strands of wire fixed to a tree. Other trees stood out stark and bare, and roughly in the middle of them was a long, single-storeyed hut. In the foreground, suspended on the wires, was a man in a grotesque position. Both legs were off the ground, one horizontal in line with the body, the other below it with knee bent. One hand stretched up to hold the wire, the other dangled perpendicularly by the tree. The head was held in position against the wire.

It was a horrifying sight but Raya kept cool, knowing that she must extract from the photograph whatever message it contained. She forced herself to study the detail then, suppressing her revulsion, she observed, "This is Yasha? The sun is behind him. Most of the body and the whole of the face is in shadow."

"It's not the sun, fräulein. It was at night. He struck the trip wire first. Every searchlight in the camp came on. That's why it looks like snow on the ground. But it was April."

"It could be anyone." Raya noticed that the right hand, the one gripping the wire, was illuminated straight across the fingers by the lights.

216

There was no sign of a ring on that hand; the other was in deep shadow.

"But it wasn't anyone," retorted Retzer firmly. "It was Jacob Stalin."

"His foot isn't touching the ground. Wouldn't he have to be earthed?"

"You're trying to reject what you see. I understand. It's not a pleasant picture. As he tripped he would have been earthed. That position is probably the result of convulsions, he couldn't have hit the wire like that. Anyway, the tree is earthed."

Raya took one last look at the photograph, memorised what she could, then sat back on the bench. "Poor Yasha. What happened to his effects?"

"Effects? You mean his clothes, that sort of thing?"

"Yes. And watch and rings."

Retzer scratched his chin. "His clothes were old, his uniform and his boots. They were probably burned. I can't remember about a watch. If he had one it would have been taken. They were hard days. I never saw a ring." Retzer's tone had become guarded.

"What would have happened to it if he'd had one?"

"Are you joking with me? Someone would have had it if it was valuable. Things like that aren't thrown away."

"Is there anyone who can tell me?"

"About a watch or a ring?"

"Only the ring. It was of sentimental value in the family."

"It's a bit late to think about it."

"What about the other guards?"

"I told you. They were killed."

"But you mentioned only two others. There must have been more."

"We were the three involved with the people in that hut. There was the camp commandant, of course, but I think he's dead too. He was already middle-aged at the time."

"How do you know the other two are dead?" Raya had failed to detect the warning in his voice.

Retzer pushed the bench back and half rose. "What is this? I thought you wanted to know about Stalin but it's a ring that really interests you. What's your game?" Retzer pulled out the gun again, his fear rising.

Raya realised that she had pressed too hard. "I'm sorry. Yasha's fate *is* what really interests me. But, as I was coming to make enquiries, my mother insisted that I try to find the ring while I'm here. It obviously means a great deal to her."

"Only now?"

"She didn't talk of it before but I believe she made enquiries over the years. It is not an easy thing to do from Moscow."

Retzer sat down slowly. "Just before I was shot, the man who had been asking me questions

218

told me he had shot the other two. He knew their names."

"What about the whores who serviced Yasha? Would they know?"

"Don't push your luck, fräulein. I've been very lenient with you."

"I'm most grateful, Herr Retzer." Raya stood up. "I'll wash up the cups before I leave."

Retzer joined her, round the table. "Where are you staying?"

Raya did not want to answer. "Does it matter?"

Retzer shrugged. "Not to me. But I might think of something. If I do, I thought you would want to know."

Seeing his growing suspicion, Raya said, "The Hotel Vannhof in Bregenz."

"Bregenz? Of course, you had my old address. Give me the telephone number."

Raya passed over one of the hotel cards which she had in her handbag.

"And your name, fräulein?"

It was too late for caution now and Retzer might get difficult again. "Raya Dubrova." She saw Retzer make a note.

Ulla needed a man. It sometimes worried her that the only time she had such strong urges was when she felt threatened and had no one to turn to. The problem could be discussed with her two partners, but it was not the same as offloading her fears. What she wanted was the comfort of strong masculine arms round her, to hear, and temporarily to believe, a soft litany of endearing lies until her needs had been satisfied.

Aware that she was displaying a side of her nature that would surprise her colleagues, Ulla tried to keep out of their way. When they did meet she assumed the role they expected from her: tough, decisive and intellectually superior.

Studying herself in the array of dressing-room mirrors, Ulla suffered a brief period of unrestrained introspection. For there was something else that haunted her, something that frightened her because it was so deeply embedded in her subconscious, that sometimes taunted her too because it was so elusive. She felt she was desperately groping for a memory that was always out of reach.

As she viewed her image, she observed her own uncertainty. Unaware that a portion of her problem was staring back at her, Ulla took a grip on herself as she picked up a jewellery box, fingered the heavy, diamond-encrusted necklace inside. Most of her exquisite jewellery was in a safe deposit in Frankfurt. She suddenly shuddered. Then her features tightened and she shut out the intrusion in her mind, almost as though she had caught someone else trying to direct it.

As Rolf Hartmann walked the Zürich streets, fast and with head down, he attempted to burn up the energy that flowed through him incessantly

There were many reasons why he must try to control himself. It was a little easier to do now than when he was young, but the sweat could still stand out on his face with the strain. If he could find the Englishman Tyler and the Rumanian girl he would enjoy enormous satisfaction.

He put a call through to a contact in Frankfurt and passed over Eddie Tyler's name and the description of him that Ulla had given them. Suddenly he realised that it was raining. It was crazy for him to walk like this when he had a Rolls-Royce and a Mercedes garaged in the city. But Hartmann had animal instincts. There was going to be trouble and it would not be like the other times. He hoped that his telephone call would produce a quick sighting of Tyler and a lead on the girl who, unknown to him, was not many miles away—along with a man he believed he had killed a long time ago.

11

EDDIE TYLER was bored to the point of recklessness. He had kicked up such a commotion that Seymour agreed to let him out for exercise, usually under cover of darkness and accompanied by Savage. But still, Eddie was confined alone for hours on end.

While he was out with Savage, and Eddie insisted that they went whatever the weather, he knew that he could quite easily run off. Savage himself had pointed this out to him, and then asked if Eddie had anywhere else safe enough to go.

There were a few compensations for his incarceration. Eddie had asked for a better television set, and had got one, and he had insisted on a fur-lined weatherproof coat and that too had been granted. He wondered how far he could go with his demands but it was a rebellious thought rather than one of gain. These concessions really confirmed to him his necessity to Seymour. And this frightened him.

"Christ," he exploded once more. "I've been here for days. What the bloody hell is going on?"

Bill Savage was in the opposite corner of the room, feet up on a stool, a plateful of chicken à la king balanced on his lap, while he watched television. He did not take his eyes from the screen, and he did not answer until the next commercial.

"Takes time, old boy, to pull the sort of strings George Seymour is pulling. Can't send you to Zürich again without the proper documents."

"Balls," Eddie emitted. "You people forge what you want."

"Not if we can get the real thing."

"I'm going home," said Eddie.

"Eat your meal first. You may not get another once you've left."

It was true.

"Sod you," said Eddie aggrieved. "Sod the lot of you. I never wanted any of this."

"It's better than Ruskies knocking on your door, isn't it?" Savage asked reasonably, briefly turning his head. He tucked his napkin further into his collar and his gaze slipped back to the screen.

Kolston's Mayfair apartment was in good taste, not over-furnished nor too brightly coloured, and the cigars were top quality.

Seymour approved. "You want my help?" he suggested, catching Kolston off balance.

The tall, lanky Texan gave a shrug and a smile. He had a pleasant, self-effacing manner, cool eyes, and a habit of hitching up his trousers by the crease when seated cross-legged. "Well, yes. I would have dropped by but I thought this wasn't too far away and I wanted to introduce myself in my own place. I hope I haven't made a gaffe."

Seymour was not fooled by the diffident manner. Kolston, the new head of the CIA's London Station, came with a high reputation. He laughed politely at the mere suggestion that Kolston could make a mistake.

"I'd better get to the point, I guess." Kolston was quick to notice Seymour's unspoken enquiry. "There's a guy called Tyler living in London who we'd like to trace. I thought you might be able to help."

Seymour adjusted himself in the chair. "There are thousands of Tylers, which one is this?"

"I believe he's called Eddie Tyler. Would that stand for Edward?"

The question was less naive than it sounded. Seymour knew that Eddie had been christened as such; he wondered if Kolston knew. "Are you sure you're asking the right person? Surely your staff could contact the police?"

"This is a favour, Sir George. I'd rather not refer it to the police."

"All right. Special Branch or MI5 then. Why me?"

Kolston smiled apologetically. "I'm not doing this very well, am I?"

Seymour, who thought he was doing it very well indeed, made no reply.

"The enquiry came to me from overseas so I thought it might be more in your direction."

"You mean this Tyler is overseas?"

"No, he lives here in London but the interest in him stems from overseas."

"Where, exactly?"

Appearing reluctant, Kolston said, "Spain. I'd rather not go further. At least not yet, not until I know more of what I'm talking about."

"You seem to feel I can help you but I really can't see this as being in my line. Are you suggesting that I might know the name in some connection?"

"Oh, no, nothing like that. I merely thought that you have enough muscle to winkle anyone out, if you wanted to."

"And what happens to Tyler if he's found?"

"Initially, we just want to talk to him."

"And after that?"

"It will depend on what he says."

"That's no answer, Howard."

"No, I guess not." Kolston nervously hitched his trousers again. "I'm in the dark. Our Madrid station put out the request . . . Oh, I see what you mean, we wouldn't do anything like that, not on your patch. My word, no."

"I hope not. You've picked up our police jargon very quickly. We certainly wouldn't take kindly to any rough stuff."

"You have my word on it."

"I'd be happier if I knew just what it is your Spanish people want from this man."

Kolston gave a good impression of being

embarrassed. "I'm not too sure myself. I'll see what I can find out from Madrid."

"It might be helpful. Have you a photograph or something?"

Kolston gave a passable description of Eddie which impressed Seymour, particularly as the American spoke from memory.

"He's young then? I wonder why I thought he would be older."

"Can you help us?"

"Only by using the sources that you seem reluctant to use. I haven't the men nor the internal know-how to do it through my own department; I really can't help you."

"The name means nothing to you then?"

"To me? I didn't realise that was your question."

"One lives in hope. I'm not yet bedded down here and I guess I'm groping some." Kolston tried his cigar; the smoke spiralled upwards. "You're in a much better position to ask Scotland Yard and MI5 on the old boy network than I am. I think they would be less surprised to hear it from you."

"And more co-operative?"

Kolston's smile widened. "That too."

"Then I'll see what I can do."

"Shave that ridiculous beard off." Seymour was barely through the doorway when he made the demand to Eddie who, with Savage, had been waiting for his return.

Eddie bristled. "It was your ridiculous idea that I grew it."

"Nonsense. The socket was faulty. Did you meet any Americans in Zürich?"

"Americans?" Eddie took his jacket off and pointedly pulled his pyjamas out from under the pillow. "I'm bloody fed up with the way you barge in here. Look at the time. You don't even knock."

"Americans," prodded Seymour, closing the door.

"Not as far as I know."

"Well, they're looking for you, so you'd better think again."

"I only met Ulla Krantz. I'm sure she's not American."

"So am I. But they know about you."

"Then it must have come from her."

Seymour did not reply. He was thoughtful as he gazed first at Savage then at Eddie. Then he said, "I was going to ask you to remove the beard anyway. The Krantz woman has seen you with it."

"So has Meisser, the bank manager."

Seymour turned to Savage. "You'd better fix him a flight and accommodation."

"Do you mind discussing me *as if I am here*," Eddie snapped in annoyance.

"We're trying to help you."

"The only way you can help me is to get me back to a normal life."

Seymour's hands were in his overcoat pocket and as he shrugged the coat flapped. "That's impossible. You've got to help us sort this business out first."

"I'm beginning to change my mind about Aunt Jane."

"You don't mean that. Anyway, everything else is ready at last. It's taken a lot of time and influence, but we've come up with something. We have a personal introduction for you to the president of the Zeitlinger Bank."

On arrival at Zürich Kloten, Eddie took a taxi to the Hotel Torsa and noticed with interest that his accommodation had now been upgraded to a three-star hotel. True, he still had two more stars to go to reach the standard of the Baur au Lac where Ulla Krantz stayed, but it was an improvement.

As his taxi drove away, a chauffeur-driven Mercedes with tinted windows pulled out after it. Ulla Krantz sat in the back of the Mercedes. She was the only one of the three who could make a positive identification of Eddie and, when she saw him, she was satisfied at last that she was getting a return for her money from the agency which had spotted Eddie at Heathrow airport. The telephone call from London had been timely and ha given her an opportunity to prepare. She had no intention of losing Eddie again.

At the airport a medium-built man in his early forties stood outside the arrival sector and watched Eddie's departure. He did not miss the Mercedes following close behind.

The man was quietly dressed in a good suit of English tailoring with a pale green silk tie. When the two cars had disappeared, he went back into the airport building to make a telephone call and then emerged to hail a taxi for the Hotel Torsa.

When he arrived he took his time to pay the taxi driver. There was no sign of the Mercedes but he had spotted a man watching the hotel on the opposite side of the street and guessed there would be another further along on the hotel side. Eddie Tyler had become hot property. He checked in, a reservation had already been made for him in a room three doors from Eddie's.

Raya studied Nakentov's list of people and addresses. One address was in Switzerland, the others in Germany. Three were men, two were women. All but one had telephone numbers.

As she put the chain of calls into operation, Raya was aware that this was not how Stevinski had intended her to operate. She had been instructed to go in person to each address as she had done with Retzer, and to extend her enquiries as necessary, on the spot. But the incident with

Retzer had unnerved her and she was beginning to dislike the whole affair.

She believed that the names she had would no longer tally with the addresses and in this she was right. Her only hope was to track down the old occupier through the present ones. The results were negative as she had expected them to be.

She went to Zürich the following day, found she was too late for a connection to Moscow, and booked in for one night at the Hotel Bernhof where she had stayed on the way in. It was almost opposite the Torsa Hotel where Eddie was staying. A man standing on the steps of the Waldorf, and who seemed to be waiting for someone, moved aside so that she could enter.

Stevinski hid his frustration. Raya was not a trained operative but she had quite clearly disobeyed his instructions at a time when she appeared to be getting somewhere. He was tempted to call in the full weight of his agents in Germany and Switzerland to end the affair quickly but he could not be sure that some were not already involved. He had even considered using the power of the State Bank to put pressure on the Swiss, but that meant showing his hand. It was best to leave matters as they were in the knowledge that only he, the Secretary General, and Raya to a lesser degree, knew about the bank account. And Raya was expendable.

He offered her tea and then admonished her.

"You were doing well. And then you deserted for no reason."

Raya did not like the word deserted. "I didn't want to face another gun. Retzer was unstable. I was scared."

"Of course you were." Stevinski assumed an air of understanding. "But take it from me, Raya, men who threaten like that never fire. They are like potential suicides who intend to throw themselves from the top of buildings. Unless they jump straight away, they can't face it."

"That's not how it was, Comrade General."

"Does something else upset you? Something you are not telling me?"

Raya shook her head. "No. Perhaps what happened to poor Yasha affected me."

"But you are not sure that it was Yasha." And then, "It was clever of you to notice that there were no rings on the fingers that you could see." Stevinski placed his elbows on the desk. "I want you to go back and carry on from where you left off. A little more effort and you'll be finished with it."

"Are you ordering me to go?"

This was a resistance in her that Stevinski had not previously noticed. He answered carefully. "I thought you were doing this as a personal favour to me. And to the memory of Pavl Nakentov and of Yasha. Of course I will not order you."

"Then I'd rather not go."

"That is your prerogative, my dear. I'm

231

naturally disappointed after you have shown so much promise. Go home and think about it. Unfortunately, you cannot discuss it with your mother, you understand? Call me tomorrow and if you still say no, then I'll respect your wishes."

It was so reasonable an attitude that Raya could not argue. She already knew what her answer would be.

Stevinski said, "Wait in the anteroom and someone will tell you when a car is available to take you back."

"It's all right. I'll use the bus."

"Raya, I wouldn't dream of letting you. I'll order the car." Stevinski took her to the door, smiling and benign. When she had gone he picked up a telephone and barked into it, "Pick up Larissa Dubrova at once, and do it openly." He flipped a pad and gave the address. "Hold her on a treason charge but give her no further information."

By the time Raya reached home, Larissa had gone but it was not until late evening that she began to wonder where her mother might be.

By eight o'clock Raya was fretting. At nine o'clock she started to make enquiries around the neighbours. Larissa had been seen in the early afternoon being escorted down the stairs by two men. KGB; everyone knew. No attempt had been made at discretion or secrecy. Practically everyone in the building had seen her being taken away and bundled into a car.

Distraught, Raya tried to contact Stevinski. She was advised that he had left his office and that she should make enquiries through the Militia. But she knew that could take days, or even weeks, as they themselves had to refer to State Security.

Raya was alone in the apartment surrounded by her mother's possessions as a constant reminder of her absence. She could not sleep. At three in the morning she realised that she had not eaten and rose to make herself a sandwich. Larissa would be terrified. Why had they taken her? What possible harm could she do to anyone? There was the rest of the night to think about it.

She rang Stevinski as soon as she thought he might be there, and, surprisingly, he was readily available to speak to her. She poured out what had happened.

"Raya, Raya, calm down. *Who* has taken your mother away?"

She was about to say, your men, but more carefully she replied, "The neighbours seem to think it was the KGB."

Stevinski laughed. "The KGB? There must be a lot going on here that I don't know about. Where are you calling from?"

Raya gave the number of the kiosk phone, the promised telephone at the apartment was yet to be connected.

"Stay there. I'll see what I can find out, but I may be a little time."

Raya had to wait outside the kiosk for over an hour in the biting wind waiting for his return call. Finally the telephone rang.

Stevinski sounded official: "Raya, your mother has been picked up on a charge of treason. I don't yet know the details and it sounds very odd to me but you must understand I'm reluctant to cut across the duties of my own men. I'm sure there is some mistake but I must not appear to show favours to friends. You understand?"

"Yes. Treason is ridiculous."

"I'm sure it is. It's difficult to imagine Larissa as an enemy of the State, you must leave it with me and be patient. But it might take a few days to unravel. Don't worry too much."

Raya was calmer now. At last the ploy was all too clear. She had worried about the absence of her mother when she should have considered the reason for it instead. Listlessly she said, "If it's likely to take some time before she's released, I may as well go back to Switzerland and Germany."

"I'd almost forgotten. With your mother on your mind I did not expect so early a response."

Hypocrite. Bastard. Raya felt the tears prick her eyes.

"Please see what you can do for mother."

"Of course. I must warn you that, if she's guilty, there is nothing I can do. Not even for you, Raya."

"I understand." Raya hung up. The final threat

had been delivered and she wondered how she could have been so blind. Only then did it occur to her that Stevinski might have had something to do with Nakentov's death.

The office was luxurious, the ornate desk at one end almost lost in the spacious room. At the other end was a semi-circular bar made of old mahogany, and an array of bottles, decanters and cut crystal drinking glasses. The chairs were mainly gilded Louis XIV but there were some modern reproductions of superb quality. The curtains at the tall windows were of burgundy velvet and hung perfectly. The pale rose pile of the carpet stretched like a desert at sunset from wall to wall.

Eddie was rarely impressed but old furniture and objets d'art were among his undeclared interests. He knew a good deal about them but could never afford them. So this was how bank presidents faced up to the hardships of their day. Poor sods.

Eric Baumann came from behind the desk with hand outstretched. "Do sit down, Mr. Tyler." He spoke in English.

Eddie sat carefully.

"I'm so sorry the president is not here in person," Baumann said. "Unfortunately he is in Japan. I'm the vice-president, my name is Eric Baumann." Baumann studied the letters of intro-duction on his desk. One was signed by the

Governor of the Bank of England; the second by the Swiss Finance Minister, Heinz Altorff. Perhaps Meisser was right. The matter was getting out of hand.

When Baumann looked up from the letters he said, "You come highly recommended. As I'm asked to help you in any way possible, what can I do for you, Mr. Tyler?" Baumann was thinking that this was a different Tyler from the one he had observed through the intercommunicating door when he had called before. The Tyler sitting in front of him now still had a beard but it was better trimmed, and he wore a passable suit and tie. He appeared respectable and the open face was honest, if touched by a twist of scepticism.

"I came before," stated Eddie, afraid to put his full weight on the chair. "I saw your manager who protected your interests very well, but did nothing for me. It comes down to this; I have every reason to believe that an aunt of mine started an account here, probably in the late twenties, and she is now dead. I'm one of the beneficiaries to her estate. Possibly the only one.'

"What was her name?"

"Jane Barnard," replied Eddie wearily. "I told your manager."

"Ah, but he didn't tell me. There was probably no reason why he should. Do you know anything about this account? It's number, for instance?'

Eddie pulled out a small notepad. "The number was 72–598–8764 and was followed by

236

Dranrab 627. I've had time to work out the Dranrab is Barnard spelled backwards."

"Indeed." Baumann was making notes. When he had finished, he glanced at the opened letters again and remarked, "You realise that these are merely requests." He picked up the one from the Swiss Finance Minister. "This is not a court order, Mr. Tyler. I think it best to point that out."

"What has to be done to make you move, Mr. Baumann? These two letters are my credentials, do I have to prove my identity?"

"No. For the moment that can be taken as given."

"What then?"

"I did not say I would not help. I merely pointed out that we are under no legal obligation to do so. Swiss banks are not as obstructive as is believed, but our main obligation is to protect our clients."

"I'm your client."

"That would have to be proved." Baumann held up a restraining hand as Eddie was about to comment. "Let me think a moment."

"I shall be back if you don't produce the answer."

"You can return as often as you like, Mr. Tyler. It won't solve anything."

Eddie held out his hand. "May I have my letters back? I'll let these gentlemen know that you don't rate them very highly."

"That is far from true. Indeed, I'm very impressed." Baumann handed the letters over. Cunningly he added, "I'm left with the feeling that you don't know either of them personally."

"That's a fact. But someone I know does, wouldn't you say? And he wields a lot of muscle. Well, will you help, or won't you?"

Baumann pressed a button on the intercom. "Let's see what we can do." He leaned towards the microphone, "Heinz, can you come in?"

Baumann rose as Meisser entered. "Heinz, I believe you've already met Mr. Tyler. Tell him what you know of Dranrab 627."

Meisser gave Eddie the facts of Dranrab as he knew them, as far as the change of code. When he had finished, he said, "There is absolutely no evidence of the lady's identity. The account was opened in complete anonymity, hence the code, and our written and witnessed introductions were that control was to be exercised through the code in lieu of signature; whoever produced the code and account number was presumed to be the client."

"That was risky, wasn't it?"

"I'm sure this was pointed out. All sorts of steps were taken to protect anonymous accounts. But really the only risk was of the client being careless. There was no more risk than, say someone leaving their signature and a cheque book around. We found that, where identity was

238

safeguarded, such clients protected their interest most rigidly."

"Except in this case."

"I don't follow."

"You say Aunt Jane opened the account and a man gave instructions a few years later."

"We cannot acknowledge that it was your aunt, Mr. Tyler. The gentleman produced the code, records show that he did no more than give witnessed instructions for us to invest the money. He made no withdrawals."

Meisser turned questioningly to Baumann. "I've really gone much further than I should. I'm not happy about it." He turned back to Eddie. "How did you come by the code?"

"Aunt Jane had made a note of her account together with the amount. Twenty-one thousand; in which currency wasn't clear."

Baumann and Meisser eyed each other. "You're still a very long way from real evidence," Baumann pointed out. "On what you've given us no court of law would agree to a positive ownership of the account."

"Who changed the code? And who operates it now?"

Meisser smiled. "I know you don't expect us to answer that. We've been very good about this."

"You've told me damn all." Suddenly Eddie looked up, eyeing one then the other. "I know Ulla Krantz is involved and I know that you told her I had called in. As to identifying my aunt as your client, it is easy. I can produce specimens of her handwriting, even early writing, and you can produce the document she signed as Dranrab. Not much, but a handwriting expert can sort the rest out."

"Mr. Tyler," Baumann answered heavily, "you really are missing the basic point. Even if it was your aunt, her instructions regarding proprietorship were quite specific. The code was the key. You have the old code which is no longer relevant. Without the new code, your claim is void."

"So all I have to do is to find the new code and you will then be obligated to honour it."

"No," said Baumann coldly. "Signatories have since been established. Now, if you don't mind, Mr. Tyler . . ."

When Eddie had been shown out, Baumann remarked, "That man means trouble."

Meisser was pleased that the vice-president was at last agreeing with him. "He's not on his own. There's too much we don't know."

Baumann did not answer. He stared despondently out of the window.

Thirty yards up the narrow street Ulla Krantz watched Eddie leave the bank, saw him look for a taxi, then told her driver to follow. She decided to deal with Meisser later.

12

EDDIE went back to the Hotel Torsa. He
was at last beginning to believe that
George Seymour was right; Dranrab had
belonged to Aunt Jane. He had enjoyed his
morning; penetrating the starchiness of Baumann
and Meisser gave him a sense of satisfaction which
temporarily erased his personal fears. In spite of
himself, he was becoming deeply interested. The
Swiss bankers were worried and there must be a
good reason. What was really hooking him to the
project was the gnawing sense of deep injustice
and that was something he had never been able
to tolerate. He was filled with the increasing
certainty that Aunt Jane had been swindled.

He paid off the taxi, still riding on a minor
wave of euphoria. He was not sure why he felt so
pleased, but he was more sure of himself and of
what he was doing. He had achieved enough to
make him want to see it through, to see justice
done to a frail old lady he had liked and respected.

The hotel was much better than the pension
had been and as he trod its carpeted corridors his
sense of well-being continued; the refined quiet-
ness was agreeable. He fumbled with the room
key as the hotel name plaque got in the way.

Afterwards his recollection was of a faint

suggestion of expensive perfume, and soft footsteps behind him before he opened the door. Suddenly a gun pressed hard into his back and Ulla's coaxing voice said, in German, "This time you don't get away."

When Eddie recovered from the first shock, he fumbled the key out of the lock and said in a dry voice, "After you, madam."

Ulla jammed the gun hard against his spine. "You're so full of ideas. In you go and don't try to slam the door in my face. The gun has a silencer."

Eddie had not seen the gun but was satisfied there was one. He went in and stopped in the small lobby.

"Good boy. Don't move except to hold up the key in your left hand."

Eddie held up the key. Ulla took it and he heard her locking the door behind her. Fear suddenly seized him and he remembered that the stakes were high.

"Right inside," said Ulla. "*Sei vorsichtig.*"

Ulla pushed him forward. "That's better. Stay this side of the bed. Good. Hands on your head."

"Oh, come on, Ulla. I'm not armed."

"*Hands on your head.*"

Her tone forbade further banter. The way she spoke chilled him.

"Turn to face me."

He turned. She stood opposite him, unfeeling

eyes watching him steadily. His arms had already begun to ache.

"I think you should know that, if you do try to run out, you'll take several bullets with you. Even if you evade me you cannot win. The hotel is being watched back and front. Now tell me why you've been enquiring at the bank?"

"What difference does it make? I got nowhere."

"I want to know what started you asking questions."

"It would help if I knew how much *you* know."

"I know enough to spot a lie so don't try one. Why have you been making enquiries?"

"It all started with Aunt Jane . . ." His hands jerked as someone knocked on the door. It was a natural reaction but for a terrible moment he thought Ulla was going to fire. She raised the gun and he saw her finger tighten inside the trigger guard; then she whispered an inaudible instruction and his gaze lifted fearfully to hers.

Ulla's eyes were stone hard. Her lips formed the message: "Don't answer." She stepped nearer and the gun was barely three feet away.

There was a knock again and a man's voice called in English, "Anyone in?"

Eddie was transfixed. He had no doubt that Ulla would fire if he shouted for help, so he kept his lips tight.

Another knock. Ulla indicated that he should sit on the bed, and be careful not to make a

243

sound. With dread, Eddie realised why. If she shot him as he stood he would make a noise falling. Slowly he lowered himself on to the bed, praying that it would not creak.

The man outside tried the door handle. Ulla stepped back slowly to the door and with her free hand inserted the key in the lock. Eddie reluctantly admired her nerve. The key did not even scratch the lock as it went in; Ulla then half turned it and held it there. If the man tried to insert another key he could not, and, if he tried to turn the inside key with tweezers, he would be unable to do so.

Ulla put her head close to the door. There was no more knocking and she gave a sign that the man had moved away but she remained where she was for some time. When her breath escaped very slowly, Eddie realised that she was as tense as he was.

Very slowly, Ulla edged back into the room. "Who was that?"

"How would I know?"

"He knows you are English."

"He *spoke* in English. I haven't the slightest idea who he is. I know nobody here."

The obvious truth made Ulla relax a little. She smiled at Eddie. "Tell me why you went to see Meisser."

So he told her about Aunt Jane. But he did not mention Nurse Hayes, the Russian connection or Special Branch's involvement. When he had finished he said, "Now tell me why you wanted to know."

"So that I know what to do with you."

"Shooting me will only complicate things." His throat was dry.

"Why?"

"Whoever knocked on the door must know you are here."

"Why?"

Eddie was sweating. "All right, but what *good* will it do?"

"It will stop you poking your nose into other people's affairs."

Ulla backed away from him. Without turning she fumbled at the lock until the tumblers turned. She faced him squarely and raised the gun two-handed.

Eddie was frozen; he could see her cool eyes quite clearly along the line of the barrel and could not tear his gaze away. Fear had locked his muscles but suddenly the will to survive galvanised him into action. He dived to the floor with the bed between himself and Ulla. As he moved he heard the plop of the gun, a bullet's impact and a splintering of brick and plaster. He lay crouched, for there was nothing he could do. He pulled himself to the end of the bed and cautiously peered round. Ulla had gone.

Eddie rose slowly. He turned the key in the door, made sure it was locked, then leaned against the wall in relief. Where his head had been against the headboard was a suspicion of a hole. When he pulled the bed out, padding spilled from the back of the quilted board. Where the bullet had embedded itself into the wall the plaster had splintered in a series of fine cracks spreading out from the central crater. Brick dust lay at the foot of the wall. He poked the stuffing back into the headboard then pushed the bed back to hide the damage. He prodded at the entrance hole with a nail-file, moving the threads until it was almost invisible.

Eddie sat in the only chair, shaken and worried. He decided that she had merely fired in warning, or she would have stayed to finish the job. But the accuracy of the shot, and the timing of it as he had moved, was frightening enough.

A knock at the door made him stiffen. He had no intention of answering. Another knock, quiet and speculative. And then a voice, close to the woodwork. "Mr. Tyler? Are you all right?"

It was the man who had knocked earlier: Eddie bawled, "Go away or I'll call the police."

"I'm a friend of Bill Savage. I'm supposed to keep an eye on you."

Eddie was in no mood to believe anyone but he doubted that Ulla would know of Bill Savage. He went to the door.

"Stand the other side of the corridor." Eddie opened the door a fraction and peeped through the crack. The man was standing as instructed and held his hands up to show that they were empty. English-cut suit, quiet, pale green tie, open face.

Eddie pulled the door back. The man stepped forward as Eddie said, "Not in the room. In the bar."

"Of course. You don't want to feel trapped. My name's Ray Barrow."

They went down the stairs together. Barrow observed, "You look a little worse for wear. What happened?"

"I was shot at."

"Ah! Difficult."

"Can you prove you're an associate of Bill Savage?"

"I could show you a passport but it wouldn't prove my identity. But if I tell you where you are staying in London, give you a description of Bill, and the name of the Detective Agency who had someone on the lookout for you at London Airport. That should do it, shouldn't it?"

"For starters."

"I came to Zürich with you the first time, too." They entered the bar. "Let's find a quiet corner."

They found a corner table and Eddie noticed Barrow's gaze scanning the room.

"You expecting Ulla back?" asked Eddie. Barrow was making him nervous.

"That should be my question. The place is being watched back and front. Perhaps inside, too, but that's more difficult to determine."

"Ulla said it was."

"Tell me what happened."

Eddie told him.

"So she told you the place is being watched?"

"Yes."

"Had she believed your story, she'd have killed you. She must suspect you're holding back or not acting alone."

"If she didn't before, she does now with you here."

"You're on a leash, Eddie. She wants to find out where you are going to lead her."

Barrow raised a finger and a waiter came over. "Your call," said Barrow to Eddie.

Eddie ordered two large Scotches. "I know I'm in a trap. I'm worried sick."

"Did you get anywhere with the bank?"

"Dranrab has changed its format. And its owners, I would guess."

"Call on Ulla at the Baur au Lac if she's still there."

"Why, for God's sake?"

"Tell her some story. Anything. Stir it up."

"Are you kidding? I don't want to stir a plate of custard. It's too damned dangerous."

"Has it occurred to you that she's more worried than you are?"

"No. She's got the gun."

"I can arrange for you to have one."

Eddie lowered his drink. Barrow had not changed his tone and his eyes were still roaming, but Eddie realised that he was quite serious.

"Jesus," he exclaimed, "you're mad. I wouldn't know what to do with one."

Barrow seemed unaffected. "You just point the bloody thing and fire. I'm beginning to think you need one."

The impression of a garotte round her neck with the loose end stretching back to Moscow, was so strong that Raya fingered her throat as she sat back in the plane. It was easy for her now to see that the trap had been gradually sprung on her. And poor Larissa. Raya did not know which prison her mother was in; her request to see her before leaving Moscow had been refused. The one good thing that Stevinski had done was to bring mother and daughter closer by the way that he had used them. But now that just made matters worse, for they would constantly be worrying about each other.

Raya was having difficulty in coming to terms with the crumbling of a lifetime of belief. It was not easy. Emotion was supposed to play no part, but it did.

Raya arrived at Zürich Airport for the third time in as many weeks. Stevinski had arranged for her to draw a credit on the Zeitlinger Bank. Stevinski obviously wanted her to remain involved with the bank though Raya couldn't see how that would help.

She checked in at the Hotel Bernhof and was given the same room as before. After dinner she walked down to the Neumuhle Quay on the River Limmat. She could see the lights lining the park across the river and the dark spires of the museum which subdued the sounds of the Bahnhof behind it. It was so peaceful, so beautiful and free that she had the urge to stay. But that was impossible. She continued walking until she was tired.

The next morning she left early for Berne. By lunch time, she had discovered that the address was a dead end. No one knew of Hans Kruger, the name on Nakentov's list. But she persevered, calling at many houses in the street, feeling foolish and realising that she was drawing attention to herself, but knowing that Stevinski would settle for nothing less.

She went to the Post Office, checked through the telephone directory, rang all the H. Krugers she could find and came to another dead end. She caught a late train back to Zürich, missed her dinner, and went straight to her room. She sat before her dressing-room mirror combing her short cropped hair and planning her trip to Germany the next day.

Her arms were raised, the comb halfway through her hair when she had an idea. Referring to her notes, she found the telephone number of Kurt Retzer in Lindau and put through a call. There was no reply. It appeared that Retzer really had left his villa. On impulse she telephoned the hotel she had stayed at in Bregenz. A message had been left for her. It was merely a name and address with no explanation; Margo Holtmier, Pension Zimmer, at Weggis, on Lake Lucerne.

As she put down the telephone, Raya had a strange sensation of impending disaster. The name meant nothing to her. The woman could be married or single, young or old. There was nothing to indicate who had left the message but it could only have been Retzer or Frau Linten. If Margo Holtmier was one of Retzer's old associates, why had she not been shot with the others?

The Swiss address did not surprise Raya. The higher echelons of Nazis who had escaped from Germany had largely gone to South America; they had had the resources. The lower ranks suspected of war crimes had either been caught and imprisoned or, if fortunate enough to escape, had gone wherever their money would take them in Europe. Most European countries unwittingly harboured war criminals. This part of Switzerland offered a similar language—and it presented a tempting, nearby refuge.

Raya lay awake in bed for a long time before sleeping. She decided it would be better to go to the bank first to draw some money before catching the train to Lucerne.

Raya felt strange going through the huge glass doors of the Zeitlinger Bank the next morning. Stevinski must have known that there was a possibility of her being recognised. She went to the nearest bay and produced her letter of credit and passport as identification. The teller disappeared to make his check behind the scenes.

Raya waited anxiously at the empty bay. The procedure was quite normal, but she felt exposed, few clients were in so early. Out of the corner of her eye she saw Meisser's office door open beyond the end of the long counter. She did not see anyone appear but instinctively turned away.

The teller returned and asked how much she wanted to draw. As Raya replied she was certain that Meisser's office door was still open and that someone was staring at her. Stevinski must be mad, she thought. And yet, why shouldn't she be here? What wrong had she done? This subdued her a little but she wanted to get out as fast as she could. As soon as she had the money, she strode across the hall with the notes still clenched in her hand. Her back was burning. Once outside she dived into the nearest big doorway.

Raya's sensation of being watched was well founded. Meisser had been about to step from his office to consult a senior clerk in the administration area when he caught sight of Raya. It was not Raya herself who caught his eye but her coat. The light grey skin and fur trimming was familiar, though it would not have registered but for an association of ideas. Dranrab had been preying on his mind.

He noticed Raya turn away so that he could not see her face, and watched her take the money and walk quickly away before putting it in her purse.

Meisser hesitated, undecided on whether to consult the teller or to follow her. He decided to stick with the girl and strode across the hall. On the outside steps he looked up and down the street. There was no sign of Raya.

Meisser felt a fool standing there; he had never done such a thing in his life. He stepped into the street to get a better view and walked a little way in each direction. The girl had disappeared remarkably quickly. He waited a moment longer hoping she would reappear but the cold morning air and a freshening wind persuaded him to return inside.

He went to the teller's bay. "What was the name of the girl you just served?" He noticed the clerk's odd look of enquiry.

"Miss Raya Dubrova."

"Show me."

The clerk passed the slip across. Raya Dubrova. That was not the name. "A Rumanian passport?" queried Meisser.

"No sir. Russian. A Soviet citizen."

"*Russian?*" Why was he so shocked? Russian? But this time the question remained in his head. "Have you an address?"

"No, sir. She has a letter of credit."

"Let me have the details as soon as you can."

Meisser went back to his office and raised Baumann on the intercom.

Raya stayed in the doorway and watched the bank's entrance through reflection in a shop window opposite. She had to reposition to get the right angle but she saw Meisser come out and look up and down the street. When he walked up the street she was positive he was looking for her. She opened the doors behind her and stepped into a lobby. There were inner doors, and through their glass insets she could see an enquiry desk and an elevator. She stayed where she was.

When she considered it safe enough to step out, she hung back and peered round the corner of the building before leaving. She hurried off and did not call a taxi until she was some distance from the bank. She told the driver to take her to the Bahnhof.

She caught the ferry to Weggis, and was surprised how easily she was finding her way round Switzerland. Standing in the stern of the ferry, Mount Pilatus rose to her right as they left Lucerne and cut across the mouth of the U-shaped inlet leading to Kussnacht. The cloud had broken and the water reflected the patchy blueness of the sky.

The half-hour journey was tranquil and she was glad to be away from Zürich for a while. As the ferry approached Weggis on the north side of the lake the magnificent point of the Rigi Kulm came into view, overshadowing the lake. Raya observed a cable car swaying up to Kaltbad, below the peak. Out here on the water, surrounded by mountains, it all seemed idyllic but suddenly she found herself thinking of her mother and immediately her peace was destroyed.

She disembarked at Weggis and signalled a taxi. The journey took her through the tunnel under part of the small, attractive lakeside town, to the higher road. Below her, the lower road curved with the shoreline, and was then hidden by trees beyond which the lake stretched placidly across to Burgenstock, with the snow-capped Pilatus to the south.

The Pension Zimmer was some distance from the lake but had a good view of it. Part of its gardens extended across the road and tumbled down the slope in a well-planned show of cypresses and firs and shrubs. The taxi pulled into the parking space in front of the pension entrance.

Raya climbed the curved stone steps in trepidation. There were few people about, the season over, and there were already signs of decorating for the following year. It was clean and neat inside and a young fair-haired girl smiled at her from behind a short reception counter.

"I'm looking for Margo Holtmier."

"May I have your name?"

Raya did not want to give her name so she said,

"Can you tell her Herr Retzer sent me." It was a gamble.

The receptionist rang through and passed the message while she eyed Raya curiously. When she put down the telephone, she said, "Take the elevator at the end of the hall or walk up one flight. You will see a door marked 'Private'."

Raya took the stairs. She found the room at the end of the first-floor landing and knocked on the door.

"*Herein*." A commanding, elderly voice.

Raya opened the door and stepped into a large room that was part office, part sitting room with bright, chintz-covered furniture. At the end of the room, her back to the large windows, sat a big woman behind a small desk.

Raya was at once aware of the intensity of the scrutiny from Margo Holtmier. She was probably aged somewhere between sixty and seventy, the face was fat, the eyes deep set and suspicious. The carefully coiffured grey hair was tinted and swept low to soften the cheek lines.

"What is it you want?"

There was no friendliness in the enquiry and the antagonism was heightened by the way she kept her hands out of sight behind the desk. It may have been a nervous reaction but nothing would have convinced Raya then that Frau Holtmier was not holding a gun. Guns had become a prerequisite of all enquiries regarding Stalin's son. Raya's instinct was to leave but

Margo Holtmier said, "Close the door behind you."

Raya shut the door and remarked, "I'm enquiring about Yasha Djugashvili. If you knew him it might have been as Jacob Stalin. Herr Retzer told me you might know what happened to him."

Margo Holtmier rose behind the desk. "You're a liar, fräulein, Herr Retzer is dead."

Raya saw that she was right about the gun. She was sickened by the sight of it. The woman facing her was not emotionally disturbed as Retzer had been, she was ice cold and in command of herself.

"Step to the centre of the room."

Raya obeyed.

The woman came from behind the desk, gave Raya a wide berth, and went to the door. Raya, still with her back to the door, heard the key turn.

Margo Holtmier moved past Raya, backing to the desk to keep her in sight. She sat down again behind the desk, placed the gun down in front of her. "Now tell me who you are?"

"Raya Dubrova. I'm a distant relative of Joseph Stalin's son Jacob."

"You're Russian?"

All Soviets were Russian to foreigners. "Yes."

Raya had been left standing in the centre of the room. There was no cover she could reach before the frau could raise the gun. She was more

257

afraid than she had been with Retzer because this woman appeared to be so clinically calculating.

"Now tell me the truth. Lies I've dealt with all my life."

Raya moistened her lips. She had already realised that she should not have mentioned Retzer's name; she may have placed him in danger. Yet nothing but the truth would satisfy this woman with the bleak eyes and the once pretty face. Raya related the story she had told Retzer and she reluctantly mentioned his role in it. It was no use leaving parts out; the eyes opposite her were almost willing her to attempt a lie. But she gave an entirely false location to her meeting with Retzer, hoping it would be misleading enough.

When Raya had finished, Margo Holtmier gazed at her in a way that made her shiver. This woman was an iceblock, unruffled by what she had heard, and now working on the various courses she could take.

"And your interest is solely in what happened to Jacob?"

"And his effects."

"And if you find out, what happens next?"

"I go back to Moscow."

"With Retzer's name and mine?"

"Only as reference."

"It's a reference I don't want." Margo Holtmier coldly considered the position. " believed Retzer was dead. So must others. I'

258

not so important as he is but neither of us will want to raise old issues or draw a focus upon us. The past is as dead as Stalin. You're working alone?"

"Yes."

"That in itself is suspicious. That you are here at all. A Russian. From my point of view it would be better to kill you."

Raya's legs were weak and she was having difficulty in standing. She tried to speak but her mouth was dry and then she managed to blurt out, "If you kill me Moscow will know there is something to hide; they will send others, professionals. If I return with the answers, you become no more than a name on a closed file."

"You're a clever girl. And you could be right. I don't care for it either way." Holtmier's hand went out to the gun and she placed it on her lap before leaning back in the chair, her head angled as she stared quizzically at Raya. "I'll tell you one thing, Jacob Stalin was a lousy lover."

Raya stared. *Margo Holtmier had been one of the Nazi whores at Sachsenhausen.* She was one of those who had serviced Yasha.

"You are shocked?" The smile on the plump face was bitter. "It was a service to the country not to the man. You are too young to have met him."

"Yes. My grandfather was his uncle, the brother of Joseph Stalin's first wife. May I please sit down?"

The request was a mistake. Margo Holtmier's face hardened again. "You stay exactly where you are. Retzer told you Jacob is dead; he is right."

"The photograph I was shown was so indistinct."

"Forget the photograph. He *intended* to commit suicide."

"How do you know?"

"Don't question me, girl. I'm too old to worry about assassins and, anyway, I'm not important enough."

"Why would anyone want to assassinate you just for knowing Yasha?"

Margo Holtmier said nothing for some time. Her posture and her gaze still frightened Raya.

"You are either naive or stupid like the rest of your countrymen. I don't think you're stupid but I do wonder who sent someone so inexperienced."

"No one sent me. My mother has good connections and is still in Moscow."

"I see. Well, young Raya, I have to decide, so I'll feel my way round the problem. Jacob was a strange man, never happy, but he was strong and not bad looking and was grateful for what we could give him; unlike that nasty piece of work who was Molotov's son."

"Nephew. Wasili Kokorin was Molotov's nephew."

"The two Russians were always spouting propaganda and how they would murder us and

260

the British too when their time came." Pencilled eyebrows rose contemptuously. "The two Russians were given more clean clothes than the others, and Jacob was being wooed by people high up. In the end I think he went mad."

"Did you see him die?"

"Few saw him die. It was night. You think it wasn't him?"

"I don't know."

"Then let me tell you something." A dimpled hand wagged a finger. "Jacob had a special girl, one he much preferred to me. I don't think she satisfied him any more than I did but he grew fond of her. Paula Menke. Jacob only took me when Paula was otherwise engaged and even then he'd be asking about her. He grew jealous." The hand slipped back below the desk top to where the gun was.

"Paula was with him the day he died. She was having a child by him and she told him that day."

Raya asked incredulously, "How could she possibly know that it was *his* child?"

Margo Holtmier was equally surprised. "Paula *wanted* his child. And she must have convinced him that it was his because he gave her his ring as a sort of unofficial wedding ring."

Raya could not speak. She was excited and afraid but her features must have given too much away for Margo said, "Is it the child or the ring that disturbs you?"

"I had no idea about the child. Nobody had."

"Well, it was the straw that broke the camel's back. He committed suicide that night."

"Why? If he was fond enough of Paula to give her the ring?"

"How could I know? Perhaps he saw the complications ahead. He already had a wife in Russia. Perhaps he could see the sort of propaganda that could be made against him." Margo laughed dryly. "A child by a Nazi whore; that would have been great for him. His father would have loved that."

Almost afraid to ask, Raya ventured, "Was the child born?"

"I believe so. But by that time we were split up, moved around to other camps. I lost touch with Paula but years afterwards I heard that she'd had a child but that it later died."

Against all hope, Raya asked, "How can I contact her?"

The plump form stirred, the voice was matter of fact. "By doing what she did; commit suicide."

Raya went limp. After so much, the let down. "How long ago?"

"Oh, ages, years." With sadistic satisfaction, Margo added, "She hanged herself. Only some said she didn't."

Raya was despondent, "You don't think it was suicide?"

"I don't know. But she died about the time Retzer was supposed to die, and the others. A masked assassin, I heard, but God knows why."

"And the child?"

"What about the child?"

"How did it die?"

Margo answered shrewdly, "Over the years it has occurred to me that if I knew why the others were killed, then I too would have been murdered. I don't know about the child and I don't want to. I thought your sole interest was in finding out what happened to Jacob and his effects."

Raya gestured in apology. "It is all so intriguing. The child. Paula. Hanging. It's really dreadful. Thank you for what you've told me. May I ask one more question?"

Margo placed the gun back on the desk. "You may not get an answer."

"Did Paula ever marry?"

"I don't know that either. But women like Paula and I don't marry too often. The first row with a husband and our past would be flung in our faces. I never heard that she got married, but I read about the hanging in the newspapers. It was quite a mystery, for she'd come into a lot of money from somewhere and apparently had no problems of any kind." Seeing the question on Raya's face, Margo went on, "From what I recall the child died long before Paula."

"I am most grateful to you, Frau Holtmier. May I go now?"

"I'm still puzzled about how Kurt Retzer knows I am here and why he did not die with the others." Suddenly Margo shrugged. There was a weariness about her as though recollection had tired her. She gave Raya a steely look before saying, "It is not frau but fräulein. I think I have already explained why. Take that look of pity from your face. If you're to survive as I've survived you must learn to hide your feelings. You're an open book but perhaps you've told enough of the truth." She spread her flabby arms. "I own all this and I run a good house. I am content."

Raya stood quite still, although it was now difficult for her to focus at all.

Margo glared. "Don't bring trouble to me, girl. I know no more than I've told you. Don't come back, and go now, before I decide I've made a mistake."

13

ULLA caught Meisser just before the bank closed. "I won't keep you long and I won't sit down," she said. "I've been talking to Eddie Tyler. Tell me what happened this morning."

Meisser was alarmed that Ulla had seen Tyler, it would all lead to trouble. But he told her what had happened.

When he had finished she said, "It's odd that such a man should carry high credentials from the Governor of the Bank of England and your own Finance Minister. The Eddie Tyler I've just left would get nowhere near such people."

"The letters were genuine, madame."

"I'm sure they were. But who arranged them?"

And that worried Meisser too. "Only the gentlemen concerned could answer that."

"Or Tyler?"

"Perhaps."

"You're not convinced, Herr Meisser. And neither am I. Tyler is being used. That's all I wanted to know. Thank you for your time."

"Just one thing before you go, madame." Meisser was standing near the door his hand on the handle. "I think I saw the Rumanian girl yesterday. Here, in the bank." Meisser tried to

265

pierce the expression behind Ulla's dark glasses, but failed.

"If it's the same girl, she has a letter of credit here. Her name is Raya Dubrova. Russian, not Rumanian." Meisser was startled by Ulla's stunned reaction.

"Are you all right, madame? A glass of water?"

She waved him away. "Where is she staying?"

"I don't know. She has a letter of credit and there are funds available so she will call again."

"Are you sure it's the same girl?"

"Certain enough to follow her out of the bank but she disappeared quickly. The teller examined her passport."

"And you examined the one before."

"One of my clerks did."

"So either one could be false?"

Meisser shrugged. "With funds credited, the Russian one is the more likely to be genuine. But, yes, either could be false. If I see the girl again I'll try to find out where she's staying."

"What made you so sure it was the same girl?"

"At first, her coat. She had worn it before; it was her one decent garment."

"Raya Dubrova?"

Meisser was surprised that Ulla got the name right first time. "She did not call about Dranrab but to make a withdrawal."

"Well, it's interesting. Perhaps someone has found some old papers and is trying to make a quick fortune; what with Tyler *and* the girl."

266

"You are probably right but it's impossible for either of them to do so."

Later when Ulla was seated in a cab she realised that it was time to take some drastic action. She would first put out a trace on the girl.

They met in Ulla's suite again. The two men were increasingly aware that all was not well. Survival instincts were surfacing.

"You should have killed Tyler while you had him," Rolf Hartmann complained. He was pacing the carpet in slow, pent-up strides.

"Tyler is a nobody," Ulla explained. "We need him to find out who's behind him. I'm having him watched very closely."

Hartmann stopped pacing. Almost gently, he said, "It's not like you. If you'd delivered him to me I'd have had the truth out of him by now."

"You'd have killed him before we had it. The problem is not only finding out who is behind him but why. And I doubt that he knows that, not all of it." She turned to Gustav Wegel but he anticipated her.

"We want a quiet villa somewhere out of town where nothing can be heard. I'll see to it. We'll have a place by tomorrow."

"And I want a trace on Raya Dubrova. Use as many agencies as you need. I doubt that she'll be in a four-star hotel. Try three and two star."

"She may not be in a hotel at all."

"Just find her, Gustav. And I think Tyler has someone here to help him. We need him too."

Wegel rubbed his cheek where the nerve ticked. He had received no word from Phil Gates whose London connection had obviously not traced Tyler. Ulla had done better on her own. But it did mean there was a smokescreen in London and that was ominous. They weren't up against individuals but organisations. He believed it and so did Ulla. What Hartmann believed did not matter for he bungled everything he touched.

When the two men had left her suite, Ulla raised her arms to her head and removed the wig she had been wearing. Next she opened a bureau drawer and took out a letter that had been forwarded on to her by her housekeeper in Germany. She knew what was in the letter without opening it. It was from a large and highly reputable firm of lawyers in Munich and she had received such letters twice a year since she was seventeen. They were always brief, and merely asked her to confirm to them that she was in a good state of health and had no financial problems.

The very first letter had been more explicit and had explained that a client, who had her welfare at heart, wanted to be kept in touch and to ensure that no harm befell her. Her mother had taken her to Munich to see the lawyers who explained that it was very much in her own interests to keep in touch, and, in time, would be of considerable financial benefit. From then on, she had always written a brief note back to say that she was in good health.

Her parents, now both dead, had cared for her very well, but had never explained the distant concern that was being shown to her. It was still to this day a strange experience to be watched over, as if someone was permanently looking over her shoulder. And the lawyers had been right about the finance. In 1965, at the age of twenty-two, Ulla inherited Dranrab 627. It came to her completely without explanation. The lawyers would tell her nothing about how she came to inherit a fortune.

She was suddenly rich. What did it matter where it came from? Only when letters continued to arrive regarding her well-being did she believe that she could be in some danger. It was some time later that she discovered that Dranrab had two other owners and the news came as a shock.

The manager of Zeitlinger at the time, aware that three different people were drawing on the account, had been concerned enough to take some action. Within the terms of the account, whoever produced the code had the right to draw, but he had wondered if each knew of the others. He had broached the matter first with the men when the opportunity occurred. It became clear that they knew of each other and apparently of Ulla's claim, although they seemed not to know her name. Later, he discovered that Ulla had no knowledge of the men at all. To avoid a possibly explosive situation, he had delicately engineered a meeting. From that moment there were no problems.

Twice a year, when the letters came, she would reflect on these things. Yet it was still a mystery. Her parents must have known something to accept the outcome so unquestionably. After each had died she had gone through papers, letters, anything that might throw light on a fortune so casually cast her way. But she had found nothing that made sense. It was almost as though her parents had been blackmailing somebody to protect their only child. But that was impossible too. Ulla could not visualise them blackmailing anyone.

One thing she had always accepted was the importance of answering the letters. It was a small enough chore; a line to say she was all right and to advise where she would be. No more.

Ulla tore open the envelope in her hand and read the letter, but she could have quoted the content from memory. The words were always the same; the signature often varied. Today the letter made her particularly wary. She did not know why, but believed that her mysterious inheritance was in danger. Her benefactor might yet prove to be her destroyer.

Sir George Seymour put pressure on the detective agency whose men Ray Barrow had seen watching Eddie at London Airport and they reluctantly revealed what they were supposed not to reveal; the name of a client. It came as no surprise to Seymour: Ulla Krantz.

He was now convinced that the late Pavl Nakentov had been somehow tied up with the late Jane Barnard, and that they had probably set up Dranrab. He could not believe that anyone as astute as Nakentov would have had no knowledge of it and he sensed the importance of the circumstances behind the affair.

George Seymour suspected high scandal. But more than that, he was beginning to believe that Dranrab might reveal information that could be of immense value to him. Dranrab was very well protected by a woman he had never heard of and he began to wonder whether she was acting alone. With the protection the bank had given the account, he was also wondering whether it was much larger than he had first suspected. Seymour was intrigued, and he wondered amongst other things, how the hell the Americans came to be involved. It was vital to find out who controlled the account. And then to discover *what exactly the account controlled*. Eddie had so far failed to prise loose any clues so Seymour felt obliged to take further action. As it was all taking place on foreign soil, he was encouraged to use methods he would frown upon nearer to home.

Seymour summoned Savage to his office. "Do you have any underground connections in

Switzerland?" asked Seymour as he poured two cognacs.

"Yes, but why? Do you intend to use them?"

"Yes," replied Seymour quietly.

Savage lowered his drink and stared at Seymour across the desk. "Do you mean it?"

"I do in a way. We need a bolt hole not too far from Zürich. The only way we'll get real knowledge of Dranrab is to lift Meisser."

"The manager of Zeitlinger?" The suggestion did not disturb Savage too much but the necessity did. "Is it worth the risk?"

"I believe it is."

"OK. But Meisser won't tell us anything. And he's not likely to take the files home. Do you intend to torture it out of him?"

"Yes. But not quite in the way I suspect you are thinking."

"Torture is torture. Isn't it?"

"A man must keep his pride. He must have a loophole."

Savage began to think that Seymour was going senile. Then Seymour said, "Go to Zürich. Contact Barrow but without Tyler knowing. Keep clear of Tyler. See what you can set up for a kidnapping."

"Prolonged?"

"That would be up to you."

Savage did not like it but he did not argue. It was rumoured that Seymour would be retiring

272

shortly; perhaps he wanted to go out in a blaze of glory—leaving others holding the baby.

Raya Dubrova paid a retaining fee for her room and booked a flight to Frankfurt. She had two German names and addresses to follow up. The trip proved abortive; the trail must have been dead for years.

The next day she flew to Bremen and went straight from the airport to the second address she had. When she arrived the cab driver could not find the street number, and it became clear that, where previously there had been houses, there was now a modern glass-fronted office block. She flew back to Zürich.

Raya withdrew more funds from the Zeitlinger, feeling that Meisser was watching her through a crack in his door. The teller had left his bay to check on her credit and she was sure that he had gone to tell the manager.

But, although Meisser was warned that she was in the bank, he made no move. He was convinced that Ulla would track down Raya anyway and he wanted no further part in it. He was already aware that he was inadvertently linked with some enormous conspiracy. He would do his job as manager, nothing more.

In Moscow, General Georgi Stevinski took time to consider how Raya might be progressing. He could expect no word from her until she actually

273

returned. But it did not stop him worrying. Raya seemed to have reached a stalemate and he was tempted to bring in his Swiss network. It would be so easy to set the vast machinery into operation. He fought off such urges with difficulty. There must be no cables, no open line telephone calls monitored by his own people, no traces, no knowledge—not until he was certain that there were no more Nakentovs in his organisation.

Phil Gates received a negative message from London through his resident in Berne. Eddie Tyler had disappeared off the face of the earth. Gates had never met Howard Kolston, but was aware of his reputation. If London was not co-operative then obviously something important was going on. But Gates put the idea out of his mind. Wegel always squirmed on the end of the hook.

Bill Savage flew to Zürich and checked into a modest hotel. When he had settled in, he rang Ray Barrow who came round immediately bringing a bottle of Scotch with him.

"Where's Tyler?" Savage asked.

"Last seen having dinner in the hotel restaurant. Why don't you send him back?"

"Tyler? He's too useful. He's like a magnet to Ulla Krantz. Fill me in."

When Barrow had finished, Savage said, "Just

as I thought. Ulla is worried about him, wondering what it's all about. Is she on her own?"

"I don't know. She has the hotel staked out. Probably using local agencies. Money is obviously no object."

"So she'll know that you know Tyler."

"I had to make contact."

"You should have been more discreet. Seymour wants Meisser, the Zeitlinger manager, lifted and the Dranrab details squeezed from him. That's why I'm here."

"Christ!" Barrow spilled some of his drink and wiped his trousers.

"Exactly. What's the run down on local talent?"

"Not too bad but we'd need time to make contact."

"That's what I expected," Savage thoughtfully sipped his drink. He moved away from the window. "If she knows about you, you'd better not go back to the Torsa. Stay here. I'll get you some clothes and shaving gear. Would they know you came here?"

"Their main concern is Tyler. They'll assume that, where he is, I won't be far away."

"You're not sure, though. We'll check it out. You go down later and I'll tag."

"OK. What about Tyler? He'll be left wide open."

"Blame Seymour. We're doing it on a shoestring. We can't nursemaid Tyler and lift Meisser at the same time. Eddie will have to take his chances."

"I don't like the way you said that about Meisser."

Savage drained his glass. "I should have made it clear. There's not much time. We'll have to lift Meisser ourselves, although I'll get some help from one of our own blokes."

Wegel said, "I've rented a place. You could stand outside and yodel your head off and no one would hear you."

"What about labour?" asked Ulla. "I don't think we should do it ourselves. It might turn out to be useful to be on view here while it's being done."

Wegel looked to Hartmann. "I think Rolf's the man for that; if we need help in a hurry. Obviously we need to raise it outside this peaceful little country."

What was it that Wegel knew about Hartmann? Ulla had not entertained the thought for many years. A great deal had puzzled her then. But as they formed their partnership and everything went so well, the questions that hung over the two men, and even herself, had become less important. Now, having been thrown together for survival, old doubts returned.

Hartmann said, "No problem. Tell me when we need them, how many, and where, and I will arrange it. Experienced men, reliable, and they will know how to keep their mouths shut. Who do we snatch first?"

It was clear to the others that Hartmann was looking forward to it and this worried them. Ulla said, "We'd better go for Tyler and the man who keeps so close an eye on him." Why had she not nominated the Russian girl?

Wegel almost read her mind. "The Russian is the biggest enigma. At least we know that Tyler had an aunt who may have set up the account." It was the first real acknowledgement among them that the account had been pilfered.

Ulla suddenly realised that Wegel was staring at her, waiting for an answer. She said, "The girl will be easier, surely? She can wait. Tyler's shadow must be a professional. He may be armed."

There was a moment's silence, registering that Ulla's view had won.

At last Hartmann said, "If we have the villa, I'll contact Germany now." He left the room, bristling with purpose.

When Hartmann had gone Ulla remarked, "We'll have to watch him. It's information we want, not broken bodies."

"I've always watched him," said Wegel drily. He left without further explanation, leaving Ulla wondering what the Tinsal arrangement would reveal next.

14

"THE British Consul uses it," Savage explained.

"*What?*"

"Uses it, not owns it. According to Seymour he rents it now and again to get away from it all. I understand it's always empty at this time of year."

"You understand? Great. I hope you're bloody right."

"Seymour checked it out with the consul."

"Trust Seymour to cheesepare," replied Barrow in disgust.

The two men walked round the small villa. The windows were boarded to bear out what Savage had said. It was not an illustrious dwelling but it was isolated and boasted a good road below the well made-up driveway. On high ground between Zurich and Winterthur it had little to recommend it from a tourist standpoint. But it was quiet and peaceful.

And cheap, thought Barrow. "Who owns it?"

"A Swiss character who never uses it."

"Let's hope you're right."

Savage tried the door then produced some pick locks. "Out of practice," he commented after the fifth attempt. Eventually the door opened and

278

they went in to the spartan interior. Two small bedrooms, a lounge-diner, one bath, two toilets and a fair-sized kitchen. "Ideal," said Savage. Barrow did not disagree. They went back to the car to fetch the food stocks.

Eddie Tyler missed Barrow who had told him he would be away for a day or two. It had been comforting to know that someone was keeping a friendly eye on him. There could be no safety until Dranrab unravelled, if it ever did. He was caught up in it regardless of Seymour or Savage or Barrow. He didn't think it mattered much what he did, and there was no escape that he could see.

He was accepting more philosophically that his life was in danger. It had been in London and it was here in Zürich. There was little he could do about it. *He* knew that he posed no direct threat to anyone, but nobody would risk believing him. It was all about a lot of money. And some other issue which seemed to obsess Seymour.

He finished his meal quietly and then went up to his room. He no longer felt safe to go out unless Barrow was with him. He lay on the bed and tried to read a book but could not concentrate. He had become a bait; he recognised that too. He simply could not understand why the Russians had tried to kill him. He could only hope that matters would sort themselves out and that somehow, he would survive. But where the hell was Barrow?

Meisser lived in a lakeside villa, surrounded on three sides by flowering shrubs and evergreens, with a large rear garden that tiered down to a jetty where his cabin cruiser was moored. It was an idyllic setting, clearly designed for the well-breeched middle-class of Zürich society.

Meisser was a creature of habit. He rose early, let the dog out, fed the ducks and the birds, did fifteen minutes on his exercise bicycle, then took his wife her morning coffee. The children, two girls and a boy prepared themselves for school. Meisser dropped the children off on the way to the bank, and his wife collected them later in her own car. Meisser did not bring his work home; he would rather work late in his office. But his wife had noticed, of late, that he was often preoccupied. She did not press him; it would have spoiled the sweet harmony of their family life.

A routine so regular can only be broken. And it was broken for Meisser that November morning when he opened the doors of the double garage and went to start up the Mercedes. His routine was to drive the car round the gravelled curve to the front of the villa and to give the horn three quick blasts to bring the children running from the house with their mother to wave them goodbye.

Meisser was no sooner behind the wheel than

a gun was pressing into the back of his neck and his hair was standing on end. A voice in German with a foreign accent said, "Don't move or I'll blow your neck out."

Meisser trembled. He glanced nervously at the central mirror and saw part of a masked face.

"Don't go to the front of the house," said the voice. "Go straight up to the gates, turn right and drive on until I tell you to stop. Understand?"

Meisser nodded nervously. He felt sick with shock. He switched on and moved the car out, not daring to look towards the house as he passed it on his left. He drove up to the gates and turned right keeping his speed steady. The children would think he had gone mad.

"Take the next turning left."

Meisser did so. He was a little steadier now and was wondering how the man had got into the garage; probably through the small rear door that led to the main garden.

"What do you want?" he asked in a cracked voice.

"Just drive on."

The gun was still in his neck but now at the nape of it. He knew the road, it was quiet and used only by the locals.

"Turn left."

The fools, he thought. This was a cul-de-sac with woods at its end. He drove on and pulled up but the voice said, "Drive into the woods, just clear of the houses."

Meisser swallowed and drove on. It was a quiet, residential area, houses and villas well separated and set back. Bracken crunched under the wheels as if his own ribs were being cracked. There was a pain in his chest.

"Stop."

"Close your eyes."

They were going to shoot him. The gun was pressing harder and he tried to plead but his tongue wouldn't move. Oh, my God. His heart thumped as a blindfold was placed over his eyes, but the racing pulse was partially due to relief. They would not trouble to blindfold him if they were going to kill him.

"Out."

Someone was opening the door and helping him out.

"In the back."

He climbed in feeling his way and the fluctuating terror.

"Get right down on the floor. Out of sight."

It was difficult for a big man but he did not argue. He wriggled down, intermittently feeling the gun muzzle against his head or neck or face until he was sure there was a whole battery of weapons pointing at him. The driver's door clicked, someone revved the engine and it was only then that Meisser realised there were two men. The car backed out, turned, and purred off the way it had come. Meisser gagged but nothing came out and he spluttered and coughed.

"Keep your head down," said a different voice. From then on he lay down cramped and uncomfortable. His fear receded as no one spoke to him or held the gun to his head. His mind wandered as the carpet fibres rose with the heat in the car and prickled his throat like pine needles. He could hardly swallow.

It seemed to Meisser that they had driven all morning but it was less than an hour. By the time the car stopped, he was numb. He was helped out but he stumbled and fell and tried to tear the blindfold away, until a chilling voice warned him not to. He was guided up a flight of shallow steps, through a door and then he was seated on a wooden chair; his hands tied behind his back, his legs to the chair. He had no idea how far he had travelled but was vaguely aware that they had climbed. Although both men had briefly instructed him from time to time, he had not heard them converse together.

Footsteps penetrated Meisser's cramped, dark and frightening world and then he was certain that he heard a third voice, speaking too quickly and too softly for Meisser to catch the sense of it. A door closed and there was silence. He had the sensation of being alone, not knowing whether he was being watched or whether there was someone behind him with a gun. Sweat soaked him, his wrists were slippery in their bonds but not enough to release them. And he knew that he dare not try.

"What do you want?" he managed to croak. "Money?"

But there was no answer, not even the scraping of a foot. He *was* alone. He started to pray, quietly, with the sincerity of stark fear his lips moving below the blindfold. He had not been to Mass for months. That would all change now. He had never been threatened in his life. So far as he could recall he had endured his schooldays without a single fight. Violence was for fools and the ignorant yet somehow he did not believe his captors were in either category. In the end it would be about money; it always was. But by Zürich standards he was not wealthy, so why pick on him?

If only he could see. He struggled some more. Now it was the sweat of exertion and not of fear, but it made no difference; legs and wrists remained tied. The blackness behind his eyes was disorientating. He tore at his bonds and the chair moved but the horrible scraping of its legs on the floor was a discordant warning that he was making too much noise.

A door crashed open behind him and a breech on a gun was pulled back. Meisser almost fainted. His heart raced again and the pain was back in his chest. He was too terrified to plead for mercy as he waited for the end. A gun was placed at the back of his head and he sent up a screaming prayer for mercy as he prepared for the bullet that would smash through his brain.

By the time Meisser realised that the gun was no longer there, he was trembling violently. Feeling the indignity of his reaction, he tried to pull himself together, but it was not easy. The protected life he had led from birth had not prepared him for this. Aware that he was quietly crying, he straightened his back, lifted his head. Let them kill him. But quickly.

Someone was fiddling at his ankles and he realised that they were being freed. He was helped to his feet and his legs almost gave way but he struggled to stay upright. His wrists were still tied behind him. There was a man either side of him. They turned him and then told him to walk while they guided him. His toe stubbed and he guessed he was by a wall.

"Spread your legs wide."

Meisser did as he was told.

"More."

Someone tapped his ankles. He was standing in a difficult position now. Suddenly something was thrust over his head and his fears returned as he thought he was going to suffocate.

"Move and you're dead. Keep absolutely still."

Meisser's recaptured pride was crumbling. He could barely breathe. At least the chair had supported him; he swayed and tried to steady himself. He called out but his voice echoed round the plastic bucket, filling his ears with bass reverberations. There was pressure on his ear drums. From somewhere beneath the bucket rim a voice whispered up to him. "For your own sake, keep still. There will be someone behind you all the time. You move, you die. Understand?"

With legs splayed awkwardly, hands tied behind his back, blindfolded and with a bucket over his head, the strain of keeping still was enormous. A minute was a lifetime, constant darkness, eternal terror. But, insidiously, as time passed, it was the loss of touch with reality that began to destroy him. He could feel himself swaying.

Someone behind him whistled on occasion to let him know that he was there. For how long could he remain upright? His legs were weakening and he had long lost all sense of balance. He became unaware of standing up and could swear that he was actually on his head.

Meisser could no longer think clearly or, at times, think at all. He had no idea where he was or why or what was happening; he had entered a totally inexplicable frightening world.

He had not dreamed that anything like this could happen to him; he was too ordinary. It was not his fault, therefore, that his resistance was low. He had no cause to fight for, nothing to sustain him to resist the inevitable. After three hours, he was malleable.

His mind was so empty that he was only partially aware of the bucket being removed, and of being helped to a chair. His wrists were untied, and his jacket and shirt were taken off. He believed he struggled but in fact his arms were moved for him and he offered no resistance. Helped to his feet again, he was laid out prone on some sort of table. And then his wrists were bound again, separately, his arms away from his body. His ankles were tied together.

All this was a vague sensation to him. With the bucket gone, he could breathe more easily but he was still blindfolded. He became aware of being naked to the waist and he thought he shivered. Something cold was placed on his bare stomach and he arched with shock.

Silence again. Whatever it was they had placed on him was still there but realisation was vague and intermittent.

"Tell us about Dranrab 627."

The voice seemed to come from all directions. He could still hear it, filling space and hurting his ears. Dranrab. Oh yes. The curse. Just one more enquiry. Soon it would be open knowledge. He talked about Dranrab, not sure how it came out or whether it was in the right order. What did it matter? He must have finished for there was silence again.

"Now tell us the new code and the signatories."

Meisser struggled. It was not conscious appreciation but subconscious conditioning that made him baulk at the new question. Dranrab didn't matter any more—but Tinsal did. He could not answer.

A gun pressed against his temple and he felt a

ripple of fear. Someone said, "It's not going to work." It was the first remark not addressed directly to him and part of the sense of it reached him.

There was another reason why he was resisting. Professionally, Meisser could keep a secret. He dared not reveal the existence of Tinsal, for his job and his credibility as a banker depended upon his discretion.

Nothing happened: There were no more questions and his mind drifted again, pleasantly, then at times painfully, but unimpeded. Very slowly he returned to semi-conscious thought. But the escape from mental oblivion brought back physical fear. Still nothing. He was beginning to think again; slowly, but ever more clearly.

"Tell us about the new owners of Dranrab."

God, they were back. Perhaps they had never left; the gun was at his head to remind him.

"If I tell you that I am finished." His voice shook. The continuing darkness was crucifying.

"You won't be finished. We've sent out a ransom demand for a quarter of a million dollars, and a demand for the release of two suspected terrorists being held in jail in Berne. You're covered, Meisser. You go back clean."

"I cannot tell you." His head was bursting.

"If you don't, we'll kill you."

"Killing me won't get the answers."

"We'll kill you when we're convinced that you

won't tell us. But we've one or two persuaders first."

Meisser felt pressure on his stomach. The object on his abdomen felt like a cold circle.

"You felt that?"

"Yes."

"Do you know what it is?"

"No." He did not want to know.

"It's a copper pan."

Meisser did not answer. He felt the pressure again; nothing to pain him—just a reminder.

"We put a rat under the pan," continued the voice. "Then we heat the pan from above until the pan is hot and the heat builds up inside."

Meisser wished he still had the bucket over his head; it might soften his mind but it relieved his fears. What he now felt was not fear but stark terror.

"Don't you want to know the rest?"

Meisser could not answer.

"As the heat builds up the rat gets demented. He can't get through the copper so there's only one way he can go. When he can take no more, he'll start to eat his way through your stomach, Meisser. And he'll go every bit of the way. When he reaches the table he'll meet another obstacle and then he'll tear his way out sideways. He'll rip your guts to ribbons, and he'll leave a big hole in your side taking half your entrails with him. Think about it. And what you'll be doing while he's tearing you apart."

Meisser thought about it. Blindness activated a mental image so horrific that he knew that he could not face it. He would become a screaming lunatic. They were trying to make him one now. He lay back gasping, turning his head from side to side. He made a last bid. "What sort of people are you? You must be monsters. Inhuman."

The pan was lifted and then rammed down again and he screamed as something scurried over his belly turning repeatedly within the tight confines of the copper prison. Oh, Christ, no. "No. No. Please. Please, I beg you. No . . . o." The last scream was frantic. Meisser struggled madly and the more he did the more frenetic became the scurrying. And then two pairs of hands were holding him, keeping his head and feet still, and someone was keeping the pan in place. Meisser screamed again, no pleading, no words, just a continuous scream that would eventually rupture his throat.

One of them bawled out, "We haven't started to heat it yet. Tell us and we'll take it away."

The gist penetrated Meisser. He was almost out of his mind. Even when he tried to steady himself, the demented scuttling across his stomach drove him back to the edge of insanity. "*I'll* tell you. I'll tell you." His words were almost unintelligible.

"Then keep still. *Keep still, damn you.*"

He tried to keep still. Someone said, "Mind those teeth, they're razor sharp. Watch your hands." Meisser shuddered violently. He felt one side of the pan lift, a final scuttling, then the pan removed. Sweat poured from him. The same man said, "Careful how you put him back. We might need him again."

Oh no. Not again. "What is it you want to know?"

"You know what we want to know. And don't hold anything back. Names, addresses, procedure. Everything. Oh, and Meisser, when I said you are covered, I meant it. No one will ever know you told us—your job will be safe. We simply held you to ransom for the two terrorists, and I'm advised that the bank has already agreed to pay. Now talk."

The Swiss authorities did not like being held to a ransom demand. In Germany, France and Italy such things were to be expected, but here in peaceful, law-abiding Switzerland it was a new threat. The police were puzzled. The Zeitlinger was an undoubted power in banking but why take the manager? Why not the president or vice-president whose resources were infinitely greater?

The police held speedy conferences. The kidnappers had been quick, and made their demands within two hours. The police were against payment but Eric Baumann decided to agree to the ransom. He believed the police theory that Meisser must have been kidnapped because he was a lesser and easier prey, unprotected by the security measures that safeguarded his superiors. The ransom was appropriate to the man; not too large.

A nervous Swiss government refused to release the two prisoners who were in remand. Later that day the kidnappers made contact again and reluctantly agreed to receive the money only. A breakaway group. It was really money they were after and they wanted a quick deal or they would kill Meisser.

The threat was taken seriously. Meisser's gold Rolex watch, inscribed by his wife on the back, had been left at an empty teller's cage in a plain envelope.

Instructions were audaciously delivered by hand the day after the kidnapping. A badly printed letter was put in the bank's mailbox. Baumann was warned not to call in the police, but had the sense to co-operate with them, and pass on the instructions.

The money was to be placed in a waterproof bag in the first of a chain of pleasure boats moored off shore from the Stadthausquai, between the Quai and Munster Bridges. The police began to think they were dealing with amateurs. There would be no problem in keeping the small chain of boats in constant view with excellent cover on both sides of the river. Baumann took a launch out alone and placed the money in the front vessel. From that moment it was under constant surveillance, with police launches at standby.

As darkness approached the police had second thoughts. The string of boats was sufficiently off shore to make them indistinct. The quay lights made shadows and the arc lamps could not be used without betraying police presence. They now had no doubt that a frogman would collect the money and all they could do was watch and listen. They waited all night. When they checked at dawn the money was still there.

Meisser was found in his car, still bound and blindfolded, about two hundred yards from his home. His clothes were filthy and he was obviously in poor condition. Pale, unshaven and dirty, he was in terrible mental and physical shape. In forty-eight hours, Meisser had lost more than half a stone in weight. Nobody questioned the fact that he had suffered and he was taken straight to hospital.

Savage ran his finger along the bars of the cage. The tame gerbil took little notice.

"Watch his teeth, they're razor sharp," warned Barrow with a grin. "You'd better take it back to the pet shop and demand your money back before Seymour complains."

"They can have it for free. This little chap worked wonders. Well, we'll have to wait on London for the run down on Ulla, Wegel and

Hartmann. Let's close up this place and see how Tyler's getting on."

"Do we need him now?"

Savage shrugged. "Probably not."

"So let's have a decent out-of-town lunch first before we separate again."

"OK."

By the time they reached Zürich the police were already claiming a victory. Meisser was the worse for wear but essentially unharmed, the money had not been collected and the kidnappers had fled in fear. Everyone was satisfied at the outcome.

For three days now Eddie Tyler had seen no sign of Ray Barrow and he was worried. He had asked at the desk; Barrow had not checked out. Nor had there been any sign of Ulla. Eddie had been left alone but instead of making him feel better it made him more nervous. Ironically, he was more concerned for Barrow than for himself, thinking that something must have happened to him.

When he read about the kidnapping of Meisser he found it suspect. When Meisser was released Eddie was even more suspicious.

Eddie went for a walk. For the first two days after Barrow's absence he had stuck closely to the hotel trying to pick out characters who might be watching him. But he could not stay indoors forever. He decided to go to the lake. On leaving

294

the hotel he turned left towards the Bahnhof bridge. It was morning and the streets were busy. The news stand placards still covered the Meisser kidnapping. He crossed the street and went past the bridge towards the Limmat Quai.

A car pulled up just ahead of him and a man leaned out of the front passenger seat and waved a map at him. Eddie went over.

He bent down to talk to the fair-haired, blue-eyed, young passenger when suddenly the map was pulled away and a gun was revealed.

"Climb in the back"—German, spoken in a tone with which one does not argue.

Eddie's reflexes were quick but not quick enough. He turned to run only to be crowded by a man who had come up from behind. The teutonic good looks were hard, and one hand was in a bulky jacket pocket that was raised towards Eddie. "In the back."

The young eyes and brutal mouth in front of him chilled Eddie. He climbed in. As he turned to sit on the rear seat someone struck him on the back of the head and he collapsed. Hartmann's thugs had arrived.

Raya Dubrova was depressed by inaction. She had time on her hands and was worrying too much about her mother. She was fast coming to the conclusion that she should return to Moscow but hesitated because she was convinced that Stevinski would not be satisfied with her result.

She had checked all of Nakentov's names and addresses, but was now at a dead end. What she had learned really left the matter more open than before.

Like Eddie, Raya had followed the Meisser kidnapping with distrust and an inexplicable apprehension. Somehow she felt connected with it. Really it was a ridiculous feeling, but she did not understand or trust anything any more. And for someone who, throughout her young life, had taken everything she had been taught at face value—and believed it—life was suddenly complex and frightening.

When she entered the lobby of the Hotel Bernhof and collected her key, she was handed with it a sealed envelope. She went up to her room totally unaware that she was under close observation.

In her room, Raya opened the envelope and was surprised to find a message from Heinz Meisser. It was in German and read:

Dear Miss Dubrova,
I am now aware of who you are and think it a pity that you did not reveal your true identity when we first met. You may know I've just suffered a harrowing experience, but I am recovered now and need to talk to you. In the hope that you will be free after lunch (Wednesday) I have arranged for a car to pick you up at two thirty at your hotel. You will be

brought straight here to the hospital. I have something to tell you about Dranrab 627. I look forward to seeing you.

Yours, Heinz Meisser

PS. The car will of course return you to your hotel.

Raya read it through a second time. The writing was in longhand and was shaky in parts but that was to be expected. Her spirits rose. Was this to be the breakthrough? She must at least see where it might lead. But how had he discovered where she was staying?

After lunch, always a lonely affair, she went to her room. She wanted to look her best; she remembered the opulence of Meisser's office. At two twenty she went downstairs, told the concierge she was waiting for a car and asked if he would advise her when it arrived.

She sat in the lobby ostensibly reading a newspaper but keeping an eye on the activity at the desk. So many people came and went and she knew none of them. At two thirty-five a uniformed chauffeur called at the desk and was pointed her way. As he approached, Raya could see that he was young and handsome, but very formal as he saluted and asked if she was Miss Dubrova. The car was outside.

The chauffeur walked slightly behind her as she went down the steps, but he reached forward in time to open the front passenger door of a

Mercedes limousine. This surprised her a little; Stevinski's driver had always opened the rear door for her. But she climbed in. The chauffeur went round the front of the car and climbed in beside her.

They had been driving for perhaps five minutes when Raya became uncomfortably aware of someone sitting in the back seat. At first it was merely an impression, then she was sure that she heard someone move above the purr of the engine.

She turned round. A man was sitting immediately behind her. He made no move and uttered no word. She turned back to look at the driver; he was gazing straight ahead, features tight, and gave no sign that he was aware of her.

Raya was suddenly uneasy. She glanced out of the window, at the traffic, the people. They were not speeding. It was all so normal, yet everything felt unreal. She glanced at the door catch to see how it operated; she had to be sure before she did anything drastic, like jumping out. She turned to the driver and, as evenly as she could, asked, "Which hospital is Herr Meisser in?"

The chauffeur gazed straight ahead and continued to drive.

Raya repeated the question with no better result. She turned to the man in the back. "Do *you* know?" But he did not reply either. Nor did he give any sign that he heard or wanted to hear; he remained hunched in the corner.

"Let me out!" Raya was aware of the touch of hysteria in her voice. No one took any notice, as if she was not even there.

"*Let me out.*" As she made the demand her hand reached forward for the door catch. There was no point in asking who they were or what was wanted of her. Ahead were traffic lights. She prayed that they would turn to red. They did. The chauffeur gave a slight nod and as Raya pulled at the catch the man behind her struck her violently with the flat of his gun. He had meant to catch her at the base of her skull but she had leaned away from the door as she pulled the catch and had half turned ready to jump out.

The blow took her partly on the temple and partly on the cheekbone. Her cheek was gashed and blood spurted out as she fell forward against the dashboard. The man in the rear leaned over the front seat to ensure that the front door was still closed, then unfeelingly pushed Raya out of sight on to the floor. The driver did not move or take his gaze from the road.

Bill Savage and Ray Barrow returned separately to Zürich after they had enjoyed a prolonged lunch. They had good reason to celebrate. They had succeeded in prising from Meisser what they needed to know and had signalled the information to Seymour in London. The two men were pleased with themselves. It was early evening when they drove back, in their hired cars.

Savage arrived back at the Hotel Bernhof before Barrow reached the outskirts of Zürich. He handed in his rented car, arranged to settle his account, checked flights to London and discovered there was one he could catch that evening if he moved fast enough. He was already on his way to Kloten Airport by the time Barrow reached the Hotel Torsa.

Barrow checked at the desk and collected his key. Although he was very slightly drunk he had noticed that the hotel was still being watched. Eddie Tyler continued to be under surveillance which meant that Eddie was unharmed. Had he known that Eddie had already been taken, there would have been no need for a stake out.

He went to the bar and had a lager, feeling thirsty after the whisky and wine of the celebratory lunch. He took his time. Glancing at his watch he decided to enjoy a short lie down before dinner. He paid for his drink and took the elevator to his room floor.

Barrow hesitated outside his door. Eddie's room was three doors along and he decided to look in on him after he had showered. He opened his door and went in—to sober up in a second. In a mirror by the window he could see the reflection of a man standing in the bedroom. He pulled out his gun and, holding it ready, stood very still.

The man in the bedroom heard the outer door open and close and was ready for Barrow to enter. He had assumed that Barrow was a professional and would not easily fall for the type of ruse used on Raya and Eddie; this man would be difficult to get in the open. Hearing no sound, he edged towards the door.

Barrow decided his best tactic was to get out. He backed towards the outer door and, turning in a flash, grabbed the door knob as the man bawled out, "*Max.*"

A second man appeared as Barrow opened the door and pulled frantically at Barrow's collar. Barrow tried to slip from his jacket but the gun stuck in the sleeve and he was reluctant to let go of it. By then the other man had arrived from the bedroom. He helped pull Barrow back while Max kicked the door shut.

Barrow struggled but his jacket was half off and he could not get his gun hand free. From the moment he had seen the silencer on the other guns, he knew that the two men were prepared to kill. He kicked out and when one man fell away Barrow fired through his sleeve. The man collapsed at the same time as Max shot Barrow through the back, startled by the roar of Barrow's unsilenced gun.

Barrow slipped to the floor. Max was worried about the noise. He stepped over Barrow to examine the other man who was holding his stomach with blood gushing between his fingers, and staring up in pain. He needed help but Max knew that he could not get him out of the hotel unnoticed. He picked up Barrow's gun, quickly screwed his own silencer on to it and, while his colleague stared in horror, shot him through the head. He then unscrewed the silencer, put it back on his own gun, wiped the grip, bent down and squeezed his colleague's hand round it. He cleaned the butt of Barrow's gun and returned it to the dead agent's hand.

Max moved quickly. He picked up his colleague's gun and pocketed it, checked that Ray Barrow was dead, opened the door, made sure the corridor was clear then hurried to the stairs. He had no qualms about the mess he had left behind him; the two guns that had been fired were in the room, the police could sort it out. But he did not think that Hartmann would be too pleased and that worried him much more.

15

SAVAGE rose late. He was tired but satisfied and reported to Seymour mid-morning. He went breezily into his chief's office but his smile was wiped from his face as soon as he saw Seymour's expression.

"They got Barrow," Seymour said heavily before Savage could speak.

"*Ray?* When?" It was a reflex question.

"Last night. At his hotel. There was a shoot out. Both men are dead."

"Oh, Christ. We had lunch only . . ." Savage tailed off. He felt as sick as Seymour appeared to be. "Poor Ray. Ulla's mob?"

"Who knows? It's not straightforward. A German was shot in the stomach and head. Barrow was shot in the back. Presumably Barrow shot his man first as he would have been hard put to fire when he was dead. The German, too, did well, killing Barrow while he himself had a fatal bullet wound in his head. It's rigged. There had to be another man."

"Why kill him?"

Seymour shrugged. "If it is Ulla's crowd, they must be getting very worried which means they have a great deal to hide. I want to know why Barrow died, what the Lubov connection is and whether it's still in operation." Seymour managed a brief smile. "You did well, you two . . . At one stage, I gather, with a replica gun. All the same, you'll have to go back."

"What about Tyler?"

"I was about to ask you. With Barrow gone we don't know, do we? We still need him. If his aunt was somehow tied to the account, and increasingly it appears that she was, then Tyler might prove to be the ultimate legal lever. Keep him alive if you can."

Savage said carefully, "Ulla's mob might get to him before us."

"Then fly back this afternoon. Keep in touch with Berne; you might need help."

"OK. Any news on the trio?"

"I've only had their names for two days. We've been working the clock round and we've come up with their home addresses, all impressive and all in West Germany. We're trying a run down on Tinsal."

Seymour referred to a note pad on his desk. "Wegel is the son of an ex SS man and we're now doing a trace on his father. Ulla Krantz is so far straightforward. Parents and background traced, well-off middle class, both dead. Hartmann is the enigma. We can't find any trace of him before the sixties, but it's early days yet. Needless to say, there is nothing to suggest how any of them became involved in Dranrab. But I'll send you information as it comes up. Meanwhile, play it by ear and just watch Tyler."

Savage had reached the door when Seymour added: "One thing to bear in mind. You may have fooled everyone else over lifting Meisser but I very much doubt that you fooled Ulla's crowd. And that will worry them even more. Watch your back. And get Berne to supply a gun."

Eddie's head was splitting. Every time he tried to raise it, the pain was intolerable and when he opened his eyes everything wavered and was shot with bright sparks.

Discomfort registered as well as the pain and he realised that he was lying on a stone floor. Gradually he collected his wits. Someone had thumped him in the car—it must have been with a hammer.

He made the effort of sitting upright and his vision spun. There was something behind him and he leaned against it. He was in an arched cellar. The light was poor and there was the hiss of a butane lamp, out of sight and casting strangely shaped bars on the floor.

It was a wine cellar. Rows of empty wine racks faced him and he guessed, without turning his head, that he was leaning back against one. The racks were solid, metal framed and obviously a permanent fixture. The cellar was surprisingly fresh as though it had been recently cleaned and aired. He gained the impression that it had not been used for wine for a very long time and reluctantly accepted that it made a good prison.

He looked around but the racks cut off most of his view; they seemed to be everywhere. It was only by looking upwards that he could obtain any idea of the size of the place. The roof comprised a series of spandrels, the wine racks themselves seemingly forming the piers. The light came from somewhere behind the rack in front of him. There must be steps leading up into the main house but he could not see them.

He was beginning to think again. Ulla had to be responsible for this, there could be nobody else. If Ray Barrow had been around, it probably would not have happened and he was angry about that.

The floor was slightly damp and he slowly climbed to his feet. Then he found that, although his hands were free, one ankle was chained to a rack support. A glance was enough to see that he would not be able to break it.

He eased himself down again and waited. When he delicately explored the back of his head, he found the bump and the congealed blood; as the pain gradually eased, his apprehension heightened.

Suddenly Eddie jerked. He had heard something. Somewhere in front of him and to his left a door had opened. Footsteps, shuffling at times and hesitating. It sounded as if someone was having difficulty coming down steps. Then he thought there were two people and this was confirmed as he heard men's voices, speaking in German. Were they carrying something? Someone said, "Put her here."

Her? A woman? A lock turned. Footsteps again, one pair moving towards him. A man came in view round the end of the wine racks and looked down at Eddie in contempt. He was one of the men in the car.

Eddie said, "You wait till the British Consul hears about this. You're in trouble, mate." He spoke in German.

The man said, "I'd like to be there when you die, you English shit. You're a nothing. Garbage."

"You Nazi berk. I can smell the stench of fascism from here." This time he spoke in English. Before he could move he was kicked heavily in the ribs. He yelled out in pain and tried to roll as the boot came in again but the chain held him back.

Doubled up and retching he was in such agony that he neither saw nor heard the second man race round and pull his colleague away. The guards exchanged angry words before they left. The door banged but Eddie was barely aware of it.

When he could breathe more easily he leaned back against the racks again. "Jesus." He sat back, panting. And then he began to wonder who they had brought in. When he was able to, he called out softly, "Anybody there?" But no one answered. He could hear nothing move.

A long time later he heard a chain rattle. Then there was the soft sobbing of a woman. He called out again.

The sobbing stopped but there was no reply. He tried again with the same result. And then he tried in German.

Raya heard him call but had developed a suspicion of everything and everyone. She had no idea why she was here. Like Eddie, her head was a mass of pain and the blood from her cheek had congealed on her face and run on to her neck and collar. She was afraid and felt cut off from all that was familiar. Raya dried her eyes. Never had she felt so alone.

The voice calling out from behind her seemed part of the trap. She had no intention of answering.

The voice called to her again in passable German but with an odd accent: "Have you got a chain round your ankle?"

Still she did not reply.

"Did they get you in a car and clobber you?"

She touched her cheek. The gash was wide and she wondered if it needed stitches. She dared not touch her temple which felt agonisingly swollen.

"They nearly cracked my skull in and I'm chained to a wine rack. Who *are* you?"

Raya decided to answer his question with one of her own. "Why are *you* here?"

Eddie tried a chuckle to reassure the girl and stopped when his ribs hurt. "It's all very complicated and about one of my aunts. Half a century ago she had a love affair with a Russian in London. And nobody knew about it." Eddie took a deep breath. He waited for a reaction but there was none.

Raya had gone into herself. This *was* part of the trap. Already he was talking about Russians. He wanted some information from her but she did not know what. When Eddie called out again she ignored him.

Through the listening device, concealed in an upper wine rack, Ulla Krantz heard the strange exchange in one of the main rooms above the cellar. She sat in a canvas chair, padded earphones over her head and a tape-recorder mounted on empty wooden boxes in front of her. Wegel and Hartmann were talking softly on the far side of the room by the long picture window.

The villa had been rented unfurnished; what little they had brought in comprised bare necessities. Bed rolls, a few chairs, two camp tables, gas lamps, gas cylinders to power the portable fire and the cooking rings. The villa was in need of renovation and decoration and had been on the market for some time. It was really too isolated and difficult to reach to be an attractive buy, but was ideal for their purpose.

Hartmann's imported young thugs occupied a

back room and were made to keep to themselves. They were being highly paid and endured the temporary spartan living without complaint. Now Eddie and Raya were captive Ulla was in favour of sending Hartmann's men back to Germany but he had insisted they remain. She strongly suspected that Wegel and Hartmann were at present discussing that very issue.

She had wanted to see if there was any reaction between Raya and Eddie. It was her idea to keep them in separate parts of the cellar. If they knew each other and were together they could give visual signals, warnings. As they were, they were forced to communicate aloud. Yet it had not worked out the way she had hoped. They seemed not to know one another and Ulla had always believed that there was a link between them. She took off the earphones and turned towards the two men.

Wegel slowly came towards her. "We've agreed a compromise. Two go, two stay." When he noticed Ulla's annoyance, he added, "Rolf thinks we may yet need them and he could be right."

Ulla stood up and called angrily across the room to Hartmann. "They made a mess in Zürich. Get them away before the police find them; or do you want to send for an army?"

Ulla was the one person with whom Hartmann always made an effort to control himself. Almost apologetically he replied, "You are right about Zürich." He shrugged. "I am only suggesting that we retain Max Berg and Jurgen Hohl, the two best. As soon as it's clear that we don't need them they can go. Isn't that fair?"

Ulla had to agree but she could not resist a last barb, "After all these years, I've only just discovered where your real interests lie. You've never stopped being a Nazi."

Hartmann smiled. "Aren't they useful now? Ready to hand and reliable?"

Ulla was forced to concede; she did not raise the issue of hotel killings again for fear of inflaming the issue. Hartmann had kept his personal secrets well. How many more was he sitting on? "There's no reaction from the cellar. We'd better start on Tyler first."

Hartmann left the room to give orders for Eddie to be brought up and he returned carrying a strong, straight-backed wooden chair. He placed it in the middle of the room. Producing a length of cord he tugged hard, almost breaking it with his brute force.

"I need tools," he complained. "Instruments. All I have are these." He held his big hands up, the weals from the cords marking them like razor slashes.

"Aren't they enough?" Ulla refused to show her uneasiness, she must remain in command. "Haven't they succeeded before?"

"They've succeeded well enough before, I suppose, and someone has to do this job. I can't see you or Gustav doing it."

311

Ulla bit her lip; there was too much friction between them already. And they had to avoid arguments. The sooner this business was finished the better.

Eddie was bundled in between Max Berg and Jurgen Hohl. The ankle chain had been removed but they had taken the precaution of binding his wrists. "Hello, Ulla. I've missed you."

Ulla gazed coldly at him. "Tie him to the chair."

Eddie viewed the chair with alarm. It stood in the middle of the room stiff and uncompromising as if awaiting his execution. He was pushed over to it and, when his legs started to drag, was half-carried. He was tied to the chair in a way that hurt, arms pressing into the sides of the back, legs straddled. Max and Jurgen left the room and Ulla, Wegel and Hartmann came to stand in front of Eddie.

"We want to know who has sponsored you, Eddie," said Ulla. "My colleague will get it from you one way or the other. He will enjoy doing it. We'll try to stop him going too far but, as you can see, he will be difficult to stop."

Eddie was left with little hope. He was as good as dead already. But he had no intention of suffering torture for nothing. "I've told you, my aunt is the cause. But I'm here at the expense of Her Majesty's Government."

"Explain that."

Eddie swallowed. "A man called George

312

Seymour in London sent me. He has an undeclared interest."

Wegel observed softly. "MI6."

"British Intelligence?" Ulla did not want to believe it. And how did Wegel know? "Why?"

"I told you. Undeclared interest. They're not likely to tell me."

Hartmann appeared cheated that the answers were coming so easily. They must be lies. He moved forward but Ulla put out a restraining hand. "And you just let them send you?"

"Ulla, you know *my* interest. And I'm out of a job. It was better than standing on street corners. Until now. Really, I'm no good to you."

"Who was the man you were seen with at the hotel?"

Eddie did not like the way the question had been put. *Was?*

"He'll tell you that better than me."

"He's dead."

"*Dead?*" He could see the truth written on their faces. Ray Barrow dead. He was afraid to ask them how or when. He swallowed uneasily. It did not matter now. "He was keeping an eye on me. I suppose Seymour sent him."

"Were you in danger then?"

"Come on, Ulla. Look at me." If he could keep his gaze away from Hartmann he believed he could cope.

"What about the girl?"

"The girl in the cellar? I've no idea who she is or why she's here."

"You're a liar, Eddie."

Before anyone could move Hartmann shot forward and smashed Eddie round the side of the face, his eyes gleaming. Ulla's accusation had been the cue he had been waiting for. Eddie and the chair went flying across the room.

It took them twenty minutes to revive him. His jaw was swollen and his left eye was cut and darkening. He was lucky not to have broken one of his arms against the chair in the violent fall. With barely concealed fury, Ulla explained to Hartmann that she had been goading Eddie, that she did not really believe that he was lying. It had taken both her own and Wegel's efforts to stop Hartmann going in to finish the job. Only when Ulla placed herself between Eddie and her sadistic colleague had Hartmann finally begun to simmer down.

They pulled Eddie upright but, even when he was conscious again, it was obvious that they would get no sense from him for some time.

They propped him up on the chair, dragging him back to the middle of the room.

"Bring the girl up," Ulla said to Hartmann and added, as a warning, "If you hit her like that you'll kill her. Wait till we have our answers and then do what you like. *But do nothing until I tell you.*"

Raya was brought in with her hands tied. She

hesitated in the doorway, her eyes on Eddie in the middle of the room like a grotesque centrepiece. She could see the damage and that he was barely conscious.

"Bring her in."

Raya was prodded forward. She had no idea who they were. Her gaze returned to Eddie.

"Do you know this man?" snapped Ulla.

The woman seemed to be in control; her tone was brittle. "I have never met or seen him before."

"We will do to you what we've already done to him, and worse, if you don't tell the truth."

"I don't know him." A door closed behind Raya and she supposed that her escort had left the room. She was standing opposite Eddie, near the centre of the bare room. She felt sorry for him; blood was trickling from his mouth but he seemed to be unaware of it.

"Where are you from?"

"Moscow."

"You came to Zürich to enquire about the Dranrab bank account. Why?"

"I don't know why."

"Be very careful how you answer Raya Dubrova, or you'll never be pretty again."

Raya knew that the threat was real. "I know nothing about the bank account. I was merely sent to enquire."

"Who sent you?"

"General Georgi Stevinski."

Ulla raised her brows. She hesitated as though unsure, before turning to Wegel. "Is this a name you know too?"

"Sure. Everyone should. He's Chairman of the KGB."

Ulla faltered. She was on view, she must regain composure.

"You are KGB?" she asked of Raya.

"No." And then, with insight, "They are holding my mother in Moscow. I was made to come here."

This was something everyone understood. "First as a Rumanian and then as a Russian."

"I don't know why I was sent as a Rumanian. I did not like it. I was sent back here to get more information."

"But you haven't been back to the bank to make enquiries, only to draw money."

Raya had a moment of deep fear, a conviction that she would never see Moscow again. "I also came to find out what had happened to a distant relative during the war."

"Who?"

"Jacob Djugashvili."

"What's he got to do with it?"

"The account? Nothing. They are separate issues." But she was convinced that they were not.

Raya saw Hartmann's strange reaction to her reply as he stepped back a pace. Wegel noticed too. But Ulla was standing slightly in front of them and missed it. Yet she herself was affected; she seemed to lose the trend of her questioning and appeared bemused.

Eddie, convinced that his jaw was broken, and having trouble seeing through the blood mist of his left eye, was slightly more conscious of what was happening than he revealed. He was in considerable pain but using his wits. He realised that the girl was the one he had called out to in the cellar and was surprised to find that she was Russian.

He developed an abstract pride in her as she answered the questions. Her fear was apparent but she held herself upright and answered with dignity. She looked so innocent and vulnerable yet she was handling the situation well. The gash down her face was terrible but it did not hide a high cheek-boned, Slavic prettiness. He wanted to encourage her but there was nothing he could say that might not make matters worse. So with head rolling, eyes half closed, Eddie watched the scene closely.

Who was Jacob Djugashvili? He had no idea but he at once saw that Hartmann did. He was not sure about Wegel but the nerve in his cheek had increased its beat.

Ulla was staring at Raya. Whatever her next question might have been she was unable to ask it. Her rhythm of questioning was, for the moment, destroyed. With a helpless gesture she turned to the others, at once noticed Hartmann's agitation, and wondered at what point it had all gone wrong. Why had the Russian name made such an impact on a tough character like Hartmann? Why was Wegel so seemingly at a loss? These were questions that could not be answered now. "Get them back to the cellar. We'll try again later."

She had learned something. The knowledge that two intelligence agencies were interested in Dranrab alarmed her considerably.

Hartmann rallied to call his men. They released Eddie and, on Ulla's instructions, took him and Raya down to the cellar and left them together. There was no further advantage in keeping them apart and something might come out of a closer dialogue between them. When they had gone, Ulla switched on the tape, aware that something had raised a barrier between herself and her two partners. Her unease increased because she could not pinpoint its cause.

16

THEY were chained opposite each other and forced to lie on the concrete floor.

"You are the man who called out to me earlier?" asked Raya.

"Yes."

"I'm sorry I did not answer you. I was suspicious." Raya spoke in English.

Eddie held a finger to his lips and glanced around to indicate that they might be overheard. He could see what it had cost her to retain her dignity upstairs. Small shudders ran through her frame.

"You've got a lot of guts," he said without thinking.

"Pardon?"

"Guts. Courage. I was proud of you up there."

"Why so?"

"It doesn't matter why. I was. Was it Raya, they called you?"

"Raya Dubrova."

"I'm Eddie Tyler."

Eddie was quite sure that they were not going to get out alive. He had nothing to hang on to now that Barrow was dead but, for the sake of the girl, he tried to hide his fear. There was nothing he could say to reassure her. He was curious about her, being Russian and seemingly alone and wanted to ask her a number of questions but realised that doing so could complete the job Ulla had started.

He wondered if the girl was thinking the same. He made signs to remind her that there might be a microphone somewhere and then offered a pantomime that was supposed to indicate that what he said did not matter. He pointed to the ceiling to show that those above it already knew the information he was about to give her. She gave a sign that she understood.

Eddie took his time over telling Raya why he was here, about Dranrab and Aunt Jane and everything he had already told Ulla. But he was careful not to go beyond that point. "She was obviously in love with this character Lubov. Is it a name that means anything to you?"

Raya shook her head slowly. His story fascinated her. She had felt part of it in some way. There was the common link of Dranrab, of course, and that was inexplicable. "Lubov is not an uncommon name."

He scrambled to his feet and started to examine the empty wine rack. Quick to understand, Raya did the same on her side. They searched every bottle hole they could reach. If there was a microphone at all, it would not be too far away. Raya found it by using the recesses as a ladder and climbing as far as the chain allowed.

With her feet inserted in the holes she hung on

while she tried to attract Eddie. She tapped on the rack and when Eddie turned she held a listening bug in her hand. He gave her a thumbs up and signalled for her to come down.

Raya tore off one of the sleeves of her blouse and wrapped the bug in it. She kept it in her clenched hand.

Raya smiled at him, pleased with what she had done yet understanding, as he did, that it would invoke the anger of those upstairs once it was discovered. Time was precious.

They squatted close together in the aisle and he shot at her some of the questions that puzzled him. Quickly she told him about Stevinski, her mother and grandfather.

"How did this character Stevinski get to hear of Dranrab?" Eddie persisted. "Lubov must mean something to him."

When Raya floundered, Eddie continued. "I wasn't going to tell you but I think I must. The diary was stolen. The nurse who knew about it was killed with her boyfriend and someone tried to run me down."

"Someone?"

He hesitated. "Russians. They were watching the house."

"*Russians? In London?*"

He could see that it would be difficult to convince her. "I had to be protected by British Intelligence. Here too. OK, they are just as bent as any other intelligence service, but I have every reason to believe them. The name Lubov must have reached Stevinski. You mentioned searching for information about a distant relative. Tell me about that."

And when she had finished, he said, "*Stalin's son?* Jesus."

But little flashes of enlightenment were beginning to explode in Raya's head. Yasha's mistress had come into money. It was still a long way from a connection with Dranrab but it was worth exploring. She gave Eddie all the detail she could remember.

"It's got to be the ring," said Eddie. "That's got to be the link. Why else would Stevinski raise it after so long?"

"No. *No!*"

Eddie gazed at her. She was suddenly distraught. He did not know that the ring led straight back to her grandfather, Nakentov. "OK," he said. "It doesn't matter."

Raya was reluctant to continue. Eddie could see that he had touched a nerve and that it was best to leave it alone. All that was clear was that he and Raya, from different angles, had both been sucked into the deadly vortex of Dranrab.

Without quite knowing why, he gave her an urgent signal to return the microphone. She climbed up without question, unwrapped the bug and put it back where she had found it.

There was a faint draught and, as Eddie turned his head, he caught sight of silk-stockinged feet and ankles through a corner section of the racks. The feet moved towards them and Ulla came in view. She stood near the wall, shoes in hand and stared towards them.

Eddie stared back, confused by what he saw. Ulla said nothing; in the bad light of the cellar she appeared gaunt and drawn—as if in a trance. Once she realised they had seen her, she put her shoes down and stepped into them.

Ulla's gaze strayed to the area where the microphone rested. It was impossible to gauge what she was thinking for she presented such an uncertain figure. She turned away almost listlessly and went back towards the steps. The door banged at the top.

Raya shivered, clasping her arms. Eddie said, "She was moving like a zombie."

They whispered together quietly after that but it was a strain and they could not be sure what the bug might be picking up.

After one of their frequent lulls, Raya said, "They will kill us."

Eddie searched the girl's face, liking what he saw, and was sorry for her. She accepted she was being used but had no idea why. He, at least, understood some of it.

He considered lying to her, to give her false hope, but he did not think she would be deceived. Raya might carry a strong streak of innocence founded on indoctrination, but she was also a realist.

The reason why *he* had to be killed was clear; he presented a possible legal threat to Dranrab. With lowered voice he explained this to her, and that as they were together the danger for her was the same as for him.

Raya looked at Eddie; they had been thrown together as strangers, but already the danger they faced together had created a deep understanding between them. He must be afraid too, but he seemed more concerned for her. She was grateful for his casual, comforting touch. It was almost as if none of it mattered, but she knew that was an illusion; to live mattered greatly to them both.

Ulla went back to the tape-recorder. Hartmann and Wegel had left the room. She lifted the earphones and put one to her ear without expecting to pick up anything. She guessed that they would be whispering and thought she could hear a disjointed hissing.

Ulla was deeply disturbed. She was lucky to have been wearing the headphones when they discovered the bug, and she had heard the sound of tampering. There was more to learn, she knew that, but she was not at all sure that she wanted to find out any more. It was a totally illogical reaction for she *needed* to know everything but was afraid that there were aspects she would rather not hear. She would have been happier had she been capable of giving a reason why.

She went to look for the others and found them

in the kitchen with Hartmann's thugs, Max and Jurgen. She said nothing but a caustic glance was enough for her two colleagues to follow her into the main room. There was really nowhere to sit comfortably; the hardback chair still stood in the centre of the room, the cords trailing over it.

"We need to talk," said Ulla.

No one disagreed. They *had* to talk; and yet they knew the dangers of doing so. Proximity was prising apart their unspoken secrets and none of them believed that it would do any good to air them.

The easiest thing to do would be to dispose of Eddie and Raya. The three should go their own ways as they always had, ignoring everything that was happening around them; Tinsal was inviolable. People might prod and probe and beaver away but there was nothing they could achieve. Ignore it. Let them batter their heads against the wall.

That was the theory. But it was only part of the story.

"Whoever snatched Meisser would have learned about us."

And that was what was in all their minds.

"We can make Meisser tell us," Hartmann said viciously. Red traces showed across his knuckles where his skin had broken on hitting Eddie.

"No, we can't," snapped Ulla. "If we rough up Meisser we lose the support of the bank. We take it for granted that the kidnap was to get our names and that he gave them."

She put the direct question: "Who's in favour of splitting? Going back to normal? Just let them get on with it."

"By them you mean the British and the Russians?" Wegel queried, with no intention of mentioning Americans.

"Of course."

"It would be unwise to separate at such a time."

"It could be unwise to stay together."

"That too," agreed Wegel. "We need each other, yet we might destroy each other."

"Am I supposed to know what that means?" Ulla was studying Wegel closely and she noticed that Hartmann was taking more interest.

Wegel rubbed his cheek, although his nerve was quiet at the moment. "You may not," he replied carefully. "But I think you're as undecided as we are. Are we really worried about intelligence agencies making inroads into Tinsal, which seems to be impossible. Or are we worried about what they might find out about us personally?"

It was the most honest question any one of them had ever voiced about their relationship.

"I've nothing to worry me on that score," Ulla said, flatly. "They can dig as much as they like. I came by my share of Tinsal legally."

326

Wegel smiled. "At least you had the grace not to say fairly."

"Leave her alone," Hartmann surprised Wegel.

"Leave her alone," he repeated. "She did come by it legally." He paused. "And fairly. So shut your mouth, Gustav, or I'll shut it."

Wegel stepped back but said, "You're getting reckless, Rolf."

"Yeah. We all are. We're being pushed into a corner and we're letting it happen. All you're doing is talking your way up a blind alley. There's nothing at the end of it except trouble." He sucked his knuckles where the skin was broken, then held up the hand for them to see. "That's what's happened to us. We've gone soft. Let's kill those two young bastards downstairs for starters. Let's sort things out the way they should be."

"They may still have information that we want," hedged Ulla.

"OK, then let's get it." He raised his voice, now turning on Ulla. "If you hadn't stopped me, we'd have had it by now."

"We stopped you killing Tyler uselessly." Ulla did not mention what she had overheard in the cellar. If she did tell them, Hartmann would get his way; he wanted it now as he insisted, "Let me squeeze their heads and the truth will pop out."

Wegel, not clear where it would all lead, fell back to supporting Ulla. "We may need them for bargaining. They must be killed, but it's a matter of timing. Once they're dead we've no link with whoever's behind them."

Ulla quickly saw that they were moving in circles. First one supported her, then the other. She had been afraid of this happening and she suspected that so had they. She said, "Let's leave Max and Jurgen to guard Tyler and the girl and go back to the hotel for three days to think things out. We need a line of action and it must be concerted. We must decide on what is the worst thing that can happen to any of us if the British and the Russians dig deep. And then how best to deal with it. If we can protect each other, we can safeguard Tinsal. We don't have to live in Germany to do that."

She thought they were relieved at the suggestion but she added a warning. "What we think of each other has never been important. But we've always had trust. If, to protect what we hold, means laying our souls bare then that's what we must do. It's Tinsal that matters, not what sort of people we are. So use the time to come up with something positive." Ulla checked the time. "Let's make it seventy-two hours from now, or send a message to my suite when you're ready."

Ulla switched off the tape-recorder, rewound the tape and replaced it with a new one, ready for their return. She went down the cellar steps to take one last look at the prisoners and her scrutiny was of Raya much more than of Eddie.

Before Ulla left the villa, she was fully aware that the time she had created was more for her own use than for the others; she badly needed the break from Wegel and Hartmann. In the back of her mind was the strong possibility that she might have to deal with them too. If a good thing had to come to an end, it would not come to an end for her. She would survive whoever else did not.

Yet, as she drove away, dusk staining the gulleys of the foothills, she knew that she would have to watch her back. Hartmann was unpredictable but it was Wegel she saw as the main danger. Hartmann had always backed down from her and had often been protective, like today; but she had never known what was in Wegel's mind.

She drove carefully towards Zürich, easing round the curves of the road as if she was a learner. It had taken all her nerve to deal with the situation at the villa. Now she was alone, it was different. She let her face muscles go and her features sagged. The name she had overhead Raya mention to Eddie came back to her as though it was printed on the road ahead. Paula Menke. *Paula Menke.* Where had she heard it before? And why did it haunt her now?

17

SAVAGE studied the signal in his room. "Wegel's father shot dead by unknown in 1966. Name changed to Wegel in 1960. Previously Gerhard Julich. Eastern Front, Iron Cross second class, later guard at Sachsenhausen. Wegel junior, no military or adverse record. Hartmann still no trace prior 1965. Krantz, nothing new. Still enquiring on all counts."

It had taken a little time to decode the message and at the end of it there was nothing to help. He had booked in at the Bernhof Hotel, as before, avoiding the Torsa where Barrow had been shot. The hotel killings were still a local sensation. What made it far worse for Savage was that he could find no trace of Eddie.

He had managed to examine Eddie's room, a risky business with Barrow's room sealed off and detectives still checking. He had found nothing suspicious. The concierge had told him that Eddie had gone out; he had not come back, his clothes were still in the room. First Barrow, now Tyler.

He discreetly checked at the Baur au Lac to find that Ulla Krantz, Rolf Hartmann and Gustav Wegel were all booked in there but that they too were seemingly absent.

Bill Savage rented a car and drove to Berne. It

330

would have been infinitely quicker by rail but he wanted to be alone and he needed the therapy of being behind a steering wheel. It was ridiculous of Seymour to expect him to operate alone, he needed a team.

It was not often that Savage felt sorry for himself. He was not only up against the impenetrable barrier of the Swiss banking system, but the many side issues buried deep into the core of Dranrab, and some, he suspected, much more important than the account.

There were signs of a fissure in the tough resisting crust of deception but it could close at any time, and what had already escaped suggested that an enormous explosion was needed to blast out the rest, and with it would come the smoke and steam to cover and confuse the issue. No one ever knew with Seymour; he might expect to get nowhere but the whim had already cost him Barrow, and Savage did not rate his own chances any higher.

He arrived in Berne clear about one thing: it was all a bloody waste of time and, anyway, he was not equipped for the job. He had a slanging match with the consular division of the British Embassy in Berne, before they reluctantly gave him permission to take a gun. And then he had another row in order to obtain a spare clip.

It had been a long way to come for a weapon, and, when he was seated in his car and holding the Browning flat in his hand, he knew that it was inadequate. He needed wing mirrors on his shoulders, or someone he could trust to watch his rear.

Savage began the night haul back to Zürich wherein lay the heart of the matter. And somewhere there, he hoped, was Eddie Tyler. He had grown quite fond of Eddie, who had been plunged into the deep end without being a swimmer. Savage suspected that Eddie's off-hand, flippant manner was a shield; beneath it lay guts and a genuine admiration for a dead lady who somehow seemed to be responsible for the present mess. Savage put on night glasses and increased his speed.

General Georgi Stevinski was becoming increasingly concerned. Raya must either be following a lead or was right out of the game. He had noted the Swiss press reports and, when Meisser was kidnapped and a man was shot dead in a hotel near the one Raya was staying in, he had suspicions.

The dead man's name was Barrow. A check with agents in Switzerland convinced him that Barrow was MI6. It was the sort of coincidence he did not care for. The death itself was of no consequence. The crime was still unsolved, the speculation and talk of spies continued.

His own tight security prevented him from knowing what Raya might have achieved but he was worried about her safety; not for her sake but for his own.

He still maintained the discipline of keeping the Dranrab affair to himself. He was well aware that the Secretary General was becoming impatient but there was nobody he could turn to either.

However, there were certain moves he could make without giving anything away. He sent a signal to his "resident" in Switzerland to deploy someone to check on Raya. He gave the hotel name. All he wanted was a trace—no contact—and then a report. No more.

Stevinski had taken the first move towards Raya's eventual extermination. He knew that the Swiss resident would wonder why Raya was alone in Zürich. Equally, he knew that his subordinate would not dare to speculate too far.

Gustav Wegel was relieved to get back to Zürich. His movements now were less restricted and he called Phil Gates as soon as he could. They met in the usual smoke-pocketed bar. He refused a drink and would not discuss what he had to say in the bar. Gates quickly swallowed his drink and they went for a walk.

Gates had seen Wegel agitated before but not like this. For once, he did not believe that the wealthy German was trying to put on an act. It was difficult to talk against a damp wind coming off the lake but Wegel seemed not to notice. He came straight to the point: "The man who was killed in the Hotel Astor the other day was a British agent. He was here keeping an eye on Tyler."

"Tyler's here?" Gates stopped walking to face Wegel.

Wegel wanted to move on but Gates grabbed his arm.

"I'm not trying a conversation with a bobbing yo-yo." He looked up and down the narrow street, there were few people about. "This will do fine."

Wegel said uneasily, "We'll be seen."

"And we'll be seen walking. You knew Tyler was here and you didn't tell me? After the enquiries I asked London to make? You made me look a fool—I ought to . . ."

"I couldn't tell you. It was impossible. Tyler came back and Barrow kept an eye on him."

Gates slowly released his anger. "You made a monkey of me!"

"That's ridiculous. I told you dogs were sniffing and you didn't believe me. Russian wolves and British hounds."

More calmly, Gates said, "So who knocked off the hotel guy?"

Wegel hesitated. "I don't know. We were watching Tyler, trying to find out who was behind him."

"The British?" Gates turned his collar up

against the wind. "That would explain why London didn't come through."

"We've got to cut out the danger to me, Phil. It's far worse than I thought."

"Do you realise what you're saying?"

"We can get another man on to the board of the French company when this has died down. Right now Reynaud leads straight back to me. I put him on the board. If the Russians and the French find out what he's been passing back to me for your people, how do you rate my chances?"

Gates was thoughtful. "Where's Tyler now?"

"We'll handle him ourselves."

"I can get it out of you, Gustav. Don't make me."

"Try that and you'll lose the lot. Just root out the danger in France."

"I don't like it. Not one bit."

"Nor do I. It has to be done."

Gates was not entirely convinced: he, in turn, would have to put up a convincing case to his superiors. And they would not be pleased. But, if the Russians were getting at all close, it was necessary to make sure there was nothing to find. He could not imagine what the British angle could be.

Watching him, Wegel could see that Gates was not satisfied, so he said, "We have the girl. The moment you try to find out where, we will take her out."

"The Rumanian girl?"

"She turned out to be a Russian girl."

"Shit. So *she* came back too."

"Her name is Raya Dubrova. She's the grand-daughter of General Pavl Nakentov and is here under the direct instructions of General Georgi Stevinski."

Gates stared, dumbfounded. Every time Wegel opened his mouth matters got worse. Nakentov was given a hero's burial only a few weeks ago. It was shown on television, here, everywhere.

"You'd better not be having me on, Gustav. So God help you."

"You have enough now?"

Gates nodded slowly. "It's enough."

"It needs a quick job, in Grenoble, Phil. We can build up again bigger than now."

Gates nodded again. He was numbed yet at the same time his mind was working furiously.

He turned up his collar, and hurried away without a word.

Rolf Hartmann leaned on the parapet of the Quai Bridge where the River Limmat flowed into the widening lake. His hands were clenched before him. So they now knew that he was directly involved with the underground SS. So what? But really all he did these days was to supply funds. Other wealthy men did the same.

Barrow had been a mistake; they should have done better but so far had lacked field experience.

They had got the girl and Tyler, though. Ulla and Wegel could not argue about that. The two prisoners should be killed, never mind the questions and answers. His reasoning was not born entirely of brutality.

The truth was that Hartmann was ready to cut off anything that might remind him of his past. Recollection held no fear for him; looking back, he would have done exactly as he had, and he believed that, by ignoring the past, it could effectively be severed forever. For the most part, he achieved this, but, when people started stirring the mud, they had to be stopped before they reached clearer water. He did not think they would get far but nor did he want them to have the chance.

Get rid of Tyler and the girl. If there was anyone behind them to follow up then get rid of them too. They would soon stop. And that would be an end of it.

What really worried Hartmann was the possibility of his background being examined. He could deal with any investigations that he knew were being made. But did he know about them all? He straightened, watching the coloured sails ballooning out, the ferry approaching the bridge, the wind whipping the steam from its funnel. His cruel features hardened as he pressed his hands together and the blood mounted in his cheeks. This time he had the others to help. But that did not shut out the recurring image of the woman dangling on the end of a rope.

Ulla Krantz sent two cables to America as soon as she returned to the Baur au Lac; one went to Blackfoot in Idaho, the other to San Francisco. She preferred not to check airline schedules at the hotel desk as she did not want Wegel or Hartmann to get an inkling of what she was doing. She went straight to the airport with an overnight bag. She was in time to catch a late plane to Paris and placed a request for a seat the following day on the Air France Concorde flight to New York.

In Paris she stayed at the George Cinq and rang up the Air France twenty-four hour reservation service to check that her onward flight was confirmed.

Ulla slept little that night. She was being forced to face old issues. More than anything else she was being compelled again and again, to face herself. The problem was that she never got anywhere with it. She became afraid, almost neurotic, and always encountered a mental barrier.

Yet she was convinced that the barrier was not self-created. She did not know what it was, and why she had inclinations towards certain actions that seemed to be entirely contrary to her own beliefs. Sometimes she had the sensation of being hypnotised or that part of her mind did not belong to her, but she knew that it was not so. Then she was terrified; she felt as if there was something she ought to remember, but could not recall.

Her private nightmare continued in the first-class luxury of the Concorde flight next day. Part of it was her very presence on the plane. What she had to do was vital but she did not want to do it. Ulla carried her agony of mind throughout the flight. She ate little, and portrayed a haughty, beautiful image which drew much attention of which she was totally unaware.

At Kennedy she took a cab for the Americana Hotel on 7th Ave. at 52nd St. She sat in the lounge, ordered tea, and waited. With the five-hour time difference she would be able to fly back that evening.

She sat alone facing the broad steps that led down the entrance hall. She glanced at her watch. Harper, the man she had put on the board of the Idaho bank, was late.

A medium-sized man approached with hat in hand. He appeared to be timid and, with his thinning hair brushed forward to cover the bald patches and a small moustache, the general impression was not striking. What firmness there was about him lay in his hands; they were steady and strong and positive in motion as he drew out a chair to sit close to Ulla at the low table. He placed his hat on the floor.

Before she could speak he said, "I had trouble with the flights. You gave me short notice." If his appearance and manner bordered on the obsequious, his voice destroyed the image; it was firm and there was no apology in his tone.

"What's the problem?" he asked.

"I want to close down. Destroy everything that leads back to you or me."

"*Everything?*"

"Yes."

Clive Harper shrugged. "You're sure there is something that leads back to you?"

"I'm taking no chances."

"It must be serious." Harper leaned back while the tea was placed in front of him.

When the waiter had gone, Ulla said, "I don't intend to discuss this."

"I just feel that the set-up is so cosy. Closing down will upset a lot of people."

"I'm not interested in who it upsets. Just do it."

"It's a great pity. There'll be questions."

Ulla put down her cup so carefully that there was no sound as it met the saucer. Harper's attitude played into her hands, made her more certain that what she was doing was right. "How would you feel if I sold the bank?"

"It wouldn't make any difference now. The set-up is there, the fish hooked."

"Let me tell you that the set-up would not last five minutes. I don't intend to explain. I want to know now, you take it or leave it. If you leave it, I'll get someone else. I think you are forgetting that the enterprise is mine."

"It started off as yours."

"I own it, Harper. Get that through your head."

"Something's obviously happened to upset you. Look, I'll refer back to the Centre. If they OK it then there's no problem. I can't be fairer than that."

"Are you afraid of doing what I ask?"

"You know I'm not. It would be easier if I knew why you think it necessary."

Ulla was prepared for it. She had created a monster and had become redundant in her own enterprise. It had become too valuable to Moscow.

"If you refer back, my interest is declared. The arrangement has always been that my personal involvement remains anonymous."

"That has always been honoured. I have never betrayed you." Harper noted her doubt and added, "If you don't accept my word for its own sake, then accept it because I believe that we can do this again elsewhere. We need you and if that means protecting you, then it will always be like that, but, if you destroy this, I would feel under no further obligation to you."

"Unless Moscow confirm."

"Right. I don't have to give your name to get confirmation. They know there's a secret patron."

Ulla appeared to give it thought. "All right.

341

But emphasise my belief in the necessity. It will be temporary, but for how long I can't say."

"Shall I wire you?"

"At the Baur au Lac, Zürich. I must know within forty-eight hours."

"That's a tall order."

"Then get them off their bureaucratic butts. It's urgent."

"You know what they're like. I'll do my best."

"No, Harper. You'll do as I say. Forty-eight hours."

Harper did not like the rebuke. He believed he held a trump card.

"I can get you dismissed from the bank with no trouble at all," Ulla added, observing his attitude.

"It still wouldn't make a difference." And then, quickly, "Look, I don't want to quarrel with you. You've been extremely helpful and we've always been grateful. I'll do as you say. And I'll give them the time limit."

Ulla spoke more gently. "I understand your feelings. But I'm left wondering whether you are worried about the set-up or concerned for yourself. What I've provided makes you appear much better than you are. You didn't work for it, I handed it to you on a plate."

Harper studied his flattened hands before looking up. "Really? But it still had to be handled. I'd better get moving or I won't meet your deadline." Harper rose and gave a cool little bow. He rammed on his hat and left.

Ulla sat back. She was exhausted after the exchange but it had been necessary to sound Harper's attitude.

After a light lunch, she took a cab to the United Nations building and stood on its steps watching the coachloads of tourists come and go. There was a point when she was aware of being under observation, not the usual kind, but close scrutiny. She picked out the man, different from Harper, heavily built with an expensive plain suit and wide, colourful silk tie. His eyes were deep and reflective, his skin sallow.

He approached slowly and raised his hat. "Miss Krantz?"

"Mr. Minelli? I'm sorry about the venue but I wanted to avoid the possibility of two appointments clashing."

"It's OK." He grinned pleasantly.

"Is there somewhere we can talk?"

"Sure. I keep a small apartment uptown. Don't use it often. I guess you'll have to trust me, though."

As he smiled reassuringly, it was difficult for Ulla to equate him with his profession. "We *have* to trust each other, Mr. Minelli. You've come a long way. So have I. You were recommended to me very highly by a mutual acquaintance a long time ago."

Minelli lightly took her arm. He raised his other hand and called a cab in a voice that must have reached the river.

343

"I know the acquaintance, lady, or I wouldn't be here." He rapped an address at the driver.

They wound through Manhattan, hitting the lights one after the other, until they reached Minelli's apartment in a block off Fifth Avenue. Minelli's small apartment turned out to be a penthouse thirty floors up. Lavishly furnished with long windows showing most of Manhattan and an enormous stretch of the East River.

Minelli showed Ulla to an armchair and came straight to the point. "So what's brought us both so far?"

Ulla opened her handbag and took out some photographs and a single sheet of paper. "I want these three people killed. And you've got twenty-four hours in which to do it." She took a smaller envelope out and handed it to Minelli who had crossed the thick pile to sit near her. "Open it," she said.

Minelli did so. His expression did not change as he held the bank draft between thumb and forefinger. "I was about to argue about the time factor," he admitted, "but this convinces me it can be done."

"A million dollars," said Ulla. She relaxed against the seat, one arm running along its back. "If you don't do it in the time, or if you bungle it, I will pay another million to see that you don't bungle again."

Minelli burst out laughing. He put the draft down on the glass-topped table on which Ulla had placed the photographs. "You know, lady," he said, still chuckling, "you're really something." He intertwined his fingers, gazing at her over the arch. "I've never been threatened before, do you know that? Not to my face, that is. Nobody has ever dared. I could take you out now and have that draft."

"But you won't. Not in your own apartment."

"Oh, I rent it out now and again." He was grinning, still unable to believe what he had heard. "You mean it, don't you?"

"I mean it. But there is a better reason why you won't touch me. I'm your client and you are a professional to your backbone. There is no way that you would risk losing your credibility. Do we understand each other?"

"We do, ma'am. But I oughta tell you that I don't know anybody who's capable of taking me out." Minelli's eyes were twinkling at the preposterous idea.

"There's always someone, Mr. Minelli. For a million I could get a small army."

Minelli glanced down at the photographs. "So I'm threatened before I even agree to the job. That's gotta be a first. You don't mess around do you? But you're crafty too. You've guessed that I couldn't run away from a threat? Not from a beautiful broad like you."

Ulla timed her smile. "I'm of the opinion that you're as good as I'm told you are."

345

Minelli inclined his head. Without touching the items on the table he asked, "Which one first?"

"This one." Ulla handed him the photograph of Clive Harper. "His address is on the back."

Minelli studied the photograph. "Married?"

"Yes. I'm not going to teach you your job but I think you should be aware of certain points. For these three to be obviously murdered would bring an enquiry which could easily defeat my purpose. I'm very aware that they live within a twenty-mile radius of each other. It's a disadvantage in one way, though doubtless it will help the time factor."

"So you want accidents?"

"Even three accidents close together, happening to these particular people, could raise eyebrows. Having got you, I'm not trying to put you off but rather am explaining that the very high fee is not for speed alone."

Minelli did not appear to be put out. He waved the picture he was holding. "Any kids?"

"Adult and married. They don't live with him. I'd like you to get him by tomorrow. He should be straightforward."

"Only a shooting is straightforward, lady. I want you to tell me everything you can, every detail, love life, habits, anything, about these three people. I mean, have any of them reasons to be suicidal? Suicide doesn't hold up unless the cops can uncover something to hang their shields on."

Ulla pointed to the pictures of an attractive woman and a young, weak-mouthed man, and said, "Three suicides will be as suspicious as three murders."

"Ma'am, now you *are* trying to teach me my business and I find that offensive. This guy, here, this first one you gave me, I guess he's got no cause to knock himself off?"

"None at all that I know of."

"Then, maybe we can invent one. Now leave it to me. Give me everything you've got. I'm a good listener."

18

WHEN the need arose they were taken from the cellar, separately, always with both guards and with a gun at their back. Max and Jurgen made it clear from the start that they would enjoy either prisoner attempting to make trouble.

It was their open, bullying manner which gave Eddie the notion that Ulla and her colleagues had left. And both he and Raya thought they had heard car engines. At one stage the guards came to change the gas can in the fading lamp and they took back with them one of the larger cylinders that were along the wall by the steps.

The presence of the bug still hung over them. They had conversed a good deal in close proximity whispers but it had become physically tiring, squatting in the middle of the aisle with no support, trying to keep their voices down.

When blankets were thrown at them they supposed they were expected to settle down for the night. It signalled a respite.

Raya climbed up to the bug again to wrap the piece of cloth around it, unaware that it was switched off. But they felt much freer to talk and could now lean back against the racks and obtain a small degree of comfort.

When they were reasonably sure that the guards would not return, Eddie suggested that they should look into the possibility of escape. As they were chained to the racks and both guards were armed it seemed a futile suggestion, yet they needed to believe in the possibility.

There was little they could do. The chains restricted movement to a few feet but, even so, they climbed the racks as far as they could go, examined every cavity within reach, looking for anything that might make a weapon or break the locks of their chains, but all they could find were three empty winebottles.

Eddie raised them in turn to see if there was a drop of wine left but they were bone dry. He placed them in the holes behind him.

Raya reached for her blanket and placed it round her shoulders. She shivered. It was going to be an uncomfortable night.

They faced each other. Silence set them apart again. The earlier need to talk, the comfort they had derived from it, had gone. They were left with their own thoughts and the reminder that, in spite of their common peril, they were strangers.

Eddie was not sure what had happened to produce this open despondency. He wanted to talk to Raya, to try to raise her spirits, but found that he could not. He supposed that the almost fruitless search had depressed them.

"Cheer up," he said.

Raya tried an unconvincing smile. "I was thinking of my mother."

"Apart from your grandfather being an uncle of Jo Stalin's son, what else was he? What did he do?"

"He was Chairman of the Komitet Gosudarstvennoy Bezopasnosti."

"Sounds good."

"The KGB."

"Are you serious?"

"Oh yes. He was for many years."

It was impossible for Eddie to connect Raya with such a man. He realised that he was staring at her but he could not help it.

Now she smiled more fully. "It's all right. I have the same reaction from everyone. He must have been a monster."

"And was he?"

"Not to me. He was the kindest person."

"And to others?"

"Until recently that question would have greatly offended me."

"I'm sorry."

"Don't be. I don't know about the others. If he was anything like Stevinski is now, I would prefer not to know."

"We could do with some of your grandfather's old resources now, though, to get us out of here."

Raya suddenly burst into tears. She was at once embarrassed, trying to cover her face and to turn it from him. The outburst had taken her unawares, the despair bursting from her without warning.

"It's all right, Raya." He crawled towards her.

"Stay away." The tears were flowing through her fingers. "I'm so ashamed." She moved back, easing round the corner of the rack so that he could not reach her.

"Come here," he called. "Come back." The chain prevented him from going further and his outstretched hands could not reach her. "Raya, please come here. Is it a crime to cry in Russia?" He strained at the chain and chafed his ankle. He wanted to comfort her but did not know how. From where he lay stretched out he could just see the stone steps leading up to the door. "You bastards," he bawled, "you lousy bastards." And the words echoed round the cellar, finding the hollows and the ceiling arches and overlapping as they faded to a senseless whimper.

Clive Harper flew back to Idaho with no intention of contacting Moscow. Ulla had been too perceptive when she had suggested that he was afraid for his own position. In any event, the chain of command was too complicated for him to send a signal himself. There was no way that a reply could be through in forty-eight hours and it would all be a waste of time; he knew what the answer would be.

He had been introduced to Ulla by a Russian he knew vaguely who worked in the United

Nations and was a finance expert. So was Harper, moderately, but he had left banking for reasons which were still obscure. Along the line he had done odd jobs for Moscow, nothing really important, but anything to make some money.

Ulla had been looking for someone to safeguard the interests of a client of hers who had just bought or had taken a sizeable interest in an Idaho bank. It was a small bank but to Harper it presented an opportunity to get back into banking where he really belonged.

Ulla interviewed him and obtained a non-shareholding directorship for him. He was paid on a par with the other directors but it soon became evident, not from Ulla but from the New York contact, that he was really needed for something else. He had been set up but this did not worry him in the least. On top of his director's salary, he received an appreciable annual fee from the Russians. Not directly from them, of course, it came through in various ways from occasional gambling wins to fees as an adviser to other companies.

Harper was never happier. He was suddenly affluent, had a job he enjoyed and was able to use external influence in a way that gave him considerable pleasure and extra income. He bought a secluded house, a few miles from Blackfoot. The comparative isolation was not sought solely for prestige, but mainly because of the nature of the clandestine life he led.

Once Ulla had arranged his board appointment, she disappeared from the scene. He had always assumed that she must know that the Russian of the United Nations was more than he appeared to be. But she did not interfere. For almost three years now he had been accountable only to a man in Washington; the New York contact had also disappeared from view.

Harper was musing on this background to his present situation only because Ulla had sprung to life again so unexpectedly, and, unlike their first meeting, now threatened to take away what she had given.

It had been a simple matter for him to discover, soon after his appointment, that the purchaser of the Idaho bank was the Zeitlinger Bank in Zürich. That did not mean anything; Harper knew all about fiduciary accounts. The Zeitlinger had a solid reputation. He was not sure where Ulla fitted into this until their recent meeting when she had blatantly proclaimed that she had bought the Idaho bank.

As he saw it, the worst that could happen to him was that he could lose his directorship but a dismissal would have to be explained and compensation for unwarranted loss of office would have to be paid. It would not change his other interest one bit. Not now.

So, as Harper approached his home town, he believed that he had little to lose by hanging on and in this way most likely things would achieve a status quo. Ulla could do her worst.

By the time he reached home it was late and he was tired after the flight. His wife gave him a peck on the cheek and a packaged meal and went back to watching television. His present position in life sustained their marriage; he because he needed the aura of respectability and she because he provided her needs and she could hold her own in social circles. Otherwise they led their own lives without endangering their local image. Money was the linchpin.

June Harper conveyed the quiet smug satisfaction that Harper himself disguised so well. Contentment oozed from her as she watched the screen in the undoubted comfort of the lounge, while she pecked at a box of fudge; her weakness for sweet things showed at her waistline but she was otherwise not unattractive.

The following evening was virtually the same routine except that dinner was earlier and they ate it together. June was due to go to a charity meeting later, and Harper wanted to watch a baseball game on television.

They were in the middle of their meal when the door bell rang. June Harper threw down her napkin in annoyance, glanced at her husband hopefully before getting up. She opened the front door and Minelli pushed a silenced gun under her flabby chin and said, "Don't scream or I'll blow your throat out."

June almost collapsed. Her legs lost feeling and a scream was impossible as her throat seized up.

"Back in slowly. There's a good girl." Minelli followed June into the hall and another man came in after him. When they were in the hall the second man quietly closed the front door; he was wearing gloves and he was armed.

While June was trying to recover from the shock the second man came behind her and taped a gag over her sagging mouth. The two men bundled her into the dining room from where Harper had just called out to ask her who was there. Her widened, petrified eyes above the gag stared at Harper across the table as Minelli said, "On your feet. She gets it if you so much as breathe heavily."

Harper rose shakily, holding on to the chair. "Is it money?"

"It sure is. Is there a study?"

Harper nodded. It was all he could do.

"Lead the way and don't do anything stupid."

Harper eased his way round the table unable to take his gaze from the terror in June's eyes and the gun at her head.

In the small study, Minelli said, "Sit behind the desk. Make yourself comfortable. That's it. Sam will tape you. It won't hurt."

Sam came behind the chair and taped Harper's mouth. He remained behind Harper with his gun at his head.

Minelli said to June, "Stand about there,

ma'am, just in front of the desk. That's fine."
And he shot her through the head.

As his wife collapsed in front of him Harper
rose from his seat and silently screamed. Sam
made no attempt to stop him but he kept a hand
lightly on Harper's shoulder. Minelli knew what
would happen next; reaction to terror and shock
was nothing new to him.

Harper, poised awkwardly between chair and
desk, stared in horror at the rumpled heap that
only seconds ago had been his wife. The inert
lump twitched once like an electric shock through
blubber, and then Harper collapsed back on to
his chair, paralysed with fright, his thoughts
already on himself.

Minelli unscrewed the silencer and came round
the other side of the desk to keep Harper on the
chair with one powerful hand. "Are you right
handed or left?" asked Minelli politely. Harper
could not reply but his right hand moved forward
on the desk. Minelli grasped the hand and
clamped it round his own gun.

Even at that point Harper was so numbed that
he could not anticipate what was to happen next.
He vaguely thought that they were trying to plant
his wife's murder on him. It was not until Sam
grabbed him from the other side and Minelli
relentlessly raised his hand with the gun in it that
he belatedly realised what was about to happen.

Harper's brain almost burst from sheer terror.
"*No*," he screamed, "*no*," but the tape muffled

356

the scream. He struggled like a madman but the two powerful men had little problem in clamping him to the chair. Harper fought to stop his hand coming up but he could not counter Minelli's strength. He was crying, he knew it. Everything was misted. When the gun reached his temple he was on the verge of fainting; he had never known such utter terror.

Minelli said quietly, "Move a bit, Sam, or you'll land half his brains."

There was a roar, a shattering, searing pain like a bomb going off in his head and that was the last sensation Clive Harper experienced. His quivering body fell forward on the desk as, with perfect timing, Minelli and Sam let the body go.

The professional killers moved quickly. Minelli took some glossy, ultra obscene photographs from his pocket. He laid one or two on the desk and wedged one under Harper's shattered head. He took three photographs to June, impressed her prints on them, squeezed one into a plump hand, and dropped the other two by her body.

Sam was getting agitated. "Someone might have heard the shot."

But Minelli was unconvinced. "Too far out. I couldn't use the silencer on him, the scorch marks on the temples would have been muted. And I couldn't leave the silencer on the gun, it would have looked wrong." He stared around critically. Satisfied, he said, "The cops can take it anyway they like; either he or she was the dirty pervert."

And then, "OK, let's get the tapes off. I'll do him and you do her. Make sure there's no residue of gum; rub the skin with your finger if there is."

Minelli callously lifted Harper's head up by the hair to remove the gag. With the tip of his finger he adjusted the position of the bloodied photograph under the head before letting it fall back on the desk. When he was satisfied that Sam had finished, he said, "Now we clear the dinner table and bung the plates in the dishwasher."

They moved to the kitchen, placed the half-eaten food in the waste disposal and switched it on, then loaded the dishwasher, inserted the powder, and set the programme.

Before they left, Sam gave Minelli an admiring glance; he thought of everything.

When Phil Gates arrived at Langley, he obtained a quick hearing from Lewis Turner, his departmental head. Turner did not want to hear about fatigue and jet-lag from Gates, he had had a bad night and was due for another late one. He called for the background of the matter; did Gates think his trifling problem had any significance in the grand scheme of things? Gate's operation was a sideshow on nice neutral territory. Turner downed his Alka Seltzer and blearily told Gates to get on with it.

Gates said offensively, "You sure you're ready for me? I mean, I don't want to disturb your sleep."

Turner raised his head to stare across the chrome and plastic desk. He adjusted his tie with shaking fingers and pushed back his silvering hair. "I don't like your tone, Phil."

"This insignificant backwater of mine is of considerable value and I don't want it playing second fiddle to a hangover. We've got to discuss knocking off a guy."

Turner rubbed his temple. "I'm listening."

"I'll cut the technical crap down as much as possible. There's a French company near Grenoble that is ahead of our own research in energy saving in recycling. A new hot rolling mill uses 45% less energy than a conventional mill to produce aluminium sheet. This is an enormous saving. They are also far advanced in ions. A beam aimed at metal can project on to it a thin integral alloy layer. This reduces vast quantities of expensive metals. Now I'm talking about a private company doing top secret government stuff."

"Who's your contact?"

"We have a man on the board. A guy called Wegel has an indirect financial stake in this French company and he knocked off one of our boys who was lifting too much dirt about him. Instead of retaliating we had enough on him to see the advantage of applying the black. He had sufficient holding to get a very useful man on the board. There was no problem except the delay at getting a man with the right qualifications."

Gates's throat had started to dry and he asked hoarsely, "Have you got a sandwich and a drink?"

Turner phoned through an order. He was listening closely without so far being too influenced.

Gates continued, "Now this French company exports to the Soviet Union. There's a strong business liaison between the two countries which naturally interests us."

Turner was taking more interest now. "Are you saying that the French are passing this breakthrough on to the Russians?"

"They might be. That's not my point. Our man on the board has established a good working relationship with one of the Soviet scientific advisers. We've been lifting some extremely interesting information from him. That, plus the fact that we're pilfering the French advancement and are also watching, with more than a passing interest, which way they are applying this advancement, makes the operation well worthwhile. We're gaining from both ends."

"So what's the problem?"

Gates did not answer at once. He wanted to make sure that Turner was fully aware of what he was saying. "All this is on file. I've short cut to fill you in but there's plenty more if you look it up." He closed his eyes wearily for a second. "The problem is this. Wegel is one of three who form an influential consortium. Suddenly, the

British and the Russians are sniffing around the consortium. Both, it seems, have dug up something about the original holding. Wegel is worried sick that if they dig deep enough it will all blow up in his face."

"You mean the consortium is crooked?"

"No. I don't know how they came by the money in the first place. It's not important to us. But if enquiries start branching out along the lines I've just mentioned, there could be a lot of blowback. We could get smut all over our faces, another cold war with the French, blaring propaganda from the Russians and we'd lose a valuable Soviet contact. Wegel wants to cut our tail off, dispense with the man on the board."

"*Kill him?*"

"What else can you do with him? If he's winkled out, it comes back to Wegel and to us, and the French and the Soviets will make a repeat impossible. Get rid of him. Nothing to find. When the British and Soviets discover nothing, they'll eventually back out. We wait a while; then find another man for Wegel to appoint. It's the only safe way."

Turner sat back, his hangover dismissed. There was a knock at the door and sandwiches and a can of beer were brought in. While Gates ate hungrily, Turner said, "It needs thinking about. There's a lot to lose."

"A temporary loss on the one hand, a major

blow up on the other." The words came out with bread confetti.

"Leave it with me, Phil."

"Wegel wants action."

"Maybe he's overreacting. Are you really able to pull him in for homicide."

"Oh, sure. What we don't know we can manufacture. But the guilt is there, and for more than just the murder. That's why he's been so co-operative."

"If the British will declare their interest, we may know what the Soviets have in mind."

Gates wiped his mouth, still chewing. "The British blocked us on the first enquiry. I don't know what they're at. Wegel is a hard case. He doesn't panic easily."

"Is he having you on?"

Gates shrugged. "He's tried before. Not this time. He's worried and only he knows what else he's got to hide. Look, it's too good a situation to shelve. Give him the benefit of the doubt. Cut our losses now, rebuild later. It wouldn't surprise me if Wegel has plans to take over the consortium."

"I'll have to refer upstairs. I'll let you know."

"Shit. We're gonna lose the lot. I want to know before I go back. Wegel is likely to do it himself if we hedge."

The sweat drenched Eddie. Although tall, he did not consider himself a powerful man. He had exerted every ounce of his strength to try to raise the end support to which he was chained. If he could raise it about an inch he could free the chain. It would still be anchored to his leg but he would be mobile, and could release Raya. He strained at the support until he thought his head would burst.

"You'll hurt yourself." Raya could see the veins standing out on his temple.

Eddie leaned forward against the rack, his breath rasping. "Yeah," he said at last. "The whole bloody rack is fastened to the walls but the stanchions aren't cemented in." He slid down to his knees, slowly turned to face her, and struck the ground in frustration. "There was give," he explained, head lolling from the effort. "But only just. I could spit."

"You did your best."

"Sure. Superman." He was disgusted with himself.

"Perhaps we can trick them."

Various ruses had already crossed his mind but he had dismissed them one after the other as useless.

As the sweat dried on him and his breathing returned to normal, he realised that they were exactly as they had been: chained and waiting for the return of their three captors. The only surprise was that they were still alive. Insurance, he thought, no more. He looked across at Raya, and her sympathetic expression gave him a kind of comfort he could not explain. "Was your grandfather ever in London?" he asked to break the silence.

"I don't know. He spoke good English."

They were suddenly staring at each other intensely as if locked by the same thought. Some of the inconsistencies of Nakentov's death formed subliminal patterns in Raya's mind. Eddie's voice endorsed her own wandering thoughts.

"Could they have met? In London?"

And then she remembered that he *had* been to London. Long before she was born. He had barely talked of it; rather had it slipped out one day and he had then veered from the subject. Yet he had not minded talking of some of the other countries he had visited. "He *was* there," said Raya. "I can just about remember his mentioning it. Oh, so long ago."

"In the twenties?"

"I don't know."

"We're both thinking the same thing."

"That he might have known your aunt?"

"That they might have been lovers. Nakentov could have been Lubov."

It was too much to believe. That possibility raised so many others. Raya shook her head. It needed thinking about.

"Dranrab could have been their nest egg. Before it went wrong," persisted Eddie.

"No. *No.* That's impossible." It had to be impossible for that meant they intended to elope.

And that in turn meant . . . "No. You go too far."

Observing her distress, and perhaps some of its cause, Eddie said, "You're probably right." His head shot up. "Hold it. Somebody's coming."

The front car drove on full beams, oblivious of the one behind it without lights.

In the second car Minelli had complete faith in Sam's driving. Sam had once been a rally driver and had coped with most conditions, bad lighting among them.

"If they take to a main street I'll have to use lights," Sam pointed out, "unless we want to be picked up."

"It won't matter on a main street, there'll be other cars. But if they're gonna do what I think they're gonna do, main streets are out."

Minelli was right. The front car's headlights picked out well-used tyre tracks and, as they climbed, the brush on their flanks grew higher and wilder, interspersed by young spruce that broke up the beams into light and shadow.

"Pretty," commented Minelli. "All that green stuff and the lights brushing over it. Changes the colour."

Sam smiled. "You're a goddam' poet."

"I like the stuff," said Minelli. "Soft, like feathers drooping from wings in that light."

"Jesus," exclaimed Sam unbelievingly. "Where d'you get it from?"

"Hold it," snapped Minelli. The front car's brake lights came on. Sam pulled up behind it, expertly judging distances in the dark. He switched off.

"Wait," Minelli said patiently.

The red brake lights, two sets of three, hung like warning lamps, glowing out from the pitch dark cast by night and cosseted by the forest ahead. Stars probed the higher foliage. Minelli and Sam sat still. When the brake lights went out, as though suddenly smothered by the trees, Minelli glanced at his luminous watch. "Let them enjoy themselves," he said reasonably. With Minelli everything was a matter of precise timing.

After a few minutes Minelli said, "OK. Bring the hose."

They followed the flattened tracks. There was the faintest impression, a vague paleness where the ground had lost its growth through constant use. They made little sound. As they neared the car they could hear it groaning on its springs and were surprised to find the engine was ticking over.

Minelli signalled Sam down and both men crouched as Minelli whispered, "They've made it easier for us." He grinned in the darkness. "They've got the heater on."

The two men crawled forward towards the hatchback estate, the exhaust pumping out fumes in soft coughs. Sam fixed the pipe over the exhaust. Minelli crept forward to the driver's side and cautiously peered through the window, a hand cupped each side of his face.

There was no light in the car but he could just make out the blur of partially clothed bodies, stretched out and writhing in the back. With utmost caution he opened the offside front door, wound down the window about two inches, and quietly pushed the door shut, holding the catch before slowly releasing it. He was aided by the noise of the engine ticking over and the blast of the heater fan.

Sam had crept up behind with the pipe and Minelli put the nozzle through. They then blocked up the window gap with old rags and squatted to wait, guns in hand.

Minelli reflected that it was not often that everything went so well. Rushed jobs could turn out to be easy, well-planned ones could turn sour. In the end it made no difference either way. He had expected that they would have to take the lovers from the car one at a time at gunpoint, and, while he held them, Sam would force the pipe into their mouths, afterwards putting them back in the car. They still might have to if the lovers realised what was happening but danger was far from their thoughts.

After some time the movement in the car became slower and eventually stopped. There was no hurry now; they had all night. Minelli was used to waiting, quite content to stay there without uttering a word, uninfluenced by Sam's growing impatience.

When he was satisfied he rose to shine a flashlight through the window: "Looks OK." He opened the rear door and at once could smell the fumes. The build up of carbon monoxide was enormous. Holding his breath he leaned forward to feel for each pulse on the interlocked bodies, being careful not to disturb them. When he was satisfied he drew back, slammed the door, turned his back to the car and took great gulps of air.

"What a way to go," commented Sam enviously.

Minelli opened the driver's door, pulling it right back, the pipe still gushing fumes and held in place by the window. He pulled out the rags and then repacked them from the inside of the door before closing it. "A discerning cop would know the difference," he commented drily.

They walked slowly back to their own car. Minelli said, "He's got almost a full tank of gas; it could keep going for hours."

"One to go," said Sam, his mind on the next hit.

"Let's do it now," replied Minelli. He turned in the darkness, placed a friendly hand on Sam's shoulder, "I think we're entitled to one robbery with violence, don't you? And then you can have your second fifty grand. That's top money, Sam."

Bill Savage was at a great disadvantage. He had

no idea, apart from Eddie's and Ray Barrow's description, of what Ulla Krantz looked like. Eddie had also said that she wore a wig which made recognition almost impossible. Nor was it so easy to get information from the staff of a hotel with the standing of the Baur au Lac. He needed a photograph of all three members of Tinsal; with no police record of Wegel, and the ageing Hartmann apparently only coming to life in the sixties, the task was hopeless.

All Savage could do was to hang around the hotel as inconspicuously as possible and hope to get some sort of lead.

When the elegant woman crossed the foyer the same day that Savage arrived in Zürich, she caught his eye. In a hotel like this, beauty was not rare. Dark glasses in November were. Both Eddie and Barrow had mentioned them.

Savage followed her on speculation to the airport. From the overnight bag she carried, he guessed that she was booking a short trip and was surprised to find, after his enquiries, that she had booked to Paris with an onward connection requested for the next day's Concorde flight to New York. Savage telephoned London straight away.

Sir George Seymour traded on the sometimes robust rivalry that festered between the FBI and the CIA in America. He did not want the CIA interfering with his own enquiries about Dranrab in Switzerland; he saw this as intrusion. The FBI, on the other hand, were concerned with *internal* American affairs. Not wanting to show his own hand, Seymour obtained the help of a Deputy Assistant Commissioner at Scotland Yard to telephone an equally high-ranking officer of the FBI, New York office. He gave details of Ulla Krantz and asked for a tail to be placed on her when she arrived at Kennedy Airport.

Savage's despairing hunch had better results than he could have hoped for.

When Ulla returned to Zürich, she entered her suite at the Baur au Lac to find a sealed envelope on the dressing-room table. She assumed that the maid had placed it there.

It was a note from Wegel suggesting that the two of them should meet before the seventy-two hour deadline. She had no objection to meeting Wegel alone but realised that they were beginning to take sides.

Ulla felt better for having taken care of her American problem. If Minelli did his job properly, some of her worries would be solved before they could get out of hand. She showered, and then called Wegel's room on the house phone but he was not in. Ordering a light lunch in her room, she found herself still preoccupied with the shadowy doubts she had taken with her to America.

She had just rung room service to have her lunch tray removed when there was a knock at the door. It was Wegel, who had taken a chance on her being in. When the maid had collected the tray, Ulla and Wegel sat down to talk.

"I had your note," she said. "You were not around when I rang."

Wegel gave no explanation of his movements. Nor did he ask her where she had been. That was how it should be, how it had always been, and why the partnership had worked so well for so long. And yet he was here presumably without the knowledge of Hartmann. He was uncomfortable, unwilling to start now that he was confronting her.

Ulla sat cross-legged, watching him closely, worrying because she had an inkling of what he might say. The tick in his face was like a pulse. He rubbed it as he always did under stress.

Wegel asked awkwardly, "Why are we so damned worried? We know that Tinsal is solid, properly formed and legal. So it's about Dranrab, isn't it; the forerunner? There's something about it that one of us must know. It's time the others knew. We must understand precisely what the danger is."

"I'm not worried about Dranrab," Ulla replied evenly. "I say once more, I inherited my share quite legally."

"But did your benefactor?"

And that was the point that had always troubled her. "I can't be expected to know that. It doesn't matter."

"It does matter. Your innocence does not excuse any earlier guilt on the part of your benefactor. If there is a guilt."

"Why are you here without Rolf?"

"Because I think he knows more than either of us."

"If you believe that, you must have known it all along."

"I've known some of it; guessed at some."

"Why didn't it worry you before?"

"There was no danger before. Who cared? It worked like a dream. But now it's threatened and we've got to stop any leaks before they become a flood."

"You're convinced that Rolf knows so much that it can be dangerous to us?"

"Yes. I think you do too."

"Rolf represents no danger to me."

Wegel inclined his head. "That's one of the things I've never really understood. But I don't mean personal danger; what he *knows* is dangerous. We might lose the lot."

Ulla thought it over. "You haven't told me what it is that he knows."

"I think we should face him with it."

Ulla smiled. "You think you can make him talk? Anyway, if he did, and you are right, what then?"

"We'd have to get rid of him to protect ourselves."

Very carefully, Ulla placed one hand on top of

the other to keep them steady. "Has it come to that? After so long?"

"Only if I'm right. But I can tell you one thing, his name is not Rolf Hartmann, it's Jost Schnell."

19

WHEN Wegel left Ulla he went to meet Phil Gates. Gates's message was brief. His superiors wanted time to think. Just a few days. They were not against the killing in principle but once done the damage was irreversible. The odds had to be weighed sanely.

Wegel kept his temper but insisted that they should walk again. Once out of earshot of others, Wegel swore continuously for some minutes before saying, "The stupid, blind bastards. No wonder the Russians make rings round you. I'll have to get it done myself."

"Gustav, listen. What difference can a few days make?"

"I don't intend to find out. You said you'd fix it." Wegel was spitting his words out, pale faced but livid.

"I promised my best shot, and I gave it. I believed you. I still do." And then, in despair, "For Chrissake, Gustav, I'm dealing with guys who can see their own reflections in the shine on their pants. I'm dealing with desk jockeys. Wait. Hang on a bit."

They walked on in silence, Wegel thinking rapidly. He glared at a street clock then stopped walking. He faced Gates angrily.

"Listen to me. I know that I'm right. If the balloon goes up, I'm no more use to you and you'll pull me in or have me put down. And if you don't the Russians or the French will."

"We wouldn't do that to you."

"You mean *you* wouldn't. But those faceless bastards behind you would." Wegel stopped quickly as a young couple went past. He moved back to give them room.

"I'm not losing what I've got, Phil. I'm not having leads pointing towards me. Too many people are trying to winkle us out."

Wegel turned and walked away rapidly, head down, face grim.

Once in his hotel room, Wegel moved quickly. Unless travelling by regular airline, he always carried a heavy Styer 9mm semi-automatic pistol. He had used the same gun on Phil Gates's colleague four years ago, when the American had stumbled across his background when looking into something entirely different connected to his father's past. The gun was packed in an old, gutted shaving pouch which was kept in a false compartment of one of his cases.

He checked on local air-charter companies and hired a Cessna to fly him to Geneva. He also booked a self-drive car to meet him at Geneva Cointrin Airport.

Wegel took a cab to Zürich Kloten. There was some delay there while papers were sorted out and signed and he paid in advance. He carried with him one small grip. The Swiss pilot was familiar with the run and seemed to know every peak. The small plane droned on, the weather improving as they headed south west.

The car was waiting at the airport; more documents, more cash, and then he was driving towards the French border. It was dark by now and the clouds were reassembling round Mont Blanc to shed some biting showers.

The border check was cursory and, once in France, Wegel settled down to a steady drive. The road was not cluttered but nor was it straight through the Savoie Alpes. The wipers cleared and smeared alternatively as the rain became heavier. The twin beams converged ahead, crystallising the water drops, reflecting back off the road, forming a dark tunnel either side of him. It was like being in a mobile prison and the relevance of the thought did not escape him.

He followed the signs to Chambery. In front of him the dials glowed with a phosphorus green, and he considered just how far he could influence Ulla against Hartmann without betraying too much of himself. They all had something to hide. And they all had an immense amount to lose, as well as money. They had enjoyed a good run, but from now on he would feel safer without the others.

He passed through Chambery and followed the signs to Grenoble. The rain eased and the wipers were sticking. He switched them off. During the whole drive Wegel barely thought of Reynaud, the man he wanted to see—as if he was already dead. His nerves were steady, as they always were when he was in control of his own destiny. After tonight it must be Hartmann first, then Ulla. That should steady his nerves forever. The tick in his face was quiet, a good sign.

The house was the north side of Grenoble. It was on high ground with magnificent views in daytime as far as Mont Blanc. It was a long time since Wegel had been here.

The beams swept up the tarmac drive, basting the white walls of the old house, picking up the twin stone lions straddling the entrance. The porch light was on. It was night but not yet late. Wegel circled the impressive drive and pulled up facing the gates he had just come through. He switched off the engine and removed the gun from under the rear seat.

When he climbed out and approached the wide porch, he carried the gun behind his back. Standing by the studded oak door Wegel could hear music. He rang the bell and heard the chimes, hoping that the daily help had not become a live-in servant.

The portly, middle-aged man who opened the door did not at first recognise Wegel. When he did, he seemed surprised but a smile of welcome struggled through the folds of his fleshy face. "Gustav. What are you doing here?"

Wegel smiled back but remained where he was. "I don't want to intrude. If you have guests . . . ? I'm on my way to Marseilles and it seemed silly to pass by without calling."

"Come in. There's just Maria and me. Watching television." Reynaud grinned sheepishly as if it were a crime.

Wegel stepped in and he half turned as Reynaud closed the door. "Just one drink and I must go."

Reynaud had no more liking for Wegel than Wegel had for him. But Wegel was his lifeline, even if it was the Americans who benefited. Reynaud enjoyed his position of trust and duplicity; it required a special breed. He stood back to usher Wegel forward and was shot through the heart as he did so. Wegel was on his way to the drawing room, guided by the sound of the television, before Reynaud hit the floor.

The roar of the gun brought Maria to her feet as Wegel entered the room. She turned away from the television, a slim, aristocratic, handsome woman, saw the gun, and, with dignity and a remarkable display of nerve, said coolly, "Put that ridiculous thing down."

Wegel shot her, saw her stagger back against the television set, observed the oozing blood where she held her stomach in agony. Before she folded, he fired again. This time she slumped and did not move. Her grey hair had fanned out like a veil to cover her death. He went back into the hall to ensure that Reynaud, too, was dead.

Back in the drawing room the television screen was performing a crazy pattern of coloured bars and brief disseminated images; Maria must have knocked the controls. Wegel then started on a jaunt of quiet destruction, pulling out drawers, breaking the odd vase. He removed jewellery from upstairs and money from downstairs and left two dead people and a ransacked house behind him.

As he drove back to Geneva, he was totally unaware that what he had done was similar to the final task of Minelli and Sam. They had added more refinement, like a deliberately dropped out-of-state coach ticket, to mislead investigation. But he had never heard of Minelli.

Once past Chambery, Wegel saw the splendid irony of using the same gun as he'd used on one of Gates' compatriots. Even if the French Sûreté, by some outlandish chance, passed on a ballistic report to the Americans, he did not believe they would acknowledge a match. Wegel was strongly convinced that he had broken the long chain of blackmail and that Gates would not act on his threat of reprisal. Anyway, it was done. Before he reached Geneva, in the dead of night, he drove to a quiet spot on the lake and hurled the gun into the water. He drove some miles further on and did the same with the jewellery he had taken from the house. He was back in his hotel room by late morning.

Sir George Seymour had not heard of Minelli, either, until he received the report from the Deputy Assistant Commissioner at New Scotland Yard who had been so helpful to him.

The FBI had picked up Ulla's trail at Kennedy Airport. They did not know the man she met at the Americana Hotel but they gave a description. They did know the man she met at the United Nations building: Art Minelli, a known but unconvicted hit man. He had twice been arrested as a juvenile, once for car stealing and once for GBH—an efficient, clever killer. The FBI had followed them to his apartment.

Ulla had been followed back to the airport but, although Minelli's block had been staked out, contact with him had been lost. There were a good many exits from the block and Minelli might have his own way out. The FBI were sorry about it and covered their embarrassment by adding that, when all said and done, they had only been asked to keep an eye on Ulla.

The Harper shootings hit the local headlines in the way that Minelli had intended. Had the gruesome business and unsavoury revelations not remained a local affair, the FBI might, just possibly, have tuned in on his description. But it was a long shot that never came off.

However, Ulla having flown to America to

consort with a high-class killer gave Seymour sufficient conviction that he was on the right track. Eddie Tyler had proved to be a useful weapon. A sack of worms was beginning to split wide open. He relayed the police report to Savage with an urgent request to keep close to Ulla and he sent over a Scot named Malcolm Jackson to help him.

Max came into the cellar, bored and looking for trouble. He swaggered between Eddie and Raya and softly called them vile names in German. He had pushed his gun into a pocket as if to tempt them into doing something rash so that he could justify retaliation.

It was the first time that a guard had come down alone. Closing his ears to the gross provocation Eddie wondered where Jurgen was; Max had closed the cellar door behind him.

The only way to deal with him was to ignore him. Eddie and Raya glanced at each other to convey the mutual message. Say nothing. The young neo-Nazi was boiling to go. Having tasted the blood of Ray Barrow, he wanted more.

When he saw that he was getting no reaction, he spat at both of them and called them all the filth he could dredge from the cesspit of his mind. He mouthed abuse, his cold eyes bright with hate.

They continued to ignore him and his voice rose to near hysteria. He's mad, thought Eddie, and he could see that Raya was nervous, but she had the sense not to move away because it would only incense Max further. They endured his ranting, then his expression changed, his gaze shifting slyly to Raya.

"Stand up and take your clothes off," he ordered her.

Raya stared back unmoving, glancing over at Eddie.

"Take your clothes off you Russian whore." Max spun round to Eddie who was squatting in his usual place against the rack. He pointed to Raya. "I'm going to show you the only thing she's fit for. She will be honoured."

"Don't you think you'll be tainted?" Eddie asked to try and dissuade him.

Max sneered. "Tainted, yes. But I will plant in her the seed of Aryan purity." He turned back to Raya with a swagger, careful to move beyond Eddie's reach. "Undress, you bitch, or I'll rip them off. Don't you understand I'm doing you a favour?"

Raya eased back as Max advanced. Both guards had learned the extent the chains would stretch and Max knew that Eddie was out of range. He reached forward and ripped the front of Raya's dress. Scared now, she tried to get round the corner of the rack but Max inserted a hand in her exposed bra and mockingly pulled her back. He groped at her body and, pulling her to him, pressed himself against her. She tried to get his gun but it was well wedged in his pocket. He arched back and struck her so hard across the face that she fell sideways, half dazed.

When Raya looked up at the slobbering figure above her, he was mockingly holding her bra as if it were a trophy. Her torn dress hung like an open shirt.

"Get up, you whore. Don't pretend you don't want it."

Raya climbed up slowly and caught sight of a frantic signal from Eddie who had climbed to his feet. Max started his coarse groping again and was being carried away by his own rising lust when Raya managed somehow to push him hard away from her. Max fell back several paces, his face white with rage, and Eddie smashed a bottle over his head as soon as he was within range.

Max fell to his knees and Eddie jumped on him. Blood was flowing through Max's blond hair, streaking it pink. Eddie struck at the base of the head with his clenched fist. Max fell sideways. The two blows had stunned him but he had learned his fighting in a tough school.

When Eddie realised that Max was only half out he bent down to measure another blow but Max spun on his hip and kicked Eddie hard in the ribs where he had been kicked before. Eddie doubled with excruciating pain and writhed on the floor as Max kicked him again.

Max climbed to his knees, blood dripping from his forehead and into eyes widened by madness. He watched Eddie's agony and rose to his feet so that he could kick Eddie to death. He staggered a little, put out an arm to steady himself but was too far from the racks to get immediate support. He kept his feet, and half spun round to steady himself. Raya curled her leg round in a wild kick that struck hard in the crotch.

Max screamed in agony and doubled up, hands flying down protectively. He fell to his knees again, body arched. The scream cut through Eddie's pain and he knew that it was now or never. Movement was agonising but he rose, gripped Max round the back of the neck and dug his fingers deep into his throat. Max struggled, making a supreme effort to straighten. He was a terrifying figure with hair and face bloodstained and eyes red and staring as air was cut off from his windpipe.

More powerful than Eddie, and crazed from pain and rage, Max pushed himself up taking Eddie with him. His big hands tore at Eddie's, trying to prise loose the little fingers, to break them and release the stranglehold.

Raya kicked him again, not as effectively as before but enough to bring his hands down. Then she threw herself at him, clinging to the struggling arms, wrapping her legs round his. He threw her off and reached for Eddie's fingers again but Raya dived straight back. She clung on grimly to smother his limbs and Eddie hung on with a madness bordering on Max's. The struggling eased off and still they clung knowing that he would kill them if ever he broke free. He sagged and his face coloured, peripheral veins not visible before now standing out on his head and neck. He heeled over and they held on. They clung on long after he was dead, and when they finally released him all they could do was to collapse on top of him.

Eddie, gasping with extreme pain, stretched out a hand to find Raya. He put his hand on her back and he could feel her panting. He raised his head. Her legs were still entwined with Max's. All three of them were interlocked in a grotesque tableau from which, at the moment, they could not extricate themselves. Raya's head came up slowly, inches from Eddie's, and they stared at each other in fear and silence.

Eddie stroked the back of her head, then cupped it with his hand. He could barely speak: "We've killed him."

Raya pushed herself up, unconscious of her exposed breasts now smeared with blood. She reached up to grip Eddie's arm. With hair dishevelled, dress torn, eyes questing and afraid, her appearance stung Eddie into taking her hand and kissing it. The strain of the fight and of what they had done united them in emotional understanding. Raya could find no words. She did not know what to do or to say. She rested her cheek against Eddie's hand as though it provided her only contact with reality.

They had to move. They helped each other up,

dazed by what had happened and afraid to think of the price they would pay. Max, lying between them, face towards the floor, strong hands half curled, might be dead but was still a problem. Eddie stared down, unable to believe that he had strangled a man.

Raya touched him lightly on the arm. "He was about to rape me," she said, providing the motive he so badly needed. "I'm glad he's dead."

So was Eddie, though he still suffered pain where Max had kicked him and the shock of what he had done did not ease. Raya bent down and, with some difficulty, pulled the gun from Max's pocket. She held it in the flat of her hand then passed it, butt first, to Eddie.

He took it without thinking, then said, "I don't know how to use this." He stared numbly at the gun.

"Unless you want me to have it you had better learn," Raya was recovering more quickly than Eddie. She took the gun back, made him watch, as she said, "Safety catch. On, off. Magazine." She released the catch and whipped out the magazine, checking on the number of rounds. She rammed it back again. "Breech."

He watched fascinated as she drew back the breech assembly part way.

"One in the breech, eight rounds in the magazine. She is ready to fire." Raya gave him the gun again. "Just point it."

The very words Ray Barrow had used. But he was dead.

"Where did you learn all that?" he asked.

"My grandfather was a champion shot."

"I suppose he would have been," he murmured, without thinking. "We can't leave him there." He looked down at the body.

"And we can't get him very far. Not with the chains on. Perhaps he has the keys."

Eddie shook off his numbness. He knelt down and went through the pockets, turning the corpse over so that he missed none. He found keys but none fitted the chain locks. The disappointment was sobering.

"What about shooting them off?" Eddie gazed at the gun doubtfully.

"Will you trust me to do it?"

Eddie was taken by surprise, yet he had no qualms. "You can't do a worse job than me."

"It is not easy," said Raya seriously. "The bullet must hit the right place and even then it could ricochet anywhere. There is no guarantee that the lock will break open."

"We've got to try." He handed back the gun.

"We need support for the lock. All we have are the heels of his boots. Do you think you can hold the lock in place?"

Eddie suddenly realised that she meant the lock at his ankle, not the one by the rack. "Christ." And then, "OK, I trust you." And he did and this astounded him too. "You can only shoot my foot off."

He sat down and tugged Max to a convenient position pulling forward one of his legs so that he could rest the lock on the heel of the boot. There was little play on the chain, and the lock was dangerously close to the ankle.

"You can take your hands away but make sure the lock does not move." Raya had come round behind him so there was less risk of him stopping a ricochet. "Hold absolutely still."

Eddie could not take his eyes from the gun which Raya was holding two-handed over his shoulder. He had expected her to place the muzzle against the lock but she was aiming it several inches away. She fired, and his foot shot out as the chain tore at his ankle with tremendous force. He found himself on his back, ankle throbbing, ribs searing as the chain fell away from his leg. "You've done it," he bawled. "You've bloody well done it." He clambered up and gave her a hug. She was smiling with delight.

But the explosion had roared round the cellar like machine-gun fire and, as it subsided, they turned anxiously towards the door.

"Quick," he said. "Now yours."

Max's heel was half off and they turned him over to use the other foot. Eddie helped Raya to place the lock, hoping she would not ask him to use the gun. But she coped well, her chained leg bent, the gun held between her legs. Eddie knelt behind her to support her shoulders. She fired and her leg and body jerked away. Eddie rushed forward, grabbed the lock and it fell open. Raya sat back in relief before he helped her up.

They rubbed their sore ankles and stood up, with an exhilarating feeling of freedom. Raya handed the gun to Eddie, as if to thank him for the use of it and suggesting that he would have done at least as well. He was not fooled but accepted the responsibility.

The cellar door burst open just as they headed towards it. Jurgen, about to rush down the steps, stopped when he saw them, and raised his gun as Eddie fired. The bullet sliced a huge splinter from the door. Jurgen, who had simultaneously caught sight of part of Max's body, ducked, and dived for the door as Eddie fired again. The door slammed. The key turned and there was the sound of bolts being pushed across.

They stood side by side staring up at the door, not moving. Eddie slowly put an arm round Raya's shoulders and she put one round his waist. For a little while they stayed like that, staring up at where Eddie's first shot had struck.

Suddenly the anti-climax hit them. They were still prisoners and were now known to be loose and armed. And they had only five rounds left.

Colonel Utenko rang through to ask if he could see General Stevinski on a matter of some importance. The colonel came in with a file under his arm, although he did not once refer to it. He stood in front of Stevinski's desk, straight backed and serious, and related a story like an actor who had just learned his lines but had yet to put expression into them.

"A series of strange events has just been signalled through from America, Comrade General. They are most disturbing. We had a man named Harper who was a director of a small bank at a small town in Idaho. He and his wife have been found shot dead at their home nearby. They apparently had a row over one of them finding out the other kept obscene photographs. Harper shot his wife then blew his own brains out."

"Can we replace him?"

"I don't know. The control is not ours but that of a sympathetic outsider. But that's not the immediate problem. The following night two lovers, each married to someone else, committed suicide, while in the act of love, by sealing off their car and running a hose from the exhaust."

Stevinski listened a little impatiently but reflected that Utenko would not waste his time.

"That very same night a house, the other side of town from the Harpers, was broken into, money and goods were stolen, and the husband and wife occupants, who apparently surprised the burglars, were killed: one shot, one strangled, both mutilated."

"Am I supposed to make sense of this?" asked Stevinski.

"Please bear with me, General. As far as the Americans know these deaths are unrelated. As you know, over there murder and violence occurs all the time; the number of crimes is almost incalculable. The local police might find it a coincidence that two of the dead worked at the same place, but there would be nothing to connect their deaths.

"We know better. In the Soviet cause, Harper controlled the woman who committed suicide and the man whose house was burgled. The woman bore a child by the man she died with, unknown to her husband, while he was on an eighteen-month posting in the Middle East. She disappeared from the area for several months to have the child which is fostered out in another state. The man who was shot while his wife was strangled was a homosexual. He was discreet, did not pursue one affair, but paid for his weakness whenever it overcame him."

"Not discreet enough to hide it from you, though," Stevinski pointed out.

Utenko smiled. "It was simple. Anyway both Harper's contacts worked at a United States silicon chip research centre. The work is highly secret, very advanced, and is an offshoot of Silicon Valley, in California, the largest electronic chip manufacturers in the world. All the staff salaries are paid by draft, processsed by the bank, which also holds their personal and financial records."

Stevinski sat up. "How long have we been getting these secrets?"

"Two full years of real information. Titbits prior to that. The results were passed straight on to our own scientists. It's a great loss. And no coincidence, I fear."

"You think the FBI got on to them?"

"No. They would have arrested them, made a big public show."

"How did Harper get on the board?"

"The position was created for him. The bank was taken over. As a bank, it is of absolutely no consequence. It is not corporate, has little to do with industrial investments. But it is efficient and it just happens to be there."

"Who took it over?"

"A Swiss bank."

Stevinski shrugged. "That's no surprise. But why would a Swiss bank want to put one of our people on the board? I'm losing the thread."

"The investment was fiduciary. In the bank's name but for somebody else."

"Do we know who this shy buyer is? This very helpful sympathiser?"

"Part of her conditions was that her name would be kept a secret; that it would not be passed on to us here. But that was a naive hope. Her name is Ulla Krantz, West German."

Stevinski stirred his memory. He could vaguely

recall something about this set-up. The results had saved years of experiments. "Presumably, bank records showed payments through the murdered woman's account to the adoptive parents of the child, thus hooking the mother?"

"There was a standing order. She had a separate account from her husband. At the time, Harper went through all the research unit employees accounts; the directors too. He was looking for anything that was suspect; the usual things, big drink bills, alimony, suspect cash withdrawals, anything that could be followed up by investigation. The woman was a highly placed administrator with access to secret documents. The homosexual was a scientist at one of the top secret laboratories there."

"So who killed them?"

"If we knew why, we would know who. Harper received a cable from Switzerland the day before he was killed. The police apparently don't think its relevant. The cable was not found and Harper presumably destroyed it."

"From Switzerland? You say the Krantz woman is German?"

"Yes."

"This is all very odd. Someone wanted to stop top scientific data from reaching us. If the police have taken the deaths at face value—shame of exposure followed by rage and killing, suicides, and robbery and murder—and you are right that they are all murders, then we're dealing with top professionals. We're back to the FBI and the CIA."

Utenko shrugged. "You could be right. But I don't think so. Our people over there are working on it."

"Perhaps the answer doesn't rest there. Do we know anything about this Krantz woman?"

"Very little. We've left well alone. Wealthy helpers are not new. We try not to embarrass them."

"Find out what you can about her. As quickly as you can."

"Yes, General. It's a big blow to us."

"Indeed. That sort of set-up is of immense value."

Stevinski had nothing more to say and gave Utenko a nod of dismissal. When the colonel was halfway to the door, Stevinski raised his head sharply, "What is the name of the Swiss bank?"

"The Zeitlinger in Zürich."

Stevinski froze. He sat still for so long, staring at a point between himself and Utenko, that the colonel was forced to ask, "Are you all right, sir?"

Stevinski stirred. "Yes, I'm all right. You carry on. Find out about the account, partners, anything."

When Utenko had left, Stevinski sat back and reverted to staring into space. The coincidence of the bank being involved was too much to ignore. A terrible thought entered his head; had he, by sending Raya to Switzerland, destroyed a valuable contact? Or was he reading too much into it? It was possible that Raya's enquiries had put pressure on the present holders of Dranrab, or whatever name it now went by, which had resulted in the loss of a highly valuable source of information.

Again, Stevinski was tempted to place the full weight of his organisation behind an investigation of Dranrab and all its ramifications. But the risks of doing so seemed to be increasing. He must tread carefully or he could make matters even worse. Ulla operated from the shadows of the Zeitlinger and he sensed a strange aura surrounding her.

Stevinski by-passed Utenko for his next step. He sent a cable to the "resident" in Berne ordering the assassination of Raya Dubrova. He did not need to give reasons, and the file would show embezzlement of foreign funds and defection while abroad on a compassionate family matter. Raya had done her job. But the irony of him losing such a valuable arrangement by his own action left him feeling bitter and frustrated. How much more might he lose?

20

AFTER leaving Ulla, Wegel went to the small bar to meet Phil Gates. Gates was not his usual self. As if to confirm that he had lost some of his confidence, he had not managed to squeeze into his usual place. It was Wegel who conveyed the assurance as he forced his way to the bar. It was Wegel who ordered the drinks. And it was Gates who wanted to leave the bar and take a walk. Their positions had reversed.

Wegel refused the walk, which puzzled Gates. Then the millionaire asked quietly, "Did you bring it?"

Gates nodded. "But I don't like it."

"Untraceable?"

Gates nodded again. "Guaranteed. What happened to the old one?"

Wegel smiled over his wine glass. "As if you don't know. I got rid of it after seeing Reynaud."

Gates closed his eyes. Even though he had been expecting it, he was shocked and angry; his anger was not directed at Wegel but at his principals in Langley. "So you did it," he observed listlessly. "You're a fool to tell me."

"You'd have found out."

Gates said wearily, "The company has lost heavily over this. But we can still hold the old crime over you—or take our revenge more directly."

"You don't frighten me any more. You've had your pound of flesh. Perhaps I should have done this before; given you what you wanted to keep your hands off me, then terminated the arrangement after a period."

"They won't let it go, Gustav. I warned them and they won't like being wrong."

Wegel seemed not to hear. He said, "I've got to like you, Phil. It's crazy, but I do. I intend to get matters entirely into my own hands. It shouldn't take long, and when I've done it I'll help you again, I don't like the Russians either. But it'll be on my terms."

Gates did not respond. He had never seen Wegel so confident. In a matter of a few days the man had changed completely.

"Are you going to hand it over?" asked Wegel. "Here?"

"If it's wrapped up."

Gates took a thick package from his pocket and Wegel took the gun from him. Gates was not at all sure that he had done the right thing, but it was better than doing nothing. In any event, he had given the gun a full ballistic test; it might be the only way to get back at Wegel.

Paula Menke; Jost Schnell. The two names recurred in Ulla's mind like an hypnotic suggestion. They were a key. Somewhere, at some time, she had encountered them before. She had not heard all Raya had told Eddie but the name Paula Menke had registered, together with Sachsenhausen and Jacob Djugashvili. She already knew, of course, that Raya, apart from the Dranrab enquiries, was looking into the precise fate of Stalin's son. She did not believe the two matters were unconnected. But she did believe that Raya saw them as separate issues.

Ulla was also right in thinking that there was little else to learn from Raya. The answers did not lie with the Russian girl, but she was puzzled why such an innocent young operator had been sent for such a potentially big issue.

Ulla knew she was groping in the dark, but then, so might be the Russians and the British. But something had started them off. Hartmann —Jost Schnell, rather—now in his sixties. Sadist though he might be, Ulla had always felt safe with him. And now Wegel was trying to get her to agree to kill him.

It was true that Hartmann was basically simple. He solved his problems with violence, probably thereby creating more. She had always had the feeling that Hartmann and Wegel did not like each other, but that in itself could be meaningless. In any business association there were colleagues who secretly detested and distrusted each other. Business was fraught with backstabbing.

Certain that neither man would confide in her,

and increasingly convinced that some issues were deliberately being kept from her, Ulla took a precautionary step. She contacted the detective agency she had used to keep an eye on Eddie, and obtained two listening bugs and a receiver. She then offered a hotel maid a substantial bribe to safely plant a bug in Hartmann's and Wegel's rooms.

There was little time left before all three were due to meet later that day, and she could not see any clear-cut solution to the problem of safe-guarding their account. Someone was willing to act outside the law. Sooner or later something would happen to Tinsal's detriment. She stayed in her suite with the door locked, a "do not disturb" sign outside, and the headphones of the receiver loose around her neck.

Bill Savage and Malcolm Jackson shared the duty of keeping an eye on Ulla. With only two of them, it was impossible for them to watch Hartmann and Wegel even if they knew what they looked like. The few times Ulla had shown herself she had been alone. It appeared that she and her colleagues had come to an agreement not to be seen together publicly. They were aware she had met a known killer in New York. And they did not need to be reminded of what had happened to Ray Barrow.

Jackson, a sandy-haired, thick-framed Scot, who looked as though he should play midfield for

Glasgow Rangers, had difficulty making himself inconspicuous. To justify their constant presence in the public rooms of the Baur au Lac, Savage had reserved them a twin-bedded room at the hotel—even though Seymour might have a heart attack over the expenses.

One thing Savage was sure about: the comprehensive stake out at the Hotel Torsa for Eddie's benefit was no longer evident. This could only mean that it was no longer necessary—Eddie was either dead or captive.

They searched the cellar. Against one wall were two large gas cylinders, presumably in reserve for the upstairs heaters and cooking stove, and half a dozen small cylinders for the lamp hanging from a ceiling hook.

From time to time the lamp canister had been changed by Max and Jurgen, usually in the morning or when they brought the food down. Sometime during the night the lamp always went out as the gas expired but Eddie and Raya had got used to the long stretches of darkness. Because they now needed light, Eddie unhooked the fading lamp and fixed a new canister. They had found both matches and a lighter in Max's pockets.

Taking the lamp with them, they continued to explore but only found a few more empty bottles. The only way out was through the cellar door.

Leaving the lamp with Raya, Eddie crept up

the steps to peer through the keyhole but the key was in the lock and he could see nothing but a fraction of daylight. He was satisfied the door was locked and bolted. Nor could one of them hide behind it because it opened outward from the cellar.

Eddie did not think that the two large gas cylinders would induce Jurgen to come down alone if his fuel ran out. He could easily obtain others. Jurgen held all the advantages.

Eddie returned to Raya. With a penknife found on Max she had made a small hole each side of her ripped dress and had cut a small strip from her ruined bra to tie through the holes to hold her dress together.

They were unaware of the carnage their separate enquiries had provoked elsewhere, but they were constantly reminded of the dead body of Max. Between them they carried the body up the steps and stretched it along the top at the foot of the door. There was always a chance that anyone rushing down might trip over it.

It was all they could do. They sat side by side, an arm around each other for warmth, a blanket pulled round their shoulders. Raya suddenly remembered that electric light flex was crudely stapled to the ceiling, terminating at an empty bulb socket near the hook where the lamp had been.

They scrambled up the racks. The flex ran straight across two of the arches and along the wall to disappear through the top of the door. Above the door itself was a concrete lintel forming a narrow shelf. They ripped down the flex as far as the door. As Eddie was about to cut it off there, Raya asked anxiously, "Supposing it's live?"

Eddie hesitated. "If it's live they'd have used it." He cut the flex with the penknife. They doubled the flex to strengthen it, then tied one end round one of Max's ankles. After several attempts, Eddie managed to loop the flex over the lintel and by pulling on the free end pulled Max up by one leg.

Max dangled like a carcass at one side of the door. Holding the flex tight Eddie stooped for Raya to climb on his shoulders. While he held Max in place with some difficulty, Raya tied the free end of the flex round Max's other ankle.

Raya climbed down and she and Eddie pulled at Max until he was central to the door. The sight was gruesome. The legs of the corpse were splayed, feet at almost lintel height, the body stretched down and the two lifeless arms dangled to hang just above the top step.

At the foot of the steps they could see that the body formed a crude shield and would give an immediate and unpleasant shock to anyone opening the door. The weight of the body kept the flex taut and would not be easy to dislodge.

It might provide a few seconds of time, but at

heart they did not really believe that anyone would be foolish enough to open the door.

Having planted the seed of suspicion in Ulla's mind about Hartmann, Wegel accepted a course of no return. He did not believe that the partnership could survive outside pressure. To continue as they had done for years required the same ideal conditions. From now on they would be watching each other, wondering, speculating on which one might break if pressures increased.

The equilibrium they had achieved was now extremely shaky. They could not even agree on dispensing with the Englishman and the Russian girl. At least Ulla could not, and Wegel thought she had her own reasons for not killing them. Had he known of the spate of killings that Ulla had induced in America, he would have acted more positively and much faster.

What did they know about each other? He knew something of Hartmann, but very little about Ulla. And that was part of the reason why it had worked so well. Ignorance of each other kept them apart, creating its own odd brand of mutual respect, and a little mystique that formed its own power. Now it was working the other way, encouraging suspicion.

Wegel contacted Hartmann on the hotel phone. He had tried several times after seeing Ulla, and it was after lunch when he finally raised him. He wanted a few words with Hartmann before they all met.

When Wegel entered Hartmann's suite, he realised with a mild shock that it had been many years since they had really been alone together. And yet, apart from the account, they had a great deal in common. Both were murderers, one was a blackmailer, the other an extortionist. Hartmann did not offer him a drink; he believed in showing his feelings when not under outside scrutiny. He stood in the middle of the room, hands in pockets to try to still them, and an expression of contempt on his face.

"Get it over quick," he snapped.

"May I sit down?" Wegel did not want to sit, not with Hartmann in this mood, but he had to try to change the hostile atmosphere.

Hartmann nodded indifferently and Wegel sat down.

Wegel said quietly, "Drop your aggression, Rolf. We're in trouble. We've got to talk. We're meeting Ulla in a couple of hours; we must put something up."

"I already have. Kill those two young bastards at the villa and anyone else who gets in the way. That's all that will work."

"For a time, perhaps. But we've got to level with one another. What can they come up with about any one of us that might endanger the account? It's time for straight talk, Rolf."

Hartmann stood still, his grey hair combed

back, powerful shoulders hunched, eyes brittle. "OK. I killed your father and you've been blackmailing me over it ever since. And if you hadn't been an unknown eye-witness, and cunning enough to leave evidence in your bank, I'd have shot you the same as I did your old man. That straight talk enough for you?"

The meeting was not going the way Wegel had intended. He rubbed his cheek which felt as if it had red hot wires in it. "Why raise that now? That's not what I had in mind."

"What *did* you have in mind? You want the detail on how I finished Paula Menke—or shot Kurt Retzer? Along with your old man, they were the only ones who could have known what was going on at Sachsenhausen? How straight do you want it? Let's hear from you."

"What's the point of going over old ground? It's what we *don't* know that we've got to winkle out. Ulla, for instance. She's hiding something and it might blow up in our faces. Where did she disappear to the last couple of days?"

"Where did *you* go? Leave her out of it, she's no danger." Hartmann approached Wegel menacingly. "You're the danger. What sort of bastard will cash in on his father's murder? You're worse than he was—and he would have done to me what I did to him."

"Is that what you've been thinking all these years?"

"It's what I've always thought. We made peace

because it paid us. All of us. There's no more peace and I know what to do about it."

Wegel could see that he had wasted his time. Hartmann saw the issue clearly but he had a one-track mind. Kill, kill, kill; not only when necessary, but as a general matter of policy.

Wegel made a last attempt, taking great care to keep his tone inoffensive. "Well, I'm glad you've told me that Ulla is no danger. You obviously know much more about her than I do. I must respect your opinion." And then, archly, "You like her, don't you? You're very protective of her."

Hartmann took his hands from his pockets, stepped forward, then, with immense control, steadied himself. "One day I'll get you, Gustav. One day. Get out before I do it now."

Wegel stood up, keeping out of Hartmann's reach. He had at least satisfied himself that both Ulla and Hartmann must go if he was to survive.

Ulla took off the headset and placed it in a drawer. For some time she sat at the dressing table, pale and shaken. The fingers splayed on the skirted side of her thigh were trembling. She rose, put on a jacket over her white silk shirt, and placed a small .22 calibre pistol in one of its wide pockets.

When she knocked at Hartmann's door he opened it with a snarl, which disappeared

406

immediately he saw her. "I'm sorry. I thought it was . . ."

"Gustav returning? I understand. I was listening."

"Listening?" Hartmann closed the door behind her. "How?"

"It doesn't matter how, Rolf. Who was Paula Menke?"

He could only stare at her dumbfounded. It took a lot to make Hartmann speechless.

Ulla crossed the room and sat on a chair near a side table. "You'd better sit, too, Rolf."

Hartmann lowered himself slowly into a seat opposite. Ulla observed that he was wondering what to say but she did not intend to give him time to think. "The truth, Rolf. It's time I knew. I know you killed Paula Menke and Gustav's father and Kurt Retzer, and that you are really Jost Schnell. I know something of Sachsenhausen. Just tell me the rest."

Hartmann had gone as white as a sheet. He spoke with difficulty. "I don't want to hurt you."

"You are already hurting me. The truth could not be worse."

"It could. Leave it alone."

Ulla took out her gun. "Why do you protect me, Rolf? Does it go so far as to let me shoot you? You know that I will."

"You won't kill me here, Ulla."

"Why not? Wegel's just called. Did you

407

arrange for him to meet you here? That would be convenient for me."

Hartmann shook his head, his huge hands clasped awkwardly.

Ulla added, "I'm not interested in your murders. I don't intend to hold them against you. I simply want to know where I stand in all this." When Hartmann remained silent, Ulla went on, "If I don't get it from you I'll get it from Gustav. I'd prefer it from you because I trust you."

"You trust me?"

"As far as *I* am concerned, I trust you."

Hartmann smiled a little. "I'm glad of that. I wouldn't harm you. Even . . . You've become a sort of daughter to me."

"Then it's time you treated me like an adult daughter. Who was Paula Menke?" Ulla raised the gun and she intended to use it.

Hartmann shook his head in an agony of mind before he said, "Paula Menke was a . . . She was at Sachsenhausen"

"What was she doing there?"

Hartmann twisted his hands, looked everywhere instead of at Ulla. "Whoring."

"Whoring? For whom?" Why was her stomach so suddenly tight?

"There were several of them. They entertained the VIP prisoners."

Ulla felt the gun wavering. She laid it down on the side table within easy reach. "Who were these

VIPs?" She snapped out the question and Hartmann's head shot up.

"There were two of them. Russians. One was Stalin's son, the other, Molotov's—or a nephew or something."

"So why did you kill Paula Menke?"

Hartmann covered his face. For a moment Ulla thought he was crying but he brought his hands down and said, "It might be better if you shot me."

Ulla picked up the gun, holding it two-handed to steady her aim. Just before she was about to fire, Hartmann held up a hand.

"All right. But what's the use? You'll regret it and so will I."

"Get on with it."

"I didn't kill Paula Menke until 1965. I was imprisoned for fifteen years for war crimes. And it took me another five years to trace her and the others."

"Why was it necessary?" Hartmann is right, reflected Ulla, I don't want to know. Yet I must.

"At Sachsenhausen she was having a child by Stalin's son. The night Jacob Stalin committed suicide he gave her a ring which had the Dranrab code engraved into it. Paula was always loose-tongued, and we'd all been in jail together. Julich, who was Wegel's father, knew about it and I think Retzer did too. It became a joke. Nobody believed its value until word got round after the war that Paula had come into a lot of money.

There was another whore called Holtmier who I think knew about it. I never found her but she made no move for it."

"And you killed Paula for the ring?"

"For the code on the ring. The ring was buried with her. Anyone who had the code had the account. That's what Jacob Stalin told her and he was right."

"Did she have Jacob's child?" She could hardly speak.

Hartmann faltered. "I don't know."

"If you didn't quite believe it before, you know now that I'll kill you, don't you, Rolf?"

Hartmann nodded in despair. His head swivelled on his shoulders as if he was in mortal pain.

Almost in a whisper, Ulla asked, "Was Paula Menke my mother?"

Tears welled in Hartmann's eyes. He could not face Ulla's cold, accusing gaze. He spread his hands. "She had you adopted just after you were two, and put it around that you had died."

Ulla's voice was hoarse. "To protect me against you and the others?"

"Partly. I didn't know you then," Hartmann cried out. "I didn't know you. But she knew that she could not live her reputation down. She did it to give you a fair chance."

There was silence, broken intermittently by Hartmann's strangled sobs. Ulla felt confused and strangely bitter that such a strong, murderous man should be reduced to tears.

"*How did you kill my mother?*" But the thought that screamed through her head was, "I am Jacob Stalin's daughter." And she did not argue the point. *She knew* what had come through the genes; the inconsistencies she had never been able to explain; the leaning towards her father's homeland while not wanting to be identified with it; the unexplained emotional ties. Perhaps her mother told her something when a child. Something she rejected but now had to face?

"It doesn't matter how." Hartmann wiped his eyes. He had known that one day this moment would come and he had been dreading it.

"I want it all. No gaps. This will be the first and last time we will talk about it so don't leave anything out."

Hartmann did not know which way to take that; it sounded like a death sentence though that did not worry him so much. If he was brutal, he was no coward. He had to go on now but it was the thought of the effect it would have on Ulla that was tormenting him. He pointed to the ceiling. "I strung her up."

"*Hanged her?*" Ulla almost choked on the words.

"It had to look like suicide."

"Did she . . . ?" Ulla was about to say "suffer" but it would be a pointless question.

"She wasn't like you," Hartmann tried to explain. "She was a tramp. She cashed in on you with Stalin."

Ulla felt as if the blood had been drained from her. "She was my mother. And she protected me against you more than you could ever understand."

Hartmann appeared as if he had just taken a tremendous beating. He was slumped on the chair, his massive energy gone, head down, runnels of tears lining his craggy face. "I know all about it. After she was . . . Afterwards I found a copy of the letter she had sent to the lawyers. It said that if anything happened to you, at any time other than identifiable illness, they were to call in the police and particularly look into the affairs of Jost Schnell, now called Rolf Hartmann, in relation to the possibility of murder. It meant that if anything happened to you, I would be hounded even if I wasn't involved."

"Now I know why you've been so protective. You're just rotten right through, Rolf. Filth."

"No." Hartmann held up a protesting hand. "No. Only at first. I wanted to protect you because I got to like and admire you."

"So you knew how I came into Dranrab. This whore of a mother of mine thought so little of me that she provided funds to those I had always believed to be my parents, and on her death she provided the Dranrab legacy to protect me from

412

you. Did you know that the lawyers enquire after my well-being twice a year?"

Hartmann nodded his head in agony of mind. "It was in the copy letter."

"That whore you hanged loved me enough for all that. And she must have loved my father, too." Ulla tried to quell the sob in her voice.

Hartmann said with complete truth, "They loved each other. I didn't see it like that at the time. But they did."

The frank observation probably saved his life. The gun rattled on the table as she laid it down again. She could not stop her trembling.

Ulla stared across at him, choked and shocked and totally unsure of herself. Over the years she'd speculated about her background but nothing so bizarre as the truth. As she sat there wondering how best to pick up the pieces, she vaguely recalled that the names, Paula Menke and Jost Schnell, must have been contained in some of the many papers she had sifted through after her adoptive parents' deaths.

Ulla fought for self-possession. Hartmann's presence forced her to pull herself together. She did not want to finish up a beaten wreck like him. But it was not easy. She was suffering the worst emotional experience of her life. When she was reasonably in control of herself, she said, "You're not only a butcher, Rolf, but a pathetic fool. You killed to gain but finished up with a life-long threat from my mother's grave, and with Wegel's

413

blackmail. You weren't very clever, were you? Was it worth it?"

Hartmann lifted his head fractionally. He ran his hands over his face, and answered honestly, "It was worth it. I've a lot to show for it." He tried to straighten.

Take away Hartmann's brutality and what was left of him? Ulla could not make up her mind. What he had done reviled her because it concerned her own mother. Hartmann had always been sufficiently honest with himself to do his own killing. Ulla did not avoid the fact that she had created a situation in America which had resulted in her hiring a killer, but now she understood better the impulse which had prompted her to set it up.

She rose shakily. Retrieving the gun she slipped it in her pocket. She stood gazing down at Hartmann who remained seated as though knowing his legs would not support him.

"I'll still protect you, Ulla," he said simply. "Whatever you think of me, I'll still do that."

He looked old now; old and washed up. Ulla inclined her head. She was very pale, her eyes red. "None of this to Gustav."

Hartmann's eyes sharpened. "Watch him. I don't trust him."

"I know. We're all due to meet shortly. We'd better pull ourselves together. But we've no options left now. We must get rid of Tyler and the girl. It's obvious that independently both the

Russians and the British are looking for the Stalin connection with Dranrab. We've got a fight on if we're to hold out."

Ulla moved towards the door and stumbled. Hartmann clambered up to help her but was warned off by her contemptuous expression. He had made himself a leper to the one person for whom he had ever held any real feeling.

21

WEGEL glanced in the mirror. "We're being followed."

Ulla, sitting next to him, turned her head and Hartmann on the back seat swivelled round to look through the rear window. "There's a car, all right. But we're not exactly in the desert."

Wegel kept his eyes on the erratic bends of the road. "He's been with us some time. I'm going to slow down. See if you can get a good look." They were climbing, so there was reason to reduce speed.

From the time they had left the hotel, Wegel had kept his eyes open. He had no idea that Ulla and Hartmann had met after his separate calls on them. By the time they all met in Ulla's suite she had showered and was freshly made up. As usual, she was impeccably dressed but seemed unusually restrained and weary. But that was to be expected; they all had a problem on their hands.

Hartmann had surprised him, though, for his earlier belligerence had disappeared. He had played an almost passive role during the meeting, itself surprisingly short. They

416

had all agreed on what their next step should be.

About two hundred yards behind, Savage said to Jackson, "They've spotted us." And he slowed to keep pace.

Jackson was unimpressed. "They could hardly miss us on this road."

"I mean they know we're tagging them."

"Och, that's different." Jackson patted his pockets. "One gun between us. What a bloody shower."

"If I knew where this road led to and what turn offs there were, I'd take a chance and drop back. We could climb the high ground and watch them through glasses."

"Why not overtake?"

"There's no clear stretch. It's all damn corners."

"Take a chance and drop back anyway; there's a feller using his eyes to laser beam us to death."

Eddie said, "It's heavy but we mustn't make a noise. If the other bloke hears us, he'll know something's up."

One cylinder was empty but they carried the full one up to the top step and positioned it between Max's dangling body and the door; arms, head and shoulders draped over the cylinder. "You're strong," Eddie said admiringly to Raya.

"I am a swimmer."

"Well, let's get his jacket and shirt off." It was not easy, and neither was keen on handling the corpse with so much congealed blood clotting the blond hair. They tied the jacket and shirt to the arms with strips from what was left of Raya's bra and the shirt itself.

From the bottom of the steps the cylinder was barely visible, hidden by the screen of body and garments.

Eddie turned to Raya. "Are you ready for this?"

"Yes. I'm ready."

He was disturbed by her unquestioning trust in him. He took her hands. "Raya, I'm the least practical man you're ever likely to meet. I've no idea whether this will work. Look at it." He made her gaze up the steps to the odd and gruesome arrangement. "It will probably kill us."

"At least we will have tried. They will kill us anyway." She returned the pressure of his hands to show that she understood. And then she added, "I trust you."

This from a girl who had been betrayed so blatantly. Eddie, for once, found himself speechless. He pulled her close and they rocked as they clung together; he was full of emotion, and a deep, deep anger that Stevinski could have used her so cruelly. Before releasing her, he said, "As long as you know that I haven't a clue what I'm doing."

"It's all right. Really. You are very considerate."

"We'd better get that lamp to the back and put it out in good time."

He went up the steps on his own. Vital points had already been rehearsed but the overall project was a highly dangerous gamble. He opened the cylinder valve by inserting the smallest of the penknife blades and then wedging it with broken matches. He pulled his head back as the gas escaped.

The crude screen was meant to trap a good proportion of gas within its folds but there was so much open space that both Eddie and Raya recognised its inadequacy.

He went down the steps and led Raya along the racks covering the wall in line with the door. Raya doused the lamp and they were in darkness. They sought each other's hands and hung on grimly. They knew the attempt to be reckless.

The smell of gas was already strong but it was a question of timing. Too soon could prove useless, too late could be fatal. Eddie fiddled with the lighter in his pocket and the little band of cloth that they had designed to fit over the end to keep the thumb press down once it was alight. That would be the first moment of danger; when he lit it would the gas have sunk low enough to ignite in their faces?

Waiting was a test of nerves. They held hands. The smell of gas was increasingly strong and they hoped that the larger concentration would remain by the door.

Eddie whispered, "I'd better do it now."

But Raya did not want to let him go. "I'll come with you."

"*No*. I do this alone. Here." He handed her the gun. "Just in case. Anyway, I'm no damn good with it."

She took the gun and he bent down to peck her cheek. She reached up and kissed him warmly. He broke away with an effort. "You stay here. Keep back against the rack."

He knew the run of the racks well enough but the lamp had made all the difference. Now he groped his way along, wondering whether he had left it too late. Did the smell of gas mean that it would ignite all around him? As long as Raya stayed where she was she stood a good chance of survival.

He reached the back of the cellar, counted the alleyways to the middle and tried to get the line of their direction away from him. In theory he was facing the door.

The gas seemed to be clogged in his nose, everywhere. He turned round, trying to perform a correct one hundred and eighty degrees. He pulled out the lighter and was sure his hand was shaking. He hunched as if, by having his back to the door, and his body arched over the lighter, he could keep the gas away. With his thumb on the catch, he suddenly became cold and frightened. The hissing of gas behind him filled the cellar. When it came to pressing the catch, he found he could not do it. I'm a bloody coward, he thought despairingly, and forced himself to push downwards. The tiny light flared into his face, as bright as a beacon in the darkness.

He regained his nerve. Raya must be able to see something of the light. He whipped the band over the catch to hold it down, surprised now how steady his hands were. He turned, hand over the flame. The light was sufficient for him to line up on the racks. With great concentration he lobbed the flaming lighter towards the door, hoping it would not go out.

The idea then was to fall flat on his face, but he was not given the time. A rush of blue flame flared upwards and outwards like sheet lightning, intensifying as it went and then bursting into a red, concentrated ball of fire that exploded in front of him, searing his eyes, robbing him of his sight and putting enormous pressure on his ear drums.

Eddie was thrown back by the blast, from the centre of which large fragments of ruptured metal screamed lethally in every direction. Something whined over his head as he fell towards the floor —and then he was airborne, arms and legs flailing, before there was a tremendous crack on the back of his head, and darkness again.

Wegel was thinking of the best way to deal with

Ulla and Hartmann. It was not something that could be easily planned. Opportunity would be the thing. He was not forgetting Hartmann's thugs up at the villa, but once the two prisoners were dead and disposed of, they would be paid off. He would have to wait and see. Meanwhile the following car had disappeared, so he must have been wrong about that. Still, he kept a close eye on the mirror, and Hartmann, too, was looking back from time to time.

Savage had done his job well. He had pulled up close to Wegel's car, sounding his horn on impossible corners, once waving a fist when the front car refused to pull over. But it made no difference. After a while he had dropped back, and then, on spotting an almost blind entry to a distant property, had swung up the dual tracks, stopping behind a hillock.

Jackson climbed to the crest of the rise and raised his field glasses. As Savage joined him, Jackson said, "No sign. I can only see fragments of road." Jackson lowered the glasses. The tinkle of cowbells came from a pasture across a small valley. The tracks they had followed most probably led to a farmhouse, at present out of sight.

Jackson looked around him. "The damned light is going."

"Keep looking."

"I've got them," said Jackson. He swung the glasses up and adjusted the focus.

"OK. I'll back the car down. We'll have to take a chance and keep well out of sight; the dusk will help."

"What are we looking for? A villa? Hut?"

"Anything where Tyler might be holed up."

"Och, he's probably dead."

"You could be right. Climb in."

Someone was propping the back of his head and his cheek was resting against warm, firm flesh. He opened his eyes and realised that Raya was cradling him. He was strongly tempted to stay there, but stirred to let her know that he had come round. The back of his head felt as if it was wide open. She carefully helped him up.

Raya, who had rushed to help Eddie, saw the damage with him for the first time. The explosion had seared his sight. Everything was misty but Eddie saw enough to understand what had happened. Brick and plaster and metal and wood were strewn everywhere. The smell of gas was still strong and parts of the cylinder had been blasted all over the place. The doorway was a rough hole, both door and frame blown out. Some of the woodwork was on fire, smoke spiralling through flickering flames that had yet to take a complete hold.

Max had disappeared from the doorway to lie at the bottom of the steps. Raya retched at the sight of his dismembered body, charred and still burning.

Cautiously, they picked their way forward, Jurgen must be somewhere close-by. They crawled up the stairs, Raya with the gun in her hand, and flattened themselves to peer over the top step. The door was lying some distance away, blown straight out. The room was a debris littered wilderness, windows smashed, and the few items of furniture scattered and broken. But there was no sign of Jurgen.

They entered the room, the smell of gas was here, too, odd pieces of wood smouldering, chunks of cylinder lying like war souvenirs. They resisted the tremendous temptation to run straight from the villa, for, when they stared out of the broken windows, there was nothing but hills and open country, and no transport. The villa had been well chosen; off the beaten track it was miles from anywhere. And Jurgen must still be around.

It was difficult to tread quietly through so much debris. They moved towards a door already ajar, which they thought might lead to the kitchen, when suddenly it was kicked open and Jurgen stood in front of them with raised gun.

He seemed as shocked as they were. He was bleeding down one side of his forehead and face, and the sleeve of one arm was hanging in shreds, blood oozing from the exposed flesh. He leered at them. "Thought you were all dead down there. Drop the gun, fräulein."

Raya had the gun hanging at her side. She

knew that she could not raise it in time. Standing close to Eddie, she felt his finger tapping her hand. She did not know what he meant but was immediately alert.

"Drop it or I'll shoot you dead right now." Jurgen's voice was slightly slurred. "Move back."

They stepped back into the main room and, as Jurgen followed, it was clear that he was not quite sure what he should do with them. Eddie took advantage of Jurgen's indecision and dived fast to his left, away from Raya. Jurgen's aim followed him, the gun roared, and Raya fired a fraction of a second later. Jurgen fell to his knees still holding the gun and then, glassy eyed, fell forward.

Eddie scrambled to his feet aware of how close the bullet had been, but his sight was returning. He took one look at Jurgen, and then saw that Raya was rooted on the spot, shocked at what she had done. He grabbed her free hand. "Let's get out."

They ran to the door but as they passed the broken window Eddie saw the car which had just pulled up and Hartmann, Ulla and Wegel climbing out. "This way." He swung Raya round and they ran back to the kitchen. As they passed Jurgen, Eddie tore the gun from his hand.

They left the kitchen door ajar so that they could peer through the gap. While Raya kept watch, Eddie tried the back door but it was locked. There was no other way out except by breaking the locked windows and there was already the sound of the three entering the front door.

"Oh, my God." It was Ulla surveying the destruction.

Watching through the crack of the door Eddie and Raya saw all three go to the gap which had been the cellar door. When Ulla clutched at the jagged brickwork and heaved, they knew that she had seen the bloodied remains of Max. All three of them held guns.

Wegel turned to Hartmann. "We'd better go down and see what's left. They might be waiting down there."

Hartmann was unaffected by the carnage. He agreed with Wegel and together they went down the steps. So far as they knew Eddie and Raya were still chained to the racks, and were probably now dead.

There was sufficient light in the cellar to see the extent of the damage. They found the broken chains and, covering each other, traversed the alleys between the racks. It was obvious now that the prisoners had escaped. Wegel said, "We'd better tell Ulla," and, when Hartmann nodded and turned towards the steps, Wegel shot him in the back. "That's for killing my father." He fired once more as Hartmann collapsed.

Knowing that Ulla could not fail to hear the shots, Wegel bawled out, "Keep away from the door, one of them's armed." He raced up the

426

steps, turned and fired when he reached the top, and then burst through the gap to dive round the side of it. "They got Rolf," he panted.

Ulla was shocked. Everything should have been under tight control, but it seemed to be going wrong.

Jurgen scraped at the floor. Ulla, seeing that he was still alive, quickly crossed over to him, telling Wegel to watch the cellar.

Jurgen was trying to speak. Ulla bent her head down, and strained to listen. When she finally caught the whispered words, she was aware that Wegel was approaching. She fired at him almost without looking up. As she straightened, Wegel was standing with a stunned expression on his face, his nerve ticking like a metronome. He was swaying.

"You killed Rolf and were just about to do the same to me," accused Ulla, expressionless. "You think we can no longer survive as a team? That only one of us stands a chance?" She was very pale, very dignified and totally impersonal as she saw the wounded Wegel struggle to reply. "Perhaps you are right, Gustav, but you'll never find out." She shot him dead, turning away rather than watch him fall.

She walked over to the shattered windows, looked down sadly at the waiting car. With her back still to the kitchen door she called out, "You can come out now. Jurgen warned me you were there." She kept her gun at her side and turned slowly as Eddie and Raya emerged. She smiled as she saw the guns. "You don't need those."

"When we are convinced we don't we'll put them away."

Ulla looked directly at Raya. "Raya Dubrova. I think we are distantly related. I am Jacob Stalin's daughter. I have just lost two partners. It might solve all our problems if I had two more."

"Who'll finish up like the last two. Ulla, give up." But Eddie was stunned by Ulla's claim to be Jacob Stalin's daughter. He could sense that Raya was too.

"You saw what happened here. Wegel was going to shoot me after killing Hartmann. Otherwise I would not have touched him."

The strange thing was that Eddie believed her.

"You won't join me?" Ulla asked in surprise.

"No way. Unless Raya sees it differently."

Raya shook her head slowly as if still bewildered. "If we are related, I would prefer not to know." And then, in understanding of the past, of how it must have been, she added, "I'm sorry it happened the way it did. My grandfather was very fond of Yasha. It couldn't have been easy for you."

Ulla shrugged, her eyes hard. "I don't need your patronage. It's too dangerous for me to use the account again without your help. Unless we can do a deal to change its structure, Tinsal is dead. It was good while it lasted, but I can survive without it."

Ulla dropped her gun on the floor. "I couldn't kill both of you—even if I wanted to. But I'm leaving, and I'll need the car. If I'm not mistaken there should be another one along soon."

She moved towards the door, stopped halfway, then turned to face them once more. "To stop me you will have to shoot me."

Neither Eddie or Raya moved.

Savage and Jackson gazed round at the havoc. Both had been fascinated by Raya's presence; neither had known a thing about her. Eddie briefly explained.

Savage came back from the cellar looking sickly and annoyed that he had not sent Jackson down there instead. "It's a bloody mess," he said. "You two make quite a team."

"Are you going to look around all day or are you going to take us away?"

Savage gave a wry smile. "That sounds like the Eddie I know and love. We can't leave it like this but we can take a leaf from your book."

They closed the outside shutters over the broken windows, stuffed the gaps where they could to make the villa as airtight as possible. While Eddie escorted Raya to the car, Savage and Jackson went into the kitchen and released the valves of the gas cylinders there, then left to join the others. There were sufficient small fires and embers to ignite the gas when it had built up. If the place did not blow to bits it would burn, but

429

with the amount of wood on the ground floor, it would probably do both.

Savage switched on the beams when they were halfway to Zürich. "So Ulla just vanished?" he queried once again.

"Straight out of the door," replied Eddie, squeezing Raya's hand.

"And you didn't try to stop her."

"She had a gun."

"I saw it on the floor. You had two."

"But she was a much better shot. You should have seen her."

"You certainly haven't changed," commented Savage, dryly.

Savage swung in towards the Hotel Bernhof and then pulled sharply on the wheel to swing out again, to a blaring of horns and flashing of lights. Eddie shouted in alarm but Savage drove on. He pulled up some distance from the hotel, swung round in his seat and said to Raya, "Your troubles aren't over. I spotted one of yours outside the hotel. The light just caught his face."

"One of mine?"

"Uncle Stevinski's KGB. I knew him in London. If they're out looking for you, Raya, it's not to shake hands."

"You are serious?"

"I'd say you've served your purpose. That man's a killer."

Eddie said, "Christ, there's no end to it."

"There is but not one you'd like." Savage placed an arm over the seat back. "What's your room number?"

Raya told him.

"Passport still in the room?"

"Yes. With some money in the small suitcase."

"I'm glad you mentioned money. We've got to get you back to London and we're short of the ready. Look, leave it to Malcolm, he's good at this sort of thing." Savage turned to his colleague. "Passport, money and a change of clothes. OK? We'll wait here."

Seymour was charming to Raya and offhand with Eddie. He had been fascinated by her story and had even listened carefully to Eddie until the narrative was complete.

They had spent the previous night at the British Embassy in Berne because Savage considered anywhere else unsafe. They had flown back from Geneva as an extra safety measure and now they were in the safe house in London.

But both Eddie and Raya were deeply worried. If Stevinski had put out his killers, and that meant a more intensified search than before for Eddie too, they were no better off. One danger had passed to give way to a more deadly, much more organised one.

Yet Seymour seemed undismayed. He showed them a copy of a signal he had sent directly to

431

General Georgi Stevinski. "This was sent in cypher, of course. What you have there is the essence."

They read: Will exchange unsullied memory of hero Lubov for deportation of Larissa Dubrova and permanent well-being of daughter and Tyler. Call off your dogs and Lubov will rest in peace. Krantz and company gone forever. So has Dranrab. Reply most urgent.

While they read it through again, Seymour said, "We'll have a signal back tomorrow. It's an offer he dare not refuse."

He addressed Eddie, "Zeitlinger are now sitting on a fortune with no immediate claimant. Tinsal, within the terms of its formation, was open only to Krantz, Hartmann and Wegel, as I understand it. Ulla Krantz was right when she said she dare not use it. It would make her too traceable and she has too much to answer for that we know about and probably a lot that we don't. I would guess that Ulla Krantz has disappeared off the face of the earth, and that her own money was never in that name."

Seymour adjusted his position at the table at which the three of them were sitting. He seemed to have lost a little weight, but his jowls wobbled noticeably as he continued.

"I think we can induce Zeitlinger to come up with something for you. It will be like getting blood from a stone, but there's a lot of stirring that can be done which I'm sure they would prefer to avoid. And they know just how much they've got away with." He did not add that he would be content for the Swiss bank to keep most of the money, provided they could influence certain matters for his benefit as they had already done for Tinsal's.

Seymour rose. "It might be prudent for us to arrange a change of identity for you both. Once I hear from Stevinski you can safely leave here." He turned pointedly to Raya. "There's a separate room adjoining. I'm quite sure you would prefer to be alone to rest. I'll show you the way."

"No thank you," said Raya pleasantly. "I don't want to leave Eddie. We have much to talk about."

Seymour appeared to be disappointed. "Oh well. Perhaps you've decided to carry on where Lubov and Aunt Jane left off. I hope you enjoy better fortune than they did."

Other titles in the
Charnwood Library Series:

THE NAKED ISLAND
by Russell Braddon

The Naked Island has been acclaimed as a classic of World War II. Employing understatement and fierce humour alternatively, Russell Braddon describes the disastrous Malayan campaign of 1942 and the long captivity that followed it. For almost four years his Japanese captors—believing that only death could redeem those who had "dishonourably" surrendered—subjected their 40,000 prisoners to a pitiless regime of starvation and slavery. Theirs, however, was not a code to which the author and his comrades were prepared to subscribe. Instead, drawing upon unsuspected resources of hatred, humour and defiance, they battled to survive.

NORTH AND SOUTH
by Mrs. Gaskell

Quite a group of novelists in the forties and fifties of the last century used their work as a medium for setting forth, in no uncertain voice, the sufferings of the poor. The author took her place as a staunch defender of the distressed Lancashire operatives by her first novel *Mary Barton*. *North and South,* which the author once admitted was her favourite story, and described as one of the finest novels of modern English fiction, is a north country story of daily life in a manufacturing district.

KENILWORTH
by Sir Walter Scott

The story is based on the tradition of the tragic fate, in the reign of Queen Elizabeth, of the beautiful Amy Robsart, daughter of Sir Hugh Robsart of Devon. Beguiled by her charms, the Earl of Leicester, the Queen's favourite, has secretly married her and established her at Cumnor Place. Caught in a net of ambition and intrigue Leicester is forced to acknowledge that Amy is his wife, thereby calling down on himself the furious anger of the jealous Queen. A sycophant, Richard Varney, convinces Leicester that Amy is guilty of infidelity, and in a passion Leicester orders her death.

CAPTAINS COURAGEOUS
by Rudyard Kipling

The story of how an accident changes the character of a rich, spoilt boy called Harvey Cheyne. Swept overboard from a liner bound for Europe, he is picked up by a trawler and forced to work hard to earn his keep. The skipper, Disko Troop, refuses to turn his boat around and land Harvey, so it is nearly a year later when he is reunited with his parents. His father, an American millionaire, is pleased to find that this "unsatisfied dough-faced youth" has become a respectful, and healthy young man.

WINTER KILLS
by Richard Condon

Fourteen years after the assassination of Tim Kegan, late President of the United States, his extraordinarily wealthy and powerful family learns, at a death-bed confession, that their beloved brother and son had not been murdered by a lone, psychopathic killer but had been the victim of a conspiracy. Satirically it is a revelation of a people who had been able to accept the death of their leader as an entertainment event; as something to be accepted and forgotten. Tim Kegan's family were no different—but they were forced against their wills to follow the chains of actual and false evidence.

THE JUDAS TREE
by A. J. Cronin

The story of a man who ruins his own life, and the lives of the four women who have the misfortune to come under the spell of his charm, by his selfishness, weakness, and capacity for self-deception. David Moray begins his professional life as a medical student, and it is then that he falls in love with Mary Douglas. They agree to marry; but Moray is persuaded to throw Mary over for the sake of a tempting business partnership, with marriage to another woman as part of the bargain.

A STONE FOR DANNY FISHER
by Harold Robbins

A novel of the seamy side of New York life where flick knives and bare fists were the passport to wealth and position. The story of a young man who was born into a family of modest means and respectability, but was gradually driven downward into the world of crime, racketeering and poverty. Danny was a boxer—a potential champion—and he might have gone straight had the fight promoters not tried to exert pressure. But he could not escape the gangsters, and later he became deeply involved in the black market and then in the slot-machine rackets.

BLAKE'S REACH
by Catherine Gaskin

The events taking place in the last decade of the 18th century, when England was stirring uneasily in the wake of the French Revolution, did not bother the pretty head of young Jane Howard. She was determined to enjoy life and raise herself from the lowly position she occupied as maid at the ancient hostelry, The Feathers, to the social rank and riches she felt were rightly hers. Her determination to fulfil her aim became symbolised in Blake's Reach, the old family manor house which stood on the high ground overlooking the wind-swept Romney Marsh.

FOLLOW THE DRUM
by James Leasor

India, in the mid-nineteenth century, was virtually run by a British commercial concern, the Honourable East India Company, whose directors would pay tribute to one Indian ruler and then depose another in their efforts to maintain their balance sheet of power and profit. But great changes were already casting shadows across the land, and when a stupid order was given to Indian troops to use cartridges greased with cow fat and pig lard (one animal sacred to the Hindus and the other abhorrent to Moslems) there was mutiny, changing the lives of millions for ever.

THE MATLOCK PAPER
by Robert Ludlum

James Matlock, Professor of English at Carlyle University, is assigned by the United States government to investigate what seems to be a large-scale dope and prostitution business. Matlock has a motive for accepting the assignment, his younger brother had died from an overdose of heroin. But would he have accepted if he knew the mental and physical agony it would bring his beloved Patricia? Would he have accepted if he knew the terror and violence it would bring to his own life and to the people around him?

SWEETHEARTS AND WIVES
by C. L. Skelton

This sequel to *The Maclarens* tells the story of a new generation of the famous Highland clan—its regiment, its wars, its loves, its honour. *Sweethearts and Wives* follows the Maclarens through the Egyptian Campaign to the Boer War. A credible tale of battle and bravery, and of what men call cowardice: a tale of officers and men, and of the women they love. For Donald Bruce it begins when he is unable to give the order to kill one of his own men. For Ian Maclaren, eldest son of the Laird, it begins with his passionate love for Naomi—a half-caste, a bastard and forbidden. This is their story and that of their fathers—proud men with their strong memories of the past.

MAN ON FIRE
by A. J. Quinnell

Creasy and Guido had served together in the French Foreign Legion. They knew all about discipline, guns and grenades, and were first-class soldiers. Now Creasy had no purpose in life and was fast becoming an alcoholic, until Guido finds him a job as a bodyguard to the daughter of a rich Italian family. A close and happy relationship develops and Creasy enjoys life once more. But then something terrible happens, and Creasy sets out to exact a fearful revenge.

I KNOW MY LOVE
by Catherine Gaskin

Ballarat, Australia, 1854 . . . a bleak encampment of tents in a valley. Here 30,000 men scramble for the gold under their feet by day—and every night drink it, gamble it away, or spend it on their women. Strange circumstances at Ballarat bring two of these women together. Rose Maguire, ravishing and flamboyant, who meets life with open arms and a calculating brain . . . Emma Brown, lonely, shy and gentle—who has killed two men. Their lives are inextricably tangled when they fall in love with the same man.

BREAD UPON THE WATERS
by Irwin Shaw

Allen Strand and his family were ready for dinner, except for his teenage daughter who had not returned from a tennis match. When she finally did, it was in the company of a very bloody stranger whom she had rescued from muggers in Central Park. The stranger, an eminent lawyer—and a lonely man—was strongly attracted by the harmony of the Strand family. As his involvement with the family increased, so did his desire to use his influence and wealth on their behalf. For Allen Strand it becomes a struggle for the survival of his family against the overwhelming efforts of their would-be benefactor.